CORAL MOON

CORAL MOON

BY

CRAIG GODFREY

www.penmorepress.com

Prologue

Cooktown, North Queensland. Mid-December 1897

Government Wharf, as it was named, was a shallow harbour with a large tidal range popular with crocodiles. Sharing the wharf with the 280-foot, 986-ton paddle steamer *Cassowary* were three pearling luggers and a bêche-de-mer boat. The town had been home to thousands of gold diggers in the 70s and 80s, but with the gold depleted the miners had left in droves. Most had drifted away to where the soil was richer, although quite a few never left.

In 1897, with the new century just around the corner, Cooktown was base to pearl shell and bêche-de-mer fishers and guano gatherers. The 60 pubs had dropped to a handful. Twenty eating houses had dwindled to four. But one thing that never changed was the weather. It was still oppressively hot, especially now in the wet season.

Chapter One

Samoa made her way ashore, off the *Cassowary*'s gangway and onto Cooktown's docks. Stepping into the shade of a shipping company office, she shared the shelter with an old Chinese man selling mud crabs from wicker baskets, the crabs' powerful claws bound with coconut fibre. A sign scrawled on a board in Cantonese and English read 'sixpence each.' The old man gave her a toothless, happy grin and together they watched Samoa's porter negotiate the gangway with her luggage—one travelling trunk and four large crates destined for the Pacific Islands.

Further inland, along the Endeavour River, Samoa noticed Chinese junks and sampans resting in the mud exposed by the low tide. The Chinese had been a driving force during the gold rush years and many had stayed on, adapting to the trade in bêche-de-mer, or sea cucumber, a delicacy in the Orient. Now the Chinese vessels, with their exotic brightly painted hulls and fully battened sails, were built in Cooktown in large numbers.

Movement in the mud caught Samoa's attention and she realised the junks weren't alone. She noted many crocodiles wallowing in the mud and lazily enjoying the sun, most a dozen feet long or more. They *all* looked hungry.

'Where to, lady?' The shipping porter snapped Samoa from her reverie.

'Oh … ah …'

'Ya got a place to stay?'

'Not yet.'

Samoa was pleased her ship had docked when it had. Out at sea, the dark sky that had looked menacing an hour earlier now formed storm clouds in which splinters of lightning speared the horizon.

'There's the Lutheran lodgin' 'ouse just up the street,' the porter suggested. 'Probably the best place for a respectable lady like yerself.'

'Fine. Thank you.'

The porter took up the strain of the luggage trolley, leant forward and pulled ahead like a carthorse. 'Then follow me,' he wheezed.

As they prepared to cross the main thoroughfare of Charlotte Street, their path was temporarily blocked by a Chinese funeral procession marching slowly, silently, up the middle of the road. Two dozen Chinese men—wearing ankle-length robes and sandals, their hair in long, plaited queues, some descending to the backs of their knees—followed the coffin, which was aboard a covered four-wheel buggy pulled by two horses.

The porter noted Samoa's interest in the parade.

'That's ol' Wong Hing, lady,' he said, taking the opportunity to rest. 'He was a shipbuilder 'ere—upriver. Built them junk ships yer can see lying in the mud. Old bugger, 'e were, nearly a hundred, they reckon.'

Like an omen, the clouds burst their seams over the township minutes after Samoa had taken cover at the lodging house. With a bed secured for the night and her crates stowed in a locker room, she tipped the porter one shilling and started making enquiries …

She was looking for a man.

The warnings had been there all morning. The sky had been a shade of tarnished pewter, the swell in off the Coral Sea building, and squalls were assaulting the horizon. Now the clouds burst overhead and the heavy tropical rain beat down on the White Horse Hotel's iron roof like a cheering drum. Cooktown was taking a drenching.

The proprietor of the White Horse, Ma Breaker Bentley, a brash bull of a woman who shaved occasionally, looked at the pendulum barometer nailed to the wall behind the bar. Barometric pressure was falling fast, the needle below 30.

A tropical storm was imminent.

'Batten down them hatches, Harry,' she ordered Harold Bone. He was part aborigine, part Christ knew what else. Harry was a deckhand on Frank Morgan's bêche-de-mer trawler. When he wasn't at sea he was at the White Horse nearly every day and did odd jobs for grog.

Skipper Tatsuo Gaston swung back on his cane chair to swallow the white rum challenge in one hit, and immediately thought better of it as one of the chair's legs splintered loudly. He'd been warned by Ma Breaker before. They'd all been warned: *Don't swing on the bloody chairs.*

Tatsuo caught the publican scowling, swung forward and slammed his empty glass on the table. He flicked the tumbler through a pool of spilt swill towards the empty bottle at the centre of his table.

'Your hook, Spider,' Tatsuo told the wiry-limbed, bug-eyed sea captain of the coastal trader *Seaboard Queen.* Spider snatched up the empty bottle and dragged himself drunkenly to the bar, swapping the empty for a full one and leaving Ma Breaker a hundred-mark note on the counter.

'I told yer before, I want sterling,' the publican huffed.

Spider dragged the bottle towards himself before launching his raw-boned carcass back towards the table.

'I get paid in marks, you get paid in marks, savvy?' he said in his habitual bad-mannered drawl.

If Ma was angry, she bottled it. There was a storm afoot and she had other issues. She cast an iron-clad glance around the taproom. Business had been down today and there were only a dozen drinkers under her roof. They were all regulars—well, mostly. She guessed two foreigners drinking quietly by the window were sugar plantation owners from the south, up here in the north recruiting blackfellas for the upcoming harvest. The others were locals, like skippers Tatsuo Gaston and Spider, and their deckhands—seventeen-year-old Willy

Maynard off Gaston's *Mystery* and Jack Spinner off Spider's *Seaboard Queen*; and then there was Selma, the *Mystery's* fifty-year-old cook. They'd been imbibing since noon, but they held their grog like true seafarers.

Ma liked Tatsuo Gaston. He'd been living in Cooktown a few years now and traded throughout the Coral Sea islands and into the Pacific. He was half Japanese, half French. A 'mongrel' his mates would jest. But a tough bastard any man would want at his side on the battlefield. Tough and fair. His crew loved him. So did the women of Cooktown, and those of the islands, for that matter. He was a good-looking bloke, more European than Japanese, with high cheekbones, a chiseled jaw, a pencil-thin moustache and a hint of sloe eyes. Enough of a hint to give him that exotic look. He had a strong youthful figure for a middle-aged man and was tanned the colour of a coconut husk. Ma knew he was forty-seven years old and that he had once had a partner named Dhia, a stunning Malaysian woman. They'd been together a dozen years—never married for some reason, although they'd been inseparable. Rumour had it that the Oriental beauty couldn't have children. Then on a journey to Malaita Island in the Solomons, hostile natives had speared Dhia over a misunderstanding, no fault of her own. She died in Tatsuo's arms on the beach. In the nearly ten years since then he had never had a full-time relationship.

An explosion overhead captured everyone's attention. It seemed the thunderclap had hit the iron roof of the single-storey timber pub, rattling the very foundations. Ma shot Harry the evil eye and the aborigine hastened battening down the hatches. A gust of wind hurled a shower of rain through the front window like someone outside had tossed a bucketful of water. The sugar men ducked aside and laughed at their folly. This was north Queensland; they were in the heart of the tropics. Harry slammed the shutters and latched them shut.

'You're sailin' for Thursdee Island, ain't yer?' Spider asked Tatsuo.

'Thursday Island ... Sure am.'

'Well, mate,'—Spider looked through hooded eyes at the streetscape out the front door, where Charlotte Street was two inches under water already—'I wouldn't be surprised if'n this 'ere storm is the front of a cyclone,' he said as Harry closed the door.

'Nar. She'll blow over.'

Truth was, Tatsuo had an important rendezvous on Thursday Island, four days' sail north. A meeting with a ship from India, and if he was late he would have a serious problem.

The two men shot another white rum and slammed their glasses on the table. Tatsuo sucked in a breath through clenched teeth … and grinned. Spider knew he was beaten, *this bloody hybrid mongrel was a legend.* He peeled off three one-hundred-mark notes from a roll, dropped them onto the table and stood, swaying. Tatsuo eyed the German bank notes; he would put them with the other five notes he had won at cards this day.

Tatsuo feigned concern. 'Leaving us already, mate?'

'You've got hollow legs,' Spider slurred.

'What about another hand of poker?'

'Forget it. Yer won at cards and yer won the game. Yer a lucky bastard, Gaston.'

At that moment the squall passed and the rain stopped as suddenly as it started. It was like that in the wet season. Immediately, intense tropical sun steamed the shutters.

'And now it seems the gods are smiling down at yer,' Spider went on. 'The storm's passed.'

'Told you. I'll see yer next time I'm in port, my friend,' Tatsuo said. 'Au revoir.'

Spider donned his peaked cap—a souvenir Royal Navy officers' cap with the insignia unstitched—and staggered to the exit on unsteady legs. He threw the doors open only to be blinded by the sun after the gloom of a darkened bar room. Jack Spinner, Spider's deckhand, hurried after him.

Tatsuo watched the man land in a deep puddle before veering off down the main street.

'Easy money, eh?' Tatsuo passed his cook Selma and William a note each. 'Not bad for an afternoon's work.' He drained the remains of a pint of ale to chase the rum and stood groggily. 'I've business out the back,' he said, heading to the latrine.

Samoa Plum, for that was her full name, was used to turning heads. The five-foot-ten beauty was in her mid-thirties, athletically slim with long blonde hair and Pacific-blue eyes. As she stepped into the pub and approached the White Horse bar with confident indifference she even caught the eye of old Selma the cook. As it was rare any woman entered the White Horse alone, Ma Breaker made no bones about her position. She stroked the stubble on her chin and looked the beauty up and down, head to toe. 'What can I do for yer?'

'I'm looking for Tatsuo Gaston.'

'Hmm.' Ma was protective of her regulars, and in a small community strangers stood out like the proverbial dog's nuts. Especially when the request was from a beautiful woman. *Was this one of Gaston's past indiscretions come to fleece him?*

'And why would yer be wantin' to see Mr Gaston?'

'Personal business.'

'Oh … and …?'

'Is he here or not?'

Ma twitched. *Cheeky minx.*

Samoa looked about the taproom as heads disappeared back into glasses and conversations resumed.

'Because I was told at the Post Office he was here,' Samoa said. Then, as if hinting she was familiar with skipper Gaston, Samoa added, 'His boat *Mystery* is in dock.'

The proprietor jerked her head towards the back door. 'He's out back.'

Tatsuo looked at the latrine and screwed up his nose. *Jesus Christ, Ma, it's about time you got it sorted.* And now the passing storm had overflowed the sinkhole of shit. As Tatsuo never wore shoes he was careful where he stepped and, positioning himself before a chest-high pile of empty grog bottles, he relieved himself.

'Tatsuo Gaston?'

The voice was husky yet unmistakably that of a female. Tatsuo looked over his shoulder, unable to stop his business, business he had put off too long in the bar.

The voice persisted. 'Well?'

'Christ, lady, do you mind?'

Samoa liked what she saw. She had heard stories of this legendary skipper and had been told by local women that he was, maybe, a nine out of ten, but … well. Now here he was in the flesh in his three-quarter seafarer britches and calico shirt with sleeves rolled up past the elbow and open to his belly button, wearing a sweat-rag necktie—red, naturally. And bare feet, of course. Samoa turned her back and called over her shoulder, smiling to herself. 'Are you Tatsuo Gaston? Yes or no?'

'Yes.'

'Then we need to talk.'

Ma Breaker had predicted Tatsuo's thirst, and pint mugs of ale for him and his two crewmembers awaited on the counter.

'What's your poison?' Tatsuo asked the blonde.

'I don't drink.' The striking woman looked at Ma, behind the bar, who stared back like a guarded Rottweiler. Samoa sighed. 'Ginger beer.'

'I didn't catch your name,' Tatsuo said as Ma pulled the cork from a stone ginger beer bottle with her teeth.

'Samoa Plum.'

'As in Samoa the island?'

'Yes. I'll explain another time.'

'Please do.' Tatsuo slid a hundred-mark note towards Ma, who, again, shook her head with disgust at the foreign note and deliberately searched out a handful of Deutschland silver 20-pfennigs as change. Tatsuo feigned indifference, pocketed the coins and scooped up the three glass tankards. He nodded to Samoa to bring her ginger beer with her and join him at the table.

'Selma and Will, this is Samoa.'

Selma brightened. 'Samoa—what a lovely name. Same as the islands, huh?'

Samoa was no stranger to this question.

'She'll explain another day,' Tatsuo answered for Samoa as she sat down opposite him. Samoa instantly felt something cold and wet against her leg, only to be greeted by a three-legged red setter bitch sniffing her. The dog looked up, tongue protruding, demanding introduction.

'That's Pearl,' Selma said. 'She's one o' the crew.'

Samoa leant over to stroke the dog and noted the missing leg. 'Oh, you poor thing—what happened?'

'Fight with a croc.' Tatsuo looked serious, nodding sagely.

'A croc … ? You mean a crocodile?'

'Yes.'

'Oh, don't believe him, lovey,' Selma said. 'He's pullin' yer leg. It was amputated 'cos she had a cancer.'

Tatsuo untied the sweat rag from around his neck and wiped perspiration from his face. The wet season was always oppressive, and the grog wasn't helping. He had a moment to notice Samoa Plum's thin cotton blouse was struggling to hold sweat at bay. She had already loosened her top buttons inadvertently revealing cleavage to pert breasts. And wearing the full-length skirt with boots wouldn't help either, he surmised.

'Well, Samoa Plum,' Tatsuo said after a deep tug at his drink, 'what can I do for you?'

Samoa looked at Selma and William. The hired help stared back with undisguised curiosity. Neither of them were going anywhere soon. Samoa fiddled with the silver bangles about her left wrist. Tatsuo responded to the silent request for privacy. 'We don't keep secrets,' he said. 'Me and the crew.'

'Then I'll get straight to the point.' Samoa sipped the ginger beer. It was warm but sated her initial thirst. 'I asked about town and your name came up on more than one occasion.'

'Oh?'

'You own the *Mystery*, yes?'

'That's correct.'

'Then I would like to hire you to take me to Mist Island …'

'M-Mist Island! You serious?'

Samoa reddened. 'Of course I'm serious.'

'Mist Island is amongst the Solomon Islands.'

'So?'

'Lady, Mist Island is amongst the islands of the Roviana peoples. They're headhunters.'

'I know this.'

'But why on earth would you, a woman, want to go there?'

Samoa leant forward in her chair staring down the skipper. 'Don't patronise me, Mr Gaston. I might be *a woman* as you so cleverly observed, but I can handle myself as well as any man.'

'Alright. So let's say that is true. Why the hell would you want to go there?'

'My brother's missing.'

'Your brother?'

'Yes, Rennison Plum. He is my younger brother. He is a missionary with the Lutherans and I have not heard from him in nearly 14 months.'

'And you believe he was on Mist Island, as a missionary?'

'I know he was there. He sent me a letter via the *Eagle*, an American whaler that called at the island a year ago.'

'And not a word since?'

'No.'

'Well I suppose there's hardly a post office there.'

'Look,'—Samoa grew impatient—'Can you help me or not?'

The heat and booze were sneaking up on Tatsuo and evening approached. He gazed at his ale in deep thought. He had sailed to the Solomons on many occasions and found some natives were friendly, but many more were prone to murderous violence. He had lost his partner to a beachside skirmish in the Solomons. The islanders had an inherited mistrust of the white man, as the foreign dogs had abused them over the centuries.

Samoa broke the reverie. 'I'll pay you 500 guineas.'

A month's earnings!

Selma and William sat up and listened. Tatsuo tried to show little interest. He emptied his glass and looked to William, who sprang to his feet to fetch another. 'Get a rum too, Will.' The skipper looked at this stranger—this siren sitting opposite him—and speculated that there might be an alternative motive.

'I hate to say this, lady, but your brother's most likely dead.'

Samoa's reaction was immediate. 'Forget it.' She stood abruptly. 'I'll find another, more suitable skipper, maybe one who's not a drunkard.'

'Whoa, easy up, girl!' Tatsuo sprang to his feet so fast he impressed even himself, but the sudden move made him light-headed. He swayed slightly, adding fuel to Samoa's last comment. He grabbed her wrist. Samoa scowled, staring at his hand before answering.

'"Girl"!' she said. 'I think not.' She wrenched her arm free and stormed out onto the street.

'Wait up! Wait!' Tatsuo skipped precariously down the steps onto mud. Samoa played the game. She turned to face him, delivering a solemn face.

'Sorry about the "girl" comment,' he said. 'Truth is, I call all women "girl." I don't mean to be derogatory.'

Samoa crossed her arms.

'I'll do it for 1500,' Tatsuo said.

'Twelve.'

'Thirteen.'

'Twelve and a half, not a guinea more.'

'Pay up front.'

'Half now. Half when we return, with or without my brother.'

'Done.' Tatsuo offered his hand and Samoa accepted.

'How soon can we leave?'

'We leave at dawn.'

Tatsuo watched Samoa Plum hitch her ankle-length skirt above the mud line and cross the street to the bank, before twisting back to the White Horse where Selma waited in the doorway. 'You met your match there, skipper.' The old cook laughed.

5.30 AM

Samoa was ahead of herself, arriving before sunup at a deserted dock that had been a hive of enterprise and industry the afternoon before. Further towards the estuary, in deeper water, Samoa noticed a single-funnel steamship, three times the size of any lugger. There was no sign of the *Cassowary* paddle steamer. A cattle run had been erected along the wharf parallel to the shoreline. Otherwise there was no sign of life. Behind Samoa, facing the sea, the police station was shuttered up, yet to open, but Bouel's Café de Paris next door showed some light at the rear kitchen, where smoke spiraled from the oven chimney.

Looking back up the main street, everything was deserted from the two-storey Burns Philp building to the new post office built to replace the one destroyed by fire a few years back. Grass Hill dominated the landscape behind the town, where those with a few more bob than the poorer folk—the elite of Cooktown—lived, back from the foreshore. Here, spacious bungalows with broad, shuttered verandas offered cool, breezy interiors overlooking tropical gardens. Closer to the shoreline lived the waterside workers—labourers, gardeners, pickers and those relying on the sea for a living. To the east the sun edged over the horizon like the yolk of the perfect three-minute egg.

Samoa's porter, a young red-headed lad from Brisbane hired by the Lutheran-owned lodging house at the west end of Charlotte Street, unloaded the four crates and one leather trunk from his porter's barrow and departed a silver crown richer. Samoa paced the wharf impatiently. *Mystery* was tied up before her but there was no activity. Samoa eyed the single-masted cutter that would be her transport and accommodation for the next several weeks.

The shallow-draft 40-footer—with its 12-foot beam and fore and aft schooner rigging—had been built in Freemantle in 1886 as a pearler, by a shipwright named Charles Walker. Built of jarrah, over a white gum frame, she had karri pine deck and topsides. Samoa thought the vessel could use a lick of paint.

Someone approached. Samoa turned sharply.

'Can I help yer, miss?'

The bare-footed aboriginal man was coal black, tall, slim to the point where he looked undernourished. He was bare-chested and wearing only three-quarter trousers, with his long matted hair tied back under a red bandanna.

'Oh … ah … ah, yes. I'm supposed to be meeting Mr Gaston here, now, at dawn.'

'Tatsuo?'

'Yes. I was to meet him here at *Mystery,* but there's no-one about.'

'Oh them buggers'll be below deck, Missy, asleep.'

'Asleep!'

'Yes, sleepin' off the grog, I should think. You must be Miss Sam … Samsao …'

'Samoa.'

'Yeh, that's it, Samoa, like the island, eh?'

'How did you know?'

'Oh, Skipper Tatsuo tell me you might be 'ere at sparrow fart, but I wasn't expectin' one so …. so ladylike, if'n yer knows what I mean.' Samoa couldn't help but smile. 'That's s'posed to be flatterin' by the way,' the aboriginal added. 'Eh?'

'And you are?'

'Skipper call me "Reaper."'

'Reaper?'

'Yes, Miss, like that Grim Reaper bugger, 'cos 'e reckons I'm a skinny bastard like the Reaper 'imself.'

'Well, that's not very nice.'

'Oh, I don't care, miss. Skipper's a good man, most o' the time.'

'Are you saying you work for Mr Gaston?'

'Yes, Missy, I'm 'is first mate. I'm his only bloody mate.' Reaper hacked a laugh.

'What's your real name?'

'Horace.'

'Horace.' Samoa laughed, but didn't mean to.

'Yeh, I know.' Reaper laughed back. 'Horace funny name for blackfella. I'm happy with Reaper, but ...'

Reaper dragged the trunks across the gangplank to the for'd hatch, ready for storing below decks. The travelling trunk was lighter. This activity on deck finally woke the crew, and Tatsuo's face was the first to appear from the companionway.

'You made it alright, then?' he said, smacking his lips as if he'd eaten something with fur on it.

'Of course,' Samoa replied. She scrutinised the man unashamedly. 'A little the worse for drink, are we?'

Tatsuo didn't bite, but pointed a finger at the deck and made a rotating motion for his passenger to turn her back. Samoa was slow to react, so Tatsuo simply unbuttoned the fly of his britches. Now Samoa turned her back and the skipper relieved himself over the port guardrail. It was at this moment that Pearl the red setter hobbled from her sleeping quarters under a small tender.

'Great guard dog, eh?' Reaper shook his head. 'She's deaf as a post, but it's a wonder she didn't smell yer.'

Pearl brushed up against Samoa's leg and sniffed at her unashamedly. Samoa smiled. 'Well, Pearl, do I meet with your approval?' she said, roughing the dog's head.

'She'll let yer know if you don't.' Tatsuo buttoned his baggy three-quarter britches. He looked to Horace. 'Those supplies arrive?'

'Aye, Boss, half an hour ago while youse were snoozin'.'

'Selma happy below decks?'

'Aye, Boss.'

'Then what are yer waiting for? Let's get underway.'

'Aye, aye, Cap'n.' Reaper hammed up the reply to the order for Samoa's benefit and she thought how out of place he seemed aboard the cutter.

As William jumped ashore to loosen the ropes, Reaper loosened the ties on the furled sails and Samoa felt the outgoing tide drift the boat away from the docks.

Immediately the steel-hulled merchant trader docked alongside sounded its horn. *All hands on deck.* What had appeared to be a deserted ship ten minutes earlier was coming to life.

Tatsuo caught Samoa's' interest. 'That's the SS *Mary Smith* from Rockhampton, up here for cattle.'

'Cattle?'

'Yeh.' Tatsuo nodded towards Grassy Hill and the top end of the main street, where 200 head of cattle were rushing towards the docks, wrangled by half a dozen cowboys. Samoa looked on, fascinated, as the hooting and rumbling brought the sleepy township awake. It was like a stampede. The dust storm approached faster than she'd expected and the wranglers drove the animals along the wharf towards the steamship.

'The boys bring them overland and rest them overnight a few miles outside town!' Tatsuo yelled over the racket.

They watched as the cattle were led through a narrow race and into stalls on the lower deck of the *Mary Smith*.

'They do it early morning, before it gets too hot. They're running late today.'

As they watched Tatsuo allowed *Mystery* to drift with the tide while Reaper and William set the jib. Within a minute he steered the cutter close by the steamship for Samoa's benefit. She was clearly fascinated.

'Have a look over the side!' he called to her from the helm.

'What?'

The skipper motioned for his passenger to look at the water below.

'Oh my God!'

'Big buggers, eh?'

As they looked on, at least a dozen crocodiles barked and hissed, thrashing in anticipation. The prehistoric monsters instinctively knew they spooked the cattle.

'Occasionally one of the cows will panic and jump the race, falling into the water.'

Samoa was thrilled and terrified at the same time, gaping at the unusual spectacle. She had never seen anything like it.

'Some of the larger beggars reach 16 to 20 feet, they say. But no one has ever been brave enough to measure one.'

As if doomed to his fate, a young bull—panicked by the clatter of machinery, the yelling and the crocodiles gathered under the ship— leapt the rail, plunged into the water and was lost in a flurry of thrashing tails and muddy water.

Sickened, yet mesmerised, Samoa looked on in silence while a steady southerly blew *Mystery* away from Cooktown Harbour and the Endeavour River estuary. Tatsuo spun the wheel, steering east towards deeper water, and *Mystery* soon ploughed north, into a moderate swell in from the Coral Sea, and on a heading for Thursday Island. Samoa allowed the skipper space. She knew north of Cooktown was littered with dangerous reefs and coral shoals and any self-respecting seafarer needed to keep his wits about him.

'Don't be worried, Missy,' Horace said, noting Samoa's concern. 'He's a bloody good cap'n, is our Tatsuo.'

'I'll take your word for it.'

With the sails set to a stiffening breeze, Horace and William the deckhand sat at the bow, their legs over the side, enjoying the ride. Below deck interesting aromas, some identifiable, others more exotic, escaped from the cowl over the galley below, where Selma prepared breakfast and simmered a curry for later. Samoa was content to hang onto the main sheet and enjoy the view, including that of the skipper, who clearly knew his way through the myriad of coral cays making up Cook's Passage, or the Great Barrier Reef as it was now commonly called. For her part, she attracted the skipper's attention, her long blonde hair loosened into the wind and trailing off the stern like the main of some fairy-tale unicorn.

'So tell me,' Tatsuo yelled above the cracking of canvas, the slapping bow waves and hissing spray, 'I meant to ask, what's in the crates?'

'Bibles.'

'Bibles!'

'Yes. When my brother Rennison wrote me last he ordered 500 bibles for the missionaries on Mist Island.'

'You really still believe he is on Mist—'

'Yes, why shouldn't I?'

'I told you why yesterday. You know what I believe.'

'You don't know Rennison, Mr Gaston.'

'Tatsuo, please.'

'Tatsuo. My brother is a resilient man.'

'So are the bloody islanders.'

Samoa was silent a moment. If she was to endure this man for several weeks, she thought she had better befriend him rather than antagonise him.

'So, Tatsuo Gaston,' she finally said, 'what's your story? You have a two-fold name, yet you sound like a true Queenslander.'

'Well I *am* a true Queenslander.'

'So what's the story behind the name?'

'My father was a French sailor, from Marseilles, and a born seafarer. My mother was the daughter of a Japanese pearl diver—one of the deep-sea divers using the hard hat gear.'

'Interesting. Where are they now, in Cooktown?'

'No, my father died when I was sixteen. So my grandfather, Yoshi Sato, became my surrogate father. He taught me hardhat diving and swearing in Japanese. I'm pretty good at it, too, if you don't mind me saying so.'

'What, swearing in Japanese?'

'No.' Tatsuo laughed showing off pearl-white teeth and a handsome countenance. 'Hard hat diving. It's a whole different world down there.'

'And your mother?'

'She lives with my half-sister in Brisbane. She's well into her eighties and suffers from memory disease.'

'Oh, I'm sorry.'

'Don't be—she doesn't remember me at all.'

Samoa was about to ask further questions when Tatsuo steered the conversation away from himself.

'The time has come. Tell me about yourself, Samoa Plum.' Samoa was contemplative for a moment. 'It *is* Samoa, as in the island,' Tatsuo continued, 'right?'

'Yes. My brother and I were found on a beach … and, yes, a deserted and remote beach on the Samoan island of Savaii.'

'Found?'

'Yes. That was in 1871. I was not two years old. My brother was eight months old. We were castaways from a wrecked ship, found by natives of the island and taken to missionaries of the London Missionary School on the main Samoan island of Upolu, where we were brought up in their faith. We were both eventually sent to London for schooling, but no one really knows our origins. I have been told I appear Scandinavian.'

'Yes, I can see that. So how did two babies survive on a deserted beach?'

'We were washed ashore with our mother who apparently died from loss of blood. The story goes that she was cut up badly on a reef swimming us ashore. Saving our lives. That's all I know.' Samoa watched a pod of dolphins gambolling across the cutter's bow and felt at ease. 'Marseilles, huh?' Samoa asked.

'Sorry?'

'You said your father was from Marseilles.'

'Yes.'

'Do you speak his language?'

'French?'

'Yes.'

'I do, actually. Do you?'

'No. But I do speak a little German, taught to my brother and me by a Bavarian nanny we had in London. My brother speaks it more fluently. He is interested in anthropology, you see, and studied the German scholars, especially the ones whom he found to be more controversial, like Karl Marx.'

'Oh, well, if he speaks German it could come in handy with the Germans claiming territories in Southeast Asia and the Pacific, like northeast New Guinea.'

'So, did you inherit this boat?'

'Good Lord, no. I purchased her from the widow of a pearler washed overboard and lost at sea three years ago. The *Mystery* was built for speed, with the pearling fishery being so competitive.'

'Yet you don't use her for pearling—you trade.'

'Aye.'

'Trade what exactly?'

'Oh, this and that. Anything to make a quid.'

'Do you always wear a gun?' Samoa asked, looking at the Enfield revolver, Mark 1, quite at home holstered on Tatsuo's right hip.

'At sea, always. And on land, too, if I smell danger.'

The wind picked up and both the mains'l and the billowing jib pulled *Mystery* across a choppy sea at what Tatsuo estimated to be six knots. Samoa became nauseas, her stomach knotted.

You alright?'

'Not really. Haven't got my sea legs yet.'

'Go see Selma, she has sugared ginger that the Chinamen use. It'll settle your stomach.'

Tatsuo watched Samoa turn to face him as she descended the companionway. They exchanged brief smiles and Tatsuo thought about how his passenger was such a breath of fresh air, especially after the hardened lasses of the north who usually vied for his attention.

Below deck Selma was cooking the curry for later that day. Although Selma had celebrated her fiftieth birthday only weeks earlier, Samoa recognised Selma would have been an attractive woman in her youth—before 30 years of life at sea, tropical sun, and many hours of recreation in the hotels of Queensland had taxed her body. And Selma took a shine to Samoa. She'd liked the assertive young blonde woman the moment she'd spoken confidently to the skipper at the White Horse Hotel. Selma figured the lass called a spade a spade.

Samoa stood unsteadily in the galley, where the confined humidity did nothing for her nausea. Selma could see immediately Samoa was pale. 'Crook, huh?' Samoa said nothing, nodded.

Now for the first time she noted Selma's teeth were stained red, like her gums were bleeding badly, but realised the cook chewed betel nut, or *buai*, as the natives called it. The narcotic was addictive and gave the user a rush of energy—a rush of energy, Samoa guessed, that the cook needed in order to work where she did. That also explained the splotches of red on the deck where Selma's excess spit didn't make the spittoon.

The air below deck was oppressive and made Samoa feel worse, particularly in the galley—it was like a hot box, where the cooking aromas that had teased her appetite at the helm now had the opposite effect.

'Here.' Selma uncapped the porcelain lid of a bulbous blue and white Chinese pickle jar and used chopsticks to pluck a large piece of ginger from its syrupy bath. 'Eat this, it'll settle your belly.'

Samoa took the ginger and bit into it. It was sticky, sweet and spicy, and more pleasant than she'd expected. 'Now go up into the fresh air,' the old cook prescribed. 'And tell the skipper breakfast is on its way.'

Samoa looked at the iron skillet grilling over the flame and thought Selma had burnt something. Selma caught her interest. 'Blood pudding, lovey—yer want some? I'm serving it with fried bread and tomato relish.'

Samoa shook her head.

'Well, soon as you feel better you need to eat, otherwise you'll fade away.'

'Thanks.' Samoa looked at the stew bubbling on the stovetop. Whatever it was smelt exotic, but she had definitely lost her appetite. 'What's that?'

'Curry, lovey. It's a mutton stew I learnt from Indians in town. You better get used to it 'cos Tatsuo loves his curries, and that's all you'll be getting' until Thursdee Island.'

'Thursday Island?'

'Yes, lovey. With this wind we should get there in under four days.'

'Wait, you said Thursday Island!'

'Yes.'

'But we are going to Mist Island, in the Solomons.'

'Not this leg, we ain't. Maybe next week.'

'Next week!' Samoa spun on her heels and mounted the gangplank. Tatsuo had no warning as she stormed the helm. 'Selma tells me we are heading for Thursday Island.'

'Aye. That's right.'

'What?'

'I have important business there.'

Samoa looked at the binnacle and then at the sun high overhead. She should have realised they were now sailing north, but in her own defence she'd thought they were still negotiating the reefs.

'You turn for Mist Island … NOW!'

Tatsuo was not one to be intimidated, especially not by a woman, goddamned beautiful or not. 'Sorry, Missy …'

'Miss Plum!'

'Miss Plum. Like I said, I have important business on Thursday Island, then I will sail directly for Mist.'

'You lied to me!'

'W-Wait a moment. No one *lied* to you …'

'You didn't tell me you had to go to Thursday Island first.'

'You didn't ask.'

'Why would I ask? I assumed you were sailing direct.'

'Ah, well, there you go. You should never assume.'

'Bah!'

'This is Northeast Queensland Miss … Miss Plum. This is the last frontier. Anything can happen. I have to make the most of what opportunities come along. I have to make a living. I am responsible for the welfare of my crew. I …'

'*Bullenscheisse!*'

'Pardon?'

'You heard. Bullshit. You had a duty to inform me of your plan.'

There was something very attractive about a woman so angry and swearing in a foreign language. Tatsuo stifled a laugh. Samoa grew angrier.

'Hey, I'm sorry, alright?' he capitulated. 'I should have told you, yes. But I do have a very important rendezvous on Thursday with a ship sailing in from India.'

'What ship? What's so important?'

'Can't say, I'm afraid.'

This answer only made Samoa angrier. She took a huge breath in, savoured the fresh air, and expelled. The swell had picked up and this altercation had made her forget her mal de mer. Samoa stepped to the starboard guardrail and, leaning on the rail, she stared out towards the eastern horizon. In the distance the sky was a hazy silvery-grey and she thought she caught, albeit briefly, a faint wisp of lightning.

'How long to Thursday Island?' she asked over her shoulder. Her tone had softened and her words threatened to vanish into the wind. But Tatsuo had keen hearing.

'Should be there day after tomorrow.'

More *bullenscheisse*, Samoa thought. Selma had told her under four days. *Under four, day after tomorrow—what's the difference?* She would just have to tag along.

Samoa pushed away from the guardrail and caught the stern sheets before she stumbled. The waves were now crashing over the bow and *Mystery* was riding growing seas. Immediately Samoa read the concern on the skipper's face. He, too, studied the eastern horizon.

'Are we in for a storm?' Samoa asked, suddenly concerned.

'You could say that.' Horace joined Tatsuo at the helm and together they studied the barometer. It read less than 29.

Samoa positioned herself forward, sitting on the cabin skylight amidships. The weather was sultry and the spray hissing over the bow did not bother her. Better to enjoy the fresh air, Samoa considered, rather than the oppressiveness below decks or, God help her, enduring the company of the annoying skipper at the helm. Pearl, the ship's mascot, wobbled on her three legs to join Samoa and fetch a pat. Moments later Samoa barely heard Will the deckhand approach. Planting his feet apart for balance, he held a large pad on a clipboard and seemed to be sketching her with a lump of charcoal as he said, 'You alright, miss?'

'Yes.' She looked up at the young man. He was handsome enough, but she figured he was a little slow upstairs. 'Yes, thank you, William. What are you drawing?'

'You, Miss.'

'Oh.'

'I'll show you when I finish.' Will kept working on the portrait. 'You can call me "Will,"' he said in a slow drawl. 'Or Willy some calls me.'

'Alright. Will it is.'

Will's hair was not unlike hers, long and white; his was just unkempt and knotty, sticky with salt air. She tried to study his face but he had the sun behind him, creating a silhouette. Samoa shaded her eyes. 'Been with the *Mystery* long?'

'Since I was fourteen, Miss. I used to run errands for Burns Philp, but they pay me fuck all.'

Samoa spontaneously laughed. She hadn't expected such strong language. 'Oh, so Mr Gaston offered you a job then, when you were fourteen?'

'Yes, Miss.' Will suddenly twitched. He tried to continue sketching but the tic was winning. His neck snapped and his head jerked sharply. He punched the air with his fist. 'Fuck!' he yelled. 'Fuck you, fuck them.' Samoa jumped. He twitched violently, ticking for several seconds.

Samoa kept her seat and waited patiently.

'Sorry, Miss, I can't … fuck … hel-help it … fuck!'

A realisation suddenly dawned on Samoa, sparked by the spontaneity of the lad's movements and uncontrolled language. Before leaving London she had visited the hospital of the London Missionary School where a French doctor was working with the English doctors diagnosing this very same hysteria. It even had a name, Tourette's syndrome, named after the French neurologist who'd pioneered the study of the affliction that same year Samoa was there, in 1885.

'Will! Will!' Horace appeared from nowhere and grabbed the lad's arm. 'Enough o' that talk. Get for'd.' Horace released his grip. The lad revealed his sketch. It was almost finished—and undeniably a portrait of Samoa.

'That's wonderful, Will,' she said.

'I'll give it to yer when it's finished,' he said, and skulked away.

'Sorry, Missy,' Horace said. 'Will's a mad bastard sometimes. Sayin' all them words in front of a lady.'

'It's alright, Horace. I understand it's a sickness of the mind and he can't help it.'

'Really.' The aborigine studied Samoa cautiously. 'You understand them things, why he cusses an' all?'

'Yes. I learnt all about it in London, in a hospital.'

'You a nurse?'

'A little. I know enough to wrap a wound or splint a broken leg.'

'Then maybe you can fix the little bugger.'

'Oh, there's no cure, I'm afraid. It's something he will have to live with all his life.'

Reaper watched Will negotiate the bow, positioning himself behind the mainsail locker for cover from the spray.

'No cure, huh? Poor bugger. Him get into fights with drunks what don't understand.'

'Then maybe he should stay out of bar rooms, Horace.'

'Who, William? Nar, don't think so, Missy. Him like the grog too much.'

A brief waterspout spiraled into the sky from a reef a few miles out to the east, catching their attention. Further out to sea a rainbow broke up and dissolved. Samoa caught Horace shivering involuntarily. 'Hmm,' he said 'big storm comin' our way.'

'Oh?'

'Yes, Missy. You see 'em big rainbow out to sea?'

'Yes.' Samoa concentrated back towards the horizon but the rainbow had totally vanished.

'Bad omen, Missy Samoa. Rainbow see, rainbow gone, bad omen. It mean storm comin', an' big bugger, eh?'

'How big?'

'Maybe big wind blackfella call willy-willy.'

'You mean cyclone?'

'Aye, Missy.'

Samoa cast the anxious eye of a landlubber towards the dark sky in the east. There certainly appeared to be some truth in Horace's prediction.

'When … I mean, how soon?'

'Tomorra maybe, maybe next day. Willy-willy build up and head for land sure as I'm blackfella.'

Exhausted from her journey to Cooktown the day before, the oppressive heat, and an early morning—matched with sea air and Selma's hearty curry and potatoes—Samoa managed to fall into a very deep, dreamless sleep. And her berth was surprisingly comfortable in the stern, alongside Selma, who was snoring like a bullock driver.

But Samoa woke to high seas. Waves twice the height of yesterday's, rolling in from the northeast and crashing across the starboard bow. Samoa made the deck with difficulty. Overhead was overcast and off to the east the grey horizon, now a darker shade, seemed closer. Like a lantern in a London fog, the sun battled to penetrate the gloom. Horace was at the helm dressed in a sou'wester oilskin, fighting to hold the wheel steady to keep the cutter on its northerly course. Samoa gripped the companionway rail. One moment she was looking towards the sky and the next she was peering into the canyon-like trough between mountainous white-capped waves. Samoa felt her heart race. She had sailed through a huge storm south of Ceylon some years back, and whilst it had been terrifying, this had the makings of being a lot worse.

Instantly Tatsuo was directly behind her on the steps leading to the deck.

'Stay below!' he cried out over the howling seas. Samoa didn't need to be told twice. 'There's cheese and dry biscuits for breakfast, and some fruit. The galley fire's been doused,' he said, squeezing by her on the steps. But the last thing Samoa could think of was her hunger.

Back in the galley-saloon Samoa found Selma had finally crawled from her bunk. William slid from one side of the bench seat to the other and back again, seemingly enjoying himself while eating mangos.

'Biscuits, cheese and mangos!' Selma shouted over the din of hanging pots, pans and utensils crashing against each other like tuneless church bells.

'What was that?' Samoa shouted back.

The old cook didn't bother to answer, she simply pointed to a small wooden box of tropical fruits, a bag of ship's biscuits and a ball of Edam cheese threatening to roll off the table.

The crazy seas continued unabated all that day and throughout the night. By day three Tatsuo and Horace were exhausted. Finally, with a cyclone now imminent, Tatsuo steered into Newcastle Bay in Torres Strait, to the lee side of Turtle Neck Island. They were a day's sail south of Thursday Island, but, as Tatsuo told the others, riding the storm out at sea amongst the many shoals, reefs and islands, was not an option. They would have to take their chances with the shallows and mangroves of Turtle Neck Island. Here on the bay the barometer was reading well below 29.

'At least we're not alone!' Tatsuo cried from the helm, over the screaming wind, as they anchored in 20 feet of water a hundred yards offshore. Three other vessels had made the same decision—drop anchor, batten down hatches and pray to your god, whoever that might be.

Tatsuo recognised the bêche-de-mer cutters *Victory's Prize* and *Emily*, being acquainted with the captains of both vessels. The *Emily's* skipper, Andy Mulgrave, had his wife and infant on board. A more ambitious skipper, known only as Bligh because of his tyrannical reputation, owned the *Victory's Prize*. They exchanged nervous waves. But the two-masted merchant vessel, whose nameplate he thought he read as *Jamaica Prince*, was a stranger. And by now, even here in Newcastle Bay, the seas were picking up. It was clear they had the worst of the winds to come. It would be every man for himself. It was going to be a long night.

The willy-willy was on its way.

Dawn

The vortex of death and demolition entered the Torres Strait with the destructive force of a dozen undisciplined armies ... *Take no prisoners, destroy all in your path.*

Tatsuo looked across the bay to the other three vessels. The barometer had earlier dropped from 29.66 to 28. Suddenly the wind shifted to northeast by north. Already the *Jamaica Prince* was dragging its moorings. But closer to shore, and in more danger, *Victory's Prize* and *Emily* both decided, as the tide was full, to weigh anchor. They would blow ashore into the mangroves, where the ebb would hopefully leave them high and dry and the crew could evacuate to safety. The option was to risk being blown ashore at low tide and foundering on rocks in shallows, only to be totally lost as the tide returned with massive waves crashing the shoreline.

Emily made the first move. She slipped anchor and bore away on the wind, her captain aiming for a narrow inlet between thick mangroves. But they hit rocks and swung broadside to the inlet. The cutter tipped 45 degrees with her deck listing seaward where huge seas washed over her. As he watched through blinding rain, Tatsuo saw the helmsman wash overboard. Terrified at witnessing what had just happened, skipper Bligh, aboard the *Victory's Prize*, was having second thoughts. But it was too late. His vessel, lighter than the rest and drawing only six feet of water, lifted on a huge wave. Fortunately Bligh had the bow to shore. The cutter surfed on the wave before grinding to a halt on the sandy bottom. They were in less than a fathom of water.

The next wave was a rogue. It rolled beneath *Mystery* like a giant whale, gathering speed as it reached the shallows. It then lifted the *Victory's Prize* like a toy, carrying it up into the mangroves, where skipper Bligh was slammed against the deck, but fortunately survived.

The *Jamaica Prince* was not so lucky. As the eye of the cyclone passed several miles offshore to the southeast there followed a change of wind direction. The captain took this opportunity to slip the anchor cables and go with the wind. As Tatsuo watched helplessly, waves rolled the old merchant vessel onto her port side, listing her dangerously, threatening to capsize her. The vessel righted briefly, but the next wave took her the hundred yards to the shore, smashing her against rocks. She broke up immediately.

The wind was now at its most destructive. Tatsuo held firm at the helm, where Horace had lashed him to the wheel. He noticed the barometer was still falling. The *Mystery* rose and fell. But so far her anchors were holding, although they dragged several yards towards land, while huge seas rolled beneath them, thundering ashore.

Two hours later.
The cyclone finally passed, displaying terrifying lightning flashes as the winds shifted yet again. Still the *Mystery* drifted landwards and Tatsuo had to make the awkward decision to risk weighing anchor himself on the next full tide and surfing ashore, or riding it out. He watched the other vessels splinter into scrap, pounded relentlessly by huge waves, and decided to stay put.

His resolve paid off. By nightfall the willy-willy had passed and torrential rain peppered the flat sea about them for half the night. It was pitch black on the bay, they had lost their tender overboard, and there was nothing they could do except wait for first light.

Tatsuo, Selma and William settled on deck, passing around a bottle of rum. They were soaked through with the fine persistent rain. Samoa joined them, drinking from the bottle.

'I thought you didn't drink,' Tatsuo said.

The rum burnt Samoa's throat but she took a second swig before passing the bottle. 'On occasion,' she managed to say, staring at the destruction ashore.

'Aye.'

Fifty yards or so inland, a freshly lit bonfire flared. They all watched in silence, wondering how many had made it. Nobody spoke. They sat, exhausted, in shock, and waited for dawn.

First light appeared about 5 AM. It was eerily silent. The rain had stopped, yet a heavy mist lingered. William was relieving himself over the stern when he heard oars dipping into the calm bay.

'Ahoy, *Mystery*,' the raspy voice of a man who had spent the last 24 hours shouting, called out as the boat approached. It was skipper Bligh off the *Victory's Prize*.

Tatsuo appeared on deck looking the worse for wear. Bligh didn't look much better, especially with the burden of a bandaged head and his arm in a splint. 'Cap'n Bligh.' Tatsuo managed to grin. 'We live to see another day, huh?'

'Only just, Captain Gaston. Only just. I don't want to live through anything like that again in a hurry.'

'We've been in worse, but I must agree with you. Sorry about the *Prize*,' Tatsuo said of Bligh's boat.

Young William took the line thrown him by the tender's oarsman and acknowledged the man they all knew as Brannon. Brannon, a surly man in his forties with a real chip on his shoulder, had a large hooked nose and a generous pointed chin, which reminded William of a crescent moon when the man was in profile. Brannon also had a bald pate, while greasy hair sprouted from the back of his skull and cascaded to his shoulders like the mane of a man desperate to keep his hair. Horace appeared at Tatsuo's side and helped the wounded skipper on board. Brannon joined them. The two skippers shook hands like old mates and stood for a moment in reverent silence. They observed the shore where flotsam and jetsam and maritime wreckage was strewn for hundreds of yards in both directions.

'Mulgrave lost his infant,' Bligh finally said quietly.

'No!'

'Aye, little fella was only eight months. A boy—Jason.'

'Oh, Jesus. How is Mulgrave?'

'He's coping, but his wife Molly's a mess.'

Now that the light was improving Tatsuo thought he could make out Mulgrave's wife sitting before the campfire that had been blazing hours earlier. The two seamen studied the wreckage as Tatsuo said, 'The *Emily* looks a total wreck—what about the *Prize*?'

'If I get carpenters down from Thursday Island I reckon I can salvage her. And I've got a hold full of pearl shell.'

'Good, that's a bonus.'

Samoa and Selma appeared from below deck, Samoa turning Bligh's head.

'Miss.' He went to tip his hat. 'Huh! Forgot. I lost me hat in the big blow.'

Tatsuo introduced the new arrival. Bligh and Brannon both knew Selma.

'Samoa, huh? Pretty name. Would that be Samoa as in the islands?' Bligh asked, not disguising his eye for the ladies, even though his wounds pained him. Samoa nodded. Samoa's first impressions were that the man fancied himself as a libertine, yet at sixty years of age she thought he should know better. He reached in to shake Samoa's hand, which she obliged hastily, only to catch Bligh's foul breath. Tatsuo would tell her later the captain was terrified of the dentist.

'Nice to see such beauty amongst such destruction.' Bligh panned an eye from Samoa's bosom to the company on board *Mystery*. 'And amongst such ruffians,' he said in jest.

'Careful, Bligh.' Tatsuo professed offence. 'I do believe it is us ruffians that are your only ticket away from here.'

'Aye, yer right, o' course. But, as yer can see, it's your tender we found washed up,' Bligh said. 'So can we row yer ashore for a parley?'

The tender sat low in the water with seven passengers on board. Tatsuo heard the *Emily* had lost three of her crew as well as baby Jason. *Victory's Prize* had lost two.

'Did you know anyone aboard the merchant?' Tatsuo asked, referring to the *Jamaica Prince*.

'No, no one,' Bligh said. 'Sam and Bill, two of my boys, went to investigate and said there was no sign of life. There is, however, a bounty of tinned produce to salvage, but we have a croc problem. There's some big bastards in the mangroves around where she broke up.'

As if on cue, thrashing in the water close to shore put everyone on edge.

'Jesus! Will you look at that?'

As they all watched on anxiously from their tender they saw drifting in shallow water, still some distance from shore, two huge crocodiles fought over human remains. Hands on the clinker's gunwale were smartly retracted, while Brannon rowed even harder, nosing into an inlet where they could wade ashore.

No one loitered.

It was midday by the time all survivors and their few private possessions were stowed aboard the *Mystery*. Thursday Island was a day's sail away, where skipper Bligh planned to charter another vessel and return to salvage what they could. While some men stood guard with long clubs and rifles to ward of the crocodiles, others stacked as much of the *Jamaica Prince's* cargo as possible above highwater mark. Although Tatsuo had other business and would not be able to return any time soon, it was agreed he would share 20 per cent for his efforts. That is, of course, if Bligh could be trusted. All they could do was hope no one else discovered the cache before they returned.

Half an hour past midday Tatsuo heard news from Horace, news he simply did not wish to hear.

'The rudder's jammed big time, Boss. Bloody thing got somethin' stuck in 'er.'

Tatsuo climbed over the stern, lowering himself into position where a brief inspection revealed the problem. 'We've got a dead mangrove root wedged between the shaft and the skeg,' he called up to his mate.

The tide was returning. With only the bow anchor mooring the *Mystery*, the stern swung towards the shore. Tatsuo cast a wary eye across the calm waters of the bay. Only 50 yards away hungry crocodiles were cleaning up the carnage. He looked up to the anxious faces peering back down at him, relying on him. There were no volunteers. There was no option but to drop into the water headfirst and cut the root free. Horace appeared amongst the faces holding a handsaw from the tool chest and a pair of goggles. Tatsuo shook his head. This was madness. 'William!'

William looked down, terrified. 'Y-yes, Cap'n?'

'Get rope and tie my feet.' Tatsuo attempted a brave face. 'Then secure the other end to the rail so I can't disappear into the drink, savvy?'

'Aye, Boss.' William's voice regained confidence. For a moment there William had thought *he* was to go in the water. Tatsuo's ankles were tied with the rope, the other end looped about the guardrail. While Selma and Samoa watched for predators, William and Horace positioned themselves, ready to haul the boss up immediately, should a crocodile approach. Armed with the handsaw Tatsuo took a deep breath and lowered himself headfirst into the water, down to his knees.

All of those on board held their breath, too.

Tatsuo worked fast. Feeling about in the murky water he attacked the root, first on the port side. The root was thick and gnarly and the saw blunt. Tatsuo twisted his body about, wriggling back to the surface for air. Through his goggles Tatsuo saw Horace looking down at him nervously. 'Hurry, Boss.'

Tatsuo snatched a second breath. On the third attempt he severed the port side of the root. He tugged at the thick, two-inch knotted tangle. It was stuck fast. He started hacking and sawing at the starboard side. Once that length fell away, he reasoned, it wouldn't be too difficult to loosen the remainder. Tatsuo came up for air, dived again. Finally severing the other side, he positioned himself to extract the remaining lump, holding the rudder in place.

Neither Samoa nor Selma noticed the crocodile.

Attracted by Tatsuo's splashing, the 20-foot croc slid soundlessly into the muddy water. It was less than 30 yards away. Samoa caught a glimpse of what at first she thought was wreckage, a large log maybe … 'Crocodile!'

The monster submerged. Skipper Bligh, catching the briefest glimpse, moved fast. 'Jesus! Pull him up. Pull him up … NOW!'

Tatsuo, upside down, waist deep, felt the urgency. The rope pulled taut around his ankles. One last desperate tug … One—last—*bash* … Tatsuo thumped at the root. It held. He pulled, bashed …

Yes! It dislodged. It pulled free.

Tatsuo's body was hauled from the water the moment the huge crocodile appeared back on the surface.

It was eight feet away and attacking.

'Pull, pull!' Bligh was shouting. Samoa joined in the tug of war. Suddenly William's bare feet slipped along the deck. He lost his grip. Samoa and Horace were caught by surprise. The rope shot through their fingers and Tatsuo dropped back into the water.

Tatsuo had no idea how deep he submerged. But the water was clear enough to see the croc attack … Its massive jaws were about to crush his chest. Something glanced close by. Tatsuo caught a glimpse in his peripheral vision.

Another croc?

The croc closed in … Three feet … Two … Tatsuo gaped down its throat.

Pink gums … Hundreds of teeth. He closed his eyes …

On board, all available hands hoisted him aloft. Tatsuo was airborne the moment the crocodile struck. Yet all aboard heard a sickening crunch. Someone screamed. Someone else cursed. Tatsuo opened his eyes. Inches away the massive jaws crushed a sea turtle as Tatsuo was hauled over the rail, landing on deck like a freshly caught tuna. Bligh rushed to the guardrail as the huge croc and its prey dropped back beneath the surface in a plume of water. It was over in seconds.

Tatsuo, lying on the deck like a trussed hog, broke into a sudden laugh, a maniacal laugh.

'Christ!' he finally managed. 'Never a dull moment, eh?'

Samoa stood about with the others in total admiration of the skipper's bravery. No one spoke, and at that moment Samoa had a whole new respect for this crazy seaman.

Late afternoon

Comfortable with the fact that land was within sight to the west —Cape York, in fact—Samoa drew Tatsuo's attention to smoke and what seemed like civilisation five miles away, in a remote bay.

'That's Somerset,' Tatsuo said.

'Oh, I didn't realise there were any communities north of Cooktown.'

'There're several, in fact, mostly the bêche-de-mer fishers and guano getters.'

'Guano. You mean the fertiliser?'

'Fertiliser, bird shit, whatever.'

'Somerset, is it a port?'

'Yes. It was settled back in the mid-70s. It's not as busy now as it was ten years ago. These days, it's Thursday Island that attracts all the villains of the Coral Sea. But there's still a magistrate, police quarters, customs house, medical officer, hospital and a barracks for marines there. But I hear the town is falling apart.'

'Falling apart?'

'Yes. Literally. The wooden buildings are being eaten by termites. It's a godawful place.'

'You said marines?'

'Yes, for law and order and all that. Although I heard many have been replaced by educated blackfellas from down south.' Tatsuo thought a moment. 'But I'm told the only guns they have to protect themselves with are vintage, double-barrelled, muzzle-loading carbines. The percussion caps are so old that only one in five fire when they pull the trigger, so I'm told.'

'They shoot their own kind?'

'Yes. There's no love lost between the two. The aboriginals in north Queensland are notoriously warlike. The Yardaigan Tribe up here is particularly unfriendly.'

'Really?'

'Yes, and they attack on a regular basis. They are headhunters, you know, like their Pacific Island neighbours. Trouble is, in the past the pearlers and bêche-de mer men have stolen their women and burnt their villages, and destroyed their crops, causing havoc, and the natives on the islands about the Coral Sea take retribution on any white men they can for that reason. Some are friendly, but most are warlike.'

'You seem to know the area well.'

'I should do, I've worked it for years.'

Samoa looked to *Mystery*'s bow where Bligh sat with his mate Brannon and his six Islander divers and deckhands who were busy cleaning their valuable diving suits salvaged from the wreck of the *Victory's Prize*.

'Is he one of them?' she asked Tatsuo.

'One what?'

'One of the guilty ones, a pearler who harasses the natives?'

Tatsuo studied the old seafarer barking orders at the natives to do a better job cleaning.

'I've known Bligh some time now and I'd rather be his friend than his enemy. I've heard stories, sure, but I have no evidence.

Trouble is, it's like a sport up here, kidnapping the young aboriginal girls and the like.'

Samoa looked horrified. 'Are you … have you ever …?'

'Christ, no, Miss, what do you take me for?'

Chapter Two

Port Kennedy. Thursday Island. December 1897
Peripheral winds from the willy-willy persisted all day and into the night. Tatsuo made the most of these and by early morning the following day the *Mystery* had left Cape York, the northernmost tip of mainland Australia, 24 miles behind them, and was sailing amongst the 274 islands that dotted the Torres Strait.

'There she is,' Bligh noted proudly, stabbing a finger at Thursday Island amongst the archipelago. He looked to Samoa standing in the bows keenly scanning the shoreline as if she was searching for something. This blonde beauty had tempted his lustful thoughts since he'd first laid eyes on her and that had not go unnoticed by Samoa— or the others on board, for that matter.

'Thursday Island,' he said. 'It's only one-and-a-half square miles with the highest point the taller of them hills, Milman Hill … there.' Bligh pointed to the hill behind the township. 'Only 340 feet high.'

Samoa avoided conversation.

'Do you know who named it Thursday Island?' Bligh persisted.

'No,' Samoa finally answered wearily, her eyes glued to the island.

'They say it was Captain Bligh.'

'You mean the real Captain Bligh, the hero?' Samoa said, intentionally discourteous.

'Yes.' Skipper Bligh was wary. He was old, short and stocky with a weathered face and unpleasant disposition. During their short time together on *Mystery* he had learnt that this mysterious woman named Samoa after the Pacific islands was unattached, and past conquests during his years of travelling suggested it was worth a try.

'Hero, yes,' Bligh responded to Samoa's challenge, 'but he *was* also a tyrant, was our Captain Bligh.'

'I think history records he was more a disciplinarian rather than a tyrant,' Samoa said. 'You were saying?'

'Hmm. Well, apparently he discovered the island on a Thursday. Imaginative disciplinarian, eh? He called the neighbouring island Wednesday,' he added, as if to make a statement. 'And that one,'—Bligh pointed to a nearby island to the southwest—'he named Friday.'

Immediately the sails were furled. William pushed in front of Samoa to unsecure the forward anchor. They watched in silence a moment as the chain whipped through the hawsepipe and they moored amongst the pearl fleet in shallow water in Port Kennedy Harbour. It was late morning. After the persistent winds at sea, the contrast of the oppressive weather of a sheltered tropical island in the wet season enveloped them. It was like being in a glasshouse in summer after the plants were watered, someone suggested to Samoa. Dozens of vessels surrounded them, mostly pearl luggers along with their schooner motherships to supply them. There were also the vessels of the bêche-de-mer fishermen, a few merchant traders and the larger clipper ship, *Star of India*. The port was unexpectedly extra busy.

'There's been a big pearl shell trade here since the mid-80s,' Bligh told Samoa. 'I know for a fact that over 200 pearlers call Port Kennedy home. They're mostly Asian, from the Philippines, China, Japan to Malaya and India. Even some Jamaicans and Spanish. Real big mix, I reckon. I'm one of the few whitefella skippers.'

Samoa listened but showed no signs of attentiveness.

'The golden lip oyster shells are used mainly for making buttons, you know.'

Of course Samoa knew this. 'Really,' her tone seeped sarcasm but the skipper was none the wiser. Or chose not to be offended.

'Mostly the shell is exported as raw material to London.' Samoa knew this also. 'Pearls are rare, though; they are a bonus. I've managed to secure eight these past few months.'

Bligh took a small leather pouch from his pocket. 'Care to see?'

Now he commanded Samoa's attention. He took her open hand and tipped the pearls into her palm. Samoa admired the unique rawness of the pearls, their lustre. They were the size of plump peas and all were spherical except one that was ringed. Seven were the standard iridescent silver one would expect; however, one was golden and larger than the others.

'Beautiful, aren't they?'

'Yes. Yes they really are.' Samoa's words communicated a reverence Bligh did not expect.

'Tears of the sea,' Bligh said, using the moment to shuffle closer, enjoying the opportunity of his hand caressing hers as she held his pearls. 'That's what the more romantic amongst us call them.'

Bligh attempted to look into Samoa's eyes, awaiting her response, but she avoided eye contact.

'These are all South Seas Keshi pearls,' he went on. '"Keshi" means poppy seed in Japanese. I don't really understand the name myself, but that's the way it is.'

Immediately Samoa realised she had been hoodwinked into close contact. 'Thank you,' she said abruptly, returning the pearls.

Bligh pocketed the pouch and caught Samoa watching a diver on the nearest lugger washing down his hardhat diving suit with fresh water.

'Most of the pearl shell fields are in shallow water, 20 feet or less, and the divers free dive. But those suits are used in the deeper water. They need air pumped down to them with compressors.' Bligh pointed to the box-like compressors with their duel hand-turned wheels for pumping air below. There were three on board each pearler as each lugger had three divers: stern, amidships and bow. Dozens of pearlers depended on a schooner for supplies, enabling them to remain at sea for longer periods. Once a shell bed was cleared they moved on.

'Attacks of the bends are common for the deep-sea divers, too,' Bligh said. He scanned the moorings. 'This lot have all sailed north to take shelter from the cyclone.'

Looking towards the shore and the township Samoa noted the nearby beaches of the shallow-water bay. Here were shipwrights' slips, chandlers and marine suppliers. To the left was the township itself, not dissimilar to Cooktown in layout.

Voices behind broke Samoa's reverie.

'Aha! Good,' Samoa overheard Tatsuo talking to Horace. She looked over her shoulder. *'Star of India's* here already,' Tatsuo said, collapsing his spyglass and jumping from the aft locker hatch cover. Clearly he was referring to the clipper ship moored amongst three schooners half a mile away to starboard.

'So tell me, Captain Gaston,'—Samoa loosened her blouse; it was already adhering to her skin in the heat—'How long are we stuck here?'

'One day should do it.'

Samoa was immediately aware the man was staring at her breasts. She clasped at her chest. Tatsuo blushed. Or was that the heat?

'We ...' Tatsuo cleared his throat. 'We need fresh supplies,' he said, suddenly diverting his eyes elsewhere. Samoa enjoyed the discomfort she caused. It had been unintended but she felt it gave her an advantage. The oldest advantage in the world—seduction. Tatsuo looked back to the clipper *Star of India.* 'I have a cargo to transfer from another ship.'

'Cargo?'

'Yes. Over 50 crates and barrels. I suggest you go ashore with William.'

Now Tatsuo was keen to dampen Samoa's curiosity.

'You can spend the night at the Grand. That's one of three hotels on the main street. Mrs Alva Jones runs it. Her husband's a merchant and always at sea. She got bored so she bought a hotel. You can at least get a bath there.'

'Are you saying I need a bath, Captain?' Now Samoa was being impertinent.

'N-no … no, Miss, not at all.' The skipper blushed. 'But should you wish to enjoy a bath, well, I was just saying, you can get one at the Grand.'

'And a decent feed, too, Missy,' Horace added. 'Mrs Jones, she do good tucker, eh?'

Samoa waited behind—there was no rush. She sat under a parasol dangling her legs over the bow, where the outgoing tide tugged at the bow anchor pointing *Mystery* landwards. It took an hour for William to transfer the cyclone survivors ashore, and whilst she felt for the *Victory's Prize* crew, Samoa struggled to pity skipper Bligh, especially when he called out to her, 'Au revoir … until we meet again, mademoiselle.'

From where Samoa enjoyed watching the hustle and bustle of this tropical harbour she could see most of the southern part of the island, including the main street directly ahead and the shipyards and a cemetery off to her right. The beaches were white sand and the shoreline lined with frangipani and palms.

'William'll see you ashore next, Miss.' Tatsuo's bare feet had not betrayed his approach. Samoa looked up into the early afternoon sun directly behind the skipper. His face was eclipsed, but his outline was unmistakable. For Samoa, Hercules came to mind. She felt a hot flush, disguising it with a warm smile.

'Where will you …?' Suddenly the question seemed unnecessarily inquisitive. *Why should she care where he slept?*

'We always sleep on board, if that's what you were asking. Can't leave the *Mystery* unattended in port, not with all these rogues and villains about.'

Instantly they heard drunken revelry and a loud splash as someone nearby was heaved overboard for a lark.

'I believe there is a telegraph on the island?' Samoa asked, thinking of the underwater cable running from Paterson Cape, on the

Cape York Peninsula, to Thursday Island, which Samoa had heard had been completed eight years earlier.

'That's right.'

'Because I need to send a telegraph, since there has been a change of plan and I am on Thursday Island and not yet on my way to Mist Island.'

If there was a hint of derision, it was deliberate.

'You'll find the Cape York Telegraph Line office down from the Grand.' Tatsuo directed a nonchalant nod towards the small town. 'You could hardly miss it.'

Samoa was grateful to rent a vacant room on the first floor of the Grand Hotel, a timber, two-storey hotel with shuttered windows, boasting an electric overhead fan in each of the four upstairs bedrooms. Samoa even shared a balcony from where she could gaze out to sea; here the turquoise ocean rendezvoused with azure skies, making for a wondrous palette of blues, speckled with cotton balls of white cloud.

Now at late afternoon a welcoming sea breeze heralded sunset. The hotel taprooms were full of imbibers and the street full of inebriated gaiety while the island's two brothels, one owned by an American and called The Honey Pot, and a Japanese bordello called Yokohama, were both doing a roaring trade. A visitor could be forgiven for thinking they were witnessing a gold rush. And in a sense it was a gold rush, with over 200 pearlers calling Thursday Island home in these lucrative times.

Samoa that learnt 210 vessels, employing 1,500 men, worked from this port. The permanent population was around 1,600, more than half of which consisted of Europeans. The remainder, nearly all associated with the pearling or bêche-de-mer industries, were Filipinos, Japanese, Chinese, Malays, Aborigines, South Sea Islanders and Torres Strait Islanders. There was also a sprinkling of Cingalese, American Negroes, West Indians, Sudanese and Africans.

Samoa left her travelling satchel on the bed and ventured out to find the telegraph office. The bar of the Grand Hotel, one of two hotels on the island—the Hotel Metropole being further up the hillside—overflowed, with drinkers spilling out onto the main street.

The pearler *Dolphin* had recently returned with a good haul of shell and pearls and the owner, Daisuke Yamamoto, a generous captain, was celebrating with champagne in the bar. This tradition, Samoa was told by the landlady, always attracted hangers-on and drunkards in for a free drink.

Adding to the prosperity of Thursday Island, mail steamers destined for East Asian ports also called into Port Kennedy. The passengers flocked ashore for refreshment and an exotic experience, such as sampling one of the barbecued turtle steaks hanging from bamboo poles, offered by Chinese street vendors, or maybe a roasted seabird, the boobie, provided in the many eating-houses.

Samoa found the single-storey, timber telegraph agency next to the post office on the main street—the only street, in retrospect— then retired to the safety of her room. Here she observed the world from the balcony. The township below was not a place she wanted to be. From her elevated position Samoa had an unobstructed view of the main street and the harbour. But of particular interest were Tatsuo, Horace and William making several trips to the clipper, *Star of India*. Samoa watched intently as on each trip they returned with the tender laden with cargo—dozens of barrels and many crates of all shapes and sizes—which they stored below decks.

Soldiers at the recently completed Green Hill Fort west of the township, provided law and order on the island, the landlady told Samoa. The fort, completed five years earlier, in 1893, had been originally built to stave off the threatened Russian invasion that thankfully never eventuated. The fort's four heavy gun emplacements stood guard over an underground general storeroom, shell store, cordite room, lamp room and artillery store, all built with two-foot-thick concrete and stone walls beneath the emplacements. A 20,000-gallon reservoir stored water beneath the ground.

'The fort might offer *some* law enforcement,' Samoa thought. But as the moon traversed the sky, making its routine passage to the west, and the cool of night prepared for the heat of the new day, an observer would have noted that the soldiers appeared as drunk as the seafarers and islanders.

In the morning Samoa reflected that, for the most part, she had slept well. Mrs Alva Jones, the innkeeper, had been protective of her respectable single houseguest, delivering a tray of grilled chops, potatoes and lemonade to Samoa's room. And Samoa had indeed managed the bath, as Tatsuo had suggested. As she'd dropped into a deep sleep it was the image of Tatsuo that Samoa last envisaged, , the image of a man she knew she had wisely chosen for the task ahead.

Tatsuo had been the last customer to be locked out of the general store at the end of the day. He'd bought his necessities—a new pig-bristle toothbrush with a fancy bone handle, three small jars of cherry tooth powder and a jar of bear-grease hair restorer for the slight balding patch he vainly noted on the top of his head. He also purchased 50 pounds of Lucky Strike, an American tobacco, for trade. That would be delivered to *Mystery* first thing in the morning. As the merchants wound down business for the day, the inns and saloons on the island were just starting.

Tatsuo heard the revelry spilling from the bars and was contemplating refreshment when he heard a familiar voice. 'Tatsuo!' He turned to face Briana Pledge, the twenty-four-year-old daughter of General Christian Pledge of Her Majesty's Army.

'Briana!' Tatsuo looked about surreptitiously. The last time he'd been with the general's daughter all hell had broken loose. And it wasn't his fault the young lady was infatuated with older men, especially the likes of Tatsuo Gaston. 'Fancy seeing you here,' he floundered.

'Why? You know I come here often, with daddy.'

Tatsuo knew the redheaded, slim, buxom firecracker was based in Darwin with *Daddy*, *Mummy* having died many years earlier from consumption. Briana rushed into Tatsuo's rather stiff arms.

'Oh, sweetheart,' she said, 'it is so lovely to see you—what a surprise.'

She raised herself on her toes and kissed him on the lips.

If Tatsuo was honest with himself, he had to admit she looked stunning in her two-piece emerald green suit showing off her perfect, corseted waist, with the extra-wide sleeves puffy at the shoulders. This evening Briana had chosen a red bodice, which paired spectacularly with her deep green eyes. Her flame-red hair was tied back under a large feathered hat.

Tatsuo weakened. 'You look beautiful.'

'You don't look too shabby yourself,' she lied, slapping his chest with her silk fan. The fact that he looked exactly like a seaman *fresh* from the sea did not bother Briana; it was the man beneath the attire she wanted. 'How long are you here?'

'I was about to ask you the same thing,' he lied.

'Well?'

'Just tonight.'

'Really?' Briana didn't disguise her disappointment. 'Buy me a drink.'

'Briana I … I … ah, have to get back to the *Mystery.* The crew are waiting for me and I have work to do.'

'Tonight?'

'Sorry. We sail early and I have cargo to load.'

'Oh, sweetheart—one drink. One quick, little drink at the Metropole.'

The Metropole Hotel had a discreet ladies' parlour amongst the rear rooms. Then, again, very little was discreet in such a small island frontier town. Tatsuo was sorely tempted. But there was more at stake than Briana's reputation.

Tatsuo noticed they were being observed from across the street. Three soldiers in khaki uniforms, their faces shaded beneath pith helmets, stood watching. They were hardly tactful. Tatsuo knew they were from Green Hill Fort. And the British garrison was under the command of Army Captain Gerald Rafferty Reynolds, Briana's fiancé. A proper bastard at the best of times, and a man Tatsuo had the misfortune to have as a foe.

'We're being watched,' Tatsuo said.

Briana shot the soldiers a glare. They looked away temporarily. 'They'll run and report to Gerald. But I don't care.'

'Briana, you are engaged to be married to Gerald … ah, Captain Reynolds.'

'So daddy thinks. But I don't know if I'm ready.'

Briana slipped her arms through Tatsuo's and pulled him close for another kiss but Tatsuo pushed her away. Tonight, of all nights, he didn't want any trouble from Captain Reynolds and his soldiers.

'We'll have a drink next time,' Tatsuo promised, walking backwards. 'Word of honour.'

'Promise.'

'Yes. I promise,' he called back, turning and hurrying to the jetty.

8 AM

The rap of knuckles on Samoa's hotel door was expected. She was dressed and her satchel was packed. It was Miranda the native housemaid. 'You 'ave a visitor, Miss.'

'Thank you.'

'He's waitin' for yer in the dinin' room.'

9.20 AM

Young William rowed ashore for the second time that morning. On the first trip he noted their passenger, the attractive, blonde Samoa, was dining with a gentleman, and he decided to afford her privacy. William drifted in the tender a while just offshore, indulging himself in his favourite pastime, rendering rough sketches with charcoal on his pad, mostly of the ships in harbour. Now, one hour later, he returned to fetch the passenger.

William ran the tender aground on a sandy beach in front of the township. He dug the anchor flute into the sand above the high tide mark and was starting off through the reeds when three British soldiers in khaki from the garrison at Green Hill Fort intercepted his path.

'You off the *Mystery*?' one asked.

'Who … who …'—the intervention sparked William's Tourette's —'Fuckit, fuck you! Fuckem! Fuck!'

'Alright,' another soldier said, stifling a snigger, 'don't shit yer pants, yer moron—Jesus!'

William's upper torso twitched and he fought his affliction. He pinched his own arm to try and stop the tic. 'Fuckit …!' As profane as his language was, William looked intimidated—scared, even.

'Hey, watch yer mouth.'

'Christ,' the first soldier said, 'if'n yer goin' to swear, matey, we'll chuck yer in the cells.'

William struggled with body twitches and finally settled. 'Wh-who wants to know?' he managed.

'We do, yer idiot.'

'Leave him be, Doug,' the third soldier ordered. 'He's got a mental problem.'

'Yer mean he's fucked in the head, cheeky sod?'

'Yeah, he can't help it. It's a mental disorder. I have a friend back in Plymouth whose brother has the same problem.'

William stood silently, fighting his demons.

'He looks harmless enough,' the second soldier said.

'You *are* off the *Mystery*, are you not?' asked the third man.

William stared at the sand and nodded.

'Then tell your skipper he's to come to the fort. Captain Reynolds wants a word before you sail.' William remained silent.

'Captain Reynolds, got it?'

William nodded again.

'Go on, then.' Doug shoved William in the back. 'Go about yer business, then, and go change yer britches.'

'Captain Reynolds, remember?' the third soldier reiterated. 'That's an order.'

Twenty minutes later William rowed Samoa towards *Mystery*. Samoa thought William looked a little the worse for wear and smelt like he could use a wash, or a swim, at least. He offered little in the way of conversation, so Samoa made the most of the peace and quiet, alone with her own thoughts, about the past and the future.

Tatsuo leant from the top rung of the Jacob's ladder off portside, holding onto the sheets amidships, and took Samoa's hand, hauling her aboard.

'Welcome back, Miss.' He showed all the signs of genuinely meaning it.

'Thank you, Cap'n.' Samoa used the colloquial, feeding off the skipper's early morning joviality, surprised he wasn't nursing a sore head from drinking.

Tatsuo took Samoa's satchel from William.

'Sleep well?' he asked his passenger.

'Yes, very well.'

'It's a wonder. They don't call this *Thirsty* Island for no reason. The lads can get rowdy.'

'I even managed the bath you so highly recommended.'

'Good for you. Me and Reaper had to make do with a swim.' Tatsuo winked at his aborigine mate. Horace grinned back.

'A swim? After what you endured at Turtle Neck Island? I thought you'd be wary of diving so soon again.' Samoa peered over the side where she could clearly see the sandy bottom.

'Well, as you can see, Miss, we are anchored in less than 20 feet of clear water. Sure, there's sharks about, but you just have to be vigilant and avoid dillydallying.'

'I must confess, it does look inviting.'

'You swim, then?'

'Of course, and I'm not too bad at it, either. I might have been brought up in England but I have spent plenty of time in the warmer climates also.'

'Very good. If you haven't eaten, Selma has saved some hash fries.'

'Thank you, but I ate at the Grand.'

'So you did. Will told me he saw you dining with an older gentleman.'

Samoa stiffened. What was Tatsuo suggesting—that she had met someone on the island, had a romantic liaison?

'Ah, yes …' Samoa stalled briefly. 'I met an old acquaintance … He's a trader who happened to be on Thursday purchasing shell.'

Tatsuo held Samoa's eyes a moment—he knew she was hiding something. She looked away.

'German,' Tatsuo fished, biting his lip as if in thought.

'Pardon?'

'Will said he was certain he heard you speaking German.'

'My, my …' Samoa looked down the deck at William and Horace, who were talking while standing by to haul the tender aboard and weigh anchor. 'How astute that boy is. He may have heard the odd word or two, but I assure you I cannot converse fluently in German. Did you send him ashore to spy on me, perchance?'

'S-spy! Spy on you? Good God, Miss—never.'

There followed a brief moment of silence. Just the mewling of Pacific gulls circling overhead searching for food and the medley of various other nautical sounds—the cracking of canvas, the snapping of rigging, and cussed orders as dozens of craft prepared to sail. Tatsuo watched his two crewmembers, animated in conversation. 'Hoy!' he called out from the helm. 'Get that tender aboard.'

Horace hurried aft. 'We have a problem, Cap'n.'

'What? What problem?'

'Will says soldiers tell 'im on da beach you have to go ashore and see Cap'n Reynolds at the fort.'

Tatsuo knew exactly what it was all about. He and Captain of Her Majesty's British Army Gerald Rafferty Reynolds went back a ways. Reynolds had been born in 1849, the youngest of the 11 children of the curate of Cripplegate Parish Church in London. He'd risen to the rank of lieutenant in the East India Company's Indian Navy, and when that navy had been abolished, back in '62, he'd migrated to the Australia Colonies and subsequently joined the army. From Cooktown he was stationed in Somerset and finally in Green Hill Fort on Thursday Island.

Tatsuo called William aft and his deckhand told of the altercation. Tatsuo looked towards the fort on Green Hill. He had no doubt he was being watched through a telescope as they spoke. The skipper weighed up his options. There were still 30 or 40 luggers anchored in the bay. And, fortuitously, between them and the fort, a three-masted schooner was setting sails for departure, and the clipper *Star of India* was turning on the tide, obscuring some of the view.

'What we gonna do, Cap'n?' Horace guessed going ashore, was not an option.

'Will …' Tatsuo placed a hand on his deckhand's shoulder.

'Aye, Cap'n.'

'Pull the tender to port, so the bastards can't see it. But take care to tie her near to the stern. With haste, now, yer hear?'

William fed the tender's towrope around the shrouds, manoeuvering it to the port side of the lugger. 'Now set the sails.'

'Aye!' Horace leapt onto the sail lockers and worked at releasing the furled sails. William joined him. The morning breeze was with them, the canvas filled and, with Tatsuo at the helm, they tacked away from the bay, keeping as many vessels in the fleet between them and the fort as possible.

Locked onto the wheel with one arm, Tatsuo managed to raise the spyglass to his eye. 'They're onto us!' he yelled over cracking canvas.

With the jib billowing out, Horace had a chance to look towards the fort. His sharp eye warned him the men in the fort was preparing to fire one of their artillery pieces. Tatsuo spun the wheel to fill the sails, beating into a strong southerly. He was forced to sail south before turning east with Horn Island off to starboard. They saw the puff of smoke before they heard the boom. The fort's six-inch Armstrong gun had fired. A geyser of water lifted skywards 50 feet directly ahead of the bow.

'Jesus!' Tatsuo shouted. 'They mean business!'

Samoa's head appeared from below deck. 'What's happening?'

'Stay below.'

A second artillery round landed closer. Its plume exploded skywards 50, 60 feet high.

Horace checked the tender, which was bouncing along in their wake. 'What yer goin' ter do, Cap'n?'

'Run, mate, run.' Tatsuo saw the terror carved into the old aboriginal's face. 'Don't panic, Reap, they won't sink us. Those're just warning shots.'

'Shouldn't we turn back, Boss?'

'No bloody way. You know we can't.'

As Tatsuo had suspected, there were no more shots fired. Besides, they were soon out of range. Samoa approached the helm, arms crossed and wearing a scowl worthy of preserving on canvas.

'What was that all about?' she spat.

'Port dues.'

'Port dues?'

'That's what I said.'

'What do you mean "port dues"? Did you sail without paying the harbourmaster?'

'That's it, Miss. You hit the nail on the head.'

'And you want me to believe the fort fired their gun at us because you failed to pay, what, five pounds?'

'Two pounds, actually.'

'T-two pounds!'

'Yes.' Tatsuo's infectious smile returned, the smirk of a serial rake. 'Crazy, isn't it?'

Captain Gerald Rafferty Reynolds at the battlements of Green Hill Fort clamped his fingers and squeezed hard in anger until they hurt.

'Another round, Captain?' Chief gunner Sergeant Andrews was enjoying himself—anything to break the monotony. The captain was seething. Right here, right now, he would reintroduce public flogging! That mongrel bastard Tatsuo Gaston would be strapped over a gun barrel at this very minute and *he*, Captain Gerald Rafferty Reynolds, would wield the cat-o-nine-tails personally ...

Fifty, one hundred … no, two hundred lashes. The insubordinate mongrel cowboy bastard. Pirate! That's what he was, a fucking pirate.

'Captain?'

'What?'

'Will I fire off another warning shot?'

'No point—he isn't turning back. You'd have to sink him.'

'That *can* be managed, Captain.'

The captain harrumphed. The sergeant noted the captain's eyes were bloodshot with rage.

'But I'll catch that bastard sooner or later,' Reynolds swore. 'Mark my words, Sergeant, you—mark—my—words.'

Truth was, the navy gunboat HMS *Pride* was in maintenance on the Navy slipway right now. The 270-foot, 6,540-ton, conqueror-class ironclad, with its four 12-pounder guns, two four-inch guns and torpedo tubes was having repairs to the port steam engine. Interestingly, the bow of the HMS *Pride* even had an iron ram. The ram, however, had never been put into practice. It was considered obsolete, although the ship was only ten years old.

The whole vessel is obsolete, Captain Reynolds thought to himself, *that's why the British Government sent it to the colonies, but, by God, what I would like to do with that ram right now!*

The captain wheeled about and turned on the nearest corporal.

'Get me an updated report on HMS *Pride* from the slipway … on the double, now.' He turned to the sergeant. 'I want soldiers on that clipper, the *Star of India*, now. Drag the captain here in irons if you have to.'

With a fair southerly, *Mystery* enjoyed excellent sailing conditions between Horn Island to their south and out of Torres Strait towards the deep blue water of the Coral Sea. Tatsuo was keen to leave the coral reefs behind as shallow waters, shoals of the numerous islands and strong currents sometimes required two at the helm to keep the vessel on course. And the reef, Tatsuo knew, was fraught with dangers where coral rocks rose almost perpendicularly out of deep water.

'Take the helm,' Tatsuo ordered his mate. Horace shuffled behind the wheel and planted his bare feet well apart for balance. This was truly a savoured moment. 'We won't be going back to Thursday any time soon,' Tatsuo told the aborigine. Horace simply grinned. He loved this mad whitefella. Life was never dull with him. Tatsuo glanced along the deck to where Will remained at the bowsprit, one leg dangling either side, watching for coral reefs. Samoa had her back turned. She was clearly unhappy.

With the skipper below deck, Samoa joined Horace at the helm. 'New Guinea's directly north from, here is it not?' Samoa asked.

'Yes, Missy, 'bout 300 miles.'

'Have you ever been there?'

'Only once me and Cap'n go ashore on the south coast, but them blackfella there don't like 'em whitefella. Up north not so bad since German Empire come, but the blackfella on the coast, he kill 'em whitefella at the drop of a hat.'

'There are cannibals on many islands, I heard.'

'You heard 'em right, Missy. Blackfella here in Torres Islands and down coast north Queensland, many many cannibals. Headhunters, Cap'n call 'em.' Horace coughed a laugh—he found something humourous. 'We sail to Darnley Island sometimes to pick up shell. Them deep hard hat divers, they dive there real deep, 40 fathoms, but water dangerous and many divers they die from bends … You know what that is, Missy … the bends?'

'Yes, and it's a terrible way to die,' Samoa said of the decompression sickness that afflicted divers spending too much time in deep water and not decompressing as they returned to the surface. The bends could cause paralysis and death.

'Bloody oath, Missy. Anyways, Darnley Island is just north o' here. Many years ago a Dutch ship sent men ashore to fill water barrels and the blackfella, well, he was not bothered at first. The whitefella fill his barrels at the only place where them savages get fresh water all year, see. But when the whitefella start washin' clothes and swimmin' in the water, blackfella tell him no. But whitefella say fuck 'em … Excuse me, Missy.'

'That's alright—I've worked with many men.'

Horace smiled; he was growing fond of this whitefella sheila. 'So a fight started and blackfella spear everyone. Three days later the Dutch ship send 40 men ashore to look for whitefella mates and find they's all dead. Now angry, they burn village, canoes and crops. After this, all whitefella are enemy.'

Samoa knew it was only too common for castaways from shipwrecks to be slaughtered on principle, and after hearing stories like Horace's it was easy to imagine why.

'"Treacherous Bay" it's called now, 'cos o' them killin's.'

When the *Mystery* dipped into a deeper trough than normal the wave exploded beneath the bow and the deck was awash with spray. Will let out an excited *'Whoop!',* while Samoa and Horace at the stern were doused in a fine spray. This combined with the breeze and Samoa felt a temporary chill. She hugged her shoulders.

'Tell me, Horace,' she said, patting herself dry, 'what is Tatsuo's story?'

'What you mean, Missy?'

'Well, he told me his father was French and his mother Japanese. His father died when he was sixteen and he was really brought up by his Japanese grandfather, Yoshi.'

'Aye.'

'Well, Tatsuo is a diver, is he not?'

'Yes, tough bugger an' all. Hard hat diving, very dangerous.'

'I can imagine.'

Horace shivered. 'Yer wouldn't get me down there, Missy.'

'He appears to be a free spirit. Does he not have a wife somewhere?'

Horace looked serious a moment. He checked his heading on the compass and the sun for good measure. 'He was in love, you know. She were beautiful. A Malay woman a few years older. She come from plenty rich family, father a Chinese merchant. Him real angry with Tatsuo for takin' daughter away. But they was in love … real love.' Horace stared off to the horizon down memory lane. 'I met Tatsuo not long after they run away. That be 20 years now. Twelve years with Dhai …'

'Dhai, that was her name, right?'

'Aye. But we were sailin' the north coast o' Guinea when big storm took our rudder. We anchored in a bay to fix rudder. On shore the beach looked deserted so Dhai and Tatsuo take tender ashore before we sail, to collect some coconuts. That's when blackfella come from jungle and spear Dhai. Tatsuo had gun. He shoot two blackfella when they attack. He lift Dhai into tender but she die before he get back to *Mystery*.'

Samoa thought she saw a tear roll down the aborigine's cheek.

'We bury her at sea. She love the sea, always say that's where she wanted to be. Tatsuo also, he say same thing.'

'And they never married?'

'No, although them two, they was always together.'

Samoa thought of the pistol always holstered on the skipper's hip. 'Hence the need for the pistol even today?'

'Yes, Missy. Cap'n know all about guns. He bloody good shot, too. Before he met Dhai, back in the '70s, he travel Australia desert with Frenchman whitefella … ah … Bourdain.'

'Really? Bourdain? I've heard of him,' Samoa said. 'Henri Bourdain, Expeditionary Adventurer.'

'That's him, Missy.'

'Yes, I've read about him. He's quite famous.'

'Yeh, that's 'im, Henri. Anyways, Henri collect specimens for the Paris Zoo Tatsuo tell me. He even travel to Tasmania island in the south to catch wolf tiger, and that's where he got pretty good with 'is pistol.'

'He's had an interesting life, then.'

The aborigine faced Samoa with nothing less than pride in his eyes. 'Tatsuo, him have good life. Him good man, Missy. But sometime he wrestle with the devil.'

'Oh?' Samoa's curiosity was piqued.

'Nuthin' I can say, but Cap'n he have secrets … But he good whitefella.' Horace paused to consider his last words. 'Well, half whitefella, anyhows.'

It was clear the conversation about the skipper had come to an end. For now, anyway, Samoa thought. 'So where did you meet?'

'Me an' Cap'n?'

'Yes.'

Horace ground his teeth and rubbed the wiry stubble on his chin, giving Samoa the impression he was uncomfortable with his past maybe. But the aboriginal ship's mate liked what he saw of this no-nonsense whitefella woman. He felt he could trust her, talk to her, not like Selma, the bloody old cook who chastised him an' Will and grumbled all the time.

'Reaper like the drink too much,' he finally said quietly. So quiet, in fact, that Samoa stepped closer to hear the man's words over the wind and hissing spray.

'Drink?'

'Aye, Missy. Every day for many, many years, I dunno how many, I got meself pissed. Drunk as ten men Cap'n say when he found me by the jetty in Darwin.' Horace laughed at the analogy.

'He saved you, huh?'

'Aye, Missy, got me off the grog. Dry ol' Reaper out, 'e did.'

'Good for you.'

'It was a mission an' God an' all that whitefella bullshit for me, or come with Cap'n Tatsuo.'

'Then you clearly chose wisely.'

'Aye.' Horace turned the bow into another irregular wave before maintaining course. 'Bloody hard work, though, givin' up the grog. I got a taste for it still, but Reaper strong blackfella.' He chuckled again, showing off his pearly white teeth. 'Grim Reaper!' he called into the wind. 'Skinny, bony blackfella bastard, eh?'

'What's in the boxes?' Samoa asked in a casual, throwaway fashion.

'Boxes, Missy?'

'The long boxes amongst all the cargo you stowed below, off the *Star of India*?'

'Oh, them. How did you know?'

'I watched you rowing back and forth from my hotel balcony.'

'I see.'

'Well what's in them?'

'Nuthin' much, Missy.'

'Oh? Like what? I mean they wouldn't be why the British Army were firing artillery at us, would they?'

'Huh!' Horace choked a nervous laugh. 'Jesus, no, Missy. Them boxes full o' spades and picks an' tools for the plantations on the islands.'

'Oh!'

'Cap'n, he trade anything he can make a quid on. Other boxes full o' grog mostly, like them barrels.'

'And what islands will you trade with?'

'New Hebrides, Solomons.'

'Solomons?'

'Aye, the friendly islands, that is. Not them islands with the cannibal blackfella. Still many islands angry with whitefella.'

'And Mist Island is friendly, yes?'

'Last time we sailed there it was.'

'Then why was Tatsuo so concerned?'

'Concerned?'

'He told me he wasn't keen on sailing there but I made him an offer he couldn't refuse, as they say.'

'Oh. That'll be it, Missy … Cap'n loves his money. That's why.'

Samoa looked to William, content at the bow, watching for hidden reefs, although Horace assured her they were heading into safer seas. 'So what's William's story?'

'William? He good lad, just got the devil in 'im sometimes.'

'You know he can't help it, don't you?'

'That's what Cap'n says … but … Reaper don't understand.'

'It's called Tourette's syndrome, named after a French doctor who studied it. It is a mental disorder.'

'Yeh … well. Cap'n catch 'im sneekin' on board an' nickin' stuff. On board *Mystery* one day in Rockhampton.'

'What kind of *stuff*?'

'Tucker, mainly. Tucker an' grog.'

'When was that?'

'He were fourteen, so three year ago. But Willy be a good lad, really, just 'is gob what gets 'im in trouble.'

'Didn't he have parents, a family?'

'Yeh, Cap'n seen 'is father—useless bastard mongrel, 'e said. Drunkard. Told Cap'n to bugger off, that he couldn't care less 'bout 'is boy. So Cap'n take 'im to sea and 'e took to it like a duck to water, as Selma says.'

Horace checked their heading once more on the compass and turned the wheel to starboard a few degrees. 'Selma like mother to Willy. She looks after 'im. Feed 'im good, but Willy's like old Reaper, eat and eat and never get fat.'

'Selma's been on the *Mystery* some years now too, I imagine?'

'Aye. Too many years. Sometimes she cranky ol' woman. But, as Cap'n say, she got a heart o' gold. She were a shearers' cook for years, then she cook on pearl luggers out from Broome out west. That's where she learn them curries and spicy stuff.'

Pearl the three-legged hound appeared above the companionway. First her black wet nose, then her long, drooping ears, and finally her protruding tongue, dripping past her chin. She looked about, sniffed, and with a friendly shove from Tatsuo she landed on deck, making her way immediately to the helm. Samoa gave the dog a head scratch as Tatsuo appeared, noting his mate and passenger in earnest conversation.

'Getting to know each other, then?' Tatsuo asked, running a wary eye over Samoa.

'Yes, I asked Horace where you two met.'

'*Horace*, eh? Then you *have* become familiar.' Tatsuo's expression changed to one of joviality once more.

'Well, I'm a little uncomfortable calling your mate by the name you bestowed upon him.'

'What? Reaper?'

Reaper smiled warmly. 'I tell Missy, Horace, Reaper—e's a skinny blackfella either way.' Horace looked at his skipper. 'I tell 'er how you got me off the grog.'

'Aye. A regular drunkard, weren't you, Reaper?' Horace nodded. 'See,'—Tatsuo checked the compass reading—'he doesn't mind. Everyone gets a nickname at sea.'

'And yours is?'

'"Cap'n."'

'Of course. Have you got one for me yet?' Samoa asked.

'I'm working on it.'

'Then something nice, if you please.' Although Samoa was inwardly smiling, she left the men at the helm with Tatsuo wearing a serious expression.

'What were you two really talking about?' Tatsuo asked Horace.

'She asked me what was in them boxes and if'n them artillery shots had somethin' to do with it.'

'Sneaky minx. Typical woman, huh? How did she know anyway?'

'She seen us from the hotel balcony.'

Tatsuo joined Samoa amidships where she reclined in the sun reading a book. Pearl was curled up at her feet, also enjoying the sun.

'You've made a friend there.' Tatsuo squatted to pat his dog.

'Do you mean Pearl or Horace?' It had not gone unnoticed by Samoa that Tatsuo and Horace had been talking about her a moment earlier.

'Both.'

'I like to think I make friends easily.'

Tatsuo smiled warmly. 'Good book?'

'Passes the time.'

Tatsuo read the title aloud. '*Little Women* ... Hmm ... Interesting title. What's it about, midgets?'

'Hardly. No, it's about the lives of four sisters.'

'Fascinating.' If Tatsuo was being cynical, he made little effort to conceal it.

'Clearly it's not your cup of tea,' she said.

Tatsuo shrugged and grinned.

'Do you read, Captain?' Now Samoa was ridiculing.

'Do you mean books, or do you mean *can* I read?'

'Books.'

'Of course.'

Samoa sat upright on the sail locker, closing her book a moment, using her finger as a bookmark. 'So, what floats *your* boat?'

'What floats my boat? You mean what do I like to read?'

'Yes.'

'"What floats your boat?" I like that.' The skipper's disarming smile lingered. 'Ah, I read *Moby Dick* recently. When I say recently I mean last year. I don't get much spare time to read, you see. But when I do, I like anything to do with the sea … That's what floats my boat.' Tatsuo suddenly experienced a pleasant memory. 'Oh, I know! *Treasure Island*. Now there was an adventure story and a half. You ever read it?'

'I know of it, but I can't claim to have ever read it.'

'Well, you should. It's a jolly good read.' Tatsuo looked pensive a moment. 'Written by a Scotsman by all accounts … ah … Stevenson. Aye, that's it, Robert Louis Stevenson.'

'A bit of a lad's book, I should imagine,' Samoa said politely.

'Aye.' Tatsuo focussed once more on the cover of Samoa's book. 'As *Little Women* is a bit of a girl's book, huh?'

'Touché.'

'Your brother,' Tatsuo steered the conversation to more pressing business. 'Rennison, isn't it?'

'Yes.'

'A lot can happen in 14 months, you must realise. Do you honestly expect to find him on Mist Island?'

'I told you before—yes, I do. He is resilient and he has a gift of, shall we say, being accepted. Gift of the gab I think the Irish call it.'

'He'll need more than the gift of the gab if he lands on the wrong island, and Mist Island is in the middle of some of the Solomons' more dangerous islands.'

Samoa gazed out to sea. Everything seemed so idyllic at this moment and although she had her own thoughts about her brother's capabilities, she didn't want to think about the possibilities at this point in time.

'When did he become a missionary, anyhow?'

'About six years ago. He was recruited by the Lutherans' Mission.'

'Interesting.'

'Interesting, why?'

'Well, you were shipwrecked here in the Pacific, you were brought up in England and returned to the islands.'

'That's my brother's choice, not mine.'

Tatsuo thought a moment. 'Some of these islands are more dangerous than others, you know, and the problem is, often you don't know which ones are which until it's too late.'

'We will just have to be vigilant.'

'Vigilant!' Tatsuo touched his holstered pistol. 'And very careful.'

Chapter Three

Day ten. December 1897.

The sky was clear—a heart-warming Persian blue reflected across the gentle swell, a perfect sea for sailing. The winds had been favourable for days and progress had been brisk yet leisurely, which was rare in the monsoon season. Tatsuo watched Samoa combing her long, blonde hair. She was struggling with her grooming more than the crew. Her magnificent long, blonde mane had become a burden in this sultry weather and was not immune to the salt and humidity of a tropical sea. The skipper watched in silence a moment, before fetching his passenger a tin mug of hot black tea from the galley and joining her amidships. They had grown to know each other since their altercation after leaving Thursday Island over a week ago. The woman was bright, and they discovered they had much in common, like politics and, of all things, a love of natural history.

'How would you like a nice bath with soap and fresh water?'

'Pleeeease.' Samoa dragged the word out. She threw the tortoise shell comb onto the hatch cover, accepting the tea with a grateful smile.

'Because we'll be at Bona Bona tomorrow morning.' Tatsuo studied the sky. 'Early, at this rate.'

Samoa knew of Tatsuo's plan to stop at the small island off the southeast coast of New Guinea, and she had reservations. But in reality she knew she had no choice about the matter. Tatsuo had made it clear from the start he had business along the way; otherwise he would have to have charged her triple the amount for her passage.

'Have you known Ah Sin long?' Samoa spoke of the Chinese bêche-de-mer fisher, merchant, adventurer and self-proclaimed ruler of his small domain, Bona Bona Island.

'A dozen years or more.'

'What's he like?'

'What's he like? In one word? Shrewd. Ruthless. Cunning.'

'That's three words.'

'Aye, one word at a time, and he's all three.' Samoa looked troubled. 'Oh, he's as charming as he is shrewd, ruthless and cunning. And he loves the ladies. He has his own harem.'

'What?'

'Well, sort of. He likes to call it his harem, but he hires out their favours to passing travellers.'

'You mean he runs a brothel.'

'Let's say a bordello. "Bordello" sounds so much more ... ah ... *je ne sais quoi.*'

'So does this self-made emperor have a palace?'

'Aye, of course.' Tatsuo laughed at the thought. 'If you can make a palace from timber and corrugated iron, with a surrounding village out of grass and bamboo for your minions. Don't worry, you'll get along just fine.'

Tatsuo had told Samoa previously how the Chinese bêche-de-mer fisherman had sailed from Canton 15 years earlier and soon learnt that there was easier money to be made as a merchant for those in the bêche-de-mer trade, rather than actually practicing it himself. Now he processed bêche-de-mer in a smokehouse on his island. It was then sent aboard one of his three sailing junks to Sydney, where he received 80 pounds per ton. He also purchased pearl shell from pearlers desperate to sell at Ah Sin's deflated prices. As time passed he built up a reputation for Bona Bona as a port of recreation with a tavern, bordello and trading post. Ships could even leave mail there to be passed on, for a price. The man was an entrepreneur extraordinaire in the true meaning of the word.

Coral Moon

Next morning, just after dawn.

Mystery anchored in the bay on the southern coast of Bona Bona. Two of Ah Sin's junks were anchored closer to shore and there was a lugger, the pearler *Helena*, which Tatsuo recognised as belonging to Zamir the Albanian. The tropical sun rose above the mountains of New Guinea's mainland peninsula to the east, bathing the waterfront village in golden light. With *Mystery*'s anchor clawing the sand only 15 feet below the cutter, and the sails furled, those on board were absorbed in the sounds of the jungle. The air was filled with the screeches, hoots and squawks of a dense and wild landscape that was well and truly alive.

'Is that monkeys?' Samoa asked, referring to the racket and keen to see one.

'Sorry to disappoint, but there're no monkeys in New Guinea.'

'Oh. That jungle sounds so … so alive.'

'It's alive, alright. I'll tell you now, Miss, you wouldn't want to get lost in there.'

'Oh?'

'Not unless you want to meet the venomous taipan, the death adder, the deadly moccasin snake, the black snake, giant tarantulas, jumping spiders, scorpions, monster cockroaches—in fact all the insects here are monsters.' Tatsuo had a secret fear of spiders. 'Did I mention the Chinese bird-eating spider twice the size of a man's hand?' Samoa thought she detected a slight shudder. 'Then there's the saltwater crocs, and if you survive that lot you could get your guts ripped open by a cassowary.'

'Cassowary, what's that?'

'A giant bird, Miss. Like an emu but far more dangerous. They jump at you and claw your belly with razor talons.'

Samoa leant on the guardrail studying the small community. Her shoulders drooped. It had looked so inviting a moment ago. Now it sounded like a labyrinth of death.

The village was perfectly situated above one of the few places where it was easy to reach the shore. A small landing jetty afforded some assistance for loading and unloading. Ah Sin's 'palace' was in the centre of a dozen grass huts with steep roofs, the palace being a sturdy cabin-sized dwelling on stilts with iron sheets for walls and a thatched roof. There were similar, larger huts scattered about, which Tatsuo explained were the smokehouse, a bath house, two storage sheds and the bordello, where Samoa had already noted several young, scantily clothed native women gathering on the porch to observe the new arrivals. The only other sheet iron structure had a bright red- and yellow-painted pagoda decorating the front of the building.

'That's a Chinese joss house,' Tatsuo explained.

'He has a temple?'

'I suppose you could call it that.'

'Then Ah Sin is religious?'

'Let's say superstitious. His temple here is dedicated to Kwan Kung, god of war and prosperity.' Tatsuo explained how Kwan Kung was believed to be a wise judge, guide, protector and provider of wealth. A perfect mentor for a man such as Ah Sin.

Further west, almost overtaken by the jungle, were open shelters where the pearl shell was stacked in great piles, and an enclosed warehouse for the cured sea cucumber, or trepang, as the Chinese called it, which, Tatsuo explained, had to be kept dry in bags and elevated on bamboo racks for storage. Directly behind the village the steep rising hills offered what appeared to be an impenetrable backdrop to an unfolding drama … the jungle.

It seemed the entire village had come to welcome the new arrivals at the water's edge. And they probably had. Samoa ran a curious eye over the crowd of 40 or 50, a real community with babies, women and men, mostly natives, yet a quarter looked Asian —Chinese, most likely, Samoa thought. As the humans gathered, pigs and chickens gained confidence, appearing from under the stilted dwellings and the undergrowth of the nearby jungle.

Samoa was looking for Ah Sin when a personable figure stepped through the beaded curtain of the main entrance to the palace. He gazed back at Samoa with the keen eye of a serious Lothario. He liked what he saw. Blonde-haired, light-skinned women were a rarity in these parts, a rarity indeed. As Samoa stepped ashore off the tender, she thought the merchant was tall for a Chinaman, and extremely handsome, especially as Tatsuo had told her the man was well into his seventh decade. He was slim and well built, wearing a dark blue robe with a colourful pattern of red, gold and green with yellow silk trousers.

Two beautiful but rather intimidating women met them on the beach and demanded Tatsuo's pistol, which, as he expected this demand, he handed over graciously. They emptied the cylinder and checked the breach, pocketing the bullets. Samoa was engrossed.

'Ah Sin's bodyguards,' Tatsuo said.

Samoa eyed the two attractive women as they walked back towards the village. 'Really?'

'Oh, don't be fooled, they know their business.'

While Horace rowed back to *Mystery* to watch and await further instructions, Tatsuo and Samoa were ushered up from the beach to the palace, where Ah Sin himself waited in the shade. The man had a long thin moustache drooping well below his chin on either side of his mouth. His traditional queue reached down to his tailbone and was tied in a leather bow. Around his neck he wore a gorget made from hundreds of tiny shells, a gift from a local chieftain, Samoa was told. He gave Samoa a searching stare through horn-rimmed glasses.

'Ah Sin, old friend,' Tatsuo began, 'I see you still don't trust me.' He gestured toward his pistol, now in the safekeeping of one of the guards.

'Please forgive me, Tatsuo, but last time you were here you shot my son's favourite pet hog.'

And that was true. Tatsuo had spent the night drinking rice wine with his Chinese host, who was far more accustomed to the potent beverage than he.

'But it was most entertaining, if my memory serves me correctly.'

'Entertaining, this is true,' the Chinaman said in his fluent English. 'But you nearly shot my son in the leg also. No, my friend, your pistol shall be returned to you when you leave.' Ah Sin stood with his hands together, hidden within the generous cuffs of his robe. He looked to Samoa with a disarming smile. 'And you have come to trade, yes?'

'I have Indian rum, Irish whiskey, Virginian tobacco and the usual commodities to trade, my friend.'

'Is that all?' The Chinaman kept his eyes on Samoa. His meaning was as clear as the water of the bay.

'That *is* all … Ah Sin, I would like to introduce you to my fiancée, Samoa Plum.'

'Fiancée!' Samoa *and* Ah Sin said in chorus.

Tatsuo pressed a finger into Samoa's lower back. Samoa swallowed hard.

'Yes, yes,' Samoa amended, going along with the charade, which she hoped had a purpose. 'Nice to make your acquaintance.'

'Enchanted.' Ah Sin did not hold back the charm. 'I never thought I would see the day when Tatsuo would marry.' He looked to the skipper. 'Congratulations are in order. We must celebrate.'

Ah Sin released a hand from his robe and waved his guests into his palace. Samoa entered first, just as a small hog rushed squealing by, brushing her right leg and disappearing down the steps.

The inside of the structure was larger than it had looked. The log-beamed ceiling held a dozen brightly coloured Chinese lanterns made of paper. A low dining table was encircled by cushions, no chairs. To one side was Ah Sin's bedroom partitioned by a colourful silk curtain. Samoa recognised a shrine, and several well-manicured potted plants attested to the man's love of plants and flowers.

Ah Sin picked up a small brass bell to summon a servant, which was hardly necessary with so many prying eyes peering in from every available gap in the airy dwelling.

After a breakfast of fried dough topped with chili-bean sauce and toasted sesame served with green tea, Ah Sin insisted on showing Samoa the trepang smokehouse down by the water's edge.

'Sea cucumber are smoke-dried for preserving, you see,' the Chinaman told her. 'They are cured over smoke from coconut husks.

The smoke must be mild and not too hot, otherwise the skin of the sea cucumbers becomes too hard, which will retard drying. Then I cannot sell them.'

'What is so special about them?' Samoa asked. 'What are they used for?'

'They are used as delicacies, condiments for soup, noodles, salad, or we eat them fermented. They are very popular, in China especially.'

Ah Sin stood close to Samoa, allowing the back of his hand to caress the back of hers, slowly. Deliberately. Samoa shifted away, ostensibly to study the open racks of bamboo smokers, which had recently been emptied. The thatch and bamboo were permeated with the not unpleasant aroma of smoked fish. 'How long does it take to smoke them?'

'Several days. They must be dried rock hard to prevent mould when stored.'

Suddenly Samoa's attention was drawn to movement— something crawling in the shadows along one of the racks. Ah Sin noticed and turned to face the bird-eating tarantula. It was a beast, a gargantuan spider with an 11-inch leg span and weighing six ounces. It moved ever so slowly, yet with purpose, apparently unaware humans were nearby. As it crawled along the bamboo, Samoa shuddered at its hairy legs with retractable claws for climbing. At the top of its head tiny black eyes were following an unsuspecting gecko.

Ah Sin's face broke into a broad smile. 'Ah, you see the bird-eating tarantula.'

'It's huge.' Samoa had an immediate urge to look about her for others, and to distance herself from close proximity to the racks and walls of the smokehouse.

By the time she looked back, Ah Sin had his hand out and the monstrous spider crawled onto the back of his wrist.

'Wh-what are you doing?' Samoa stepped back. Ah Sin enjoyed the power this tomfoolery afforded him.

'If you treat them with respect they will treat you with respect. Would you like to touch it?'

'Maybe some other time,' Samoa said. If he was trying to impress her, he was succeeding. Samoa disguised her fear. Spiders as a rule did not bother her, but this beast was terrifying.

'So tell me,' Ah Sin said casually, placing the arachnid back on the bamboo to go about its business. 'How long have you and our intrepid Captain Gaston been engaged?'

'Six weeks,' Samoa answered without weighing up the question. 'No ... no more like four.'

'Well, what is it, four or six?' he spoke slowly and deliberately.

'Four.'

'Where did you meet?'

'Cooktown.'

'Cooktown ... ah, I have many Chinese friends there. Where exactly did you meet? I find such love stories irresistible. I am a hopeless romantic, you see.' Ah Sin cast a lascivious look at the length of Samoa's body in a disturbing display of flirtation. He was acting like a prize rooster, feathers and all, strutting in his colourful garb.

'Where did we meet? In the bank ... Yes ... we met in the bank.'

'Which bank?'

'Queensland National Bank,' Samoa said smartly, having used the bank for her services when she was there. 'So where do you store the fish once they're cured?' she asked, steering the conversation away from herself.

'Come, I will show you.' Ah Sin liked what he saw, and she was smart, too.

After she had inspected the warehouse, where tons of the smoked bêche-de-mer were stored in tightly sealed calico bags, well off the ground for ventilation, and also to keep rats at bay, Samoa had Tatsuo alone briefly.

'Fiancée?' she hissed through grinding teeth. 'I assume that was for my protection and not some fantasy of yours ... some bravado in front of *Emperor* Ah Sin?'

'Fantasy? Don't be delusional.'

'Me, delusional?'

'You were right the first time. I did it for your protection. Ah Sin is used to getting his own way, and he has the sexual prowess of several Casanovas.'

'I could see that.'

'What? Did he try anything?'

'I can look after myself.'

'I'm sure you can. However, for the sake of your safety I suggest you go along with the charade.'

The day was spent pleasantly enough. Business first. Haggling over the quality of the Indian rum, which was notoriously inferior to Caribbean rum, but much cheaper. The Irish whiskey fetched a better price than Tatsuo had expected. And the sugar, flour, salt, paraffin and numerous household commodities were in high demand. Then, of course, the wily Chinaman wanted to trade in bêche-de-mer rather than gold.

'I think you love your gold more than you love your mother, Ah Sin,' Tatsuo declared, smiling at their host.

'Have you met my mother?' Ah Sin grinned back. The Chinaman was happy—he had traded well and the truth was he loved to bargain hard. It was in his blood.

Transactions and deliveries went on into the evening and Ah Sin was feeling sociable. 'Don't forget we have prepared a feast for you this night. The Bona Bona Island favourite, the pig pit.'

Ah Sin spoke of the whole gutted hog, wrapped in banana leaves and dropped into a pit of hot coals where it was covered with dirt and left to cook slowly within the earth for three hours.

'I wouldn't like to leave your beautiful island, Ah Sin, without the mandatory sampling of your cook's wonderful repast.'

'So eloquently put, Tatsuo. Pass on the invitation to your crew and please be certain to bring your beautiful fiancée. I'm afraid we don't have a turkey for you, but the cook has prepared you a roasted cassowary for your Christmas celebration.'

'Christmas! My god, Ah Sin, I forgot. We all forgot.'

It was the 25th of December and no one aboard the *Mystery* had realised.

'Well, as you know, my friend, the Chinese do not celebrate your Christian calendar. Was today not the day your god was born?'

'Something like that. I was raised as much Shinto as Christian. Cassowary, huh?'

'Yes, marinated and basted over the coals, cooked slowly with soy sauce, honey, ginger, garlic, lemons and sweet peppers.'

'Sounds wonderful.'

'I do hope you enjoy it.' Ah Sin looked serious for a moment. 'Because the cook had to run fast to catch the bird.'

The Chinaman kept a straight face for three beats before bursting into laughter. Tatsuo laughed along, but, jokes aside, Tatsuo knew it was an honour, as cassowary was indeed a fast and dangerous bird, best stopped with a bullet.

A brass ship's bell, recovered some years back from a coral shoal wreck, echoed its peal about the bay. It was the summoning for all and sundry to the pig pit banquet. The sun had set, giving way to a balmy, still evening with a half moon, a clear sky and a galaxy of fireflies for company. From the deck of the *Mystery* the village looked romantic, inviting. Chinese lanterns lit the pathways to guide the happy diners to a clearing on the beach set for the feast.

'Merry Christmas, everybody,' Tatsuo greeted the crew who had tidied themselves up for the occasion. They returned the greeting.

'I can't believe we forgot it was Christmas Day,' Selma said. She had managed a skirt and blouse with a bonnet for the event, most chic.

With the crew ready to go ashore, Tatsuo slipped down the companionway to find Samoa. She looked stunning, having made use of the bathhouse in the village during the afternoon. Samoa had dressed in a pink cotton blouse and an ankle-length calico skirt. For modesty Samoa had fastened her hair into a chignon, securing it with a whalebone comb. She had deliberately avoided perfume, however Tatsuo still managed to identify the fragrance of frangipani, the petals of which had scented her bath water. Tatsuo stood to admire Samoa a moment. In the soft light of one lantern she looked like the blonde-haired, blue-eyed beauty of a thousand dreams.

Tatsuo stood, mouth open.

'Didn't your mother tell you it's rude to stare?' Samoa said, keeping her face straight and concealing the delight she felt.

'Ah … oh … was I staring? Sorry.'

Samoa was secretly delighted. As the days had passed by her attraction to this adventurer had strengthened. There was simply no denying it.

'Ah Sin's invitation,' Tatsuo went on. 'You are joining us, are you not?'

'Of course. Pig and cassowary,' Samoa said, trying hard to keep her straight face, 'how could I resist?'

'Well … I …' Tatsuo said, floundering.

'I jest, Captain. The slow-cooked cassowary sounds particularly interesting. This will be a Christmas dinner to remember.'

'Aye, it will.'

'Will there be other women there? I mean I don't want to insult Ah Sin, but he is a lecherous tyrant.'

'"Lecherous tyrant." I like that. Yes, the whole village will be there.'

'And all the whores?' Samoa had counted six in all, four local natives, a Malay and one from the Philippine Islands. And they had been a rowdy lot all afternoon, entertaining Zamir the Albanian and his pearl lugger crew.

'Yes,' Tatsuo said. 'And all the whores.'

Samoa was secretly looking forward to meeting them. 'Do you …' Samoa stopped to re-phrase the question. 'Whores… have you … you know?'

Tatsuo knew exactly what Samoa was asking. 'Know what?' he teased, trying hard to keep a straight face. 'What are you trying to say?'

Samoa blushed. Now the *skipper* was enjoying himself.

He relented. 'Are you asking if I have ever slept with a whore?'

Samoa pinched her lips and nodded gently. 'Would it bother you if I had?' he said.

The cheek. Samoa grew defensive. 'Paying underprivileged women to have your wicked way with them is degrading.'

'For the man?'

'No. For the poor woman.'

'Oh, I don't know …' Tatsuo was on a roll. 'They most likely enjoy it.'

'You have, haven't you?'

'Had my wicked way with a whore? I'm not saying, Miss. I am not a kiss and tell sort of fella.'

'And that's something else that annoys me.'

'What. Kiss and tell?'

'No.'

'What, then? Come on. Let it all out.'

'"Miss." Will you stop calling me "Miss"? Horace calls me "Missy."'

'Alright then, how does "Mademoiselle" sound?'

'Much better.'

'I'll call you "Mademoiselle," then. Assuming you've never married.'

Samoa stared into his eyes a moment. They were dark and exotic and she thought she could see the slightest hint of Japan. He really was a most handsome man.

'Am I right? You have never married?'

'No.' Samoa's voice had softened. Her heart accelerated. *Why the interest?*

'Such an attractive woman. Why? You have other priorities? You prefer the company of women, maybe?'

'Why do men immediately assume for a woman not to have married at, say twenty-five, that she is an old spinster or a zami? I've just never found the right man.'

Samoa did not appear overly insulted by Tatsuo's insinuation. Besides, the two had traveled in a confined space for nearly two weeks now and were accustomed to each other's nuances.

They had slept in close proximity.

Samoa had lain awake at night listening to Tatsuo's snores. Snoring like a mountain lion. And if she had been honest with herself she had fantasized, on many an occasion, lying next to this man, tight in his embrace. Yes, he was much older, but Samoa craved maturity and security. She had been courted by men her own age but found them, on the whole, quite dull and mostly puerile.

For Tatsuo's part, he had listened to Samoa's breathing during naps, while he lay alone dreaming of coupling with this remarkable young woman, a woman he knew he was falling for. But there was more than physical attraction. Much more.

They had discussed politics at length and found they both had a love for natural history. They were both appalled by whaling and sealing and had a love for music. Now, during this rare moment alone, they shared their mutual attraction, helplessly drawn together like the opposite poles of a magnet.

Samoa's warm reaction to Tatsuo's compliment, as brief as it had been, dissolved into yearning more. And this unexpected reaction from Samoa was the lure Tatsuo so hungered for. The moment was right. He took a step forward. Samoa stood her ground. She felt her breathing quicken. They were alone and, by God … love was in the air.

Samoa met Tatsuo in the shadows cast by the light of the single lamp. He placed his hands on her shoulders and gazed into her eyes briefly. They connected. Samoa closed her eyes and Tatsuo's powerful hands tightened …

At that moment Horace called down the companionway, 'Boat's ready to go ashore, Cap'n.'

A beach party. It really was one great beach party. The deckhand off the pearler played the fiddle and one of the three divers played a banjo. They sang and danced and ate, and drank too much. The pig meat fell from the bone while the pigskin had crisped over the coals. They ate with their fingers and washed their greasy hands with sand in the ocean.

Against his better judgment, Tatsuo drank rice wine, not the sake of his ancestors, but the Chinese rice wine. Mijiu rice wine was made from the fermentation of sticky glutinous rice and was almost as strong as whiskey. Samoa sat close by, the sober voyeur. It looked like it was going to be a long night.

Reclined on what Samoa could only think of as a beach chaise longue, Ah Sin reclined like some Caesar with his rice wine. Discreetly, as Samoa did not wish to attract their host's attention, Samoa watched one of the whores bring him a long pipe, the bowl carved like the head of a poppy flower.

Tatsuo noticed Samoa observing. 'Opium,' he whispered.

'I guessed so.' Samoa looked away before Ah Sinn noticed her staring. The other guest who had caught Samoa's curiosity was Zamir the Albanian, off the pearler *Helena* in the bay. He, too, had been the discreet voyeur, keeping an eye on the two of them. Finally Samoa asked Tatsuo about him.

'He's a bit of a dark horse, that one,' Tatsuo said. 'You've seen how he walks, I assume?'

'Like he has a wooden leg.'

'Exactly. He lost it in a boating accident. He had a prosthetic leg fitted from the left knee down.' Tatsuo took a drink from his rice cup and wiped his mouth on the back of his hand. 'There's a great story about how he likes to scare natives by sticking his hunting knife straight through his leg.' And Tatsuo demonstrated. 'In here and out the other side, straight through his trousers as well.' This had Samoa's attention. 'You see there was a gap in the prosthetics that allowed him to do this. The natives thought he was a devil and used to get really excited about it.'

'I should imagine they would.'

'Until one day a chieftain decided he wanted to test it himself and came up behind Zamir with a spear, sticking it in his backside.'

Zamir caught Samoa's eye, laughing, and finally having had enough of the squealing, giggling whores for company, he came and sat on the beach with Tatsuo, a bottle of whiskey under his arm. Tatsuo and Zamir had caught up earlier in the day and laughed about old times. They hadn't always seen eye to eye. Once, years back, in Port Douglas they had had a minor altercation over fresh water supplies.

'Christmas cheer, old friend,' Zamir said. Tatsuo returned the greeting and they saluted drinks. 'So, Tatsuo,' Zamir said, staring only at Samoa, 'are you going to introduce me to your beautiful companion?'

'My fiancée, Samoa,' Tatsuo continued the charade.

'Yes, Ah Sin told me you were to be married. About time, old friend.'

Zamir reached in front of Tatsuo and took Samoa's hand.

'Enchanted, mademoiselle,' he drawled. It was almost embarrassing. 'Zamir.' He shamelessly held Samoa's hand longer than necessary. '"Zamir the Albanian" they call me.'

Samoa pulled her hand free, dropping it to her side where she cleansed it in the soft sand.

Zamir pulled his knees up to his chest, hugging them. 'You traded well with Ah Sin, I take it?' he asked Tatsuo, with one eye on their host, who was content in the company of Madame Opium.

'Aye. Yes. I'm happy.'

'I'm glad for you, my friend, because he is a tough negotiator.'

'That he certainly is. He wanted to pay me with bêche but I insisted on gold.'

'That's sounds like our Chinaman.'

'You know, I told him he must love gold more than he loves his mother, because he was loath to part with it.'

Zamir laughed and took a swig of whiskey from the bottle. His crew were a mixed bag of ruffians, mostly natives with little English, and he craved intellectual company. Now the whiskey stimulated his tongue. 'Speaking of gold, you've been sailing the Coral Sea some time now, have you not?'

'Aye.'

'Do you remember the *Bao Zheng* or *Coral Moon,* the ship the captain named after himself?'

'The gold ship?'

'Aye.'

Tatsuo looked over at Samoa, who had been joined by one of the palace beauties who was keen to practise her English once more, after their meeting earlier in the day.

Everyone in Cooktown over the age of 30 remembered the *Bao Zheng*. The owner, Bao Zheng, was a Chinese sea captain from Canton whose adventures were legendary. But his greatest coup was when he and 20 other Chinese gold miners accumulated 20,000 ounces of refined gold from the goldfields around Cooktown and Hodgkinson River to the south, and left Australian waters for Canton without paying taxes or informing the authorities of their departure. Value: 215,000 pounds. There were also rumours of pearls on board, some said as many as 1,000. But the Cooktown-built, three-masted junk never made it back to China.

'That was 20 years ago, in 1877,' Tatsuo said. 'Many searchers went looking for it, from Thursday Island to Indonesia, Philippines to Hong Kong. But it vanished from the seas without a trace. No wreckage washed up, no islander folk stories, nothing.'

'That is correct.'

'What made you mention the *Bao Zheng*, Zamir?'

'I was anchored off Dauan Island six weeks ago for supplies when the steamer *Bandicoot* anchored nearby,' Zamir said. 'There was a storm threatening, you understand.'

'Yes?'

'Well, I got friendly with the first mate who told me an interesting story about wreckage from a junk being used in the building of the chieftain's house on the north-east coast of Nggela Sule Island.'

'In the Solomons?'

'Aye. It was washed up wreckage salvaged 20 years earlier after a willy-willy flattened part of the island, he told me. The *Bandicoot* took missionaries to the island recently, you see, and some of the crew visited the village.'

'But it could be any Chinese junk.'

'Ah, yes. But the *Bao Zheng* had the timber stern painted purple and red. The shipwreck timbers used in the village were also purple and red. Into the bargain, there were private possessions washed up on the beach and salvaged by the natives at the time. One item was a trunk with some clothing. Inside was a document seal that the village chief wore around his neck, and the *Bandicoot's* cook, a Chinaman, identified this seal as belonging to Bao Zheng.'

'Really?'

'Really.' Zamir passed the whiskey to Tatsuo who stared into his rice wine cup a moment, before tipping out the wine and filling it with whiskey.

'That's half a ton of gold almost. Half a ton, my friend.' The Albanian hugged his knees tight to his chest and was lost for a moment, staring across the still black waters of the bay.

'Well, good luck to anyone who wants to look for it,' Tatsuo said. He was feeling immediate effects of the whiskey and joined Zamir in his romantic reverie. 'Nggela Sule Island is directly opposite Malaita and the natives there eat whitefella for breakfast.' Tatsuo took another long swig from the cup. 'It's a good story, though, but why would Bao sail east from Cooktown?'

'Simple. Bao Zheng was a very clever bastard. He knew the Royal Navy would sail from North Queensland to track him down. And he knew they would assume he had sailed west through the Arafura Sea and Celebes Sea between Borneo and the Philippines, then onto Canton. He had all the time in the world and a lot of gold, so he sailed east around New Guinea and into the Solomon Seas before sailing north, then northwest for China.'

'It's still only hearsay,' Tatsuo commented.

'Is it?' Zamir looked into Tatsuo's eyes, his own eyes glazed by the romance of treasure.

'I mean the mate on the *Bandicoot* could have been pulling your leg.' Tatsuo immediately realised his faux pas.

'Which one?' The Albanian laughed at his own expense. 'The good leg or the prosthetic one?' Zamir filled their glasses. 'Yes. What you say is true. But I'm a good judge of character. All seafarers love a good treasure story, right?'

Tatsuo was a little befuddled with drink, yet confused as to why the Albanian would tell him this news.

'And you are telling me this because …?'

'You are diver, are you not?' Zamir said.

'Aye.'

'Well, I thought that is why you were sailing to the Solomons.'

Ah, Tatsuo thought, *so he is fishing for information.* Tatsuo looked at Samoa, but she was deep in conversation with her new friend. He turned back to Zamir, deciding to settle the issue there and then.

'I'm taking my fiancée to meet her brother on Mist Island, that is all.'

And there he hoped the matter would rest.

Tatsuo, in the stern quarters of *Mystery*, was awoken from a drunken slumber by the hand of William, shaking him vigorously. Nursing a crushing hangover he sat bolt upright, cracking his head on the deck beam only two feet above his upper bunk. 'Christ!'

'Fuck,' William replied, his tick having been triggered. He fell back, laughing at the Cap'n cracking his head and swore again, struggling with his affliction, finally dropping the smile. 'Mor-mornin' skipper … tic …'—a muscle spasm shot through the young man's upper body—'S-sorry. I'll tell Selma t-to get yer c-coffee.'

Tatsuo could not stay angry for long. And William had a good heart. Selma heard the commotion from within the galley.

'Yer awake, then. It's about time.' She projected a glob of spent betel nut into the galley spittoon. 'Will yer be wantin' lunch, Cap'n?'

'Lunch?' Tatsuo smacked his lips. His mouth was dry as bark. He splashed water over his face from a china bowl in the cabin and slipped a calico shirt over his head. 'What's the time?'

'Time we were sailin'.'

'And?'

'Nearly eight.'

'Jesus, Selma … lunch?'

'It got yer up, didn't it? I managed to get a dozen fresh eggs from the island. Fancy some fried?'

'Later. Where is everyone?'

Selma jerked her head upwards. 'I'll bring yer coffee.'

'Thanks.' Tatsuo mounted the companionway nursing a sore head with a bump to match. On deck his sober crew waited. Samoa was trying her luck fishing. Horace knew what to expect when the cap'n had a sore head from grog. He stepped up to the stern to make a cursory scan of the bay for any fish larger than man. A loud splash echoed about the still bay and Tatsuo surfaced seconds later, spouting water from his mouth like a whale. Now he was refreshed. He rolled onto his back and floated a moment while Samoa looked on.

'Coming in?' Tatsuo called out, his charm returned. 'The water's just fine.'

Samoa looked at Horace. 'All good, Missy, I'll keep an eye out.'

Samoa loved swimming and she was a strong confident swimmer. Without hesitation she dived over the side, blouse, three-quarter sailor's trousers and all. Horace and Will watched her descend towards the sand and coral before twisting at two fathoms and swimming back. She surfaced next to Tatsuo.

'How's the head?' she asked.

'Fine … *now.*'

'Got company,' Horace said casually. Tatsuo followed Horace's sight line, his hand shielding the sun. 'Starboard bow, hundred yards. Might be dolphin, but … I dunno, Cap'n.'

Tatsuo steered Samoa to the Jacob's ladder on the portside and the two climbed back on deck. Moments later a curious tiger shark swam by the lugger. A relatively small female, yet big enough to take a chunk out of someone's leg.

'Plenty tucker in the bay for them buggers,' Horace said as they all watched the magnificent fish snatch the remains of last night's pig's head floating just below the surface, 30 feet off shore. It was not like the islanders to discard scraps in the bay like that, for this very reason. Maybe he hadn't been the only drunkard last evening, Tatsuo thought.

'The water kegs are full Cap'n,' Horace said, showing little interest in the shark, now joined by others vying for the pig scraps.

'Then let's set sail.'

As it was customary to fire a shot into the air as a departing gesture, Tatsuo remembered his pistol … and the fact that he left it ashore. Horace however, had been waiting for this moment.

'Here, Cap'n.' He passed Tatsuo his Enfield revolver. 'Ah Sin's ladies gave it to me when they carried you back to the tender.'

'Carried me?'

'You were plenty liquored up, Cap'n.'

'Ahoy there!' Zamir the Albanian's distinct voice was crystal clear over the idyllic water as two crewmembers rowed him towards the *Mystery*.

Tatsuo leant on the rail, watching the tender pull alongside. 'Morning, Zamir.'

Samoa joined Tatsuo, drying her long blonde hair on a towel.

'Morning, beautiful lady,' Zamir said. 'Fiancée to the lucky Captain Gaston.'

Samoa nodded curtly. There's something … something sleazy— yes that was the word, 'sleazy,' about this man, she thought.

'Enjoy your swim?' Zamir asked.

'Most refreshing. You should try it some time,' Tatsuo said, knowing only too well that Zamir never entered the water, leaving all the diving to his Filipino crew. The possibility of any thrashing of a large tail disturbing the water nearby was all the excuse he needed.

'Swim? Not this morning, my friend. We have unwelcome visitors.'

'We're about to sail, Zamir, so what is the purpose of your visit?'

'Ah, Tatsuo, always straight to the point. That's what I like about you.'

As Horace and William were already preparing to raise the anchor and unfurl the sails, Tatsuo did not particularly want Zamir on board.

'You have guns to trade, no?'

'I don't trade in guns, Zamir, you know that.'

'Oh! I thought …' Zamir caught the look of denial on Tatsuo's face. Clearly he wanted to be discreet. 'That's a pity, because I am in the market for … say … two new rifles, and we both know how scarce they are out here.'

'Sorry, Zamir, I can't help you.'

'Of course the natives on Bougainville are desperate for arms,' Zamir said. 'Did you know that?'

Tatsuo shrugged his shoulders.

'And if a man was enterprising enough there is money to be made there.'

Tatsuo nodded indifferently.

'The Germans are stealing their land, see, bit by bit, and I know for a fact the natives want to fight back.' Zamir waited for a change of heart from Tatsuo that was not forthcoming. 'Alright, my friend, safe voyage … You're heading to Mist Island, are you not?'

'Yes. Samoa has business there.'

'Aye. So you said last night.'

Zamir's oarsmen were about to shove off when Zamir feigned an afterthought. 'Oh, I nearly forgot.'

'Yes?'

'You should know there is a German gunboat in the area, the *Prinzessin*. She's been creeping about the South Pacific for weeks now, and the word is they are here to force Bougainville to become a German protectorate.'

'Oh, well, that's progress, I would have thought.'

'Yes, but the Germans! Like I said, those poor islanders could sure use guns, if you know where any can be found.'

With the undulating seas rolling beneath *Mystery*'s keel and the Solomon Sea on the horizon ahead, Samoa released her hair to the wind. Her clothes dried almost instantly, hugging her body, and pleasing to the eye of young William, who struggled with subtlety. Samoa held onto the stern guardrail, reveling in the warm sun.

'Did you enjoy the pig roast?' Tatsuo, at the helm, asked.

'Delicious.'

'Did you know that's exactly how the headhunters, the cannibals of Malaita Island in the Solomons, cook humans?'

If Tatsuo was trying to revolt Samoa he wasn't succeeding. Samoa had read about cannibalism. She'd studied the islanders of these areas on her voyage from Europe, hoping to understand better why her brother Rennison would want to join the missionaries here. He'd never been overtly religious, for one thing, a matter she kept to herself. Samoa read copies of accounts of Captain Cook's voyages and the published diaries of castaways who had survived living amongst these islanders, having brought several books with her amongst the bibles. She was indeed well read, surprising Tatsuo with her response regarding cannibals. 'It makes sense, really, that they should cook human's the same way as they cook pigs.'

'Aye.'

'So, do tell.'

Tatsuo stared into Samoa's eyes and she held his gaze. First the swim, now this conversation. The woman never ceased to amaze him. 'Well, just like a pig they disembowel the body and remove the head. This is done by the women, of course.'

'Of course.'

'The carcass is cleaned and filled with breadfruit, bananas, yams and taro roots. The liver and heart are placed outside on the chest and the body wrapped in banana leaves.'

'Like the pig.'

'Aye, like the pig. The body is then lowered into the hot pit, covered with coals and topped with earth, where it is left to cook slowly for three hours.'

'Same time as the pig.'

'Then the ceremony begins. They dance and chant and invoke the spirits, working themselves into a frenzy for the feast. When the 'long pig' is cooked—for that's what they call human meat—the roast is removed to the women's cooking hut once more, where it is carefully portioned to be dished out according to rank and desire. By desire I mean, if one warrior has weak legs, then he is given leg meat to eat, in the belief it will make his legs strong. The brains are given to someone who needs intelligence. The eyes for better sight, and on and on it goes. The inner thigh is deemed the best cut.'

Samoa enjoyed the challenge. If the skipper was trying to revolt her, she wasn't going to let him succeed. 'Like I said,'—Samoa smiled—'delicious.'

Thursday Island

A small foundry on Thursday Island managed to cast a new lock collar for the piston connector rod for the gunship HMS *Pride*'s Rennie inverted steam engine. Leaving Sergeant Andrews in charge of Green Hill Fort, army captain Gerald Rafferty Reynolds insisted he lead the pursuit to catch 'this damned insolent pirate Tatsuo Gaston.' HMS *Pride*'s captain, Captain Jonathon Bourke, wasn't so impressed.

The no-nonsense Bourke, born in Australia of English parents, who had joined the Royal Navy back in the 50s, was old school. Having recently celebrated his sixtieth birthday, he had witnessed plenty of action, including, as a young Jack tar, the Siege of Sevastopol in the Crimea. And at six-foot-four he looked much more the colonial than the Royal Navy stereotype. Bourke twisted the ends of his generous moustache, a hairy slug of a thing his wife Clarabelle hated. But it helped hide a shrapnel scar from Sevastopol on his left cheek.

Three days after *Mystery* avoided the wrath of the British Navy, HMS *Pride* slid into the high tide of Thursday Island's harbour like an armour-plated saltwater crocodile. Recently slipped and free of barnacles, she would move through water like a torpedo.

With the gunboat capable of maintaining 14 knots, as compared to the *Mystery's* four or five knots if the wind was favourable,

Reynolds was confident he would hold Tatsuo accountable for his suspicious actions and insolence within a week or so. And his enquiries at the telegraph office had confirmed that his adversary was headed to Mist Island in the Solomons. That fact alone made the army captain confident he was onto something important, important enough to spend Her Majesty's sterling in pursuit.

And, more exciting still, was the fact that the most attractive visitor seen entering the telegraph office—a Miss Samoa Plum, the telegraph operator had informed him—had sent a message to a German consular representative in Sydney. A subsequent telegraph to Garden Island Naval Precinct, also in Sydney, was answered only hours later with orders to the effect that a Rennison Plum, assumed relation of Samoa Plum, was a fugitive, to be arrested with all haste. It was also assumed he was travelling somewhere in the South Seas.

'At last,' Captain Rafferty Reynolds crowed, 'a purpose on this godforsaken island! Something to sink the teeth into.'

But those close to Reynolds knew there was a more sinister reason for the army captain's determination: jealousy.

'We are betrothed, Briana,'—Gerald Rafferty Reynolds's voice was breaking—'We are to be married, and you humiliate me so … talking to that, that … damned scoundrel, and in public.'

'Why? Would you rather me talk with him in private?'

'No!' Reynolds answered only too swiftly. 'No, I would not. As a matter of fact, I forbid you to talk to him at all.'

Briana was incensed. She did not give over to orders so readily, especially as she was daddy's little girl and daddy was General Christian Pledge. 'Forbid me? You can't do that.'

'Oh, but yes, I can.' Reynolds straightened his shoulders. 'And your father would readily support me.' And this was true.

'Oh, Rafferty,'—Briana changed tack and purred, preferring to use Reynolds' middle name—she detested the name Gerald— 'Rafferty, my darling. You are being quite silly.'

Her eyelids fluttered over her green eyes and Briana stroked her fiancé's arm.

Reynolds weakened. 'You were seen talking to *him* in the street. My men saw you, and you were acting most improperly.'

'But I've known Tatsuo Gaston some time now. At least a year.' There was no mention of his buying her champagne in the past. 'And he is always the perfect gentleman.' Suddenly Briana feigned shock, horror. 'Why? Don't you trust me? Oh, Rafferty!'

'Of course I trust you, my darling.'

'Well, then, stop this nonsense.'

Chapter Four

Seven days' sailing from Bona Bona Island. Late December, 1897

Mist Island, egg shaped, about ten miles from top to bottom, lay northwest in the archipelago of the Solomon Islands, a 600-mile line of scattered islands. 'Right here,' Tatsuo said, pressing a finger against the chart.

'Note only the name "Mist Island,"—those two words only—written on this map, no other landmarks,' Tatsuo informed Samoa. 'That's because no one has ever explored the island—well, not and lived to tell the tale, that is. I asked about Mist Island back at Thursday Island and all I could find out is that there are only two safe places to row ashore, one on the north side and another on the southeast, where the Maanoa Indians live.'

'Are they friendly?'

'I couldn't find out if they are friendly or not.' Tatsuo rubbed his chin. 'I did discover that they trade with the Malai'ta natives.'

'Malai'ta people … Who are …?'

'They are confirmed headhunters who occupy Malaita Island in the southwest. They are not inhabitants we want to meet. The other closest islands to Mist are the Duke of York Islands, named by the British during the last century, but Germany declared a protectorate over them in '85.'

'So they are German territory.'

'Well, I guess they are, against the natives' wishes. But by all accounts the Mist Island natives are friendly. The blackbirders have been going there for a few years now.'

'Blackbirders?'

'I don't know if you are aware of this or not, but cheap labour is sought in the islands, to harvest sugar cane and cotton in Queensland.'

'You mean slaves?'

'No, Samoa, not at all. These men are paid on a three-year contract that includes taking them back to their home island at the end of their term.'

This wasn't entirely true. Tatsuo knew only too well that many were taken unwillingly or by deception. It was known that some natives, naturally curious folk, were enticed on board some boats with the offer of coloured calico or fish hooks, only to be kidnapped and sold in Queensland.

Samoa wasn't terribly convinced. 'I bet they aren't paid much.'

'Maybe not as much as the whitefellas, but they do get paid.'

'And what do the slave traders get?'

'Blackbirders, not slave traders. The blackbirders are paid ten pound a head to transport them to Australia.'

'Hmm. Anything else I should know?'

'Yes. Mist's coast is rugged and storm-battered. There is one mountain rising steeply from the coast, probably an extinct volcano, and it's covered with impenetrable rain forest.' Tatsuo paused for a moment. 'I did hear one other titbit of information from Captain Zamir, back at Bona Bona.'

'Oh?'

'Aye. There *is* a mission there.'

Samoa let out a cheer. 'Why didn't you tell me before?'

'I wanted to surprise you.'

'Surprise me? And leave me wondering all this time?'

'Well, there is one question.'

'What?'

'The missionaries are German. Would Rennison work with Germans?'

'He wrote in his letters that he was with Lutheran missionaries, so the answer must be "yes."'

Mist Island appeared, like a mirage on the horizon. With the equator only a few hundred miles north, the wet season humidity hung like a sultry cloak. To add to the oppressive weather the wind dropped during the approach to land, and the final miles to the northern settlement—where Tatsuo surmised they would find the mission—were covered at less than one knot.

Samoa's excitement grew. Not a day had gone by when she had not thought of her younger brother Rennison. The questions mounted. He had some explaining to do. About not writing to her often enough, for one thing, and when he had written he had divulged little of his life with the missionaries.

With the mainsail barely catching any breeze, Tatsuo had time to share Samoa's excitement. She had spoken daily of her brother Rennison and Tatsuo felt he knew the man reasonably well. Since Bona Bona Island, the chemistry between them had strengthened. But the confines of living in close proximity with the crew aboard the cutter did little to aid a blossoming relationship. Certainly they flirted when the occasion arose, but Tatsuo wanted more. Much more.

It was time to move on, Selma kept reminding him.

And Tatsuo thought Samoa had the courage of his partner Dhai, who had been taken from him without warning by the point of a native spear.

Yes, it's time to move on.

Tatsuo had no doubts now; he had fallen in love with the intelligent, confident and often cheeky woman and, despite their age difference, he knew Samoa wanted more also. But the reunion with her brother loomed like a dark cloud overhead and Tatsuo wondered what her intentions would be after she found her brother.

Tatsuo watched Samoa leaning on the bow guardrail, studying the island as they approached; her long, straight blonde hair trailing down to her waist. For comfort she had cut and stitched sailor's britches just below the knee like Tatsuo wore his, and more often than not she was barefoot.

Selma spat betel nut juice over the side into the calm water. Although they could see smoke spiraling upward from the island they had yet to recognise a village.

'Nice view,' Selma said straight-faced, catching her skipper staring at the rear view of their most attractive fellow traveller.

'W-what? What was that?'

'The island,' the old woman said with a smirk. 'Nice view?'

'Oh, aye.'

Selma was no fool. She could tell the captain was smitten. 'She's a gooden,' Selma said quietly.

'The island?'

'No, you daft bugger.' Selma nodded to Samoa. 'She's turned out alright.'

'Aye.' Tatsuo pretended to be nonchalant.

'We'll miss her, eh?'

'Miss her?'

'Aye, when she finds her brother. She'll stay with him, will she not?'

'I don't know, Selma. Don't know what her plans are.'

Selma waited, but the captain was not forthcoming.

'Jesus, you're slow,' Selma finally grumbled.

Although Selma was only a few years Tatsuo's senior, she had grown to be the motherly figure Tatsuo had missed in his life.

'What do you mean, "slow"?'

'I've seen how she looks at you … and you look at her.'

Tatsuo wanted to say: *Christ, Selma, isn't she gorgeous? And we get along so well. Maybe it is time I moved on and shared my life with another.*

This wasn't the first time Tatsuo had thought about his future. He had recently looked at buying property in Cooktown, although that meant selling *Mystery*. And at forty-seven he was not too old to enjoy a family.

Samoa approached and Selma gave the skipper a slight elbow, before bunching fresh betel nut leaf wrapped around areca nut into the corner of her mouth, and leaving the skipper alone.

'Mist Island,' Samoa said, in a reverent voice that made the destination seem a lifelong ambition.

'Aye.'

'What else did you learn, then, from Zamir, about the missionaries?'

'Not a lot. Just that missionaries moved here in about '85 and started ramming the fear of God down the natives' throats.'

'Do I sense an element of cynicism?'

'Aye, that you do, Mademoiselle. I've never had much time for God-botherers.'

Samoa narrowed her eyes to study the coastline. They were still a mile out to sea and Samoa imagined her brother on the beach waiting.

'Why are some islands friendly and others filled with headhunting savages?' Samoa asked.

'Well, to start with, all the islanders of the South Seas are headhunters—they hunt trophies. The heads are revered souvenirs of their prowess in battle. And, yes, they eat their victims, but this is not because they particularly enjoy eating the meat, it's also a spiritual thing, gives them power over their enemies.'

'Still doesn't answer the question why many islands are so aggressive towards outsiders.'

'Alright, I'll give you an example. Basilaki Island to the southwest of here. In July of 1885 two sailors came ashore looking for water. The captain and his carpenter. They were immediately killed by natives in retribution for two islanders killed by whitefellas earlier. The crew out in the bay on board the schooner *Lallah Rook* saw everything and escaped. Three months later, in October, three ships returned to look for the men's bodies. Two of the ships were Royal Navy. They found the two men's skulls but not the rest of their bodies, and buried them at sea. Then one of the Navy ships returned, HMS *Diamond*, and destroyed every village along the shoreline in revenge. It's just a vicious circle. This is what causes the natives' resentment.'

'Oh, then that is understandable.'

'Aye.'

'What else do you know about Mist Island?'

'I'm thinking the missionaries here are Jesuits, not Lutherans. However, they are all tarred to the same bush, eh? Bloody Germans taking over the Pacific and the Coral seas. They already occupy northern New Guinea.'

'You don't like Germans?'

'I don't like their arrogance.'

'And the British aren't arrogant?'

'That's different.'

'Oh, is it?'

'Up until '89,' Tatsuo said, 'Thursday Island had its share of sauerkrauts, as my mates call them. The sisters of the convent were on the island to convert Filipinos working the pearlers and using the island as a headquarters for their points of departure all over the South Seas. Then came the Lutherans and the Rhenish mission, but the Queensland government made claim to the island and made them bugger off. They moved to Yule Island off the south coast of New Guinea. I heard the Filipinos, already Catholic, had a lot to do with converting the savages to Christianity, as they were trusted by the natives.'

'Isn't that a good thing?'

'Maybe. Or maybe we should leave the poor devils alone.'

An hour later the mist lifted as mysteriously as it had blanketed the lush green island earlier. With *Mystery* drifting on the tide, Tatsuo prepared to anchor at what he considered a safe distance. And only now, slowly, did the jungle come to life with natives gathering on the beach.

'Well, they look friendly enough.' Tatsuo waved to dozens of children who were up to their waists in water just off the shore, squealing and laughing, waving frantically at the new arrivals. From the deck of *Mystery* the scene ashore seemed idyllic. The ship was now positioned off a rocky promontory in clear view of native huts on stilts framed by tall coconut palms and cultivated gardens. The anchor was lowered. By the time the sand around the anchor settled in the crystal-clear water, dozens of adults had joined the children.

Rowing ashore Horace was first over the bow, but having misjudged the depth he landed up to his neck in water, much to the delight of the laughing children.

'*Guten morgen, guten morgen,*' called a large, heavy-set, suntanned man, easily mistaken for an overweight native, who was wading into the surf. He reached out and took the anchor from Horace, who threatened to lose balance and go under completely. '*Herzlich willkommen!* Hallo.'

Horace understood 'welcome.' 'Thanks, boss.'

'Well,' Tatsuo said out of the corner of his mouth to Samoa, 'you're in luck. They *are* Germans.'

'*Ah, Englisch, ja,*' the fat man said.

'Australian.' Horace smiled awkwardly, showing his perfect white teeth. He pinched his black skin. 'One hundred per cent Aussie blackfella.'

'*Na sicher* … of course, *Australisch* native … *ja, ja, gut.*'

The tender caught a gentle wave and easily slipped nose-first onto the beach, where Samoa, Tatsuo and William bailed over the side before the clinker was surrounded and dragged by well-wishers above the tide line.

Samoa imagined there must be a hundred people on the beach, all shoving and giggling, vying for position, curious to inspect their visitors. Clearly new arrivals were scarce.

A harsh voice forced the crowd apart and another overweight man, in his sixties, approached. He was wearing a native woven grass hat with a brim wide enough to double as a parasol, a grubby, mended white suit coat—donned especially for the new arrivals, Samoa guessed—an open-neck shirt, and white trousers folded at the cuff above the ankles; his feet were bare.

'Hello, hello. Welcome to Mist Island,' he greeted them in heavily accented English.

Tatsuo stepped forward and took the chubby, hairy hand in his own.

'Thanks … My name's Tatsuo Gaston.'

'I am Jonas Hartzer. I am head of our small, yet ever important Society of Jesus, here on the island… *ja*?'

'Jesuits, huh?'

'*Ja, und* at your service, Herr Gaston.'

Tatsuo presented the others. 'This is Horace, my mate, and young William. And the pretty lady is Samoa Plum.'

'Rennison Plum?' Samoa skipped the greeting, impatiently asking about her brother while other missionaries gathered about them. 'Is he here?'

'Rennison?'

'Yes. My brother. Rennison Plum.'

'Well, bless the Lord. I believe I can see a likeness … *ja*.'

'Is he here?'

'*Nein*.'

Samoa's eyes searched the gathering. 'No? *Is* he on the island?'

'N*ein, fräulein*. Rennison sailed from Mist Island … oh …'—he looked to his subordinate, exchanging a few words in German—'a good year ago.'

'A year ago. Are you certain?'

'*Ja*. Actually, he left under duress.'

'Duress? What do you mean?'

The old priest studied Samoa briefly with the eye of a celibate man. Something weighed on his mind and now was the time to release it.

'Come, *boot ist* safe here. We can talk at ze mission … *ja*.'

Several raffia huts on stilts had been built back from the sea against a backdrop of coconut palms and dense jungle. Pigs, chickens and mongrel dogs lived in harmony, sniffing, rooting and pecking in a constant hunt for food. Jonas Hartzer led the group over a sandhill to the largest hut, used more as a community hall, Tatsuo surmised. Horace and William stayed with the tender. Alongside the hall was the communal church, a tropical affair built with bamboo and reeds with a slender spire crowned with a wooden cross that looked as if it would blow over with the next gust of wind. Waiting on the porch were the womenfolk, four European and two native women of various ages. The three other missionary men who had met them at the beach followed behind.

'This is Clara, Mila, Gretel and Monique,' Jonas introduced the women. '*Und* Elias, Moritz *und* Hans,' he said as the men joined them.

Tatsuo introduced himself and Samoa.

The interior of the hall was unexpectedly spacious, with ample openings at ceiling level, where the walls met the grass roof, letting in a flow of cooling air.

European furniture, such as a dining table, bureaus, a large cottage dresser displaying a full china dinner set, even a smoker's stand, along with various German home comforts like tinware, jars of pickles and tableware were scattered about. *Jesuits maybe,* Samoa thought, *but they are not averse to a little luxury.*

Jonas noticed Samoa looking about inquisitively. 'Home from home, *ja*? Clara,' Jonas called to one of the younger women, a shy-looking German in her early thirties, 'please, bring our guests some coconut beer.'

'Beer?'

'Oh, it is not alcohol, you understand. We call it beer because we make it like ginger beer, *ja*.'

They stood about a moment in uncomfortable silence, watching Clara, now joined by the other women. They fussed about at the open kitchen at the far end of the elongated hut. Samoa noticed many of the islanders had gathered outside, curious about their visitors. She grew restless.

'Rennison, my brother?' she asked.

'*Ja*. Take a seat … please.'

'Rennison, he depart this island like I said, about one year ago,' Jonas said as Samoa and the menfolk took chairs around the dining table.

'*Dein bruder* … ah, your brother, he did not have his heart in our mission,' Hans added. 'He lost his path with his God.'

'Oh.' Samoa wasn't all that surprised. She had gotten over the surprise years ago, after her brother had told her he was off to join missionaries in the Pacific Islands. Now *that* had come as a surprise.

'Where did he go? Did he say?'

'Ah, no.' The four men looked at each other and nodded silently in agreement. 'We feel as though we failed your brother,' Elias said.

'Why?'

'Rennison lost his love for the Lord Jesus, *ja*.'

Moritz grew impatient. 'He was tempted by the devil,' he said in a raised voice and looked to the heavens, making the sign of the cross.

Jonas sighed. 'He was lured from the flock … plucked from the Lord's arms by the hunger for gold.'

Gold!

Now the meeting had Tatsuo's attention. 'Gold, huh?' He cleared his throat. 'Excuse me, gentlemen. What's this about gold?'

'We had some visitors here, you understand, some 14 months before. A schooner …'

'*Shetland*,' another said.

'*Ja, Shetland.* Rennison make friends with some of ze crew …'

'He started drinking,' Moritz said, shaking his head.

'*Ja*, well,' Jonas continued, 'they feed him stories.'

'Stories?'

'Stories of lost ship.'

'Chinesen ship.'

'*Ja.* Chinesen junk,' Moritz said.

'*Ja, ja*, junk. Apparently lost in ze Solomons 20 years ago …'

Elias weighed in, his eyes wide and serious as if it were a mortal sin to discuss the matter. 'But I feel he vos looking for ze gold all along, that he used us.'

Tatsuo tried to remain nonchalant. 'The ship?'

'*Ja*. It was on its way back to Canton, laden with gold.'

'Ze Chinesen ship … she vos named after its owner, Bao Zheng,' Jonas said. 'He vos a wealthy businessman from Canton. The story vos that gold vos taken from ze Queensland and smuggled out of Australia.'

'Two tons of gold, they say,' Moritz elaborated.

'It vos not that much, Moritz.'

'But it vos much, much gold, *ja*?'

'Why the sudden interest in gold?' Samoa asked.

'It sounds a bit far-fetched to me,' Tatsuo said, pretending to lose interest.

'Oh?'

'Every seafarer dreams of finding gold,' Tatsuo scoffed, doing his best to dampen Samoa's interest and change the subject. 'Lost treasure and all that. The seven seas abound with such nonsense.'

'May the Lord bring brother Rennison back to us,' Hans said reverently.

I shouldn't think so. Samoa knew her brother better.

'Here, here!' Tatsuo piped up. 'May he return to Jesus.'

Now he was going too far. Samoa shook her head slightly. 'You said the schooner was here 14 months ago.'

'*Ja. Und* two months later our supply ship, das steamer *Bavaria* arrive *und* Rennison bid us *auf wiedersehen* und departed with ship.'

'Where to?' Samoa said impatiently.

'Well das *Bavaria* is based in Batavia in ze Dutch East Indies. It makes regular voyages around ze Pacific and Coral Seas. It even services our brothers in North Queensland, you know.'

'So where would it normally go from here?'

'Well, usually ze next island would be Bougainville Island, ze largest of the Solomons islands.'

Samoa looked to Tatsuo. 'That's a day and a half sail,' he said.

'Then it's best we be off.'

'Whoa. Not so fast—we just got here.' Tatsuo looked at Jonas. 'Where can we fill our water kegs?'

'Moritz will organise it for you. There are many hands to help around here.'

'And, the bibles?' Tatsuo reminded Samoa.

'Oh, of course.'

'We have 500, do we not?'

Samoa pulled an extraordinary face. 'One hundred,' she said without thinking.

'Rennison ordered 100 bibles,' she told the Germans.

'But you ...' Tatsuo began.

'One hundred, Captain,' Samoa reiterated.

Tatsuo guessed something was afoot.

'One hundred it is. I'll have the lads row them ashore with the empty barrels.'

Mila overheard the conversation as she dressed the table with glassware. 'You're not leaving again immediately, are you?' she asked.

'Well ...' Tatsuo hesitated.

'You must stay,' ordered Clara. 'We rarely have visitors.'

Gretel and Monique joined the table with a hefty jug requiring two hands to pour.

'Samoa spoke for Tatsuo. 'We must leave. And I must find my brother before he does anything ... rash ... or foolish.'

Jonas shrugged. 'I understand,' he said. 'Then maybe we can hold hands in prayer, a prayer for our fallen brother, and ask for God's hand in bringing him to his sister.'

'And,' Gretel said, 'back into the flock.'

'Amen to that.'

'Tell me if I'm wrong,' Tatsuo said to Samoa as they rowed back out to the *Mystery*, 'but I was under the impression you had 500 bibles and they were all to be delivered to ...'

'To Rennison, yes. He paid for them with his own funds. I'll let these people have 100 only. The rest are for Rennison when we find him.'

Tatsuo wanted to say 'if we find him,' but thought better of it.

'I trust you did not mind me telling them we were leaving immediately,' Samoa said.

'Not at all, *fräulein*,' Tatsuo jested. 'I could not bear spending a night with that pious lot.'

'Amen to that.' Samoa grinned, raising an eyebrow.

In the hold Horace stood back from the cargo lifting high a hurricane lamp that afforded barely enough light for the purpose. Samoa squeezed between boxes of cargo in the semi-blackness, searching for her crates, unaware she was observed by a tall, menacing figure. It loomed from the shadows.

'Oh, my God!'

'What is it, Missy?'

Samoa caught her breath. The figure wasn't moving. What was this folly? Was some prisoner chained to the hold timbers?

'You alright there, Missy?' Horace called out, still holding the lamp, yet out of sight. Samoa realised her error. She was staring at a deep-sea diving suit. Now that her eyes were adjusted to the light, she recognised the brass helmet, weighted boots and all the paraphernalia for diving.

'I just frightened myself, Horace,' she said with a nervous laugh. 'There's a diving suit hanging there.'

'Huh! He won't bite yer,' the aborigine replied, chuckling.

'Whose is it?'

'The Cap'n's, Missy.'

'Really?'

'Aye.'

Samoa was impressed. 'What other dark secrets does this man have?'

'You knew the Cap'n were a diver, didn't yer, Miss?'

'Yes, but I … well, I didn't expect to see a diving suit on board.'

'Oh, the Cap'n wouldn't go anywhere without it. That belonged to his granddaddy, that did.'

Samoa found her crates. 'Can you bring the lantern closer, please?'

'Better I don't, Missy.'

'What? Why?'

'A flame shouldn't get to close to some o' dem boxes.'

Samoa cast a wary eye over the rectangular crates taken on board from the *Star of India* at Thursday Island. 'What's in them?'

'Cap'n's business, Missy.'

'What business? Is it dangerous?'

'You could say that.'

'You said they were shovels and picks to trade with the natives.'

'Aye. I did say that.'

'Well?'

'Well what, Missy?'

'Don't beat around the bush. And,'—Samoa grew angry—'stop calling me "Missy."'

'Sorry, Mis …'

'What-is-in-these-boxes?'

Silence.

'HORACE!' Samoa shouted.

'Guns!'

'Guns?'

'That's what I said, Mis … Miss Plum.'

'And I assume there is gunpowder to worry about as well?'

'Ah … dynamite, actually.'

'Dy-dynamite.' Samoa's bottom jaw dropped wide open. She froze on the spot. *Why in God's name are we carrying guns and dynamite?* Samoa thought briefly. 'Don't tell me—to trade with the natives.'

'It's actually to protect the natives,' Tatsuo said. He appeared in the doorway. Having heard the commotion he'd dropped into the hold to see what all the fuss was about and heard the conversation. Tatsuo took the lantern from Horace. 'Which box is to go ashore?' he asked. Samoa finally read the label. She said nothing, touching the lid of one of her crates.

Tatsuo whistled out for William. 'You and Will take this ashore for the missionaries,' he ordered Horace. 'And fill at least two barrels of water, savvy?'

'Yes, Cap'n.' Horace was only too happy to return on deck.

Samoa planted her hands firmly on her hips. 'Please explain.'

For a rare moment in Tatsuo's life, a woman was humiliating him. 'I planned on telling you.'

'Telling me what? That you're a gunrunner? Is that why the fort was firing artillery shells at us as we escaped Thursday Island?'

'Well, I can't tell a lie …'

'No you can't.'

'It was always my intention to sail to Bougainville; meeting you by chance and your chartering my ship was a bonus, Mist Island being so close and all.'

'Fine. But gunrunning?'

'Listen, the Germans are infiltrating the Pacific Islands; they are intimidating the natives. They are nothing but imperialist thugs wanting to rape the land for nickel, gold, guano and any other riches they can take back to the Vaterland.'

Tatsuo held up two fingers on each hand and mimed inverted commas in a satirical gesture. '*The Vaterland,*' he reiterated.

'You're inciting war,' Samoa pointed out.

'Only a small one.'

'Tatsuo Gaston, that's almost an act of treason.'

'How? Treason against who? The land belongs to the natives of Bougainville, no one else.'

'So who pays for the guns?'

'They do.'

'Oh?'

'I deal with a middleman, a woman actually, Hatsie Raven. She's a Maori who's lived with these people all her life.'

'Hatsie Raven, huh?'

'She shunned her Maori name for a whitefella one.'

'And how does this Hatsie Raven pay for the guns?'

'In gold.'

'And I assume you make a profit from this, that you aren't doing it for charity.'

'I make a little profit,' Tatsuo admitted. Samoa stared into Tatsuo's soul. 'Alright, so I make money out of it. If I didn't do it someone else would.'

'Gunrunner!' Samoa sighed. 'I'm in cahoots with a gunrunner. What's next? Slaves?'

Tatsuo hadn't seen that coming. He reddened, and with the lamp close to his face it did not go unnoticed.

'You're not ... no! You're selling slaves as well, aren't you?'

'I'm not selling slaves ...' There followed a moment's pause, then Tatsuo said quietly, almost ashamedly, 'It's called blackbirding. We've already discussed this.'

'So you don't deny it, then?'

'I'm doing the natives a favour. They are on three-year contracts; I take them to Rockhampton where they get paid wages. They're not slaves.'

'But they get slave wages!'

Tatsuo shook his head in frustration. 'And I bring them back after their lease expires.'

'Lease, huh?'

'Aye. Lease.'

'And what's in it for you?'

'I get ten quid a head, for each one delivered to the sugar fields.'

'Gunrunner and slaver.'

'Look, they get paid and return to their islands after three years, wealthy men.'

'Wealthy by their standards, not ours.'

'Yes, well. Everyone's happy. The natives get money and the farmers get reasonably priced labour.'

'Cheap labour.'

Tatsuo bit his lip. He thought it best to remain silent.

At sea, sometime later.

'So, does Tatsuo dive often?' Samoa asked Horace when she caught him alone in the galley chewing on a stale crust dripping with plum jam.

'Not a great deal, Miss Plum.'

'Call me Samoa, Horace. I'm sorry I yelled at you earlier.'

'Alright, then. Samoa. It's a beauty name, same as dat island.'

'You ever been there?'

'Samoa? Aye. A few years back.'

If Horace could only have spoken honestly, he could have told Samoa how he and Tatsuo delivered guns to the island to help with a civil war between two chiefs there, as recently as five years before.

'Is it pretty?'

'Same as all dem 'cific islands—palm beaches, sand, savages an' coconuts. I s'pose they's pretty to some folk.'

'If the captain doesn't dive much anymore, why does he keep the suit on board?'

'Oh 'e wouldn't go nowhere without it, Miss … Samoa.' Horace poked the last morsel of bread and jam in his mouth and spoke with a mouthful. 'Besides, yer never know when yer might need it.' Horace wiped jam from his chin. 'An' 'e's a good diver an' all.'

'Is that where he got the money to buy his own boat?'

'Yes. But 'e 'ad a run o' luck 'bout 15 year ago, before I met 'im.'

'What sort of luck?'

'Gold. 'e found gold.'

'What's gold mining got to do with diving?'

'Oh, it weren't on the goldfields where 'e found his riches—it were on a sunken ship.'

'Oh?'

'Aye. Back in '82, thereabouts, 'e dived on the passenger ship *Kimberley.*'

'The *Kimberley!* Really?' Samoa had read about the *Kimberley* back in Europe and she told Horace so.

There had been an article on shipping disasters in the Antipodes she said, in *The Illustrated London News,* a popular magazine. The

500-ton screw steamer had sailed from Palmerston in north Australia on its way to Adelaide with 80,000 pounds' worth of gold in the hold. The *Kimberley* was also transporting several miners on their way home after success at the gold diggings. Most of these passengers wore their gold about their persons, in money belts under their clothing. All was plain sailing until they reached the Torres Straits. Here they encountered bad weather and at 7 PM, with the ship rolling in heavy seas, the *Kimberley* struck a reef.

Initially, although the ship was stuck fast, there was no panic. The captain ordered water kegs thrown overboard to lighten her. Some hours later, with the tide at its flood and the engines at full steam, the ship slid off into deep water. However, a sudden gust of wind swept her broadside back onto the reef. The *Kimberly* heeled over and started taking water. The boats were lowered and they began abandoning ship. There was no time to save the gold. But many on board who had the gold strapped to their bodies, refused to jettison their treasure, and in attempting to jump into lifeboats many fell overboard, only to sink onto the reef and drown.

But the gold bullion on board the *Kimberley* was eventually salvaged Samoa had read. Now she had the vision of Tatsuo in his brass helmet and diving gear stashing gold bars inside his suit.

'How did Tatsuo benefit from the wreck?'

'Well, I ain't sure the boss would like me to tell yer that.'

'Oh?'

'Well … ah …' Horace looked beyond Samoa. He could hear the captain's voice on deck. He spoke quietly. 'When all the gold was salvaged it were common knowledge on Thursdee Island that lot's o' men drowned with the gold strapped to their bodies, eh.'

'Oh, of course. I read that also.' Immediately Samoa realised where this was headed. 'He didn't, did he?'

'What?'

'Rob the dead?'

'Them's harsh words, lass.' Horace looked about for the boss, but he was nowhere to be seen. 'You gotta understand, there was a sudden rush, see? Rival pearlers and dem mad bastards, the bêche fishers, they rush to the reef, see, to search for them drowned buggers with them money belts.'

'I understand. Rob the dead.' Samoa repeated her slur, but this time it was not with malice, but with admiration for Tatsuo's ingenuity.

Horace recognised the comment as praise. 'The Cap'n,' he continued, ''e find two or three bodies …'

'Horace!'

The aboriginal spun about to face Tatsuo. He had entered the galley from a forward hatch where he'd caught the tail end of the conversation. 'You telling the young lady porky pies?' he said, supporting himself on the bulkhead.

'Sorry, Boss … Cap'n. We was jus' …'

'William's at the helm—go check him if you would.'

'Aye, Cap'n.'

Samoa watched the ship's mate head back on deck. 'Is it true?'

'What? That I took gold from the dead? Well, yes. If I didn't, someone else would have.'

'I'm not judging you. But you did say something back on Mist Island about seafarers' stories and gold and lost treasure and all that, and here you are, a successful treasure hunter.'

'Well, I …' Tatsuo was lost for words.

'I think that was most businesslike of you, searching for money belts,' Samoa said. 'Entrepreneurial—yes, that's the word.'

'You do?' This lass never ceased to amaze Tatsuo.

'Yes.' Samoa imagined the situation. 'How long was this after the salvage?'

'About three weeks.'

'So the bodies were …'

'Bones. The sharks and fish had picked at them, but the heavy money belts lay on the seabed 60 feet down. Lying there for the taking. Mind you, I spoke to some of the divers employed by the insurance company. They saw some horrendous sights.'

'Like?'

'Well, one fella I spoke to in the tavern told of how he peered into some of the cabins of the sunken ship, this is only days after the disaster, and he saw bodies of women, their arms rising and falling with the water movement and their long hair floating like seaweed. Then there was the story of the shark killed on the reef and when it was cut open there was jewelry in its stomach, along with human remains.'

'Fascinating.'

Tatsuo was impressed that the whole scenario did not disturb Samoa.

'So that's where you got the money to buy this boat, huh?'

'Yes.'

'I'm impressed. But I still don't condone gunrunning.'

'Yet you condone Germany claiming the islands for their Vaterland? I don't.'

'Excuse me. How do you think the British got their Empire?'

'That's different.'

'Oh, how?'

'If you can't understand that, then I pity you.'

'Pity me?'

'Sorry.' Immediately Tatsuo realised he had riled Samoa. 'Maybe pity was the wrong word.'

'Then I will accept your apology.'

On board HMS Pride. Somewhere on the Coral Sea off the tip of eastern New Guinea

Captain Jonathon Bourke sat in the bridge on his captain's swivel chair, its heavy iron legs bolted to HMS *Pride's* teak deck. Through the bridge window he could see nothing but blue ocean and empty sky, an endless mass of undulating water and turquoise blue. At his side Army captain Captain Gerald Rafferty Reynolds had gone quiet. For the past hour he had spoken of nothing but his damned fiancée, Briana Pledge, the Admiral's twenty-four-year-old daughter. Bourke, of course, knew of the 'red-headed firecracker,' as she was called behind Reynolds's back, being an Admiral's daughter and all. But her reputation was not exactly squeaky clean. One of the reasons she had stalled her marriage to Reynolds was to enjoy the life of a free thinker in matters other than religion. But daddy would have no more of it and she was to be married, and soon, to the only fool who, it seemed, had been crazy enough to fall for her.

Now Reynolds sulked. The ship's captain had had enough of the army captain's ranting about Miss Pledge and said, quite heartlessly, something along the lines of, 'She has a bit of an eye for the lads, I hear.'

He might as well have struck the poor sod in the heart with a metal stake.

An officer broke the barrier of silence that had befallen the two men. 'Message from the radio room, Captain.' The officer passed the slip of paper to Captain Bourke. Bourke read in silence.

Proceed immediately to Bougainville Island. Have intelligence German Navy pressing forward north of the island at Wakanai Bay. Intercept at all costs. Proceed with caution. Discretion paramount. Must not spark diplomatic tension.

Rear Admiral A.J. Baker

Captain Bourke passed the memo to Reynolds.

'How long?' Reynolds asked Bourke. 'How soon can you get us to Wakanai Bay?'

Captain Bourke loved the challenge already. He looked once more at the clear blue sky.

'We should arrive there by tomorrow,' he said twisting one moustache end and then the other. 'Providing this weather holds.'

Chapter Five

Wakanai Bay. Bougainville Island.

Late the next day, Tatsuo poked his head down the companionway.

'We'll be sighting Wakanai Bay any time soon,' he called down to the galley. He spoke of the small village where his old friend Hatsie Raven the Maori lived on the east coast of Bougainville Island.

'Thanks, Skipper,' Selma called back.

Tatsuo wore an infectious grin. 'Tell our passenger, Mademoiselle Plum, this is where we drop the guns and dynamite off.' He said, keen to stir the pot.

'Aye, aye, Cap'n.' Selma went along with the charade. 'The captain told me to tell you …'

'Yes, I heard. Thank you, Selma.' Samoa watched Tatsuo's shadow vanish from sight above deck. 'Go ahead!' she shouted after him. 'Arm the natives and they'll probably shoot *you* before they kill each other!'

'Don't be too hard on the cap'n, love,' Selma said. 'He's a good man. Mostly.'

'Tatsuo, you Samu-wi bastard son of a smuggler!' Hatsie Raven barked with her speech impediment. The Maori thumped down to the water's edge on shovel-sized feet, hoisting Tatsuo from the bow of the tender like he was a child. The New Zealand native had arms and legs like a huge wild bear. There wasn't a part of her body not tattooed in some way, especially not her face, a geometric whirlpool of stippled circles and swirls, all awarded to her after various battles won. Even her chin was tattooed in a design reminding Samoa of an ancient Ionic column, which she thought exotic in some wild, savage way.

On the left of Hatsie's chin a mole the size of a grape sprouted a tuft of grey bristles. Her long, ghost-grey hair was pulled back in a bun, not unlike a chignon, with bone hairpins to keep it in place, surrounded by a *tipare*, or headband. Tatsuo would tell Samoa later the hair pins were carved from human bone. Hatsie's only clothing was a flax skirt and a sailor's calico shirt, and she wore a greenstone tiki about her neck. The woman carried a club as long as half the length of her body, a mean, gnarly, knotted piece of tree root, carved in Polynesian geometric patterns. It was not an ornament.

Within minutes they were surrounded by islanders of all ages who were excited to have visitors, and all eager for a small gift. Dropping Tatsuo onto the sand, Hatsie Raven took the captain by the shoulders with her gorilla-sized hands and rubbed noses in a traditional Maori greeting.

'Well, look at you,' she sighed, 'you old smuggler, you.'

'Smuggler, Hatsie?' Tatsuo acted modest. 'Enough of that smuggler talk, if you please. I'm an honest trader, I'll have you know.'

'Oh, yeh! I bet yer still got that little smuggling locker for gemstones and other waluables hidden under the keel,' she laughed, her obvious speech difficulties adding to her peculiar charm.

Tatsuo looked shocked.

'Don't give me that look,' Hatsie went on, winking at Samoa. 'Does he still eat fish eyes with them chopsticks?' She cackled. Samoa broke into a smile. Hatsie turned back to Tatsuo. "Look at yer —yer still 'andsome as ever.'

'And you, too, Hatsie,' Tatsuo said. 'I swear to God you get more beautiful each time I see you.'

''Ah … always the womantic, eh? I swear one day I'll sweep you off yer feet.'

'You just did, my love.' These words had them both laughing.

'Well, ain't yer goin' to introduce me to yer lovely?' Hatsie asked.

'Sorry, this is my passenger, Samoa.'

'Samoa, like the islands, eh? Is 'e bein' kind ter yer? Has 'e been a gentleman?'

'Most certainly.'

Samoa noted the woman's eyes were bloodshot and she soon discovered why. 'Here, yer ol' bastard,' Hatsie said to Tatsuo. She unhitched a leather gourd hung over her shoulder and passed it to Tatsuo. 'Dwink.'

'Arak!' Tatsuo said.

'Yeh, well, I'm out o' rum, eh?' Hatsie hacked a laugh. 'An' tobacco, too. Hope yer got Hatsie some baccy.' Her friendly grin exposed several missing teeth in both jaws. Tatsuo took the drink, the alcoholic juice of the sugar cane, a product whose fermentation began with human spit, like yeast for bread. He swigged generously before passing it to Samoa who had now stepped onto the beach.

'Drink,' he ordered. Samoa hesitated. Tatsuo turned his back to their host briefly. 'It's her way of welcoming us to the island and it would be an insult not to take a sip.' And he meant it.

Samoa took a draw at the gourd. The neat brew stung her throat and tasted muddy. She feigned appreciation and nodded to the Maori.

Hatsie Raven now went straight to business. 'And you bwought the guns?'

Tatsuo avoided Samoa's gaze. He took the Maori's arm and led her up the beach, leaving Horace to deal with Samoa and the gathering natives. Instantly Horace was the centre of attention, handing out baubles and coloured glass beads to the islanders. Clearly they had done this before and it was expected. Now Samoa's attention returned to Tatsuo and Hatsie settling in the shade beneath palm trees to discuss business.

'Why is there a New Zealand Maori here as chieftain of these people?' Samoa asked Horace.

'She arrived here as a kind of castaway gettin' away from missionaries on the North Island of New Zealand.'

'Escaping missionaries? Pray tell.'

'Cap'n tell me Hatsie's tell him them missionaries in New Zealand was, ah … what's the word 'e used?' Horace looked to the sky as though the word he sought would be written on a cloud. 'Zealots! Aye, that's it. Bloody zealots. She was a youngun, thirteen maybe. She left with her parents but them two drowned in the surf paddling their canoe ashore the night they arrived.'

'But how did she end up the chief?'

Horace told how Hatsie Raven had grown to be adored and revered by the islanders, and now, three decades later, she was feared and respected as their leader.

'Twelve crates, 20 rifles in each,' Tatsuo told the Maori chief.

'These better not be made in India like some of the last lot you sold me.' Hatsie Raven looked into Tatsuo's eyes. She was not a person to cross.

'You only get what you pay for,' Tatsuo replied, matching her timbre.

'And?'

'These are Martini-Henrys. And, yes, they did come from India, but …'—Tatsuo paused for effect—'… but they are British, made in Enfield in London, not copies made by the Indian black marketeers.'

'Bwitish made. Good. How old?'

'They were all manufactured in the early 80s.'

'Ammunition?'

'Twenty thousand rounds.'

'Good, vewy good.'

'They … ah … fell off the back of a wagon, so to speak.'

Hatsie Raven laughed and belly fat undulated beneath her shirt. Suddenly she turned serious. 'How much?'

'These are far superior to the last lot, you know. These rifles …'

'How much?'

'Four pounds each.'

'Four!'

'Four for the rifles and you can have the ammunition for three pence a bullet, let's say 500 pounds.' Hatsie whistled. This was expected. The large native woman fixed her stare on Tatsuo, a stare as cold and hard as that of an Easter Island statue. 'And a case of whiskey?' she demanded.

'Of course,' Tatsuo always threw in a case of cheap whiskey. He went on, 'You know, I risked heaven and earth to get these. The British took shots at me as I left Thursday Island.'

'What's a few bullets? You're used to that.'

'These weren't bullets, my friend. This was artillery.'

'Artillery. Well, well, you are going up in the world.' Hatsie was thoughtful a moment, watching the islanders fighting over trinkets at the water's edge. 'I wouldn't mind a big gun,' she said. 'Army field gun would be nice.'

'Yes, well. That's not going to happen. I do have some dynamite, though. Two boxes.'

'Dynamite!' Hatsie Raven was impressed. Suddenly her weathered, tattooed face scrunched. 'I've never used it, but ...'

'I'll teach you. Most importantly, though, you must learn respect.'

'Respect? For you?'

'Not me—for the dynamite. Otherwise you might blow that pretty head of yours off your lovely shoulders.'

'You tiger!' Hatsie Raven slapped Tatsuo on the back. 'Always there to compliment a beautiful woman, eh?'

Samoa had waited long enough. She caught Tatsuo's eye and shrugged her shoulders impatiently. Hatsie Raven noticed.

'You have a very beautiful woman here with you. Have you met your match at last?'

'Me?' Tatsuo harrumphed. 'Met my match? I don't think so.'

But Hatsie thought differently. 'Samoa, pretty name.'

'Aye. Samoa Plum. She's contracted me to help her find her brother Rennison …'

Hatsie stiffened. 'Wennison Plum?'

'Aye. He's here, then?'

'The bastard was here. He got one of the village women here pwegnant and sailed away.'

Tatsuo sighed. 'Where to?'

'Don't know. He was looking for something but he would never tell us what. He lived here for maybe seven months, about a year ago now.'

'That sounds about right.'

'And he was quick with the women on the island. He knew a lot about stwategy.'

'With women?'

'No. Stwategy for fightin'. He advised us on fortification and the like—that's why I let him stay.'

'Fortification?'

'Aye. An' warfare. He knew a lot about fighting. Said he fought the Amewicans and the Bwitish in Samoa eight years ago.'

'He what?

'He fought with the Germans against the Royal Navy and the Americans. It was a civil war …'

'Yes, I know what happened in the Samoan Islands.' Tatsuo knew only too well. It had only been in the late 1880s that the Samoan Islanders had started fighting a civil war over who was to be the king: Malietoa Laupepa or Mata'afa Iosefo. Tatsuo had sold arms to the Samoans in '92.

Rennison was looking less and less like the picture Samoa had painted of him. 'The man I'm talking about would have sailed from the Duke of York or Mist, about a year ago.'

'That's him. Tall, white hair, good looking. I was thinking of taking him for one of me husbands.' Hatsie Raven roared at her joke.

Now Tatsuo was confused. 'Are you certain?'

'Aye.'

'And he fought alongside the Germans, not the British?' Tatsuo asked.

'I'm as certain as I am hungwy right now. Come, let's get the cwates safely ashore while my servants cook up a storm, as you whitefellas say. I tell them, cook up a feast, when I see *Mystewy* anchor in me bay.'

Samoa was more annoyed about Rennison's activities. 'My brother was always a womaniser,' she told their host and Tatsuo after a full belly of yams and some small roasted birds, each about the size of a plucked blackbird.

'And here was me thinking he had given himself to God and all that,' Tatsuo said. 'A missionary, no less.'

'He gave himself to all the women 'ere,' Hatsie Raven said, still eating. 'But I never seen him pway to no god.'

'Yes, well, I must confess I was surprised when I heard he had joined the mission in the first place.'

'Look, Samoa,' Tatsuo said, 'I've got to ask you, what was Rennison doing fighting with the Germans?'

'I honestly don't know. I think there is a mix up.' Hatsie Raven looked affronted. 'I think you may have misunderstood,' Samoa told her diplomatically. 'And that he meant he was fighting alongside the British.'

'I know what he said!' Hatsie Raven reared up like a disturbed cobra.

Tatsuo dived straight in to defuse the situation. 'How long is it since you last saw your brother?' he asked Samoa. She was quiet a moment. 'You said you received a letter from him last, when, fourteen, fifteen months ago?'

'Yes. But I haven't actually seen him for five years.' Samoa said. 'I would like to talk to the woman he … ah … the woman who is having my brother's child.'

'She lives in the next village,' Hatsie Raven said with a full mouth of food, pointing with a bone. 'Near the weef. I'll 'ave someone take you there.'

'Thank you.'
'You might want to collect his belongings while you're there.'
'Belongings?'
'Aye, 'e left clothes an' a few books, nothin' of walue.'

Tatsuo had nothing but admiration for Rennison's taste in women. The islander who carried his child was a Pacific Island beauty. Maybe it was the hint of the Orient about Safina, her high cheekbones and slightly sloe eyes. Whatever it was, she was not pure-blood Bougainvillian. But with the whitefella sailing the vast Pacific Ocean more regularly these days, multi-racial people were hardly rare. Tatsuo only had to look in the mirror.

Samoa felt instant empathy with Safina, who lived with three sisters and their aged mother in a grass hut built amongst palms, back from a reef. The location was idyllic—the constant pounding of the surf, the clear blue sky and the tropical vegetation. They lived in romantic poverty. Or was it bliss? They wanted for nothing. They knew no better. They had little idea of the whitefellas' folly of greed and desire.

Safina was made to understand the situation with the aid of Ratal, Hatsie Raven's assistant, translating into Pidgin English. And Samoa immediately bonded with Safina. There was a common thread connecting them. Sure, at first Safina was wary, but with time she too felt a bond with this equally attractive woman from the other side of the world.

'Yes, he arrived one year ago,' the translator said. 'They fell in love. Rennison promised Safina the world, but he was restless. Safina got with child, then Rennison left not long after. That was many months ago now.'

'How did he leave?' Samoa wanted to know.

Ratal and Safina spoke quietly and Samoa noticed a tear roll down Safina's cheek. Ratal turned to Samoa. 'Safina,' he told her in Pidgin, 'she heard that Rennison walked across the island to the west where he met fisherman from Georgia Island. But the man who tol'' her say many times the Georgian islanders were headed to Vanguna Island, south of Georgia. It is believed that was their destination.'

'To Vanguna Island?'

'Yes.'

'I know where it is,' Tatsuo said. 'The natives there are very primitive. It's better known to those who are well-traveled as Rat's Nest Island.'

'Rat's Nest?'

'Because the biggest rats in the word breed there, like … rats.'

'Are there missionaries there?'

'Not that I'm aware of. Just lots of rats.' Tatsuo was showing no enthusiasm. None at all.

Samoa turned to the translator. 'Is there a mission on Rat's Nest Island?'

'I hear of a small group who sail there some months ago. But have heard nothing else.'

'Oh.' Samoa had a thought. 'Could you please ask Safina if she still has the trunk … ah ... the box belonging to Rennison that he left behind?'

Safina nodded and was only too happy to oblige. She sent one of her sisters to fetch it. The dented tin trunk was smaller than Samoa had expected. She opened it in front of everyone, but clearly it had been rifled. It seemed to contain nothing of importance, not to the natives, anyhow. But there were some clothes, mainly undergarments, three novels and a diary. Samoa took up the leather-bound diary.

'This is so like Rennison,' she said nostalgically. 'Always kept a diary.' She eagerly opened the bible-sized book. The chronological entries were mundane; she was skimming through the pages when one word caught her attention. 'Is that the French word for treasure?'

'What?' Tatsuo ears pricked like a burglar's in the night. Tatsuo looked over Samoa's shoulder to where her finger underlined the word '*trésor*.'

'*Trésor. Oui* … I mean, yes.'

'Thought I recognised it.'

'Let me see that.' Tatsuo didn't mean to snatch. But he did. He cast a rapacious eye over the page. 'It's in French,' he said, translating the lines before and after the *magic* word, treasure.

'Isn't that the French word for gold?' Samoa pointed to '*or*.'

Tatsuo muttered something and translated '*navire d'or*' as the words 'golden ship.' 'Oh … huh … yes,' Tatsuo continued, putting on a face of disinterest. 'That old chestnut,' he puffed out his cheeks. 'The golden ship, it's *that* old sea tale. Been going about the Pacific for years, like the pox … ah, if you'll excuse the comparison.'

Tatsuo took a sly look at the faces of all those in the hut, including the translator, who, he noticed, had an eye for the younger sister. No one else seemed to bother with the word 'treasure,' or 'gold.' He gathered up the books and diary, throwing them back in the trunk, leaving the underwear behind.

'We better take this stuff and be off, then,' he told Samoa. She quickly realised something was afoot. She unclipped a silver-plated bangle from her wrist, presenting it to Safina, who was delighted with the gift. They bid farewell.

'Nice touch,' Tatsuo said as he trudged back across the dunes towards Hatsie Raven's village with the tin chest wedged under his arm. Samoa and Ratal were directly on his heels.

'Nice touch?' Samoa asked.

'The bangle. Trinkets. The natives love trinkets.'

Samoa ignored the comment. 'What's in the diary that's so interesting?'

'I don't know.'

'What's the hurry, then?'

Tatsuo stopped so suddenly Samoa walked into him. 'Look,' he said, his face the most serious she had seen it, 'do you want to find your brother or not?'

'Of course I do.'

'Then come along. Hurry.' Tatsuo hurried ahead. Back at Hatsie's beach Tatsuo shoved the small tin trunk into Horace's arms and leant close before Samoa was in earshot. 'Guard this with your life. Do you hear me?'

'Aye, Cap'n.'

'Keep a sharp eye on it.'

'Whose is it, Boss?'

'That woman's.' He alluded to Samoa approaching fast. 'It's hers, but see it's safe, savvy?'

'Savvy.'

Samoa caught up. 'Well you certainly are in a hurry.'

'Yes, well, look at that sky," Tatsuo replied. "Lovely evening for a sail, eh, Horace?'

'Aye.'

'Row Mademoiselle back to the *Mystery*, please,' he ordered Horace. 'And then come back for me.'

'Where are you going?' Samoa asked the skipper.

'I have unfinished business with Hatsie Raven and I've got to collect payment.'

Bank of England sterling and a bag of assorted gold coins awaited, sovereigns and guineas, mainly.

'You're leaving in a huwwy,' Hatsie Raven's slurred words were scented with cheap whiskey. She reclined in a huge cane chair with armrests and an oversized rounded fan back that almost reached the ceiling. 'My throne,' she called it. Stacked beside her were 19 crates, 12 of rifles, one of dynamite and six of ammunition. Her massive feet were hooked up on another crate of dynamite. On the side table, next to her, a half-empty bottle of whiskey and two glasses waited.

After the dynamite demonstration that scared every bird in the jungle for a mile radius Hatsie was keen for another drink. She also insisted on showing her visitors the fortifications Samoa's brother Rennison had advised the islanders to build. These rock-walled defenses were on strategic hills close behind the village. Others were like stork nests at the top of coconut palms, single-man sniper lookout posts.

'I'm afraid I have to leave.' Tatsuo folded the banknotes and tightened his purse strings, pocketing his payment with the satisfying sound of jingling gold. 'I'd love to stay a day or two—you know I would—but there is a possibility the brother of my passenger, Samoa, is on Rats' Nest.' Tatsuo knew he wasn't going anywhere until he had had the customary farewell drink and clearly Hatsie Raven had started without him. She flicked her fingers towards the bottle. Tatsuo filled her glass and then his.

'You'll be passing by when?' she asked, back to business.

'I'm not certain.'

'Not certain when or not certain if?'

'If.'

'Because I have 20 stwong men who want to sign up for Queensland,' the woman said. 'They are waiting in another village.'

'Sorry, Hatsie, blackbirding is a bit of a touchy subject at the moment.'

'That woman, huh?'

'Aye. She accuses me of being a slaver… as well as a gunrunner.'

'Huh,'—Hatsie Raven laughed out loud—'you're both gunwunner and slaver, my fwiend.'

'Yeh, well, I'm under contract to find her brother.'

Hatsie stood unsteadily. The whiskey had made her playful. She took up a rifle from the top crate and rammed a bullet in the breach. 'I'm goin' to need these sooner than later, I'm thinkin'.'

'Oh, why's that?'

Hatsie swung the loaded rifle across the hall aiming out through the main entrance. Those in the firing line ducked and weaved.

'The word is there's a German gunboat with mawines heading this way,' Hatsie said, shouldering the rifle butt and sighting down the barrel. 'The bloody sauerkwauts have alweady helped themselves to land in the north of Bougainville and they want more. Much more.'

Someone outside shouted a warning and natives scattered. Hatsie pulled the trigger. Her giant body absorbed the recoil and across the way a human skull hanging on a post outside the next hut exploded into hundreds of bone shards.

'Doesn't it seem strange to you,' Tatsuo said to Samoa back on board *Mystery,* 'that your brother told Hatsie he fought with

Germans, and then he shows these islanders how to defend themselves against them?'

'He may have been thinking about any country taking over this island, for that matter,' Samoa answered defensively.

'Maybe.' But Tatsuo wasn't so certain.

Somewhere on the Coral Sea Captain Herr von Schlumpf stood on the bridge of his beloved ship, the SS *Prinzessin*. He was a proud navy man, born and bred in the industrial German port city of Emden. Now at fifty-eight years of age he was at the top of his career for a commoner. Captain of the 407-foot passenger steamer converted into a gunboat with the sole purpose of claiming Pacific islands for das Vaterland. The all-white SS *Prinzessin,* with her two tall slim funnels amidships, rounded stern and richly decorated clipper bow featuring a figurehead of a German princess, was capable of maintaining 15 knots with her quadruple expansion steam engines. The 120 cabins and luxurious staterooms had been converted to military purposes half a dozen years earlier. When the vessel had been assigned to the Pacific region she'd been fitted with guns: one 15-centimetre SK L/35 on the foredeck and two Maxim guns mounted under cover at the stern. Although orders came from Rear Admiral Alfred von Tirpitz himself, the SS *Prinzessin*—which technically should have been called the SMS *Prinzessin* of the Imperial German Navy—was not officially a Navy ship. Many suggested espionage was afoot.

Tatsuo had sailed by her several times over the past two years. The SS *Prinzessin* now proceeded at full steam ahead, across the Coral Sea.

'Final destination, *Kapitän*?' the navigator asked, seeking instructions.

Captain Schtumpf waited for orders from Admiral Gustav von Stosch, a sixty-nine-year-old veteran of several battles standing alongside him on the bridge. The old admiral, a large man fond of the dinner table and bar, twisted his generous moustache—a well-waxed growth above his upper lip that resembled the letter 'W' … 'W' for Wilhelm II, his Emperor, the crew jested behind his back.

Stosch looked at the chart before him. The island of Bougainville, approximately 100 miles long and 25 miles wide, had been in Germany's sights for some time. He ran a finger across the map where intelligence had recommended a cove in the middle of the eastern side of the island, and studied it briefly—Wakanai Bay.

But there something was bothering the Admiral. For the past year many of the islanders were managing to secure arms, mostly English rifles—the famed and feared Lee Enfield, although some were Indian copies.

'There is something else we need to do, *Kapitän*,' Admiral Stosch told Captain Schtumpf.

'Admiral?'

'I want every cutter, lugger, pearler, and bêche-de-mer fishing vessel stopped and searched.'

'Would this be looking for smuggled arms, Admiral?'

'Exactly.' A gaseous belch escaped with the admiral's affirmation and an invisible mist of garlic sausage permeated the bridge.

The captain stepped back, feigning a necessity to check the compass reading. 'Forgive me, Admiral, but I don't think we have a legal right.'

'Damn it, man, someone is selling the savages guns. Guns are killing Germans. I don't give a rat's arse if it is legal. We are on the high seas, man, I … *we* are the law.'

'Certainly, Admiral.'

An officer ascended the companionway onto the bridge. 'Admiral, sir, a message from the radio room.'

Admiral Stosch snatched the paper, scanned the Morse coded message carefully, and harrumphed.

'Anything urgent?' Captain Schtumpf asked.

'We have an agent to retrieve on our travels.'

'Oh?'

'Horst Schwarz, remember the name?'

'Yes, I actually met him once.'

'Good. Intelligence notified the admiralty he was living on Mist Island amongst Lutheran missionaries. That was his cover. But he's been reported last seen on Nagho ni ara and he has no authority to be there. I suspect there is more afoot than we know, Captain, and I suspect I know what it is.'

'Oh?'

'I'll fill you in. However, right now, the top brass want him escorted back to New Guinea.'

Captain Schtumpf knew this to be the island west of Bougainville.

The ship's navigator interrupted. 'Admiral?'

'What?'

'Final destination, if you please, sir?'

Admiral Stosch inspected the charts once more, struggling to pronounce the words. 'Nagho ni ara,' he finally managed.

On board the Mystery. Rat's Nest Island.

Rat's Nest Island was less than a day's sail from Bougainville. In this case an overnight sail. Tatsuo knew the island to be five miles long and roughly three and a half across. Mostly, it remained unexplored by Europeans. The island was dominated by a volcano Tatsuo estimated to be nearly 4,000 feet high, and although it was believed to be inactive the islanders spoke of a live volcano under the sea less than 20 miles south. Kavachi, they called it. Tatsuo also knew neighbouring islanders, cannibals amongst them, frequented the island, for it was rich in resources, although infested with the giant rats that made life difficult for inhabiting islanders.

'So why would Rennison come here?' Tatsuo asked Samoa. The two scoured the landscape from where they were moored in the deep water of the bay. The wind had died, but the jungle slopes reaching up to the volcano's pinnacle were alive.

Mystery's anchor chain rattled through the metal-framed hawsehole creating enough racket to reverberate about the bay like a Viking landing. Their voices carried across the water. There was no sign of human inhabitants, although grass and bamboo huts in disrepair, some destroyed by fire, could be seen amidst the encroaching jungle where Mother Nature reclaimed her own.

'It's eerily deserted,' Samoa said.

Horace agreed, his furrowed brow signaling vigilance.

Selma joined them at the guardrail. 'What are yer thoughts, Cap'n?' The old cook, too, looked cautious. Tatsuo did not answer. He stood firm, training his spyglass along the shoreline.

William's tic broke the unearthly silence in his usual profanity. He twitched two or three times before going quiet.

'It is a bit like that, eh, Will?' Tatsuo made light of the young man's affliction, communicating that there was no cause for alarm, no reason to apologise. Will took a deep breath and squeezed the guardrail until his knuckles whitened.

Without warning a lone figure burst from the jungle, plunged down a six-foot sandbank and rushed onto the beach, waving frantically.

'What the hell?' Tatsuo framed the figure in his lens. 'White male, white hair!'

'It's Rennison!' Samoa shouted across the water. The figure continued waving but did not respond verbally. 'Renn—'

Tatsuo cupped a hand over Samoa's mouth. 'Quiet, girl.' Samoa protested, but the captain was resolute. 'Keep quiet. Something's amiss.'

'What?'

'Don't know, but he looks scared.' Tatsuo waved back silently before carefully searching the landscape for trouble. 'Horace.'

'Yes, Cap'n?'

'Launch the tender.'

They watched silently as the clinker was lowered onto the water and unshackled from its davits. 'Stay here. Horace and I'll go ashore. Will, you come with us and stay with the tender.'

'I'm coming,' Samoa was adamant. 'That's my brother.'

'No. Something's not right. I need you to stay ...'

'I'm coming. End of story.'

Tatsuo followed Samoa to the stern where she had one leg on the Jacob's ladder already. 'Jesus!' Tatsuo argued. 'Then I insist you do as I say. Savvy?'

'Fine.' Samoa dropped into the boat.

'Will.'

'Cap'n.'

'Fetch rifles. The Mauser is under my bunk.'

Tatsuo handed one to Selma who was clearly comfortable handling a rifle. 'Keep a sharp eye.'

'Aye, Cap'n.' Selma rammed the heel of her hand against the bolt action of the rifle. Ready to load. But it was already loaded. William had seen to that.

Moments later William rowed the four of them ashore. The lone figure rushed into the shallows to meet them. He was frantic, constantly looking back towards the jungle, yet he maintained silence and motioned for his rescuers to do the same.

Samoa's heart sank. 'That's not Rennison.'

Tatsuo. 'Oh! Really?'

'Thank the Lord, I'm saved,' the man hissed, trying to climb aboard. 'We need to leave, now.'

'Easy there, soldier,' Tatsuo said, leaping over the bow into waist-deep water. 'Wait.'

'Who *are* you?' Samoa asked.

'Ben Rudder, ma'am.'

'We're looking for Rennison Plum.'

'Rennison? Rennison Plum? You know him?'

'He's my brother. We've been searching for him. We were informed he came to this island.'

The castaway—for that seemed to be the only way to describe this rather timid man—was quiet a moment.

'Well?'

'I'm sorry, ma'am …'

'Sorry?'

'Rennison Plum was … I'm so sorry.'

'Speak, damn it.'

'He was killed. About two weeks back. I've lost track of the days.'

Samoa fell back onto the bench seat.

Horace saw the pain the man's statement had caused and put a comforting hand on her shoulder. He said nothing.

'How was he killed?' Tatsuo asked the castaway.

'Look, I'll tell you when we get away from here. Please, let's go.'

'Answer the question,' Samoa snapped. 'How was my brother killed?'

'We were attacked by savages from another island.'

'When?'

'Like I said, two weeks ago, thereabouts.'

'Are you alone?'

'Yes, yes. But I'm afraid they will return. They stayed here only a few days after the attack and were here again three days ago. We must leave immediately.'

Tatsuo had one thought, and it had nothing to do with Rennison Plum: the gold ship lead had come to an abrupt halt.

'Where's his body?' Samoa asked, once the devastating news had sunk in.

'I buried them.'

'Them?'

'Yes, there were five of us. They were all hacked with axes, it was horrendous … Savages! There would have been 30 of them, in two war canoes. The first time they came through the jungle and ambushed us. They must have landed up the coast and walked through the jungle. And the last time they paddled right in here.' Rudder was clearly terrified, his head spinning, constantly searching the coastline.

'Who? I mean, what were you doing here?'

'We are missionaries, ma'am.' His eyes went blank briefly. 'At least we *were* missionaries. Look, can't we do this away from here?'

'What kind of missionaries ?'

'With the Lutheran Church of the Pacific. Sent here on reconnaissance, so to speak.' Screeching erupted in the jungle as a flock of parrots lifted en-masse from the trees. 'We had heard the island had a small community and the word was they were reaching out to God.'

'When?'

'Maybe a year ago. Please, can we leave this God-awful place?'

Tatsuo looked at the damaged buildings. 'There's little we can do.'

Samoa was adamant. 'I'm not leaving without my brother's body.'

'You *are* joking, are you not?' Tatsuo countered.

Samoa shot the skipper a death stare. She leapt into the shallows and snatched Ben Rudder's arm. 'Take me to my brother's grave.'

'Ma'am, please. They might come back any moment.'

'Then we better be quick.' There was to be no argument.

'You and Will take the tender offshore,' Tatsuo ordered Horace, who knew the routine. It was always best to wait in deep water. The skipper checked his pistol, unclipping it from its holster. 'And make certain the rifles are loaded,' he told the aborigine.

'Aye, Cap'n.'

'Lead on.' Agitated, but with little option than to comply with his only ticket out of hell, Ben Rudder led the trio along an overgrown path into the cool shadows of the dense jungle. Without warning, something orangey brown, fat and larger than a domestic cat shot across the path. Samoa instinctively jumped.

'That's one of the devilish rats, ma'am—ugly things, steal your food, eat everything, they will.'

A hundred yards in they came to a clearing. Here were the burnt remains of more recently built huts. Lying on the ground in front of the largest was a charcoal cross.

'How long did you say you were you here?'

'A year, thereabouts.'

'Where are all the villagers?'

'Well, that's the thing. They must have known something we didn't, because they disappeared in the night about three weeks ago.'

'Just like that?'

'Yes. All their canoes were missing.' Ben forged on through the thick jungle. 'They will have taken refuge on another island and left us to God's mercy.'

Tatsuo wanted to say, 'Well that's what you get for spreading Christianity,' but thought better of it.

They spilled into a clearing. 'There's your brother's grave.'

One single grave was covered in bracken and quite well hidden. Nearby were four other shallow graves, all empty.'

'What happened here?'

'Oh it's awful. Disgusting. When they returned the first time they exhumed the Lutheran brothers and took their bodies away.'

'Why?' Samoa asked.

'Don't ask,' Tatsuo said.

Samoa looked to the castaway. 'Why?' she repeated.

Ben Rudder looked sheepish. 'Well, ma'am, they *are* cannibals.'

'No! But they would have been … well they'd been dead three days.'

'Matters not to them,' Tatsuo said matter-of-factly.

'But my brother's grave was untouched.'

'Yes, it was well hidden by that fallen palm. I had to dig these graves with sticks,' he went on. 'Luckily the soil is soft. But I buried them to keep them away from the rats as much as out of respect. All I wanted to do was get away from here and a supply ship isn't due here for a month yet.'

'How deep is my brother?'

'Shallow, ma'am, same as these. Please, can we hurry?' Ben Rudder's fear was palpable, unnerving Tatsuo, who was more than familiar with headhunting islanders roaming this part of the Solomon Seas. He also knew they were only a day's sail from the island of Malaita, where the most notorious cannibals thrived, totally intolerant of the whitefella.

'Let's be quick about it, shall we?' Tatsuo said.

The two men started digging with sticks. Samoa looked on with mixed emotions. Tatsuo noticed her angst. 'Maybe you could gather some banana leaves,' he said in a sympathetic tone. 'We will need to wrap him in something.'

A task he was not looking forward to.

Samoa was gone only minutes, long enough for the men to uncover the body, which had been covered in less than two feet of topsoil. She dragged several huge green leaves behind her and stopped silently at the grave's edge. 'That's not him.'

'Pardon?'

'That's not Rennison. That's not my brother.'

Tatsuo looked to where he had exposed the cadaver's head and bare torso. The body was well decomposed and to him it seemed the body would have been difficult for anyone to identify.

'My brother didn't have tattoos.'

Sure enough, even though the corpse was in poor condition, the chest was generously tattooed with a sailing ship, circled with rope and a heart that read 'Sarah.'

'Maybe he had tattoos done in the islands.'

'A missionary having tattoos? Hardly. Besides, he always said how only common men wore tattoos.'

'Could he have changed his ways?'

Samoa studied the cadaver carefully. 'That is not my brother.'

'Are you certain?'

'Yes ... I am certain.'

'Then who is it?'

Ben Rudder stepped away from the grave. 'Honest,' he said, 'I knew him as Rennison Plum.'

Samoa was exasperated. 'Was there another man on this island at any time? Late twenties, blond hair, tall, slim.'

'No. Definitely not. There were only the six of us Europeans. We all—'

'Look out!'

The first spear thudded into a tree inches from Tatsuo, the same moment a second penetrated Ben Rudder's thigh. He let out a gut-wrenching squeal. Tatsuo snatched his pistol and fired two shots in the direction of several dark bodies shifting in the vegetation.

'Run!' he screamed at Samoa.

She didn't need prodding. A spear stabbed the ground where she had stood. A naked warrior appeared. Tatsuo fired and the native's head exploded in a mist of gore. Tatsuo caught Ben Rudder falling and threw the man's arm around his neck. He yelled in his ear. 'Run, man, run!'

Awkwardly, they hobbled back along the path towards the beach. Samoa hit the beach, shouting to Horace, but he had already heard the shots and shouldered the Mauser.

William started rowing towards the beach.

Behind them Tatsuo heard the whooping and cheering of a war party in murderous pursuit. Stumbling with his burden he managed two more shots. One native dropped across the pathway. Others scattered. Tatsuo reached the sand dune leading to the beach. He twisted about to heave Rudder onto the sand when a stone axe wheeled through the air, slamming into the man's neck.

Rudder died instantly.

Tatsuo cast away the dead weight and bolted after Samoa, who was waiting in waist-deep water. 'Swim!' he screamed.

Another axe whistled by Tatsuo's head.

He spun on his heels as a dozen angry savages spilt onto the beach. Horace opened fire while Tatsuo squeezed off his last two rounds. Two natives fell and a third was hit, as Horace picked off the closest assailant. Tossing his pistol aside, Tatsuo chased Samoa into the water. Spears spiked the bay all about them, but with Horace picking off targets from the tender the natives backed away. Soon the two were in deep water. Some natives waded out, yelling, but Tatsuo knew one thing about these people—they were notoriously bad swimmers.

'You alright?' Tatsuo spat seawater, swimming alongside Samoa whose strong strokes threatened to best him.

'Fine. Now I know what you mean by savages.'

'Yes, they weren't a happy lot.'

Samoa rolled on her back, treading water a moment, observing the beach where at least two dozen natives now ranted and whooped war cries.

'Where's Rudder?' she asked.

'Didn't make it.'

As Samoa narrowed her eyes in concentration she could make out naked men hacking at the missionary's body.

'Oh, God!'

'Hurry!' Horace's voice was urgent. He was still a hundred yards out. 'Hurry, we've got company.'

Tatsuo searched the shore where Horace pointed. 'Christ!' he said, gargling water. 'Swim, mademoiselle! Swim for your life!' Back towards the beach a canoe with six savages—until now hidden from view behind a promontory—pushed off across the water. It sliced over the surface with frightening speed. The two swimmers were between the canoe and the tender.

'Shoot the bastards!' Tatsuo screamed to Horace, his words garbled as he swam. 'Shoot, for Christ's sake!'

'I'm out of ammunition!' Horace yelled back.

'Jesus! Now?'

Suddenly another shot rang out across the bay. Selma was an experienced adventurer but she was a hopeless shot, especially from quarter of a mile away on the *Mystery*.

The canoe closed in fast. Ten yards … Five …

Tatsuo swam to Samoa. 'The moment they get close, dive. Do as I do.'

Samoa nodded urgently. She took a deep breath. The men in the canoe paddled alongside, clubs raised. Tatsuo and Samoa dived. Under water Tatsuo signaled to Samoa. She knew what to do. The savages gazed into the water. Watching. Waiting for their prey to come up for air. Tatsuo and Samoa were on the opposite side. They grabbed it, and with all their strength … they capsized it.

Six natives spilt into the deep bay. Floundering frantically. Hopeless as swimmers. Tatsuo dived again. Holding men under, drowning his attackers one by one. William heaved on the oars, closing the distance between them. Once alongside the canoe, Horace wielded the butt of the Mauser, clubbing any natives on the surface.

It was over in minutes.

Tatsuo helped Samoa aboard the tender and Horace hoisted his skipper to safety. And not too soon. The commotion and scent of blood had attracted swift reef sharks. Will struck out towards the cutter while behind them three natives managed to climb back into their canoe. They were defeated.

'I don't want to do that again any time soon,' Samoa said, snatching breaths.

'Now where have I heard that line before?' Tatsuo smiled.

Selma waited on deck, cocky as a rooster. She stood with one foot hooked on the hatch cover, using the rifle for support.

'By Jesus I tried, Skipper,' she said, spitting a glob of betel nut in the direction of the retreating canoe.

'That you did, Selma. Remind me to give you target practice when we make land next.'

'You sayin' I'm a crook shot?'

'At least you tried.' He took the rifle from Selma and checked the breach. 'I'll just store this below, before you shoot someone you're not supposed to.'

'I shot yer a roo once, back at Cooktown, didn't I?' she yelled after him.

'That was with my shotgun, and I nearly broke a tooth on the pellets.' Tatsuo was keen to reach deep water. 'Horace!'

'Cap'n.'

'Weigh anchor, set sail. I think we better put some distance between us and Rat's Nest.'

Chapter Six

Leaving Rat's Nest Island behind them, *Mystery*, with favourable winds, sailed through the afternoon on a short six-hour voyage northwest to safety, off the coast of Georgia Island. Here Tatsuo consulted his charts. By late afternoon they'd found a sheltered bay surrounded by high cliffs rising sheer from the sea. At the base were low-ceilinged caves. The cove was tranquil, affording them a safe anchorage for the night, away from unpredictable natives.

Tatsuo watched the anchor descend into a deep natural harbour. Any breeze soon deserted them in the protected bay and the oppressive heat returned. It was time to rest up.

'I need a drink.' Tatsuo's words carried across the still water. 'Selma.'

'I heard yer.' The old cook's voice rose from the galley. A chinking of whiskey bottles was followed by the woman's bare feet padding along the deck. Selma poured two glasses—one for the boss, one for the cook. Tatsuo looked over his shoulder to Samoa under the shade of a wide-brimmed straw hat. She looked stunning.

'Drink?' he asked, before answering his own question. 'Oh, that's right, you don't drink, do you?'

Little did he realise. Samoa also needed something after her near-death experience. It wasn't that she didn't drink. What she had meant to say when she was asked that the first time back in Cooktown, was that she didn't drink much. Samoa looked down at Tatsuo, bare-chested and sunning himself on the deck.

'Do you have any schnapps?'

'Schnapps! Now there you go. I thought … never mind. Selma?'

'*No*, we don't have schnapps.' The old cook smacked her lips. She held her glass high. It was nearly drained already. 'Whiskey?'

'Ah … What about gin?' Samoa asked.

'No.'

'White rum?' Tatsuo suggested.

'You know we have white rum,' Selma retorted.

Tatsuo caught Samoa's approving look. 'Then be a darling and fetch a bottle, will you?'

Selma shot the skipper a *fetch the bloody bottle yerself* scowl.

Tatsuo grunted. 'Will, fetch a bottle of white rum, and ginger beer and a lime if there's any left.'

The lad disappeared down the companionway. Tatsuo rose lazily from the deck to act as barman, mixing Samoa a cocktail on the sail locker. His first whiskey had hit the spot; the second relaxed him—now he felt cheeky. He passed Samoa her drink. Behind them Horace secured a sail for a sunshade while William set up a small portable card table with water kegs for seats before settling himself down with his sketch pad, discreetly rendering an image of his skipper and Samoa.

'Miss … ah, Samoa,'—Horace played waiter—'take a seat.'

'Why, thank you, Horace.'

'And what is our wonderful chef de cuisine preparing for us this evening, Selma?' Tatsuo asked the old cook.

Selma drained her glass, poured another. 'Have you thought about fishing?'

'Cheeky sod,'—Tatsuo made as if to scold Selma—'I should have you whipped. Will … William Maynard.'

'Aye, Cap'n.'

'Fetch the cat o' nine tails for me, lad.' And the laughter echoed off the cliffs.

For the first time in weeks Samoa saw crew camaraderie surface.

Tatsuo stood and stretched. The whiskey made him sweat even more. He looked over the side. The water was clear to 20 feet and already he could see good-size fish swimming about, there for the taking. He lifted a locker lid and removed a trident—a six-foot, custom-made, three-pronged spear—and a pair of goggles made for pearlers, with a vulcanised rubber seal and strap. Samoa was impressed. She was even more impressed when he dropped his britches, baring his Herculean physique. Modesty kept him in the loincloth he wore tied beneath. Tatsuo climbed the ratline to the mainsail boom and picked his moment. Horace knew his duty; he would stand guard watching for predators. Tatsuo dived, barely making a splash. The others rushed to the guardrail and watched him descend two, three fathoms before leveling out and swimming gracefully towards the cliff face, where the fish were congregating. He surfaced a hundred feet away, half way between *Mystery* and the cliffs. Tatsuo looked back at his pride and joy, the ship. It was everything he owned and moments like this he savoured. As the others watched he sucked in another deep breath and dived once more. Samoa watched and waited. Two minutes passed and she was starting to feel concerned. Horace noticed. 'Don't you worry, Miss, that bugger has lungs like a whale.'

Three minutes …

Samoa, Horace, Selma, and William were now all keeping a sharp eye. Three and a half minutes. Samoa looked to Horace who for the first time looked anxious.

'I'm going in!' And before the others could say anything, Samoa had shed her three-quarter britches and leapt over the side, striking out towards the cliffs. The others watched her progress a dozen feet down, arms together, outstretched, while she flapped her feet like a mermaid's tail. Samoa had scarcely been in the water when Tatsuo exploded to the surface, yahooing like a cowboy, with a huge fish on his trident. Samoa surfaced beside him.

'Crikey, where did you come from?' he said.

'I thought you'd drowned.'

'Oh, isn't that sweet.'

'Sweet!' Samoa pushed his head under water.

Tatsuo came up laughing. 'I should warn you, I saw a school of reef sharks down there.'

Samoa was instantly serious.

'Best we swim to that cave over there,' he said, pointing with the trident to a cave just above the tide line, 50 feet away. Samoa was first to the cliff and lifted herself onto the ledge with ease. Tatsuo was impressed with her agility, and her wet blouse and bloomers hugging her trim body did not go unobserved. Samoa turned to give Tatsuo a hand but he was out of the water and onto the ledge like a seal.

'That swim's livened me up,' Tatsuo said, casting an eye back to the *Mystery,* where the others had lost interest and Selma had gone below to cook rice for the catch.

'This is amazing,' Samoa said, looking into the cave. It was barely tall enough to enter but was clearly much larger inside. Tatsuo placed the trident and fish in the shade.

'Come, let's explore.'

Inside, the cool damp air was a pleasant relief. Samoa took in a deep breath, straightening her back and looking about her. 'Spectacular.'

'We're probably the first humans to ever enter this cave,' Tatsuo said.

'Do you really think so?'

Samoa stood ten feet in, where a shaft of sunlight from the collapsed ceiling high overhead cast a beam onto the cave floor, reminding her of a spotlight thrown onto a theatre stage. Their presence disturbed bats or small birds above. Tatsuo watched Samoa. She was like an excited schoolgirl once more, mesmerised by the cave, the sea and especially the spent adrenalin of the day's events. Samoa caught Tatsuo gazing—staring, more like.

'Would you like to take a photo?' Samoa said cheekily.

'A photo?'

'It will last longer.'

It took Tatsuo a moment to realise Samoa was joking, her face and demeanour were so straight, so convincing.

Christ! I have definitely fallen for this woman.

'Actually I was just thinking …'

'Yes?'

'How beautiful you are.'

There, he'd said it. It had been over a week since that moment on board the *Mystery* off Bona Bona Island had brought them so close. Samoa felt well flattered. They faced off for an awkward moment, both hesitant to make the first move, . Samoa stood fast but Tatsuo had the benefit of Dutch courage. *Three whiskies.*

Tatsuo stepped forward and took Samoa in his arms. Their eyes never strayed from each other. She relaxed in his hold and he pulled her tight to his body. Suddenly Samoa's arms stiffened against his rock-hard chest. She made to push him away, confused in her thoughts … *Was this the behaviour of some Lothario? Was this simply lust?*

Samoa had had bad experiences of that.

But Tatsuo held firm and stole a kiss. The man might have the chiseled face of a paragon, but his lips were supple and wet, his breath scented with Irish whiskey fuelling the sparkle in his dark piercing eyes.

Their kiss was long and sincere. Although they now held each other tightly, their bodies relaxed and desire coursed through their veins. Samoa sensed his manhood pushing against her body. She hadn't been with a man in a long, long time and craved this heated passion more than life itself.

'Cap'n …' William's voice echoed about the cave as he came looking for them. 'Cap'n … you there?'

Tatsuo groaned. Samoa stepped aside, suddenly taking an interest in the bats squealing about the ceiling.

'What is it, Will?' Tatsuo could not stay angry with the lad for long.

'Horace send me ter fetch yer in the tender.'

'Oh?'

'Yeh, yer got a big hammer snoopin' about the bay.'

'Hammer?' Samoa inquired.

'He means hammerhead shark.'

A moment later Tatsuo and Samoa followed William out onto the ledge, but not before Tatsuo took Samoa's hand behind Will's back and gave it one last squeeze.

Until next time.

Outside they watched the dorsal fin of a moderately sized hammerhead shark slice across the surface between them and *Mystery*.

'Not huge, but big enough to bite an arm off.' Tatsuo grinned, climbing into the boat while Will held the bow rope and Samoa jumped aboard.

After grilled coral trout and spicy rice, the crew retired below, offering the skipper and his lovely passenger some privacy—at Selma's instigation.

Throughout the meal and over the past few hours the two had exchanged less than subtle smiles. *Something had happened in that cave,* Selma just knew it.

Now, finally alone, with the one faint lamp Selma had left behind, Tatsuo lifted the card table aside from where they'd eaten dinner and pulled his chair close to face Samoa's. He took both her hands in his. They were silent a moment. They gazed into each other's eyes.

'Penny for your thoughts?' Tatsuo finally asked, feeling a little tongue-tied. 'That's what my mother always said.'

Samoa shook Tatsuo's hands free and stood, looking out to sea. 'My brother's still alive and out there somewhere.'

Tatsuo sighed heavily. He took in a deep breath of balmy night air and banished his lustful thoughts. 'We'll find him,' he promised rather lamely.

'Where will we go from here?'

'Let's start with the diary, see if there are any clues in that.'

'*Trésor!*' Samoa read the word aloud once more. 'Look, it's underlined half a dozen times in pencil.'

'You're right.' Tatsuo studied the page within the well read, leather-bound diary. 'It appears your brother acquired this book second-hand and has continued using it, as the first 20 pages are in French and in a different hand.'

'Interesting. Rennison always talked about learning French. We both speak some German, you know, Rennison better than me.'

'Bavarian nanny, huh?'

'Did I tell you that?'

'Yes, back in Cooktown.'

'Right. So, Mr Mysterious, what attracted you to the word "treasure" back on Hatsie Raven's island?'

'"Mr Mysterious"?'

'Yes. There's more to you, Tatsuo Gaston, than you let on.'

'Really? Is that what you think?'

'Really.' Samoa ran a soft hand down Tatsuo's arm. His muscles were tight and she followed a vein with the tip of a finger. He looked into her eyes and she teased him by pouting her lips.

'Read it, then,' Samoa said. 'Mr Mysterious.'

'Read what, the French part?'

'*Oui.*'

Tatsuo cast an eye across the pages that were in French. Now, he thought, with the Chinese golden ship seemingly a reality and with Samoa's brother a key player in finding the ship, he decided to tell Samoa what he knew. 'Your brother has written here that he is onto the whereabouts of the *Bao Zheng*, also known as the *Coral Moon.*'

'And what, pray tell, is the *Coral Moon?*'

'A ship … a Chinese junk, to be exact.' Tatsuo went on to explain about the wealthy merchant and shipbuilder and the gold seekers who'd left the Australian coast so mysteriously, with supposedly half a ton of refined gold, in smelted bars, on board. And how it went missing, reputedly somewhere around the Solomon Islands. 'Bao Zheng was the ship owner and I believe the ship was referred to as the *Coral Moon.*'

'And you told me it was a sea story.'

'Yes … Well … Ah. Maybe there is some truth in it,' Tatsuo finally said, tapping the diary with the back of his hand.

'So *"Coral Moon,"*you say—I like that.' Samoa looked at the pages written in a language she could not read. 'Well, then, you have my attention, Mr Mysterious. Read on.'

Tatsuo scanned the first page quickly in silence for a moment, to try and attain the general gist. 'Woah!'

'What?'

'He writes here that … Wait … just so I get this right,' Tatsuo reread the words written in an untidy scrawl. 'He mentions an earthquake and a following tsunami … You know what a tsunami is?'

'Of course. A giant wave.'

'Yes, well, when a tsunami hits the coast the shoreline water recedes out to sea briefly before the wave comes rolling ashore. When this happened, it says here, a Frenchman by all accounts called, ah, that's interesting … Rembrandt.'

Samoa looked the page along with him and singled out the name. 'Yes, read on.'

'It was this Rembrandt who witnessed a reef being exposed briefly, and he saw the remains of a Chinese junk trapped amongst the coral. Then the tsunami hit, the sea returned and it was lost from sight once more.'

'Wow!'

'Yes, wow!'

'One can only assume he ran like a jack rabbit up into the sand hills before the wave came ashore.'

Samoa laughed at the thought. 'So where was this? What island?'

'It doesn't say.'

'What!'

'Seriously, it doesn't say where.'

'Brilliant!' Samoa sat back exasperated.

'I reckon he has deliberately omitted it in case someone else read his diary.'

'That is so like Rennison, always secretive. So this man Rembrandt, where's he?'

'On Guadalcanal.'

'Another island?'

'Aye.'

'Great, then surely we can safely say the ship was lost on a reef on … what did you call that island?'

'Guadalcanal. Maybe it is. Maybe not.'

'Where is that island, anyway?'

'It's one of the Solomons' largest islands, about five days south from here, with the benefit of a steady wind.'

'Is this island … ah … friendly?'

'It wasn't once, but it is now. Whalers used it a lot a hundred years ago and created problems with the natives. More recently blackbirders were taking many natives from there back to Australia for the cane fields …'

'You mean slavers!' Samoa frowned.

'No. Blackbirders. Then the Germans came along and the British came into the equation, pushing the Germans out and … Well … it became the British Solomon Islands Protectorate four years ago, in '93.'

'So it's safe for us to sail there?'

'Yes. But where on Guadalcanal?' Tatsuo muttered to himself. He turned the page to where the author had drawn a crude chart. 'Ah, a map.'

'Great.'

'It's rough, but, yes, I recognise Guadalcanal, and,'—Tatsuo pointed to crude markings—'there. "X" marks the spot.'

'Treasure?'

'Huh! That would be nice. No, it's a small settlement in the northeast called Nagho ni ara. I've been there before.'

'How do you pronounce it?'

'Nagho-ni-ara. I remember the name means "place of the east wind" in the native tongue.'

'And you've been there, you said?'

'Yes, but there isn't much there except a small community of natives who trade in timber, dried fish and coconuts.' Tatsuo scanned the hand-etched map in the diary. It was rough but reasonably accurate. 'Oh, and there was gold found in the centre of the island once, but not enough to get excited about.'

'Then we can only hope to find Rembrandt, who should lead us to my brother.'

'Hopefully. In theory.'

Samoa had a renewed surge of urgency. 'So when do we leave?'

'First thing in the morning.'

At sea aboard the SS Prinzessin. Three days' steaming from Bougainville Island.

The messenger from the radio room aboard the German Imperial Navy ship SS *Prinzessin* was anxious. He stepped over the coaming from the narrow companionway and onto the bridge, whispering to himself 'Please don't shoot the messenger, please don't shoot the messenger,' for every time he presented Admiral Stosch with a message he seemed to be verbally abused.

'Ah … Admiral … Sir!' he started.

'What?' the admiral said with a mouth full of pastry. 'What now?'

'M-message, sir.' He handed the note to the admiral with a shaking hand. The admiral glared at the timid sailor. *'Grow some balls!'* he wanted to bark at the young man. The admiral lifted his large carcass from his swivel armchair, tugging a napkin free from his collar. The napkin was protecting his uniform from his fifth almond crescent kek. Sugar powder dusted the upholstered teak furniture. He snatched the paper.

'What is it?' the admiral grunted, not expecting an answer.

The sailor stood to attention, awaiting a reply. The admiral read the order and passed it to *Kapitän* Schtumft, before glaring back at the messenger. 'Well, why are you standing there? Waiting for a gratuity?' The admiral chuckled at his little jest.

'N-no, sir, just a reply.'

'Radio back "Affirmative."'

'Aye, sir.'

The admiral watched the sailor disappear faster than he had appeared, before turning to the captain. 'More troublemakers afoot, eh, *Kapitän*?'

Captain Herr von Schtumpf ran a sharp eye over the orders once more:

Proceed to Wakanai Bay, Bougainville, before Nagho ni ara. Royal Navy suspected in area. Secure and claim coast in the name of Imperial protectorate.

Days later. Wakanai Bay.

The SS *Prinzessin* dropped her two-ton anchors overboard, the heavy chains chattering through the hawsepipes and flattening any sea creatures 40 feet below that were too slow to take flight.

Commander Eduard von Seitz assembled 50 marines ready for landing. He was meticulous, proud and ruthless. And he had been commanded by Admiral Stosch to place the north of Bougainville Island under German protectorate law, under orders from the Emperor of Germany himself, Wilhelm II.

Forty-nine-year-old Seitz strode down the deck, back straight in the tropical sun, beads of sweat trickling down his cheeks beneath his black shiny leather pickelhaube helmet, complete with its steeple-like decoration and brass adornments. With his handlebar moustache, bald head and a long grey beard that reached to his chest—parted in the middle, creating two conical beards, resembling that of a walrus —he was the quintessential German officer. The unofficial marines paraded in neat rows beneath the bridge. Seitz was delighted with his command. All young, enthusiastic sons of the Vaterland. They were dressed in their navy blue, double-breasted, brass-buttoned jackets, white shirts with black neckerchief and white trousers worn loose over black leather jackboots. On their heads they wore dark blue peakless caps with ribbon cockades hanging from the black cap tally, where the name of the ship was embroidered in white. Each man was armed with a Mauser fixed with Hirschfanger bayonets, and 100 rounds of ammunition in bandoliers. Each also carried a water bottle and the standard issue for marines ashore, a bread bag. The rifles and bayonets were nearly 15 years old, but so what …

The savages will never know what hit them, he thought.

Hiding out of view in the jungle, Maori Chieftain Hatsie Raven assembled her own troops. At least 300, without counting. They were all armed with long body shields, spears, bows and arrows, and 50 of the youngest, the ones she had had time to train, were armed with Lee Enfield rifles—Tatsuo's Lee Enfield rifles, in fact. 'Savages, my arse!' she shouted, rallying her troops. 'The bastards won't know what hit them!'

A dozen of Hatsie's riflemen took up positions behind Rennison's rock fortifications on the hills behind the village, where they had a clear shot to protect their community. Four others in the 'stork nests' 80 feet up in selected coconut palms took sniper positions. Their moment had come.

German Commander Seitz slung the binoculars back about his neck. 'I can't see any life in the village at all,' he told Admiral Stosch and Captain Schtumpf. 'Strange. Normally the savages would be flocking onto the beach like sheep.'

'Strange. Strange indeed.' Seitz panned his binoculars slowly across the shoreline and into the village, his face sweating profusely and his ridiculously long, parted beard fluffing in the afternoon breeze. To the ship's captain, the marine commander looked like a bearded collie dog wearing a pickelhaube. 'No … can't see a damned thing. I trust they aren't considering resistance.'

'We want to hope the mongrels haven't been armed.' The Admiral said, twirling his moustache.

'Well isn't that why you have a small army with you, sir?' the captain said curtly.

As if that was a cue for war, a shot rang out. The bullet hit the ship's bell and ricocheted out to sea to the knell of brass.

The Admiral jumped.

'What did I just say?'

Seitz saw a puff of smoke dissipate around what looked like a huge bird's nest at the top of a palm. 'Everyone take cover!' he yelled, but already the marines were breaking ranks, diving for shelter.

'What a nerve!' Seitz yelled. 'Bastard savages have got a gun.'

'I hate to tell you this, Commander,' the captain said, squatting behind the binnacle, 'but they may have several guns.'

'How? Savages aren't supposed to have guns!'

'I tell you it's the luggers, the pearlers and the like. The bastards are selling guns to the savages.'

Commander Seitz called to his chief gunner. 'Sergeant Fischer!'

'Yes, sir.'

'Did you see that puff of smoke? From the top of the second palm on the right of the village?'

'Yes, sir, I did.'

'One round, if you please.'

Hatsie Raven paced up and down behind the communal hall. She was furious. 'Stupid bastard!' she hissed up at the culprit in his sniper's nest. 'I told you to wait for my—'

The 'stupid bastard' never heard the end of Hatsie's rant. A well-aimed, 15-centimetre SK/35 projectile killed the unfortunate native.

'*Ja! Ja!*' resonated from the ship.

Hatsie stared skywards, speechless for a change, blinking in shock as shredded palm leaves and bloodied, segmented body parts rained down. Immediately the German 'protectors' became invaders, and as the marines dropped into boats to be rowed ashore, Hatsie Raven and her fighters scattered into the jungle.

'"Dwaw them into the twees,"' Hastie had told Tatsuo their strategy, taught by Rennison. 'He called it "gorwwilla warfare."' That's what Wennison explained to me. Gorwwilla warfare—I told 'im we don't 'ave gowillas 'ere.' And the Maori chieftain roared at her little joke.

Now that armed conflict was a reality, the little joke was a joke no more. This was serious. But if guerrilla warfare worked for the underdog in other places around the globe, then, by God, it was going to work here at Wakanai Bay.

The history books are a little blurred about what happened next. Suffice to say that HMS *Pride* sailed into the bay not that long after the German Marines rowed ashore and vanished from site into the jungle.

Treading on diplomatic eggshells, Captain Gerald Rafferty Reynolds ordered the Royal Navy gunboat to anchor a mile northwest of Wakanai Bay and sent a reconnaissance crew ashore. They reported back two hours later, after witnessing the above attack.

'We're in business. The Germans are attacking these people,' Reynolds told the ship's captain, Captain Jonathon Bourke. 'Take us into the bay, if you please.' Captain Bourke, the no-nonsense, sixty-year-old sea captain and man of iron, ordered gun crews standing by the two 4-inch guns and the four 12-pounders.

He loved a fight.

In the taverns and on the sea, there was nothing like a good scrap, in his opinion. And he had the scars to prove it. The two men re-read the radio message from the Royal Navy headquarters in Sydney that was lying on the chart table, pinned to a map of Bougainville Island.

> *Proceed immediately ... Bougainville Island ....*
> *Intelligence ... German Navy ... Wakanai Bay. Intercept ... all*
> *costs. Persuade .... Discretion ... do not spark diplomatic*
> *tensions ... Locate and apprehend Rennison Plum ... repeat:*
> *apprehend British citizen Rennison Plum, at all costs ...*
> *possible alias Horst Schwarz ...*
> *Signed,*
> *Rear Admiral A.J. Baker*

HMS *Pride* cut engines and drifted to within a hundred feet of the SS *Prinzessin* before dropping anchor. Captain Bourke ordered all the *Pride's* guns directed at the German ship.

Admiral Gustav von Stosch was livid. 'What's going on?' he screamed at the German ship's captain. 'What do they think they are doing?'

'This is awkward.'

'Awkward! Awkward! Are you serious? This is a catastrophe!'

Captain Bourke stood in the open doorway on the portside of the bridge and barked into an amplifying speaker. 'Attention, *Prinzessin*. Stand down immediately. We have all our guns trained on you at this time. Show yourselves, hands in the air.'

'What do you want me to do, Admiral?' Captain Herr von Schtumpf asked his superior.

Admiral Gustav von Stosch stood, seething, slapping the side of his leg with a cane swagger stick, the corners of his mouth frothing, his eyes bloodshot, his moustache twitching.

'Admiral?'

'Damn it, man, let me think!' The Admiral looked back towards the beach. The German boats were beached. All the German invaders had vanished into the jungle. 'Our men are dispersed into the jungle,' he said. 'We can only hope Commander Eduard von Seitz will discover our situation sooner rather than later and get us out of this predicament.'

'And?' Captain Schtumpf persisted.

'They have the advantage for now. We will do as they say.'

'Ahoy!' Captain Bourke was enjoying himself. 'What's it to be, chaps?' the colonial said, hamming up a British accent. 'Show yourselves or …'

'*Ja, ja* … Ve heard you ze first time,' Admiral Stosch answered through his own speaking horn.

'Good. We are coming aboard,' Bourke said. 'Stay where you are.'

Captain Reynolds sent a boarding party of marines across to the German ship, under command of the lieutenant of the marines, Jack Anson, a ruthless bastard who hated the Hun. Twenty minutes later the SS *Prinzessin's* 60-man crew, captain and officers were under Royal Navy guard. With the German boats abandoned high and dry on the beach after the arrival of HMS *Pride* in the bay, Captain Reynolds knew the German marines had already infiltrated the village. *But where the hell was everyone?*

'I can't see a bloody soul anywhere.' Reynolds scoured the village and surrounding jungle with his binoculars. The island was eerily quiet.

Satisfied the German ship was secure, Captain Reynolds ordered 40 armed marines ashore.

Meanwhile Captain Jonathan Bourke gave orders to his First Lieutenant, Jeffrey Hanks. 'Take charge. I'm going to make a closer inspection of these sauerkrauts,' he declared as he cast a dark glance at the bridge of the SS *Prinzessin*.

Minutes later, he stepped onto the German ship's main deck, where he joined the Royal Navy marines. The SS *Prinzessin's* Captain Schtumpf and Admiral Gustav von Stosch were not welcoming to the larger than life, six-foot-four colonial ship's captain.

Bourke eyed his adversaries with a rake's eye, tipping his captain's hat to the back of his head.

'What, no piping the side?' Bourke said dryly of the Navy custom of the boatswain piping the captain on board ship.

The German captain, who spoke English, was not amused. 'Vot ees ze meaning of thees? You are breaking maritime law.'

Bourke ignored the comment and looked at the German admiral, who stood sternly erect, his back against the bridge rail with his arms crossed. The admiral did not speak English.

'Did you hear me?' the German captain repeated. 'You are breaking ze international law.'

'Nice to meet you, too, Fritz,' Bourke said with undisguised contempt, standing straight, showing off his full height.

'I demand to kno ...'

'Yes yes, keep your shirt on, Fritz.'

'I am not ze Fritz. I am Captain Herr von Schtumpf of ze Imperial navy of Emperor Vilhelm II.'

'And who's this turkey, then?' Bourke nodded to the admiral.

'Turkey?' Captain Schtumpf struggled with the translation.

Bourke jabbed a finger towards the admiral.

'Dis man ees ze Admiral Gustav von Stosch of the German Imperial Navy.'

'Pleased to meet you, Gus.' Bourke nodded.

Admiral Stosch understood enough to know this uncouth Royal Navy captain was being impertinent.

Bourke did not introduce himself. He popped a boiled mint in his mouth and, chin high, strutted to the starboard guardrail facing the island. 'How many men have you sent ashore, Fritz?'

'*Kapitän* Schtumpf!'

Captain Bourke kept his eye on the shoreline, where four Royal Navy 27-foot whalers were now drawn up near the German boats. Fifty armed Royal Marines spread out on the beach as he looked on. 'I'd say you have 40 men ashore.' Bourke was calm, patient and collected. He was enjoying antagonising these sauerkrauts. He rolled the mint from one side of his mouth to the other before licking his fingers to curl the points of his great moustache.

Less accepting than the German ship's captain was the first lieutenant, Anton Kruger, who appeared from the bridge. He was an annoying man with a small round head and too much red facial hair, reminding Captain Bourke of his cousin's terrier back in Darwin. Kruger and the admiral exchanged words and the admiral was angry.

'By international maritime law,' Kruger, who spoke good English, started, 'you are conducting an act of aggression towards Germany.'

Captain Bourke, still holding the guardrail, looked over his shoulder. Kruger continued, 'And what's more—'

'Who are you?'

The terrier pushed out his chest, raring for a fight. 'I am Lieutenant Anton von Kruger.'

'Well, Kruger … shut it.'

'Sir, you are not within rights to board this—'

'I said keep quiet, or I will have you thrown overboard … In fact I'll throw you overboard myself.' Bourke continued his discussion with his back turned to Kruger. 'So, *Kapitän* Fritz, Friesian … whatever … I estimate you have 40 men ashore. I assume they are armed. Silly question—of course they are armed. The question is, where are they?'

The Royal Navy Marines were now spread out and about to enter the jungle to surround the village, spread well back into the landscape. 'I said, where is everybody?'

'The beach was deserted when we arrived,' *Kapitän* Schtumpf said sourly.

'Because if my men are ambushed I will sink this tub of yours.'

'Captain Bourke!' The terrier started … but never finished.

Captain Bourke took the man by the seat of his trousers and the back of his coat and, frogmarching him to the starboard rail, launched him off the side. A whimpering squeal accompanied the sailor as he sailed into the water. Both Germans and Royal Marines hurried to the side of the ship to watch the German lieutenant's progress, Admiral Stosch amongst them. Kruger soon surfaced.

'At least he can swim.' Captain Bourke chuckled as lifebuoys sailed towards the fully-clothed German.

Admiral Stosch yelled something at Bourke in German.

'What did he say?'

'He says, dees ees too much.'

'Oh.' Captain Bourke exploded. He stood inches from the German admiral, so close they exchanged breaths, mint for pickled cabbage.

'Tell Gus here I suggest he sends a lone messenger onto that island to tell whoever is in charge of the men who landed in those boats to cease whatever they have been ordered to do and return to this ship, immediately.'

'*Hai!*' a sailor shouted from amidships. '*Hai! Hai!*'

Others joined in. Suddenly there seemed an urgency on the deck. '*Hai! Raus aus dem wasser.*'

'Now what?' Captain Bourke searched the water, scrutinizing the area the Germans were pointing towards while excitedly shouting. 'Hey? Hey what?' Bourke demanded to know.

'"*Hai*,"' the German captain said. 'It means "shark."'

No sooner was Kruger hoisted to safety than the first gunshots echoed from the jungle.

A quarter of a mile inland, Captain Gerald Rafferty Reynolds and his marines came under attack from a well-hidden, well-placed and well-armed enemy. They had been ashore less than 20 minutes. There was no sign of the native villagers or the Germans that they knew were ashore somewhere.

'Three men down, Captain.' Royal Marine Sergeant Baker snaked his way across the jungle floor to lie flat next to the captain. 'One serious, two with leg wounds.'

'Christ! How did this happen? This was supposed to be a discreet diplomatic negotiation. Now it's all out bloody war.'

Immediately an amplifying speaker broke the silence amongst the trees. 'Thees ees Commander Eduard von Seitz of the Imperial German Navy. Ve have got you surrounded, *Kapitän*. Surrender now, return to your ship and sail free and we will cause no more injuries, *ja*.'

'Who the hell does he think he is?' Reynolds whispered to Baker.

'Bloody sauerkrauts, sir—think they own the Pacific.'

'*Kapitän*, thees ees Commander Seitz. I repeat, surrender to us now and return safe to your ship.'

Reynolds saw movement a hundred feet away amongst heavy growth. Aiming carefully, he fired off a shot. A groan was followed by cursing in German. Clearly he was on target. This warning shot, however, sparked a type of gun battle never before heard on Bougainville Island.

For ten minutes the battle raged, with casualties on both sides, while rifle fire echoed across the bay.

On board the SS *Prinzessin,* 'Get me back to the *Pride*!' Captain Bourke yelled at his crew. 'And you!' he barked at a corporal of the Royal Navy Marines. 'You stay with the admiral here, you got it?'

'Yes, Captain.'

'And if he tries anything, shoot the bastard.'

'Aye, sir.'

Leaving the Royal Navy boarding party to guard the Germans, Bourke returned to the HMS *Pride*. Taking up the binoculars hitched about his neck, he scanned the jungle.

'Come on … Come on …' he growled under his breath. 'What the bloody hell's happening?'

The British were losing. That's what was happening. There was no doubt about it. They were out-armed and the Germans had the high ground. The situation was dire. Captain Gerald Rafferty Reynolds was paying dearly for his overconfident arrogance The Haka resonated from the jungle …

Ka mate, ka mate!
Ka or, aka ora!
Ka mate, ka mate!
Ka ora, ka ora!
Tenei te tangata pu'ru-huru
Na'a nei tiki mai whaka-whiti te
Ra! Upane! Ka …

German Commander Eduard von Seitz's pickelhaube rose vertically from behind a particularly large banana tree. His nervous head appeared one moment later. '*Was ist das*?'

Captain Reynolds looked at the men cowering around him. 'What the bloody hell is that?'

'S-savages, s-sir,' someone whispered.

With the war cry complete, Hatsie Raven came out of hiding leading her tribe into the fray, wielding her five-foot, gnarly club made from a tree root. The first poor bastard to be clobbered—a German—fell into the undergrowth. He would never know what hit him. The natives with the Lee Enfields—Tatsuo's Lee Enfields, no less—ambushed the ambushers and within minutes the Germans were fighting for their lives. They managed to regroup, but when two men perished as sticks of dynamite sailed through the air like giant firecrackers, they ran, defeated, back into the sea.

Commander Seitz was one of the first into the boats, noticeably minus his fancy pickelhaube helmet, lost somewhere in the jungle during the skirmish. They had no choice but to abandon the dead and wounded, otherwise they feared the savages would headhunt each one of them, and, worse, eat them. At the water's edge the British watched their foe hurry back to their ship like water rats. Some, left behind in the panicked evacuation, even swam … *hai* or no *hai*.

'Get our men off that German ship!' Bourke ordered. The amplifying speaker echoed with life and the Royal Marines remaining on board the enemy ship disembarked into waiting cutters.

The moment the last marine cleared the SS *Prinzessin* Captain Bourke barked fresh orders to his men, 'Gunners stand by.'

'This'll be good, Captain,' one of the Royal Navy lieutenants on the beach muttered, grinning and watching his gunner mates on HMS *Pride* prepare to open fire with the stern Maxim guns.

'I need to get a message to Captain Bourke immediately!' Reynolds yelled.

'Message, Captain?'

'Yes, a message! Cease fire!'

'What? Pardon me, Captain. I meant, are you certain, sir?'

'We will have a major diplomatic shit fight on our hands if we kill any more Germans or, God forbid, Captain Bourke sinks their ship.'

'But they attacked *us*, Captain.'

'Signal the *Pride's* bridge. Now, for Christ's sake!'

Signaling the ship 300 yards out on the bay from the beach was easier said than done. Men started jumping, waving their arms. On the bridge Captain Bourke's attention was drawn to the frantic signalers on the beach. He trained his binoculars along the line, located Captain Reynolds, and tried to interpret his message. Reynolds made several cutthroat actions, running a finger across his throat.

'What's he saying, for Christ's sake?' Bourke muttered to no one in particular, focussing on lip reading Reynolds. 'Kill them all? Is that what he's saying?'

'Kill their guns, sir, maybe,' one officer suggested.

Captain Bourke ran the glasses over the German ship. The 15-centimetre cannon fitted on the bow was an immediate threat. One well-placed shell from that gun would see HMS *Pride* sitting on the bottom of the bay within minutes. Captain Bourke decided to pre-empt this. 'Give the order. I want that forward gun destroyed.'

'Aye, aye, Cap'n.'

Bourke was focussing on the German marines clambering back on board, when …

'Captain! Their forward gun's turning about.'

Time was of the essence. Bourke watched the *Pride's* own forward gun-turret train to starboard, ready to aim. But the turn was slow. Too damned slow.

'Jesus Christ!'

The German gunner had the advantage. The *Prinzessin's* 15-centimetre cannon lowered for what would be a point-blank shot. The *Pride's* 4-inch gun was finally positioned. The gun crew took aim.

The thunderous boom of the enemy cannon at such close range was terrifying. But in the German gunner's haste the aim wasn't true. He had not allowed for the gentle swell undulating with the change of tide. The shell whistled over the HMS *Pride's* gun turret, missing its mark by mere inches. Royal Navy crew standing within feet were dusted with black powder.

Now it was the Royal Navy gunners' turn.

The head gunner took his time. He knew he had at least 20 seconds before the enemy could reload. He sighted the German gun.

It was like an old fashioned duel. If the first man to fire misses then the second can take his time …

Fifteen seconds …

'What the bloody hell's he waiting for?'

'Let's get this right, boys.' The chief gunner had the German gun sighted. He was enjoying the moment. He read the swell. He wanted this to be perfect. This was his big moment. He thought of all the lovers he had conquered, and, yes … this was like making love. *Hang in there, boys. We're almost ready …*

Wait for it, wait for it.

'NOW!"

The gunner tugged at the lanyard. The explosion was instant. The damage immediate. The German's main gun was *kaputt*.

Those closest were killed instantly, bodies cartwheeling into the bay. The Germans now had only the two Maxim water-cooled machine guns. But these were still lethal, capable of firing 600 rounds a minute. The SS *Prinzessin*'s propellers churned the seabed. From her quarterdeck her gunners opened fire with the Maxim guns, scattering everyone on board HMS *Pride*. Wooden decking, lifeboats on davits, superstructure and portholes were splintered and shattered as hundreds of bullets ripped into the starboard side.

Captain Reynolds on the beach was beside himself with anger, storming up and down the sand while the SS *Prinzessin* made good her escape. This was bad. Really bad. *Avoid a diplomatic incident at all costs … my arse*. Now he knew he was in big trouble.

But Captain Bourke hadn't had enough. 'Pop a shell in her hull for good measure!' he yelled at the gun crew.

'Sir?'

'I said give the sauerkrauts a proper send off. One more should do it, just to scare the bastards good and proper.'

'Yes, sir, Captain, sir.' No one had to tell the head gunner twice.

Reynolds snapped his head back across the bay. Another shot rang out from the *Pride*. As he watched the second shot, an angled

12-pounder struck the German ship just above the waterline, breaching a hull plate.

'Wh-what the hell's he doing?' Reynolds screamed at deaf ears.

On HMS *Pride's* bridge, Captain Bourke pumped the air with a winner's cheer.

Hatsie Raven stomped onto the beach screaming obscenities at the fleeing Germans. If Commander Eduard von Seitz had looked back, he would have seen the huge Maori woman wearing his pickelhaube, his shiny black leather helmet with its pointed spire and huge brass badge of the eagle of the Imperial German Empire. Hatsie threatened the escapees with her club held high, cheered on by her doting subjects. As they all looked on, the German ship steamed away.

'I think a celebwation is in order!' Hatsie roared, still high from all the action. Captain Reynolds looked at the woman as if she was mad. And maybe she was.

'Tell me,' Reynolds asked the Maori. 'Where did you get those guns … that dynamite?'

'Oh,' Hatsie was taken aback. 'I just saved your arse, sailor. A thank you would be nice.'

Reynolds's eyes threatened to cross with anger. 'I said, where—did—you—get—those—guns?'

'It's not for you to ask, my fwiend.'

Reynolds turned to his marines flocking about them on the beach. 'Sergeant !' he spat, 'confiscate all the guns on this island.'

'Sir?'

'Are you deaf, man? I want every gun confiscated. This is no place for savages to be armed.'

Immediately 20 native rifles were aimed at the captain.

'What's the meaning of this?'

Hatsie Raven was in no mood to be trifled with. 'I suggest yer get back on yer ship and chase your fwiends.'

Captain Reynolds shoulders deflated. He was defeated. 'Fine. Have it your way. But answer me one question. Did you purchase these guns from a man called Tatsuo Gaston?'

'Never 'eard of 'im.'

'I'll take that as a yes, then.'

On board the SS *Prinzessin* Admiral Stosch was a caged lion, stomping the length of the bridge, starboard to port, port to starboard. 'The audacity of that … that … that English pig-dog!' he roared.

'I believe he was a colonial, Admiral.'

'I don't care if he was the Tsar of Russia! I should have … should have…'—he slammed his swagger stick hard against his leg— 'should have flogged his back till it was red raw.'

Captain Herr von Schtumpf wanted to say, *Well why didn't you?* But bit his tongue.

'The cheek, the insolence, the nerve of the man!' the admiral ranted. 'Doesn't he know who I am?'

'Where are we heading, Admiral?"

'Heading?' The admiral sighed heavily.

'Nagho ni ara Island, west of Malaita.'

At sea.

The following six hours were fraught with problems. One Royal Marine and four Germans had lost their lives that afternoon on Bougainville Island. Their bodies were sewn into canvas shrouds to be buried at sea, later. The wounded, 14 in all, were transferred to the sick bay on HMS *Pride*. Under the circumstances, it was the least Captain Reynolds could do for the German wounded, as he imagined if they were left on the island … well … they might not see tomorrow's sunrise. Besides, he thought diplomatically, this would be in his favour during the court martial he was certain would proceed.

But that wasn't the only problem to plague HMS *Pride*. Chief engineer George Morrison tapped on the bridge door, his face black with grease. Captain Jonathon Bourke looked at the man and read *doom*.

'What is it, Mr Morrison?'

'I 'ate to be the bearer o' bad news, Cap'n, but the valves to the main steam pipe need replacin'. Both valve rods are worn through and the cross 'eads need replacin'.'

Captain Bourke stood at the helm, staring blankly out the bridge window at the setting sun. If there was ever a time he wanted rum, it was now. He sucked in a deep breath. 'Tell me you can repair it.'

'Aye, Captain. I can repair it.'

'How long?'

'Couple days, sir.'

'Jesus Christ! A couple of days! Why? Why does this come along right now? Can you do it sooner?'

'I'll do me best, Captain.'

Captain Reynolds made a final excursion ashore to eat humble pie with Hatsie Raven. They would need fresh produce, fruit, yams and water. Hatsie was only too pleased to oblige, for a price.

That evening Captain Bourke and Captain Reynolds buried their differences and shared a bottle of rum in the stateroom.

'I should have rammed that bastard when I had the chance,' Bourke muttered with hooded eyes, easing the cork from a second bottle. And Captain Reynolds knew he meant this literally, as HMS *Pride*'s hull was clad in iron and the bow, in particular, was reinforced, turning it into an offensive weapon, namely a ram. Reynolds also knew it had never been trialed or put into practice. In reality it was a difficult weapon to simply trial on a whim.

Days later, the natives of Wakanai Bay lined the beach and cheered as HMS *Pride* finally steamed away from the island …

But the Germans were long gone.

Chapter Seven

There was little to greet the *Mystery* in the bay of Nagho ni ara, where the relatively flat coastal land gradually climbed through dense tropical jungle into the hills and up into the mountains. The village was sparse and, although the island was under the protection of Britain, there was little evidence of European influence. Horace, armed with his Pidgin English, went walk-a-bout searching for a man called Rembrandt.

There was little Samoa and Tatsuo could do in the meantime, but wait. Selma stayed on board the *Mystery* with orders to fire off a shot if she had any trouble. Will and Pearl the three-legged dog played chaperone. Three hours had passed when Will leapt to his feet.

'Fuck-it,' he ticced. 'H-Horace …' The tics continued until a violent shake of the head brought them under control, the fit receding as fast as it had started. 'Horace!' the lad shouted.

Samoa and Tatsuo jumped to their feet. Further along the beach the tall, lanky aborigine squeaked barefoot through the crusted, wind-dried sand. He had a native woman in tow.

'This is Wiki,' Horace introduced the older native. Her face was black and wrinkled from the weather, her body round and comfortable, but when she smiled she showed off teeth as white as the sands. 'Wiki—she was Rembrandt's woman.'

'Was?'

'Rembrandt's dead!'

Samoa sat back heavily on the tender. 'It's the story of my life. I'm never going to find Rennison.'

Wiki muttered, picking up on the name immediately. '*Rennison. Rennison budgeree fella.*'

'What did she say?'

'She say, "Rennison budgeree fella." It mean good fella.'

'So she knew him?'

'Aye,' Horace said. 'That's why I bring her here.'

'Alright, Horace,' Tatsuo said, 'don't keep us in suspense.'

'Well 'er 'usband—whose real name were Mathew, by the way—was a bit of an artist, see, and liked the natives to call 'im Rembrandt. I seen all his paints and stuff back at Wiki's hut.'

'Rennison?' Samoa interrupted.

'Aye, 'e was 'ere 'til recent, like,' Horace translated from Pidgin. ''E came lookin' for Rembrandt. 'E stay here just two days, maybe. They spend much time together, fishin', talkin', drinkin', laughin', drinkin' serious, and Rembrandt, 'e tell Rennison the story he tell many, many whitefella.'

'What story?'

'The story what Rennison come here specially to hear.'

'Yes, yes. What story?'

'The story how Rembrandt was livin' one year on Malaita Island with the blackfellas there …'

'The blackfellas there are dangerous cannibals,' Tatsuo said. 'They kill and eat people, black *and* white.'

'Wiki say her Rembrandt spoke some of the blackfella lingo. An' 'cos he paint pictures of 'em—portraits, I think she means—the Malaita like 'im whitefella.'

'Jesus,' Tatsuo said. 'That's unheard of in these parts.'

'Yeh, well, he become friends. Then one day big wave wash ashore and destroy village. But Rembrandt, 'e see the wreck of a Chinese ship—trapped in the coral, it were. Then wave cover again and all was lost.'

'How did he know it was Chinese?'

''Cos 'e said there was remains of an old campsite where survivors from the wreck were marooned a whiles. Blue and white pottery and a Chinese cannon with a dragonhead.'

'When was that?'

'From what I can figure, Wiki's sayin' maybe 20 year ago. Rembrandt tell Wiki the blackfella on the island found them Chinamen weeks later and kill and eat 'em all.'

Samoa cringed. 'Charming.'

'When did Rembrandt see this, ah, tsunami?'

'From what I can gather, a coupla years ago. Rembrandt had enough of Malaita by then and moved here, where he met Wiki and they fall in love.' Horace gave Wiki a caring smile.

'Lovely story,' Tatsuo said stone-faced. 'What reef on Malaita Island? There's thousands of them.'

Horace conversed briefly with the native woman, who seemed long-winded with her answer. All Horace had to say was, 'She don't know.'

'She don't ... I mean, she doesn't know?'

'That's wha' I said.'

Wiki rattled on a few more sentences. 'She say Rennison know. Rembrandt was ill, he tell Rennison everything. Rennison leave the island and Rembrandt, he die of his sickness only short time later.'

'We're talking just days ago?'

'Seems like it, Boss.'

'How did Rennison leave this island?' Samoa asked.

'She say he was taken away by a big ship.'

'Big ship?'

Tatsuo and Samoa looked on while more pidgin was exchanged.

'Ship with engine,' Horace told them. 'Other islanders tell Wiki it was a German ship.'

Wiki muttered something. 'And she say ship had chimneys.'

Tatsuo ground his teeth in thought. 'That'd have to be the *Prinzessin*. I heard it was in the area, supposedly seeking new islands to place under the German protectorate. The captain is Herr von Schtumpf, a right bastard ... excuse the French.'

Tatsuo told the others the *Prinzessin* had been launched in Hamburg as a passenger vessel around ten years before. He'd sailed by her several times over the past two years. 'When she was assigned to the Pacific region she was fitted with guns, one 15-centimetre SK L/35 on the bow and two Maxim guns mounted under cover at the stern, port and starboard.'

'You know your guns, alright,' Samoa said, tongue in cheek. 'You've dealt in plenty.'

'Yes, well, someone has to help these poor islanders.'

'Wiki say one more thing, Cap'n,' Horace volunteered.

'Oh, what?'

'She say this Rennison whitefella was took by force.'

'By force! You certain?'

Horace and Wiki were lost in animated conversation for a short while. 'Yes. She say him tied up like pig and dragged on ship kickin' an' shoutin'.'

Samoa went white. 'Why? Why in God's name?'

Tatsuo looked at Samoa—she was seriously upset. 'You have no idea why the Germans would arrest him?'

'No! ... No, I don't. Now what?'

Tatsuo took a deep breath and looked out onto the bay where the *Mystery* swung lazily round her anchor chain. 'Let's get back on board and I'll consult my charts, see if I can work out where they might go from here.'

Thanking Wiki in a language she had no hope of understanding, the four had started pushing the tender back into the water when Wiki called out to Horace. They exchanged that ever-handy pidgin. 'Ho!' Horace sounded excited.

'What?'

'She say, don't you want to know where they have taken him?'

'Really! ... How ... does she know where?'

Horace interpreted. 'She say fishermans from this island returnin' from tradin' on other islands, seen the big ship at the Shoal of Ghosts.'

'The Shoal of Ghosts…' Samoa shook her head. 'Where on earth is that?'

Tatsuo knew all about it. 'The Shoal of Ghosts is a damned awful place. It's a coral atoll between here and Malaita Island.'

Tatsuo looked at Wiki. 'Is she certain?'

Horace translated. Wiki spoke with her hands as well as her tongue.

'She say same islanders who tell her ship white colour. Fisherman 'ere afraid to go to Shoal of Ghosts. Bad place full of evil spirits.'

'Do you know this … this atoll?' Samoa asked Tatsuo.

'Aye.' Tatsuo nodded his thanks to the native. With her confidence restored, Samoa slipped another silver bangle from her wrist and passed it to Wiki; then they hurried back to the cutter.

The Shoal of Ghosts.

Mariners in a storm at night, beware. For the horseshoe-shaped atoll ambushes the unwary. During daylight hours in fair weather the coral outcrop is readily identified by its lone 1500-metre-tall volcanic peak, steep as the Alps but with a flat top, and situated on the curve of the horseshoe. Thousands upon thousands of seabirds warn the vigilant. They circle endlessly: terns, boobies and gulls, pooping vast quantities of waste, which under normal circumstances would make excellent, valued guano for the fertiliser industry. However, the atoll, only six feet above sea level, is regularly washed over by stormy seas, leaching the nutrients from the guano and rendering it valueless.

'There is nothing to like about this island,' Tatsuo told Samoa as he passed the telescope over the coral reef, which was still a mile distant.

'See anything?' Samoa asked.

'Nothing. I don't want to sound negative, but don't get your hopes high.' He collapsed the glass, shaking his head. 'There's a lagoon on the south side which stinks of naturally occurring ammonia and sulphuric acid,' Tatsuo said. He went on to explain how waves crashed ashore creating a pounding surf, making landing very dangerous. The sound of birds constantly screeching made yelling the only way to converse. There were millions of fist-sized orange crabs that ate everything. In adiditon, the sea surrounding the atoll was plagued with tidal rips and dangerous currents. It also dropped away sharply into very deep water, and for some reason this reef was abnormally over-populated with sharks.

'We're talking several species, including hammerheads, tiger sharks and even great whites. The water is also host to masses of yellow-belly sea snakes and moray eels. Even wading in the shallows is dangerous.'

Samoa was as still and white as the marble statue of Venus de Milo. 'And my brother was marooned here?'

'We don't know. It certainly looks deserted. The only positive thing if he was marooned here is… there is plenty to eat.'

'Eat!'

'Eggs, and the birds, too, if he's fast enough.'

Tatsuo was careful to keep a hundred yards between the *Mystery* and the atoll. 'It looks deserted.'

'I must go ashore,' Samoa declared.

Tatsuo was about to try to dissuade her from the idea, though he knew it would be impossible. 'We'll circle the reef first,' He replied instead.

There was still no sign of life, but Tatsuo knew of shallow caves at the base of the volcano-shaped peak near the lagoon. These caves were barely four feet high and not much deeper—more like an area of decay in an unwholesome tooth. But they would afford some shelter, providing a storm was not pounding the reef. Here, down-wind, the stench from dead sea life and the stinking lagoon water was horrendous.

'Horace, squeeze off a shot from the shotgun—it's the loudest.' One minute later Horace aimed the double-barreled shotgun skywards and fired. Instantly thousands of birds rose in unison. Their racket was unbelievable. All aboard watched and waited.

'Will, drop anchor then get the tender over the side,' Tatsuo ordered.

But suddenly a figure appeared from the darkness of one of the deeper caves.

'It's Rennison!' Samoa shouted. She started waving frantically. 'Rennison! ... Rennison! ... It's me! Samoa!'

They were still a hundred yards off shore but Samoa was certain.

'Unbelievable,' Tatsuo shook his head. 'This is the most inhospitable place on earth.'

The others stood open-mouthed.

'Rennison!' Samoa shouted. 'Rennison!'

They could see the figure was weak—he could barely stand. The figure shaded his eyes from the glaring sun. *Was this a mirage?*

'Is that really your brother?' Tatsuo said.

'Yes, yes!' Samoa screamed into the wind, 'Rennison!'

She waved both hands, jumping on the deck to gain the castaway's attention. Although he could not hear her words, he finally recognised his sister with her long flowing white-blonde hair.

'Samoa?' the man cried out, but his call was weak, his voice hoarse and croaky, and impossible to hear over the racket of thousands of unsettled birds. 'Samoa?' he finally shouted. Excitement and adrenalin rushed through his body.

'Rennison!'

Rennison could not believe his own eyes. Disbelieving, the marooned man hobbled lamely, barefoot over jagged coral towards the water's edge.

'Samoa!'

This time his sister heard her name, carried in the wind. She climbed onto the ratlines, waving hysterically. Tatsuo studied the shoreline. The swell was up, and six-foot waves were crashing onto the reef.

'We've only one chance,' Tatsuo told Horace, and pointed to an inlet where two coral arms jutted away from the water's edge, just wide enough to accommodate the tender.

'It's tight, Cap'n.'

'I know. But it's all we've got.'

Tatsuo, with Horace on the oars, pushed away in the clinker, while Rennison looked on, troubled. He knew the dangers only too well. With the tender riding a six-foot swell 20 yards offshore, there was a very real danger of it capsizing. But Rennison was taking no chances. It was now or never. He limped to the precipice where waves crashed shoreward, washing up around his waist and threatening to drag him out to sea. The tender rose and dipped on the undulating waves rolling onto the rocks.

'It's too dangerous!' Horace yelled over the thundering surf. He was having difficulty keeping the boat in deep water. 'Can we chuck him a rope, Boss?'

Tatsuo was considering this option when Rennison waded out to the lip of the ledge, waited for the backwash of the last wave and dived in.

'Rennison!' Samoa screamed.

Immediately all the stories of sharks, sea snakes and moray eels with razor teeth rushed through Samoa's mind. She dropped to the deck and rushed forward to be as close as possible. Rennison was weakened from his treatment by the Germans and his time on the shoal, as short as it had been. But fear spurred him on and he and Samoa had both been strong swimmers in their youth.

Horace managed to turn the bow into the oncoming swell.

'Keep her steady!' Tatsuo yelled to Horace, and the experienced seaman dipped oars and held the tender steady. Tatsuo clambered to the rising-falling stern.

'Hurry, man!' he screamed at Rennison. Rennison didn't need prompting. He was well aware of what swam nearby—he had seen them often enough in the past days. A wave broke over his head, pushing him under, threatening to drown him. Tatsuo threw a rope over the stern and waited. Rennison surfaced, gasping for air. The wave had dragged him over coral and he was bleeding badly. Another wave exploded on top of him, threatening to wash him back to the shoal. Rennison fought the undertow. He weakened. Another wave hit. They were relentless. There would be no respite.

'Grab the rope, man!' Tatsuo shouted.

'Got company!' Horace yelled. Tatsuo looked over his shoulder. A tall dorsal fin sliced through the next wave. As they watched, the fin dived.

'The rope, man! The rope!'

Rennison felt the rope before he saw it.

But he was floundering and his voice was hoarse from salt water. He was lifted high on the next swell, giving Tatsuo the opportunity to pull frantically on the rope.

Precious seconds passed.

The tender lifted on a wave and Horace caught a glimpse of the shark beneath them. Rennison reached the stern, his face tight with fear. Tatsuo lent over the side, hooking powerful arms under Rennison's. The half-drowned castaway was dead weight. Tatsuo lifted and Rennison hoisted his feet to the stern panels just as the shark swam inches beneath him. Horace immediately hauled on the oars with powerful rower's arms and the tender pulled back into deep water. Tatsuo hoisted Rennison into the boat, landing him ungracefully, face-first, on the boards.

'Oh, Lord Jesus!' Rennison snatched breaths. 'Oh, Christ!'

'Catch your breath.' Tatsuo sat down heavily next to him, also short of breath. The skipper looked at Horace, facing him as he rowed. They read each other's mind.

That was bloody close.

Rennison noticed his leg was bleeding badly. 'Oh, Jesus!'

Tatsuo took a length of rope, fashioning a temporary tourniquet around Rennison's upper thigh. 'It's not as bad as it looks. We've got a medical chest on board …

It's Rennison, right?'

'Yes.'

'You've been a hard man to find.'

'And you are …?'

'I'm Tatsuo and this here old seadog is my mate Horace.'

'God, am I glad to meet you two.'

'I should imagine you are.'

As they approached *Mystery*, anchored well away from the shoal, they heard Samoa's excited voice. 'My sister, Samoa,' Rennison said meekly. 'How did you …?'

'Relax, mate. All shall be revealed. Let's get that leg seen to first, huh?'

On board, Samoa had mixed emotions. Ecstatic to have eventually found her younger brother, and then fussing over his wounds. Rennison was helped below, where Samoa and Selma attended the cuts with a needle and thread, cheap rum, Holloway's ointment and clean bandages.

Tatsuo, Horace and William wasted no time sailing away from the fearsome atoll. Tatsuo looked back from the helm as the sails filled and they nosed east. All they could see now was whitewater exploding onto the razor coral now half a mile behind them.

'God-awful place, eh?' he said. Horace agreed. 'Yer can see why it's called the Shoal of Ghosts, eh?'

'Aye.'

Tatsuo and Horace were quiet after the rescue; watching brother and sister reunite was reward enough. *Besides, the gold isn't all that far off now*, Tatsuo thought. It was some time later—an hour, at least —when Samoa joined Tatsuo and Horace on deck.

'How is he?' Tatsuo asked.

'He sleeps.'

'Laudanum, huh?'

Samoa nodded. 'We washed his cuts in rum. I managed to stitch the skin and applied Holloway's ointment before bandaging.'

'She's quite the hand on the battlefield, is our Selma,' Tatsuo said. 'He'll live to tell his tales.'

And tell us where the wreck is, I hope.

'He woke briefly a moment ago,' Samoa said. 'And drank some soup Selma made especially, before collapsing again. He would have died on that … that rock. Thank you both so much!'

'Well, he's got you to thank for being so persistent.'

Samoa now noticed the late afternoon light. The sun, low in the sky, was washing the vista with a rich golden hue, like autumn leaves in a tree-filled forest, yet the sky to the north was sharkskin grey where a squall darkened the horizon.

'Is that a storm?' she asked.

'Aye, and if I didn't know any better I'd say it's planning a rendezvous with us in the night.'

Samoa looked troubled. Tatsuo changed the subject. 'I don't suppose your brother mentioned the lost ...' His words faded away as he read the expression on Samoa's face. 'Well, either way, we're heading towards Malaita Island and hopefully will find shelter before that storm hits.'

The storm was fierce, yet moved across the ocean slowly. An hour later darkness arrived early. The sea was a boiling cauldron but Malaita was in sight. More advantageous still was a small uninhabited island with steep cliff faces between them and the larger island. If they could make the lee side of that smaller island they could ride out the storm.

Samoa found oilskins below and staggered unsteadily aft across a pitching deck, to the helm.

'Will we make it before it hits?' She was forced to shout over the wind whistling through the rigging. They had reduced sail and the land was still another hour distant.

Tatsuo held firm to the helm as hill-sized waves trundled under the keel. But *Mystery* was an experienced mistress who rode the waves like a lady of the night.

'We're heading to that island!' he yelled, briefly taking a hand off the wheel to point directly ahead. Samoa looked forward, but could only make out the whites of giant waves as they broke over the bow. She could only trust Tatsuo's judgment.

'Now get below!' he cried. 'It's not safe out here!'

Tatsuo's warning was immediately supported by the appearance of a rogue wave. The monster approached from darkness, white water frothing at its curling crest. The cutter plunged into a steep trough and the wave exploded across the deck, drenching them both. Samoa lost her footing and slid back towards the companionway just as Horace appeared from below. He snatched her ankle and dragged her to the hatch.

'Get below!' he yelled. 'Quick, now!'

Samoa dropped back below deck as Horace slammed the hatch shut behind her, to join Tatsuo at the helm.

Below was bedlam. Pots and pans cascading off galley shelves. Equipment skittering port to starboard. Lumps of cooking coal scattering along the deck like a mountain-slide, leaving a trail of black dust. Samoa sat on Rennison's bunk and held tight. He was awake but happy. After his terrifying experience this storm was nothing. He had faced his maker several times during the past days. Selma wedged herself on the bottom bunk, forward, near the cargo hold, and nursed a bottle of whiskey. She wasn't using a glass. William and Pearl lay on the bunk opposite. The lad seemed unconcerned; after all, they had been through all this dozens of times.

Half an hour passed. The din dropped in decibels. The motion became less sporadic—just an undulating sea that Samoa suddenly found peaceful. The companionway hatch opened and Horace called out, 'Will!'

'Aye.'

'Get up 'ere, lad.'

Seconds later they heard the anchors dropped. 'We're sheltering here for the night,' Selma told the other two. 'How yer feeling?' she asked Rennison.

'Believe it or not, I feel rested.'

'Good, then nurse this.' She passed him the whiskey and started cleaning up the mess. Samoa joined her.

The storm passed while they had the protection of the tall cliffs between them and the tempest. But the rain was heavy. Below decks Selma laid the galley table with cold roasted meats, pickles, some rock-hard cheddar cheese she had managed to save and two-day-old damper-style bread. Everyone was famished. It could have been a king's banquet, especially from Rennison's point of view.

Rennison said little at first. The sudden intake of shipboard tucker gave him a gut ache, but a few whiskies seemed to restore him. *Mystery* rode on her anchors, her timbers creaking with the swell—she, too, was pleased to rest. With the evening meal over, Rennison sat at the table. He had always been a slim person yet the days on the atoll had taken their toll. He was wrapped in a blanket while he shivered, although the humidity had returned below deck.

He told how the German gunboat, SS *Prinzessin*, had called at Nagho ni ara while he was there. They were actually looking for him. How they knew he was there he had no idea. 'I was arrested and locked up in the ship's brig.'

'Why?' Tatsuo asked.

'I don't know.'

Tatsuo looked directly at Samoa, who reddened. Her brother was lying. Tatsuo just knew it. He studied the twenty-six-year-old Rennison, who fiddled with a lump of cheese, avoiding eye contact. There was something about the man he couldn't quite put a finger on. Like Samoa, he was a good-looking specimen of the human race. And he was tall and fair-skinned with blonde hair. Scandinavian? Probably.

'What do you mean?' Tatsuo sounded annoyed. 'You don't know why you were arrested?'

'They sent marines ashore and I was arrested. I don't know …'

'Let me stop you right there.' Tatsuo didn't like being lied to. Especially by someone whose life he just saved.

Rennison sat upright. 'Pardon?'

Tatsuo tossed the leather-bound diary onto the galley table. 'Recognise that?' Rennison's jaw dropped. 'I … I … ah … Where did you get that?'

'From your love nest on Bougainville Island. We met Safina.'

Rennison sat back, dumbfounded. He looked at his sister, who was also annoyed that he would lie.

'You found it?'

'Ah, yes.' Tatsuo also sat back, and crossed his arms.

'I left in a hurry, leaving everything behind.'

'Including an unborn child,' Samoa said.

'I can read French,' Tatsuo added.

'You know about the …?'

'About the Chinese Junk laden with gold named the *Coral Moon* owned by Bao Zheng, who wrecked on a reef somewhere near here. Yes.'

'Okay, so I lied. Sorry. I was being cautious.'

'Cautious … huh. So, let's start again. Why were you arrested and taken aboard a German gunboat?'

'The Admiral on board the SS *Prinzessin*, Admiral Gustav von Stosch, is a tyrant. He had visited Mist Island, and the German missionaries there—the ones I worked with—told him everything. I do believe he is in cahoots with the German captain, Captain Herr von Schtumpf. He knows about the wreck and knew that I knew which reef it is wrecked on. He tortured me, you know.'

'How?' Samoa asked.

'Cigarette burns.' Rennison lifted his shirt to reveal three nasty cigarette burn welts. Samoa shook her head. Selma had already dressed them with ointment.

'I thought they looked odd,' Selma said, frowning. She had assumed they were from his stint on the Shoal of Ghosts.

'So what happened? Why were you marooned on the atoll?'

'I managed to convince him that the reef he sought was on Yandina Island northwest of Nagho ni ara. I even drew him a map.'

'Yandina Islands is two days' sail from here in a steamer.'

'Yes. And he bought it. But he sailed directly to the Shoal of Ghosts to maroon me first, vowing to come back after he had salvaged the gold.'

'Why not take you with them?'

'I don't think they had any intention of coming back for me, unless …'

'Unless what?'

'Unless they found I had sent them on a wild goose chase.' Rennison took his sister's hand. 'It's so good to see you, dear sister. But how on earth did you know where to look for me?'

'Your request for 500 bibles was the first correspondence I'd had from you in 14 months. I found Tatsuo here in Cooktown and hired his services. I was worried about your safety, and rightly so.'

'So you *did* receive my letter?'

'Of course. Otherwise I wouldn't be here.'

'And the bibles?'

'They're on board. In the hold.'

'Wonderful.'

'You're hardly a man of the cloth, Rennison Plum,' Selma said. 'Why would you go to all the trouble of having bibles sent to this part of the world?'

'As Samoa will tell you, I have an interest in anthropology. I was keen to study the people of the Solomon Islands. Besides, I just wanted to do my bit for the natives,' he said. Tatsuo found this hard to swallow.

'Why did the dead man buried on Rat's Nest Island call himself Rennison Plum?'

Rennison stiffened. 'Dead?'

'Yes, killed by savages from Malaita, by all accounts.'

'He was a sailor I met. A rather simple fellow who had a shady past. He had escaped the French Penal Colony on the Isle of Pines two weeks' sail south of here ...'

'I know where Isle of Pines is,' Tatsuo said.

'Yes, well, I suggested he assume my identity and take up with the missionaries, who were only too glad to have him volunteer. He was facing serious prison time. I also knew Safina's brothers would come after me, so I wanted to leave a false trail. Normally I would have gone back to Europe but ... Well ... the golden junk beckoned.'

'Why would Zamir the Albanian tell me that night on Bona Bona Island that the wreck of the *Coral Moon* was on a reef on Nggela Sule Island?' Tatsuo thought aloud. 'He told me wreckage washed ashore there not so long ago after a willy-willy swept the island.'

'You'd trust an Albanian?' Selma said.

'Exactly,' Tatsuo frowned. 'He actually thought I was onto the wreck. I've diving equipment on board, so he was trying to send me off on a wild goose chase. Bastard!'

'Fuck!' Rennison looked on, shocked at the young man cursing in front of the women. 'Steady on, old chap,' he said.

'It's Tourette's,' Samoa explained to her brother.

'Oh.' Rennison turned back to Tatsuo. 'Did you say you have diving equipment on this boat?'

'Yes. I'm an experienced pearler. You were marooned four days ago, right?' Tatsuo asked.

'Five now.'

'Alright, five. And it's a two-day sail for the SS *Prinzessin* to Yandina Island. Did you give them specific details about the reef?'

'He drew them a map, remember?—under duress.'

'Under torture!' Rennison corrected.

'Then the sauerkrauts will soon realise you sent them on a wild goose chase,' Tatsuo said. 'They'll be back to the Shoal of Ghosts to cut your legs off and scoop your eyes out.'

'Charming,' Samoa commented.

'Aye. Charming. I know the Germans. That means we only have a few days at the most to find this wreck.'

'So where is it, exactly?' Selma was holding the bread knife, and if she was trying to be intimidating, she succeeded.

Chapter Eight

The following morning turned out to be a magnificent, bright day in paradise. Tatsuo sailed *Mystery* towards the outer barrier reefs surrounding the west coast of Malaita Island, one of the Solomon Archipelago's largest. His charts noted the island was roughly 100 miles long and over 20 miles across at its widest point. The weather here was hot and wet and unpredictable. Malaita was a tropical mountainous island little explored, and although Tatsuo knew it had been made a protectorate under British rule two years earlier, it was still a dangerous island and home to savage, headhunting cannibals. Some missionaries, however, had managed to establish a semblance of civilisation on pockets of coastal land. But they were few and far between.

With Will at the bow, one leg on either side of the bowsprit, Tatsuo managed to penetrate the outer reef with just a jib set. Horace made soundings, calling out the depth at regular intervals. Although they were inside the reef, the shoreline was still a good mile distant.

Rennison was excited at the possibility of studying some of these savages firsthand. He was free to admit anthropology was his first love, however life had had other plans for him. And although he had spent some time in the Coral Seas, Malaita had eluded him.

'I must warn you,' Tatsuo told Rennison, casting an eye over smoke spiraling lazily skywards from cooking fires in a village several miles south, 'the skull of a whitefella is still very much prized as a trophy on this island.'

'I'm aware of the dangers, Captain Gaston,' Rennison answered, the impetuosity of youth starting to expose itself. Or was it a hint of German arrogance?

'Whoa … "Captain Gaston"! "Tatsuo" will do just fine,' Tatsuo responded. 'Although the Brits made Malaita a protectorate recently,' Tatsuo said to the group, 'and there have been missionaries here for ten years, the whalers and more ruthless blackbirders have given the tribes a hard time in the past. So whitefellas aren't exactly welcome all over the island. I hate to imagine what happened to Bao Zheng and his Cantonese survivors who came ashore here 20 years ago. They would have been butchered … and I mean butchered.'

'I think,' Samoa interrupted, 'that my brother gets the picture.'

As if initiated by the hand of some superior power, a sudden ripple scattered across the sea. It lasted only seconds but Tatsuo knew immediately. 'Earthquake.'

'Really?' Samoa rushed to the port side, peering into the calm sea where colourful fish flashed by, panicked, amongst the knots of coral in the emerald green water. 'I felt it under the boat,' she said, amazed.

'Earthquakes are common here,' Tatsuo said. 'After all, it was a tsunami, caused by an earthquake at sea, that exposed the *Coral Moon* on the reef to our friend Rembrandt, was it not?'

Rennison listened but did not respond. He studied the coastline. 'Have you kept to the directions I gave you?'

'Aye.'

'Then there should be a coral island village around that headland.' Rennison indicated a point of heavily vegetated land reaching out into the lagoon.

Although the shoreline was still the best part of a mile away, the water was incredibly shallow, only six to ten feet deep, the bottom clearly visible. Schools of angelfish, parrotfish, butterfly fish, pink coral trout, red cod and tiger-striped snapper abounded. Approaching the headland Tatsuo was sailing close to shore when the village finally appeared. Villages, seemingly sitting on stilts in the water, were dotted along this coast and Rembrandt had assured Rennison that they were friendly.

These villages were actually perched just above the waterline, sitting on foundations of rock coral, floated out onto the reef on log rafts and stacked onto existing reefs by the natives. Once complete, soil was rafted out to form gardens and grow banyan and breadfruit trees and to secure the palms. 'The roots of these plants, mostly grown about the perimeter of the villages, act as protection against the weather,' Rennison noted. 'And bind the artificial islands together, literally. It's quite ingenious, huh?'

Tall coconut palms reached into the blue sky from the middle of the man-made island, which Tatsuo estimated was about two acres in size.

'Some of these man-made islands have stockades built from vertical palm trunks bound together,' Rennison said. 'To fortify them against attack.'

For William they were the type of image one expected to see on a child's book cover, like a Robinson Crusoe tale. They were the quintessential images of the south sea islands. He was seeing the exotic south seas that most Europeans could only read about. He busily sketched on page after page, his natural talent the light of his life.

'These people should be friendly,' Tatsuo agreed with Rennison. He explained that he knew these coral communities consisted of refugees who had come here from all over Malaita—islanders victimised by stronger dominant tribes, fleeing vengeance, or escaped slaves from other villages, some even exiled by their own families, all come here to restart their lives.

'The Malaita can be warlike people on occassion,' Tatsuo said. 'It's really the inland natives we have to worry about.'

'If they're all Malaitians why can't they just get on?'

'Have you forgotten the American Civil War?' Samoa asked.

'Fair enough.'

'Well, as I said, they're naturally warlike, and racist against their own, a bit like, say, Ireland and England. The tribes on the shore allow these communities to survive as long as they keep to themselves. In return the coral people trade fish for the starch they need in their diet, like yams and taros. In times of trouble, say during conflict with other warring tribes, the refugees take up arms and fight alongside their bushman hosts.'

'It's like medieval Europe,' Rennison suggested.

'Exactly—that's a good way to describe them.'

Tatsuo was cautious. The *Mystery* dropped anchor well out from the coral village where at least 200 inhabitants lined their settlement's perimeter, calling out and chattering excitedly, making outward signs of friendship.

'They seem amicable enough,' Samoa said.

'Hmm … I trust you're right.' Tatsuo passed the spyglass to Rennison. 'So, you say this is the village of which Rembrandt spoke,' Tatsuo commented. 'If so, I assume that southern headland over there marks the reef we are searching for.'

Rennison closed one eye and studied the shoreline through the glass. 'Yes. "Half Moon Reef," Rembrandt called it, on account of the landscape.'

'Good choice of name,' Samoa said. '*Coral Moon* on Half Moon Reef. I like it.'

Rennison scanned the promontory reaching out onto the reef. 'Rembrandt spoke of an embankment where the reef joins the land.'

With the tropical sun high overhead, the land was clearly visible.

Yes! There.' He pointed. 'I can see it. That's where Rembrandt said he found broken Chinese pottery and other small items.'

'And he saw the ship where?'

'Right out on the point,' Rennison said, still glued to the telescope as he panned the instrument left. 'He told me the sea withdrew out past the barrier reef there, exposing identifiable wreckage wedged in a coral crevice. He put two and two together, but not before he high-tailed it into the foothills. He reckoned the tidal wave rolled inland half a mile.'

'Scary!'

'Very scary.'

'Was he alone?'

'No, he was with a tribe that had befriended him. He had lived here some time near then.'

'Samoa,' Tatsuo said, 'best you stay here with Selma and Pearl.'

Samoa shot Tatsuo the look he should have expected.

'Alright,' he capitulated, again 'please be vigilant.'

Horace hid rifles under a tarp in the bottom of the tender, while William fetched bags of trinkets and a dozen cheap tomahawks and knives, for gifts, along with his sketchpad and a pocket of charcoal. Tatsuo took it upon himself to row the few hundred yards to the coral village, with Samoa watching on from the stern sheets.

The coral island villagers were indifferent to the whitefella visitors. They were curious, but clearly others had been there before them, with, by all accounts, friendly results. They did, however, love the trinkets, and the iron-head tomahawks were received with utmost appreciation.

The five visitors were ushered to a central meeting place in the middle of the man-made island, entering via narrow alleyways between the grass and bamboo huts. The meeting place was a built-up mound of coral packed with earth, where four 80-foot coconut palms reached to the heavens.

Rennison made mental notes, fascinated by these people and their well organised community. It was soon clear they knew some pidgin and Horace managed a simple conversation. He asked for their permission to look for a lost whitefella ship off the reef.

'We have to find the bones of our people, so we can rest their spirits in peace,' he lied.

The chieftain came forward. He was a short, elderly, proud man, who introduced himself to Horace as Karoo. He wore coloured plumes on his head and sported arm bracelets of carved stone—maybe alabaster, Rennison thought—with a small shield around his neck. He was welcoming, insisting they take arak with him and the elders of the tribe, in the communal hall. Tatsuo insisted Samoa join them and at first Karoo was confused as to why they would want their *woman* to join them.

Although they came bearing gifts, the natives were desperate to trade as well, wanting to swap coconuts for fish hooks and iron hoops, which Will and Horace fetched from the cutter.

Several dark, canoe-shaped pods hanging vertically from the rafters of the communal hut, were of particular interest to Rennison.

'Fascinating. I've read of this but never witnessed it.'

'What are they?'

'There are bodies in there.' Rennison nodded discreetly to the pods. 'When someone close dies, like a relative, they swathe the body in a shroud of leaves, from the *barringtonia* tree.'

Tatsuo knew this tree was more commonly known as the box fruit tree, on account of its poisonous fruit. It grew in the mangroves and was very water resistant.

'See there?' Rennison pointed to bamboo tubes running from the bottom of the pods and into the floor. 'They penetrate the low water mark of the shingle and coral stones that are the foundation of this island. They stay like that half a year. They don't smell, you notice'—he sniffed the air—'because the body fluids are drained away. They then take them ashore and bury them on dry land, but not before removing the heads for, what we would call, a reliquary.'

That explained the dozens of skulls adorning the walls, and set Samoa, William and Horace more at ease.

'These skulls in here are respected. It's the ones skewered on poles out in the village that are trophies from skirmishes with enemy tribes.'

Tatsuo was growing impatient. 'Horace, ask them about a whitefella shipwrecked here many years ago,'

Horace spoke for some time. The elders nodded and grew animated. 'They say "yes," Boss—a big whitefella canoe sank on the reef jus' out there … long, long time ago. They said they was foreign devils with long plaited hair and narrow eyes.' And Horace put fingers to the corners of each eye and stretched them, denoting the almond-shaped eyes of an Oriental. 'An' their skin, they say, was not dark and not same as whitefella, more like pig.'

Karoo suddenly became sombre. He approached Tatsuo until he was inches from his face and began a long-winded commentary, doing the same, one at a time, to Rennison, Horace, William and then Samoa. He was deadly serious.

'What was that all about?' Tatsuo asked Horace in a reverent tone.

'He say this village wash away by the angry wave, many ancestors dead.'

Tatsuo made a suitably sympathetic face and Karoo took Tatsuo's hand in his own, stroking the back of Tatsuo's hand in what was interpreted as appreciation. Tatsuo looked at Rennison and Samoa. 'I think this *is* where "X" marks the spot.'

'I think you're right.'

The chief asked something of Horace. They exchanged a brief but urgent conversation.

'What is it, Horace?' Samoa asked.

'He say, why you ask about foreign devils?'

'Ah … tell him … ah … foreign devils were our brothers,' Tatsuo said. 'And we owe it to them to put dead men's spirits at peace.'

Horace spent some moments attempting to convey this message. Karoo and the elders looked on, contemplating the situation. When Horace had exhausted his Pidgin rhetoric, the wise men of the village deliberated for some time while the visitors stood by in anticipation. Finally Karoo turned to Horace, and his answer seemed positive.

'What did he say?' Rennison asked impatiently.

'He say other whitefella doin' same same, much distance north of here.'

'What?' Tatsuo asked.

'Yes, he say whitefella canoe same as the one what brought us 'ere. Man in strange clothing, he breath under water. He look for ancestors also.'

'A diver!'

'Damn it!"

'Who could that be?' Samoa asked.

'Don't know. Zamir the Albanian, possibly. He tried to send me to Nggela Sule Island. A deliberate ruse I thought at the time.'

Tatsuo's face pinched and he studied the villagers' faces. There was so much riding on this. Tatsuo took Karoo's hand and shook it whitefella way, and nodded suitable appreciative thank yous, understood in any culture.

'We better hurry,' Tatsuo told the others.

With the ceremony over, friendships established, and gifts exchanged, the Coral Islanders watched with indifference as the whitefellas rowed away from the coral village and across the lagoon, where they beached the tender. Tatsuo shielded himself from the sun with his hand, searching the steep embankment for anomalies. Something instantly caught his eye. He clawed his way to the top.

'Blue and white porcelain!' Tatsuo picked up several small shards of broken pottery, now weathered smooth by the years of exposure. He looked back down the embankment, to where the others were climbing to join him, and gold fever surged through his veins. 'This is Chinese pottery.'

'So it really isn't a myth?' Samoa asked.

'Oh ye of little faith,' Rennison said, grinning and climbing the last few feet of the steep bank on his hands and knees. 'I told you, this is where the survivors of the wreck camped.'

They gathered at the top where this headland levels out.

'That's the remains of a cairn'—Tatsuo pointed out a pile of rocks 20 yards inland—'It would have been used to light a bonfire to attract any ship that might have been passing by.'

'A rarity in itself.'

'Aye. But they were captured by the natives, were they not?' Samoa asked.

Tatsuo positioned himself to study the reef headland about half a mile back out to sea. Horace joined him. 'It's easy to see how they wrecked here, Cap'n, eh?'

'Aye, especially if the weather was bad, or if it had been a dark night. And that crafty Zamir the Albanian tried to tell me Bao

Zheng's *Coral Moon* wrecked off the northeast coast of Nggela Sule Island.'

'Who?' Rennison asked. Tatsuo told him the fabrication the Albanian pearler had told him, trying to steer him in the wrong direction. 'He thought I was on a treasure hunt. All he did was fuel my imagination. Now here we are.'

Horace was looking nervous. 'Boss.'

'Yes, matey.'

'May I suggest we get busy before the bush tribes get wind of us?'

'Fuck, fuck'—William's tics started. His body went into spasm, his face twitched and he punched the air. This was more than his usual tic behaviour. The others caught the fear in his eye.

'I think we're too late.' Samoa was looking over Tatsuo's shoulder. Behind him the palms and vegetation came alive.

At least a hundred armed savages stepped out of the jungle, their faces painted for war, their teeth purple from betel nut, spears and clubs at the ready. The spearmen looked particularly menacing, each carrying a shield in one hand along with spare spears and a club. Many had bows with poisoned arrows. These arrows were particularly dangerous. Made from palm wood set in reed shafts they had human-bone arrowheads soaked in the juices of decomposed enemy victims. If one of those arrows, with its barbed head especially carved to break off in the wound, was to penetrate the body, lockjaw was unavoidable.

More worrying still was the all-familiar *haka,* a war cry common amongst Pacific islanders. The men stamped their feet, slapped their thighs, and pawed at the ground with their feet whilst yelling out a war chant.

There was no mistaking their intent.

Tatsuo instinctively twisted back to look towards *Mystery*, but already two war canoes of 30 natives each were paddling rhythmically away from the beach ...

And in the direction of the cutter.

Each canoe was over 25 feet long with its sides inlaid with pearl-shell from one end to the other. Twenty paddles dipped into the water in rhythmic unison, soundlessly, while they sang a chant with each stroke.

'Selma,' Tatsuo whispered under his breath, 'for God's sake don't try and fight them.'

'You seem to know more about the people of Malaita than the rest of us, Rennison. What are your thoughts?'

'My thoughts?' Rennison looked about nervously. 'Ah, well, as recently as the 1870s these people were hostile to all visitors. Anyone who had the misfortune to be marooned on this island was killed.'

'That's what I thought. That's why I never visit the place.'

'Even ships who called to trade or look for water were sent running,' Rennison continued. 'But I do believe missionaries have made some headway in the past ten years.'

They were immediately overpowered and surrounded and there was no doubt about the islanders' intention.

'Maybe that is wishful thinking,' Rennison said anxiously. 'We … we're prisoners.'

Tatsuo looked at Rennison and groaned, 'Your powers of observation never cease to amaze me, Mr Plum.'

Standing close by and wearing terrified faces, Samoa, Horace and William looked to their captain for encouragement.

'I strongly suggest we do as they say … and smile everybody, smile,' Tatsuo said. 'I'm certain they aren't planning anything … ah … nasty.'

Horace put a comforting hand on Will's shoulder. This was the lad's closest encounter with savages. 'How certain of that are you Cap'n?' Horace asked.

'Um … ah, I'll let you know.'

Prodded and pushed, they were herded back into the jungle, where they marched single-file in forced silence for three miles, to a village where they were presented to the chief.

The chieftain, Sulufou, wore a necklace of red discs. Rennison had seen these before and knew them as Malaita Island shell money, carved from a small spondylus shell with a red lip. After being cut into discs they were rubbed flat, polished and pierced for threading. They were then used for buying a bride or a pig, as blood money or even to pay off ghosts seeking redemption. Even more valuable were porpoise teeth, used for larger purchases like a war canoe or land. Although these natives were cannibals who ate their enemies, they appeared more civilised than the whitefella gave them credit for.

Life in the jungle village was a tough existence. Land had to be first cleared for cultivating vegetables with stone tools. The deep roots of hardwood trees had to be burnt before the inland dwellers could remove them, piece by piece, with primitive tools. Rennison had studied these people in the libraries back in London. He knew there was little in the jungle to supplement their diet besides frogs, snails, lizards and grubs. He had read how they had a mutual agreement with the coral people, whom they called the saltwater people. They needed each other to survive.

The coral people needed starch in their diet, like yams and taro, and the inlanders, the bush people, needed fish. And fresh water on the island had to be shared.

They had a rich history that included rules, rituals and a sense of ancestral pride. As they had no recorded history, without use of the written word they were obliged to rely on meticulously accurate memories to pass down stories from their ancestors. They did not think individually, but as a group. They believed everyone had a soul, which they called *nanu*. The literal translation of this term, Rennison remembered reading, was 'the shadow of a person as cast by the sun.' They believed that when a person was asleep the *nanu* left the body. That was why they believed one must never waken someone who was sleeping.

A younger-looking version of Sulufou appeared, clearly his son. He wore a necklace of tiny red, white, yellow and black shells crocheted with fibres into decorative patterns, which hung around his neck and down to his waist. He ordered them all to go up the rock steps into the communal hall. The structure was 50 feet long by 20 wide and had a steep roof. It was totally built from bamboo and coconut palms. Inside, on an open pit fire that filled the hall with smoke, yams were cooking. The chieftain entered with his entourage. They sat in a circle and the prisoners were made to stand where he could see them clearly.

There followed much animated conversation amongst the elders who were gathered. From what Horace could make out, some tribesmen, the younger warriors, wanted to kill the newcomers there and then. But Sulufou argued he wanted whitefellas for ransom. Either way, it appeared Sulufou had the final say. He was the chieftain, after all.

Suddenly much screaming and shouting created a commotion outside and two men were carried in on long stakes, trussed like pigs for roasting. They were natives from a rival village. Immediately Tatsuo thought the worst.

'This doesn't bode well,' he whispered to those of his crew within earshot.

One of the younger warriors saw Tatsuo communicating and Tatsuo received a hearty blow with a club to the back of his legs, dropping him to his knees. The trussed captives were thrown to the floor, where Sulufou inspected them. He muttered something to the young warriors who had brought them into the hall. Tatsuo stood awkwardly. He was angry but fearing he was also being measured up for the villagers' feast he remained silent. He was prodded, his shirt lifted and his tight-muscled stomach pinched. Another warrior thrust a hand to Will's groin and squeezed his genitals. Will leapt back in shock, clutching at his privates. 'Fuck you, fuck, fuck you! ... Fuck!'

Those gathered around looked shocked. The warrior who grabbed at William said something Horace did not understand, but immediately the entire assembly burst out laughing.

Tatsuo, however, feared for the lives of his crew. But then he caught sight of several sketches—portraits, of various elders pinned to the wall of the communal hall. He recognised a sketch of Sulufou.

The portrait was done in black and white charcoal, and very professional.

'Rembrandt!' Tatsuo said aloud.

Sulufou appeared to recognise this word … this name.

'Rembrandt?' Tatsuo directed the word at the chieftain, stabbing a finger at the sketches.

The old native looked inquisitive. 'R … Rem …bran?' he muttered.

Tatsuo had a sudden thought. 'Will, show the chief your sketchpad.'

Will understood immediately. He approached the chieftain but was instantly stopped by several warriors pointing spears. Horace stepped in, talking pidgin to one of the few who understood. The message was relayed and Sulufou beckoned William to approach him.

The old man's face brightened at the sketches. 'Rembran …' he said. He understood immediately and nodded profusely, flipping page after page, inspecting William's craft.

'Sketch the man, Will,' Tatsuo prompted.

Sulufou seemed to understand and, like a prize rooster, he lifted his chin and turned slightly, as if he knew which profile was his best. William wasted no time. With his board cradled in his left arm he started sketching, creating enormous interest amongst those in the hall, who were all chattering at once, pushing and shoving. It was then that Tatsuo realised they all wanted their portraits drawn.

Art managed to cross oceans that morning. Language was meaningless. William did himself proud and the heavy pall of fear lifted. There was now a certain camaraderie that would have seemed impossible earlier. An hour and a half later William had sketched eight of the elders.

'You've done yourself proud, lad,' Tatsuo said. 'Proud, indeed.'

Chapter Nine

It was late afternoon by the time they arrived back at the *Mystery*, gratefully unscathed. But it had come at a price. Sulufou had demanded that William stay at the village and sketch all the elders. Four of Sulufou's warriors returned with Tatsuo and the others to fetch William's last sketchpad. If William was worried, he didn't show it, and his bouts of Tourette's tics, only improved his relationship with the old chieftain, who clearly took a liking to the young, pale-skinned lad.

Tatsuo anchored *Mystery* off the reef in deeper water and together the remaining crew studied the reef beneath them. On the reef, schools of fish with their startling combinations of vibrant colours swam by, curiously gaping up at the intruders from gullies and hollows amongst the coral.

Finding lost treasure at sea was every seafarer's dream. It had always been that, just a dream. But now, for the first time, it seemed a reality.

Tatsuo estimated they were anchored in six fathoms of water, although there were only two fathoms in places. There was no sign of a wreck.

Rennison frowned. 'Can't see a thing, huh?'

'Only one way to find out.' Tatsuo stripped down to his loincloth, pulled goggles over his head and dived head first over the side. As the others watched, the fish scattered. They watched Tatsuo reach the coral reef under water. He surfaced, took a deep breath and dived again. Horace kept an eye out for unwanted predators as the sun was low and the Solomon Islands played host to a variety of large sharks.

Tatsuo free dived several times in a wide arc around the reef headland before surfacing once more at *Mystery*'s stern. Horace dropped a Jacob's ladder over the side. Tatsuo climbed back on board. It didn't look promising. Samoa, Selma, Horace, Rennison and Pearl stood staring impatiently.

'Not much luck, I'm afraid.'

'What!' Rennison's face pinched. 'It has to be here!'

'The only thing I found was this.' Tatsuo held up what appeared to be a three-legged pot, about three inches in diameter. The bronze censer encrusted with small shells was missing one leg, otherwise it was in good condition. Jaws dropped.

'What is it? For cooking?' Selma asked.

Rennison shook his head in a condescending manner. 'That,' he tutted, 'is a censer for burning incense.'

Tatsuo rubbed at the encrustation. There was no doubting it was Chinese-made. He pointed out disc-shaped stamps on the side embossed in Chinese Han characters. Rennison held the pot in both hands. 'It's solid bronze, maybe a hundred years old.' It immediately dawned on him. 'Well? What else?'

'There's the remains of a ship down there, alright,' Tatsuo said. 'It's dropped off the reef and is resting in thousands of pieces in about six fathoms. I'm going to have to suit up in the diving gear. I could see it from the reef edge. That—what did you call it?—censer … was jammed in the coral at about two fathoms. There are many other pieces in the coral, broken pottery mostly.'

'And it's a Chinese junk down there?' Samoa asked anxiously. 'Definitely?'

'Well, it's hard to tell. There's not much remaining of a ship, exactly. It's covered in sand and encrustations; the coral's growing around what remains there are. But, hey!'—Tatsuo pointed to the bronze artefact—'I'll bet my last pound note she's Bao Zheng's

Coral Moon.' Tatsuo thought a moment. 'You know what else is down there?'

'What?' Samoa asked.

'Fish, and lots of them. Horace, fetch my trident. Selma, fire up the brazier, and Ren, old boy, it's time to celebrate. Selma will give you the key to the grog locker … Fetch the whiskey.'

With the night came balmy, still air. While reef fish barbequed on the hibachi brazier, a Japanese style of outdoor cooking that Tatsuo had taught Selma, they celebrated and could only hope young William was enjoying himself.

Across the lagoon cooking fires were eventually doused as darkness fell and the coral villagers drifted off into their spirit world —where they believed the soul traveled at night whilst they slept. By mid-evening Horace and Selma had retired to their bunks.

Tatsuo, Samoa and Rennison sat around the table at the stern. Across the water, beyond the beach, the jungle came alive with screeching, hooting, squealing and noisy clicking of the cicadas, or "tree crickets" as they were called. The night could not have been more perfect. Tatsuo poured what little remained in the whiskey bottle into Samoa's glass. She had grown accustomed to the Irish tipple of late. He twisted his own empty glass in his fingers a moment, lost in thought.

'It's still early,' he finally said. 'I'll be right back—don't go anywhere.'

Tatsuo returned with a fresh bottle. 'So you two haven't seen each other in five years, you were saying?'

'About that,' Rennison said.

'Where did you see each other last?'

'London,' Rennison replied.

'Munich,' Samoa said.

'London, Munich—which is it?' Tatsuo asked as he pulled the cork from the bottle and poured.

'You're right,' Samoa said to her brother, 'it was London.'

'London. I'd like to go there one day,' Tatsuo said. 'What's it like?'

'Cold,' Samoa answered.

'Busy,' Rennison said.

'Not like this, then?' Tatsuo grinned, looking across at the white water breaking over the reef.

'You have the ideal lifestyle here, Tatsuo,' Samoa said, unintentionally placing a hand on the captain's knee. Rennison was taken aback momentarily. Samoa smartly removed her hand. 'I mean,' she continued, 'would you look at this? It is so beautiful.'

'And dangerous,' Rennison said.

Tatsuo looked at Samoa. 'You told me you were taken back to London as young'ens by the missionaries.'

'That's right. The London Missionary School.'

'Aye. When you were adopted out from the London Missionary School where did you live? I mean, who adopted you?'

'We were very lucky. A professor of science, Walter Forbes and his wife, Nanette, adopted us. They had one daughter, Constance ...'

'Spoilt brat,' Rennison said.

'She was, a little. But we're very grateful to them.'

'We moved to Oxford,' Rennison said, clearly with fond memories, 'where we lived near Wolfson College.'

'We had a maid, and a cook ...'

'And remember Martin the alcoholic liveryman who would drive the coach like it was in a race.'

The two laughed at the memory.

'Rennison had an attic room and he used to sneak out at night and go to the inn.'

'And chase the girls.'

'How old were you?' Tatsuo asked, having thoughts of Rennison being too young.

'Old enough,' Rennison smiled, lost in memory lane for a moment. 'You know it was in Oxford that I became interested in anthropology, at the Pitt Rivers museum of Anthropology.'

'You mentioned Munich,' Tatsuo said. 'You told me you had a Bavarian nanny in London. Did she take you to Munich?'

Rennison remained silent, looking to his sister to answer.

'No. But we paid her a visit, ah … when?' She looked to Rennison. 'What, ten years ago?'

'I suppose it was about then.'

'What's it like, then?'

'What? Germany?'

'Germany, Munich.'

'Well it's very different to London in many ways. They eat garlic sausages and love potatoes; they go crazy with decorations at Christmas …'

'And eat pickled cabbage.' Tatsuo grinned.

'Have you tried it?'

'No. The Japanese have a pickled cabbage called tsukemono,' Tatsuo said. 'But I think the German sauerkraut is kept longer … and you need to acquire a taste for it. So after Oxford, what happened?'

'We both moved to London. I worked at Westminster Hall,' Rennison said.

'Westminster!' Tatsuo whistled. 'Parliament, huh?'

'Don't get too excited. I was in the records, with the archive. Filing ministerial speeches mainly.'

'But you did get to meet some important people,' Samoa said.

'Yes. That's true.'

'And you?' Tatsuo asked Samoa.

'We shared lodgings together in Putney. I found employment at a pharmacy and did the accounting for an importer at Canary Wharf.'

'Where did you grow up, anyway?' Rennison asked his host.

'Broome, in my early years,' Tatsuo said. 'Then all over North Queensland, really. My mother … did you know she was Japanese?'

'I thought there was a hint of the Orient there somewhere,' Rennison said diplomatically.

'Yes, well.' Tatsuo ran a finger along each side of his pencil-thin moustache. 'My mother was Japanese and my father French. But he was a seaman, a merchant navy man, and was away a lot. He died when I was young and my mother and her father, a pearl diver, Tatsuya, brought me up.'

'Do you speak Japanese?'

'A little. You must understand, my mother wanted me to grow up a whitefella, a European. She used my father's name, Gaston, although they never married. And she wasn't too keen to teach me too much about the other half of my culture, Japan.'

'Oh, what a pity,' Samoa said.

'But grandfather Tatsuya—I loved that man—taught me deep sea diving when I was twelve.'

'Twelve!'

'Yes, I could swim in the suit. It was so big, but I was tall for my age. Then we moved to Cooktown. But my grandfather died when I was twenty-four.' There followed a moment of silence as each took a drink. 'Died of the bends,' Tatsuo lamented. 'Diving off New Guinea in deep water, collecting pearl shell.'

'Oh, I'm sorry,' Samoa said.

Rennison reached for the bottle, filling his glass. 'What do you think our chances are tomorrow?' he asked Tatsuo. 'I mean, our real chances.'

'Well I can't see why it wouldn't still be there, that is *if* the gold was on board in the first place.'

'I've been around the Coral Seas some time now,' Rennison said. 'I've asked lots of people, listened to all the rumours, and I'm willing to bet there was gold on that ship and she was trying to avoid the Royal Navy pursuers at the time, by sailing the long way to Canton.'

'I'll tell you one thing,' Tatsuo said.

'What's that?'

'There is definitely a Chinese junk down there.'

'We know that.' Rennison swallowed his whiskey. 'Rembrandt saw it, for Christ's sake, before he ran like a wild hare up that hill slope … It must have been terrifying.'

'And in talking with the natives you've heard no mention of anyone having been here before, I mean whitefellas, diving.'

'So, who's diving up the coast?' Samoa wanted to know.

'Don't know. But I'm keen to get in the water tomorrow and get this over with,' Tatsuo said, standing and draining his glass. 'With that in mind, I'm going to turn in.'

Samoa was less than subtle watching Tatsuo descend below deck.

'You seem pretty friendly with our Samurai Frog,' Rennison said, when Tatsuo was out of sight.

'He's a good man, Ren. And don't you forget it.'

Rennison bunched his lips and exhaled out his nose. He poured another two fingers of whiskey into his glass and gulped it.

'Half a ton of gold,' he sighed. 'Can you imagine? Can you really, really imagine what that would buy?'

Samoa hated her brother when the drink affected him. He was not a good drunk.

'See you in the morning,' she said and retired, leaving Rennison alone with his thoughts of riches.

Samoa woke first, from a night's sleep of bizarre dreams. She was certain she heard a rooster. But looking about her groggily, half asleep, she recognised she was on board the *Mystery*. The second crow reminded her of the nearby coral village. Sound carried over water. But more ominous was the thumping against the hull. By the time Samoa had dressed Tatsuo was armed with a rifle, and padding barefoot through the galley and up the companionway. He burst into bright sunlight, instinctively shielding his eyes.

One whiskey too many, he thought, *that'll do it*.

Suddenly, excited chattering and dozens of happy faces greeted him from several canoes alongside the *Mystery*. The natives had come to trade with coconuts, yams, taro and fish. Some were offering bows and arrows and other blackfella trinkets like shell necklaces. It was too much, too early. 'Horace!'

'Coming, Cap'n.'

Horace stood next to his skipper and grinned. He'd seen it all before.

'Deal with it, would you,' Tatsuo ordered his mate. 'Selma.'

'Aye.'

'I need coffee.'

'Sure thing, Cap'n.'

Trading went on for an hour with the bartering in the natives' favour; anything to appease them, Tatsuo instructed.

After imbibing a pot of strong coffee, Tatsuo was suited up by Horace. Samoa looked on, fascinated. Tatsuo's suit was relatively new, made by Siebe, Gorman and Company in Holland. First the waterproofed canvas suit had to be fitted; this included the corselet, or breastplate, to take the weight of the heavy copper, brass and glass helmet. This suit consisted of a solid sheet of rubber between layers of tan twill. The thick, vulcanised rubber collar was then clamped to the corselet, making this connection waterproof. The twill was designed for strength against barnacles, rock or the sharp edges of wreckage. Tatsuo sheathed a diving knife into his belt, while Horace fixed lead weights onto the suit to counteract buoyancy; one worn around the chest, one on the back and one for each shoe. On deck the suit was clumsy, but once in the water it all made sense. Fully rigged, Tatsuo carried an extra 190 pounds.

'Isn't that claustrophobic?' Samoa asked.

'You don't want to think about that,' Tatsuo said. 'Just the work ahead. Say, how about waking that brother of yours. We need him on the pump.'

Rennison appeared, looking bedraggled, but Selma was on his heels with coffee and banana bread. He pulled a face, but Selma wasn't taking no for an answer and Tatsuo knew he was in safe hands.

Horace unveiled the deck pump, which had been protected from the weather under an oilskin cover, and gave Rennison a lesson on how it operated. Tatsuo, Horace explained to Rennison, was connected to the air pump with an umbilical air hose into his helmet. The air was supplied by turning flywheels to operate bellows in the compressor. The umbilical also held the lifting cable. Tatsuo could adjust his own air intake with a valve on his chest plate. Rennison would be responsible for feeding air to Tatsuo while he was on the bottom.

Horace was explicit in his direction. 'If you feel three sharp tugs at the hose, it means Boss wants to come up—*now!* You give 'im two tugs back immediately so he know you got message, savvy?'

'Savvy,' Rennison answered.

Horace caught a hint of condescension, which he put down to immaturity. Trusting it wasn't racially motivated, he made a mental note to watch Rennison with the eye of a hungry eagle.

Tatsuo and Horace knew only too well how things could go wrong. An over-inflated suit could cause a sudden ascent. Or a snag in the air hose could be fatal.

'You see, Tatsuo can only walk across the bottom,' Horace told Rennison. 'He can't swim in this suit.' Horace returned to Tatsuo who was sitting suited, except for the helmet, on the locker hatch. 'Ready, Boss?'

'Aye. Let's do this.'

Aware that there had been chemistry between the skipper and his passenger the past week or so, Horace called to Samoa, 'Samoa, come 'ere. Give me hand, eh?'

With the heavy helmet placed over Tatsuo's head and resting on the corselet, Horace instructed Samoa to tighten the 12 wing nuts, securing the helmet in place. 'Good luck, Cap'n.' Horace had the last say, screwing the glass facemask with its copper safety grill into position.

Samoa couldn't help herself—she took Tatsuo's gloved hand and squeezed hard. Her face told the rest of the story. *Good luck, be careful,* she mouthed. Tatsuo winked back through the glass.

Moments later Tatsuo stepped onto a wooden platform hanging from davits at the stern. With the cutter anchored directly over the wreck site, Horace checked the airflow while Rennison started cranking the flywheel. And with thumbs up from the diver, Horace lowered Tatsuo into the water.

At 30 feet Tatsuo felt the platform touch down. The water was clear and there was a parade of fish. Behind him the coral reef climbed steeply, almost to the surface. It was as though a volcano, millions of years before, had spewed lava into the sea where it solidified and became a home base for live coral. It was really quite stunning.

Tatsuo stepped from the platform and, careful not to snag his umbilical line, fed it behind him, taking his first steps. Thankfully the seabed was reasonably flat, an underwater desert with tufts of seagrass growing sporadically here and there, waving lazily in the current like mermaid's hair. With weighted boots, each weighing 15 pounds, Tatsuo's steps were measured. Beneath the fine sand he could feel loose coral and now he recognised the symmetrical shapes of man-made items, like shards of pottery and metal bolts, all heavily encrusted. The past 20 years of salt water, shipworms and storms had made quick work of the Chinese wooden ship.

From the few scattered remaining timbers Tatsuo ascertained that the *Coral Moon*'s port side had struck the reef. The tsunami had most likely dislodged the junk's remains, from where she had been wedged in a narrow coral gully running reef to shore.

Tatsuo started by exploring the artifact bed. This was a name he gave any wreck site where contents of the ship had spilt out through the shattered hull and onto the seabed. He found little of interest. He then moved back to the edge of the coral reef, where it met the sandy floor. Here many items of shipboard life were scattered, buried in the sand and only exposed when Tatsuo fanned the silt with his glove. Amongst them he picked up a ceramic figure of a man with a long beard, a broken rice bowl, and a ginger jar wedged under some ship beams.

No sign of gold!

He would have to work harder. Tatsuo used his short-handled pick to chip away at the coral where it met the sand, and he soon realised much of the remaining timber was heavily encrusted with calcareous deposits that refused to yield, even with a crowbar. It had been 20 years, after all. Tatsuo located the gully that ran towards the shore like a long crevice. Being deep and narrow it had trapped many artifacts of shipboard life. Tatsuo chipped and hacked at the soft coral and became more enthused as it came free in larger and larger chunks. Ceramic shards, pottery, rusted iron … more pottery. Tatsuo's arm ached. Taking a brief respite, he looked up a moment, watching the air bubbles from his outlet valve flitter to the surface. They almost danced with excitement, rising skywards, escaping like naughty children playing hide and seek before bursting into the tropical sunlight alongside *Mystery*, nearly six fathoms above.

Gold, he muttered to himself, *where the bloody hell are you?* Disturbingly, Tatsuo was having doubts. Maybe the gold was a myth after all.

Tatsuo swung the pick with refreshed energy. Its iron head shattered a lump of coral but immediately smashed open a pot behind it. Suddenly Chinese *cash* coins cascaded from the wound.

Eureka!

He had broached a ceramic pickle jar commonly used to store coins. Tatsuo knew these coins—round with a square hole in the centre, cast in bronze, and known by the name "cash"—were used extensively for trade. They were threaded on string, a thousand each, and the value equaled one tael of pure silver. Now Tatsuo could see a cluster behind the jar—other blue and white jars. Using the point of the pick he prised another free, and another. There we were five in all, but the last jar also broke and a mixture of currency spilt free. Tatsuo recognised many silver coins, mostly English crowns and florins, Spanish *reales*, French francs and German marks. There were others he could not identify. And, having been stored in jars, they had not been affected by encrustations.

Gold, however, eluded him.

But this find was a positive start and Tatsuo was enthused. Storing the hoard in an artifact net he had brought along, he stepped onto the platform and gave the umbilical three short tugs. Slowly he was winched topside. Desperate to examine them in detail, Tatsuo secured the netted coins on a hook beneath the hull, just below the surface, before he was winched on deck empty-handed. Horace unscrewed the faceplate so Tatsuo could speak freely.

'Well, Cap'n,' Horace started, 'any good news?'

'Do you want the good news or the bad news first?'

'Good news,' Rennison said, stepping away from the compressor, grateful to give his arm a rest.

'Sorry, you get the bad news first. I haven't found any gold.'

'Well, I can see that. And the good news?'

'Horace, pull up the net.'

Horace immediately realised the net was hanging under the boat. He climbed down the Jacob's ladder and retrieved it, returning with a huge grin that showed off his white teeth, accentuated against his black face.

'Huh!' he cried out, tipping the jars of coins onto the deck.

Everyone gathered about. Even Pearl was curious enough to sniff the collection.

'Well,' Samoa said, 'that qualifies as a good sign, does it not?'

'There's gotta be a few hundred quid right there,' Selma crowed. The unopened jars were smashed to reveal their contents. 'Silver!'

'They're all silver except the one with a lot of brass cash coins. My reckoning,' Tatsuo said, his voice echoing from within his helmet, 'is that these came from the stern cabin. They probably belonged to Bao Zheng himself.'

'So the gold should be there too, huh?' Rennison said.

'Not if there is half a ton. That would affect the buoyancy of the ship. No, the gold would be ballast in the lower hold.'

'Oh?' Selma said. 'Now what?'

'Well, I'm pretty certain I know where amidships lies, if I follow the stern line, and it's buried under coral. I'm going to have to use dynamite.'

'Dynamite!' Rennison's eyes widened. 'Do you have dynamite?'

'Aye, I have a whole box of the stuff remaining in the hold.'

'Dynamite! We've been sleeping next to a box of dynamite!'

'It's fine. You look after it and it looks after you.'

'Fine.' Rennison had a thought. 'Question.'

'Yes?'

'How do you ignite dynamite under water?'

'Glad you asked … Horace?'

'Aye, Cap'n.'

'Fetch six sticks—that should do it. The detonators are in the separate red box with the waterproofed wire. And then, while I'm down there, you show Mr Plum how it works.'

'Aye, aye.'

Twenty minutes later Tatsuo stood on the bottom six fathoms down, feeling pleased with himself. He ran an experienced eye over the seabed. Twenty feet from the gully exit onto the sand an outcrop of coral rose almost vertically. The shape seemed too symmetric to be completely the work of Mother Nature. After studying the mound he chiseled six inserts six feet apart, where he thought the explosives would be best applied. After inserting the dynamite, already primed on deck, Tatsuo reeled out the individual waterproofed wires leading back up to the cutter.

On board, Horace removed Tatsuo's helmet and Tatsuo alone wired the charges to an electrical detonator. He allowed extra length so the *Mystery* would not be floating over the charge.

'You've done this before, I trust?' Rennison queried.

'Many a time. Have you ever weighed anchor on a boat before?'

'I have, actually.'

'Then shorten up on the anchor chain, sailor.' Tatsuo was in high spirits. 'But just enough to allow us to drift on the outgoing tide. Then, when I tell you, drop her again.'

'Aye, Cap'n.'

Ten minutes later Selma, smiling, said, 'This'll be interesting.'

'What will?' Samoa asked.

'Well, how are those villagers across the lagoon going to handle this?'

'Don't you worry, Selma,' Tatsuo replied with a grin. 'I've a little surprise for them.'

'A surprise! Bloody hell, Tatsuo—it'll be a surprise, alright.'

With the ship at a safe distance the six connectors were fastened to the electric detonator. Six faces looked back towards the reef headland.

'Everyone ready?'

'Aye.' Horace stood next to his skipper, ready to release the switch when Tatsuo gave the nod. Tatsuo looked at his aboriginal shipmate. 'Hope I haven't overdone it,' Tatsuo whispered to Horace.

'Soon know, Boss.'

'Everyone ready?' Tatsuo yelled again, loving a performance.

'Yes.'

'Ready as I'll ever be.'

'Aye, Cap'n.'

'Louder!' Tatsuo shouted. 'I can't hear you!'

'YES!' the others shouted in unison.

Tatsuo cranked the dynamo, revving the wheel faster and faster, building up energy, creating enough electrical current to reach the explosives.

'Now!' he said to Horace.

Horace flicked the switch. There followed a terrifying delay. Then …

If the natives hadn't had an earth tremor in the recent past they sure as hell had one now. The water rippled in a 100-foot radius all around the cutter and six geysers of seawater, from the charges, joined into one plume of water 50 feet high. The *Mystery* lifted on a six-foot wave from the displaced water, while spray, coral chunks and fish rained down all about them.

'There's your answer, Selma.' Tatsuo pointed to the hundreds of dead fish already floating with the tide towards the coral village. 'They'll be barbequing, frying, baking, boiling and smoking fish for days.'

As they watched, canoes paddled away from the village to the excited chattering of villagers scooping up fish like it was a gift from the gods …

And maybe it was.

The explosion also guaranteed these superstitious people would keep away from the wreck site for some time.

The wait was maddening. As they all looked on, it took the tide half an hour to sweep the silt cloud far enough from the wreck site for Tatsuo to go over the side once more. To his intense excitement the sea floor was strewn with rusted cargo, rotting timbers and trade goods that had been on their way to Canton. There was little worth salvaging, though. Tatsuo pulled at the encrusted coral face. Corroded barrel hoops no longer held their wooden staves in place. A black mass was all that was left of some salted pork, and Tatsuo recognised pips from stone fruit that would have fed the crew on the return voyage. The variety was astounding. Tatsuo had no doubt he had found the hold. With enough of the immediate coral loosened, Tatsuo started dragging the remnants of the cargo items, some of them preserved better than others, out into more open water. Hundreds of sealskins, still tied in bundles of a dozen, fell apart at the touch. His frustration was growing when … shadows cast from overhead caught his attention. Sharks.

With so many dead fish floating about the reef, the sharks had grown curious, and were swimming into the lagoon in dozens. As long as they had fish to eat, Tatsuo wasn't overly concerned. His main worry was a shark chewing his air hose; or, more deadly still, his umbilical—he would be trapped on the seabed.

Tatsuo watched in silence for a moment, not moving. He contemplated returning to the surface. Several six-foot reef sharks swam inquisitively by. One came a little too close. Tatsuo smacked it on the nose with the handle of his pickaxe and it swam off in a hurry.

On deck, the others saw the sharks. They were worried. But Horace knew his skipper well. If it became too dangerous the boss would signal to be winched up.

Tatsuo was despondent. He turned back to the hole he had created. More barrels, their shape barely recognisable, were stacked beyond the entrance. He took a swing at the closest. His pickaxe crushed through the rotting staves like butter. Instantly a glitter caught his attention. A glitter reflected in a beam of tropical afternoon sun spearing in from above. A shiny metallic, auric sparkle …

No …

Tatsuo reached in, snatching up the heavy object. He felt his heart race.

Yes!

It *was* gold.

It has to be. Thrusting his gloved hand into the black mess, he saw another gold ingot spill from the remains of the barrel; then another, and another. *They must be packed in sugar cane, tea or hay ... bamboo leaves, maybe.* Whatever it was had rotted.

But who cared? Tatsuo had found gold. Taking one heavy ingot in his palm he rubbed at the blackened packaging with a gloved thumb, finally revealing a stamp. It was Chinese ... Han characters. Tatsuo was certain they read 'Bao Zheng.'

Bao Zheng ... Bao Zheng ... Tatsuo chanted, managing a short, heavy-footed dance. He was laughing in his helmet when a reef shark swam in front of him, catching him unawares. He stepped backwards, tripped on coral and felt himself fall, landing in sand and creating a silt cloud. With the solid copper helmet weighing him down it was difficult to stand—impossible, even—without turning onto all fours to lift himself erect ...

What the ... ?

Tatsuo had exposed a carpet of small gold ingots. *Hundreds of the bastards!* They had been underfoot the whole time. Tatsuo managed to slowly turn completely around, conscious of snagging his air pipe.

Jesus Christ!

Tatsuo yelled into his helmet. He dropped back to his knees and fanned the seabed like a madman.

Gold, gold, gold!

There were hundreds of ingots. No, thousands! These barrels must have been disturbed when the *Coral Moon* broke up on the night of the wreck, or maybe by the tsunami or some other wild storm over the last two decades.

Tatsuo bundled up all he could carry. Sharks circled, more curious than hungry, their bellies already filled with the fish killed by the explosion. He piled ingots as neatly as possible on the raising platform. There was no time to count them. Just cram them onto the platform. When Tatsuo guessed he had his body weight in gold stacked neatly on the platform, he tugged three times and stepped back watching the gold being winched to the surface.

The diving platform disappeared from sight, hitting the water with a splash and sinking quickly. Tatsuo could only imagine the excitement on board the *Mystery*. He stepped onto the platform and tugged the rope, ascending faster than usual into cheers and whoops. Horace spun the faceplate open.

'Cap'n!' Horace's face was alight. 'You done it Boss! 'You actually done it!' Horace grinned like Aladdin discovering the cave of treasure.

Tatsuo had never seen his old mate so excited. Fatigue suddenly caught up with him and he sat heavily on the locker hatch.

'There's more,' he finally managed. 'Much, much more.'

Gold fever had spread amongst the others. 'Really?'

'Yes, really.'

'How much more?'

'It is just how we dreamt of it—well, for me, anyway.'

Selma could hardly manage her words coherently. 'How much much more?'

'Selma,'—Tatsuo turned stiffly in his diving suit, throwing his arms out awkwardly to steal a bear hug, and Selma fell into his stiffened canvas arms—'the seabed is a carpet of gold,' he said lifting her off her feet with a whoop.

'Mother Mary! We've done it!'

'Aye.'

'Well, blow me down.'

'You look exhausted,' Samoa said. 'How about taking a break?'

'A break?' Rennison barked with unconsidered impudence. 'Are you kidding? *I'll* go down.'

'And drown yourself?' Samoa snapped.

'How hard could it be, anyway?'

Tatsuo felt like slipping his diving gear free and locking the man in the suit there and then *and, yes, letting him drown, stupid bastard.*

If there was one thing Tatsuo was aware of, it was that greed—kills—men.

But he was captain of the *Mystery*. He, and only he, would give orders.

'I'm doing one more dive. I figure I'm good for three lifts at four hundred-weight each lift. That's about 450 pounds each lift. I'll have had enough by then. Savvy?'

'Savvy.'

Tatsuo didn't know whether the gathering or the stacking was more tiring. But thoughts of success motivated him. By the last lift he was feeling the effort. Every muscle ached.

Finally, six hours later, Horace freed him from his suit. Selma stood by with four fingers of whiskey, and everyone sat about, staring at their haul. It was a bizarre moment. Unbelievable. Before them, stacked like miniature bricks, nearly five hundredweight of gold, smelted and shaped by Chinese gold diggers 20 years earlier, was displayed before them. A neat pile of gold! And plenty of it.

And it was now theirs.

'We did it,' Tatsuo said with a reverence only treasure seems to demand. He shot his whiskey and Selma poured him another. Tatsuo had been too focussed, too vigilant and too busy on the seabed for the realization to really sink in. Now that he was relaxed, it hit home. If he didn't want to, he would never have to work again. He could buy a new, bigger and better boat ... *No, bugger that, he could buy a* ship.

'Is that really, really ours?' Selma was lightheaded. Until now it had all been in a day's work, but now the realisation weighed on her mind.

'Finders' keepers, Selma.' Tatsuo threw an arm around the old cook's shoulder. 'You can buy that eating house you always talk about, so you don't have to go back to sea.'

Selma eyes were wide with excitement and renewed ambition. 'I could, couldn't I?'

'Aye, my love.' The skipper grinned. 'You could buy a huge hotel if you took the fancy.'

'And give dem other poor buggers the gut ache for a change,' Horace joked.

'You watch yer tongue, there, Horace, yer cheeky blackfella.'

'What *is* the law exactly, concerning finding lost gold, anyhow?' Samoa asked.

'Law?' Selma lost her smile.

'Does it matter?' Rennison swallowed his third whiskey, his eyes fixated on the hoard.

Before sunset, four coral village canoes appeared, heading toward them across the lagoon. Karoo, their chieftain, sat astern the largest canoe, a beautifully crafted vessel with its pearl shell inlay and upward curved bow.

'I wonder what they want,' Samoa said, watching the craft glide alongside.

'Curious, no doubt,' Tatsuo said. 'Just keep smiling. Rennison, Selma, make certain the gold is covered securely … smartly, now.'

'Yes, Boss.'

'Horace.'

'Aye, Cap'n.'

'We need your pidgin expertise, if you please.'

Karoo was keen to come on board and was made welcome. Tatsuo ordered Selma to bring stone bottles of ginger beer on deck and Karoo and his entourage of ten were treated to refreshments. Karoo recognised the flavour of ginger but was astounded at the effervescence of the spicy, sweet drink. After the welcoming ceremony, Horace and Karoo engaged in conversation.

'He ask me, big thunder underwater. Did we do it?' Horace translated.

'Tell him yes.'

'He ask what magic is this?'

'Tell him, "We make thunder to appease the gods and the dead men below who lost their lives byn your beautiful island." They can now go to the spirit world in peace.'

Much nodding of approval followed. The local people seemed to understand.

'Nice work, Tatsuo,' Rennison said casually.

'He wants to know what you have taken from the reef. His warriors have been watching. He say they see many shiny rocks. Coral that shine in the sun.'

'Tell him these belong to the widows and mothers and fathers of the dead. It is their sacrifice to the gods and we must take it to their temple, back where we come from.'

'Nice,' Rennison said.

Karoo seemed satisfied. But he demanded to see the shiny coral close up. 'Selma,' Tatsuo said whilst smiling at the chieftain, 'fetch an ingot, if you please, just the one. Be discreet'

Selma felt under the canvas tarpaulin, slipping an ingot free. She passed it to Karoo who studied it with reverence. He was in awe at its weight and noticed the Han characters stamped on the top. Animated, he passed it to his bodyguards who marvelled at its colour, its shine, its weight. Karoo's voice went up a decibel as he spoke to Horace. Horace looked doubtful.

'What did he say?'

'He said he wants this one trinket, as a gift from our gods to his.'

'Take it,' Tatsuo said with the best smile he could muster after such a request.

'No!' Rennison made to grab the gold bar back from the warrior. 'Are you joking?'

Karoo was taken aback by this sudden change of heart.

Greed—kills—men ...

Tatsuo turned, clamping his fist around Rennison's wrist. 'Leave it!' he said through gritted teeth.

'But ...'

'But nothing.' Tatsuo fixed Rennison with a death stare. Rennison shook his arm free and stormed for'd. Tatsuo held both open palms up to the warrior holding the ingot, and gestured he keep it. Karoo was happy. Plucking a plume from his headband he handed it to Tatsuo, and the tribespeople left as peacefully as they had come.

'What are you doing?' Rennison harangued Tatsuo in an attempt to save face. 'You just gave away two … three hundred pounds, to some … some blackfella primate.' Horace flinched. Rennison ignored the fact that he had just offended the aboriginal. 'Well?' Rennison demanded.

Tatsuo had had enough. He stood so close to the young man, Rennison felt his angry breath.

'Listen to me now and listen good. That *primate* as you call him, happens to be an intelligent and articulate human being. You're the anthropologist, for Christ's sake, you should know better. He is also the chief of hundreds of young, armed warriors. It is their custom to eat … yes, eat, their opponents. If he chose to, he could demand *all* the gold. You hear me? The bloody lot. And never, ever, question my judgment again. Savvy?'

Rennison dropped his eyes to the deck, desperate not to look the fool, especially in front of his sister. 'Well … well, I …'

'SAVVY?'

Rennison nodded, walking to the guardrail, where he watched the canoes returning to the coral village, and brooded.

The evening proved awkward. Samoa apologised for her brother.

'That's not necessary,' Tatsuo said.

'He can be impulsive. And I think the stress of being taken captive and marooned by the Germans, and now the excitement of this … this amazing discovery, well …'

'It's still no excuse, and besides it is not your duty to apologise for him.'

Silence. Another balmy tropical night, seemingly in paradise, was marred by disagreement.

Sunrise

6 AM. Selma brought Tatsuo black coffee with four spoonfuls of sugar. He drank it gratefully where he had slept on deck under the

stars, alongside the pile of gold. By 6.30 AM Tatsuo was suited up and winched down to the seabed. Rennison cranked the compressor, agreeing to alternate each half hour with Selma and Samoa. Horace was skipper while Tatsuo was below. He kept watch and stood by, waiting to hoist up the gold.

It was a long and arduous day. Once again exhausted, Tatsuo took a break in the late afternoon.

'One more dive will do it,' Tatsuo took a long drink of water through a bamboo straw. 'I've definitely collected all the barreled bars from the hold. There's mostly scatterings now, pushed away from the wreck by years of storms.'

'You done good, Cap'n.' Horace nodded proudly.

'A diver could spend weeks down there searching, but I'm confident we have most of it.' Tatsuo looked at the heap of gold bars stacked under the tarpaulin. It stood four feet high and was roughly the same in width and breadth. 'What are *you* going to do, anyway, Horace?'

'What you mean, Boss?'

'Well, you're a rich man now.'

Horace hadn't dared think too hard about it before. Selma could finally open an eating-house, if that's what she wanted and the boss could buy a bigger and better boat. But now those words from his Cap'n—'*You're a rich man now*'—suddenly hit home.

'I don't think you realise how wealthy you are now, Horace.' Tatsuo smiled.

'Jesus,' Horace scratched his head. 'What *does* a rich blackfella do?'

'You'll be the richest blackfella in Australia. You can buy your own lugger, for starters. Buy a fleet of the buggers if you want.'

'Nar. Think I'll move back to Darwin and take care of dem silly blackfellas what need a hand to get off the grog.'

'Very noble of you, my friend. Very noble indeed.'

'I'll miss yer though, Cap'n.'

'No you won't, you silly bugger,' Tatsuo tapped his gloved hand onto his helmet. 'Now seal me up—let's get this over with.'

The last haul was fewer than 20 ingots. Tatsuo was beyond exhausted. His body ached, he was fighting fatigue. But success was sweet. It was time to call it a day. Tatsuo stepped onto the platform to be hoisted to the surface, twisting his air valve to allow more air enter his suit, giving him buoyancy. Instantly his helmet filled with cigar smoke.

Bastard!

Was someone playing a joke?

Tatsuo gave three sharp angry tugs on the umbilical. Immediately the lift started. But something didn't feel right. Tatsuo leant back, an awkward manoeuvre in the solid copper helmet. He peered aloft and saw the hull of second boat, a lugger maybe, not quite the same length as the *Mystery*.

Fearing the worst, Tatsuo waited until he was level with *Mystery's* keel and gave two short tugs. Horace stopped winching.

On deck, one of the crew from the other boat steadied the Webley revolver at Horace's head. 'What are you doing?'

'The Cap'n, he signal me to stop.'

'Why?'

'Sometime he get stuck.'

'Pull him up.'

'I gotta wait for signal.'

'I'm giving you the signal now. Bring him up.'

Minutes later Tatsuo appeared at the surface. Horace hoisted the platform aloft, swinging the davit to lower Tatsuo onto the deck where Tatsuo had a moment to survey the scene. Armed men had boarded his boat and he immediately recognised the leader standing by the compressor, holding a pistol in Rennison's face with one hand and a cigar, awkwardly, in the other. The man still wore one arm in a splint from the cyclone on Turtle Neck Island. The motive was clear, and his heart sank.

'Bastard!' he muttered into his helmet.

Horace wasted no time unscrewing the face portal.

'What's going on, Bligh?' Tatsuo shouted from the confines of the helmet.

Bligh simply puffed on his cigar, motioning to Horace to unbolt the headgear. Fumbling impatiently, Tatsuo stepped from his diving suit dressed only in his loincloth. Bligh looked on; if anything, he was envious of his rival's fine physique. Tatsuo didn't hesitate; he stormed the deck to confront Bligh.

'What the bloody hell do you think you're playing at?'

'Uh-uh. Back you go.' Bligh now aimed his pistol directly at Tatsuo's head. 'Back. One false move, my friend ... One false move.'

Tatsuo hastily looked about him. He counted six men in all. Brannon, Bligh's right hand thug, and four of his native divers from *Victory's Prize*. Two others remained on board the *Beacon*. They were all armed.

'You bastard!' Tatsuo spat. 'You rotten bastard. I saved your arse on Turtle Neck Island after the cyclone and this is how you treat me. Bastard.'

'Yes, well ...' If Bligh harboured a conscience it was on vacation this day. 'That's a lot of gold there for five people. Didn't your mamma teach you to share?'

'Share?'

'Yes, I'm not a totally greedy man, Captain Gaston. I will leave you five bars, one each.'

Tatsuo rushed forward, fists balled, but Bligh fired off a warning shot and instantly two other gun barrels were trained on Tatsuo. It was hopeless. There was no point losing your life over gold.

'You know what?' Bligh huffed. 'Forget it. I'll leave you nothing. Now get aft ... all of you. Now!'

Brannon herded Horace, Rennison and Selma towards the bow at gunpoint while Bligh took Samoa by the arm. 'And as much as it hurts me to do this, I mean you, too, mademoiselle.'

'Get your hands off me!' Samoa tore her arm free to follow the others.

'Where's the moron?' Bligh asked, remembering William. 'The moron, what's his name? F-f-f-f-fuck! William, yes, that's him, f-fucking William.' Bligh laughed at his little joke.

No answer.

'Well?'

Tatsuo remained silent.

'Look below,' Bligh ordered one of his divers.

The native returned minutes later. 'Nuthin', Cap'n.'

'Where is he?' Bligh asked once more.

'He's with the natives, if you must know,' Samoa said coldly.

'Oh, is he now? Doing what, might I ask?'

'Getting a war party together to capture you and your lackeys for a banquet.'

Bligh laughed nervously. Tatsuo felt the corners of his mouth curl. *Damn, that Samoa was good.*

Bligh turned to Brannon. 'Get the gold on board … now!'

With the crew of the *Mystery* bundled at the bow, Bligh was supervising the transfer of the gold onto the *Beacon* when he noticed Tatsuo running an experienced eye over the old lugger.

'She's seen better days, I know,' Bligh told Tatsuo while Brannon supervised the transfer. 'Bought her for 800 pounds and had to borrow most of that.'

'With any luck,' Tatsuo said bitterly, 'she'll sink and take you down with her.'

'Oh, don't be like that,' Bligh tutted. 'You'd do the same if it were you standing here with the gun.'

'You think so?'

'I know so. You always had an eye for gold. What man doesn't?'

Bligh took a draw on his cigar and flicked it in a spiral over the side before turning to watch his men. They had set up a human chain, hand over hand, and the transfer was going smoothly.

'I was going to sail the *Beacon* to Turtle Neck, you know, salvage what I could of the *Victory's Prize*, salvage my cargo of shell, but I kept hearing all these rumours of this golden ship being seen in the Solomons. On a whim, I decided to sail to Bona Bona, and blow me if Ah Sin didn't tell me you had been there, and so had Zamir the Albanian who was bantering on about the ship of gold being lost on Nggela Sule Island.'

One of the men dropped an ingot. It landed on the deck with a heavy thud.

'Be careful, imbecile.' Bligh scowled. 'You lose any overboard and you'll be going for a swim with the sharks.'

Bligh watched in silence as the bar was retrieved. 'Now, where was I? Oh, yes—rumours … Of course I had heard these rumours before and guessed the sly Albanian was sending people on a wild goose chase. Then I happened by Guadalcanal Island and the talk there amongst a family of missionaries down south was that the *Coral Moon,* as I now discover is the name of the ship, was on a reef off the west coast of Malaita. So there we were diving off one reef after another when we had a visit from local savages wanting to trade and … well… here we are.'

Tatsuo was never a man to cross. 'I'll come after you, Bligh.'

'Oh, really, is that the best you can do?'

The bow of the *Mystery* afforded little shade from the noon sun. The heat was softening the pitch between the decking planks and frying Tatsuo and his crew. The request for water was denied. Finally, after two hours, the gold had been transferred to the hold of the *Beacon.* Now Bligh ordered his masterstroke. Two men were lowered off *Mystery's* stern, where they crippled the old pearler by smashing the rudder into splinters.

'Think yourself lucky I haven't sunk this tub,' Bligh said, stepping towards his own vessel.

Tatsuo seethed. He wanted retribution, but knew he was outnumbered, with four native crewmembers training rifles at them. And half a ton of gold was definitely worth killing for. Tatsuo thought himself lucky to be alive. Bligh would have to wait.

The crew that had been left on the *Beacon* unfurled sails while the others prepared to board. Bligh, Brannon and two divers remained on the *Mystery.* Tatsuo shot Brannon the look of death. *Ugly as ever*, Tatsuo thought. Forty-something Brannon ran a hand over his sunburnt, bald pate and through the greasy hair hanging to his shoulders. His tongue rested on his bottom lip, salivating through yellowed teeth … Tatsuo knew what was coming next.

Bligh gave Brannon the nod. Brannon pounced, fastening an iron fist around Samoa's arm. She screamed out. Tatsuo leapt forward, but Bligh fired a warning shot over Tatsuo's head. Tatsuo felt the lead sizzle close by … damned close.

'One step further … !' Bligh shouted. He took three steps towards Tatsuo. His eyes were black, soulless orbs of avaricious evil. 'One—more—step.'

Tatsuo was looking straight down the barrel. Death was a split second away.

Greed—kills—men …

'Leave her, Bligh,' Tatsuo said with as much calm as he could muster. But there was no masking his anger.

Bligh jerked his head hard and two native divers took Samoa from Brannon, dragging her across to the *Beacon*—screaming, shouting, kicking and punching—where she was thrown to the *Beacon*'s deck before being dragged below.

'Don't do this. I'm warning you—don't do this, Bligh.'

'You're warning me? Huh!' Bligh jumped aboard the *Beacon*. Brannon was still on *Mystery*.

Tatsuo leapt to reach him before he could board the other boat, but the man was ready. Twisting suddenly, he cracked Tatsuo across the head with a lead cosh. Tatsuo lost his footing and crumpled, dazed, onto the deck. Rennison made a last-minute attempt to pursue Samoa.

A gunshot exploded.

Bligh's bullet splintered the guard rail. A second shot slammed into the hull. 'Those were warning shots!' Bligh shouted, aiming his Webley at Rennison's chest, only feet away. Rennison froze. 'I don't want to have to kill anyone, savvy,' Bligh said coldly. 'But, by God, I will if I have to.'

Rennison was shaking. 'She's my sister. Please … leave her be.'

'Sister, huh? Well, she's a fiery one, that's for certain.'

'Let her go, I beseech you.' Rennison lowered his tone. 'Take me instead.'

'I don't think so.'

The mooring lines securing the *Beacon* to *Mystery* were loosened and the lugger drifted free. Horace stepped forward with a bucket of seawater and threw it on the captain. Like a dose of smelling salts, the water revived the skipper. He stood groggily with Horace's help.

'No, Bligh! Don't do this!' Tatsuo shouted across the water. 'You've got the gold, damn you. Leave Samoa.'

'Oh, don't trouble yourself, Captain Gaston,' Bligh called back. 'She's only collateral. She's in good hands. I'll set her free in … ah … Tahiti … or somewhere nice. Au revoir, Frenchman. Or should I say "*Adieu pour toujours*"?'

Tatsuo leant, dazed, on the rail for support, fixing an angry glare at the *Beacon*. His bloodshot, angry eyes scrolled up to face Bligh, who was still staring back, smug as ever, but now 20 yards distant.

'Horace,' Tatsuo called, a drizzle of blood trickling over his left eyelid.

'Aye, Cap'n?'

'Fetch rifles.'

'Aye.'

Rennison. 'Rifles? What on earth are you planning?'

'Planning?' Tatsuo scowled, his face deathly serious. 'I'm planning on putting a bullet hole in that bastard's forehead, that's what I'm planning.'

'You can't shoot at them … Samoa's on board. They'll kill my sister.'

Jesus!

Of course Tatsuo knew Rennison was right. Horace hovered over the companionway, waiting to drop below, awaiting further orders. Waiting to fetch guns. Tatsuo looked at his old friend and devoted crewman.

'Belay that order,' he groaned.

'Boss?'

'Belay that order. Fix the bloody rudder so we can chase the bastards.'

'We have to fetch William first,' Selma said.

'Oh, Christ!' Tatsuo buried his face in his hands. With Samoa in trouble he'd completely forgotten his young deckhand, alone with a village of savages. Even if he was revered for his artwork.

'Where's Pearl?' Tatsuo suddenly remembered his dog.

'I'm gettin' her, Cap'n,' Horace called out descending below. 'She bit one of Bligh's men and they locked her below.'

'Good girl,' Tatsuo said with the thinnest of smiles. 'At least someone fought back.'

Horace wasted no time crafting a new rudder. As he went about his work on deck, Tatsuo climbed over the stern and dismantled the broken steering gear, salvaging the bronze fittings. A happy Pearl looked on, her tail wagging her pleasure. Meanwhile Rennison took the spyglass and climbed the ratlines to watch the *Beacon*. She was now under full sail near on a mile away, beating out across the lagoon towards the opening through the reef … and out to sea.

'Rennison!' Tatsuo called out. Rennison looked down to face Tatsuo, his face grey with worry. 'I need you to come with me in the tender to fetch William.'

Rennison nodded solemnly and took one last look through the telescope. Tatsuo turned the cook. 'Selma.'

'Aye.'

'Watch Horace's back.'

'Yes, Boss.'

'Wait!' Rennison yelled out.

Tatsuo stopped. 'What is it?'

Rennison was immediately animated, his eye fixed to the spyglass.

'You may want to see this,' Rennison called out anxiously.

'What is it, for God's sake?'

'Oh … Jesus …'

Tatsuo swung up onto the rigging. He narrowed his eyes, staring out beyond the lagoon, beyond the crashing surf. The *Beacon*, he guessed, was now over a mile away, her bow dipping into the trough of an incoming ocean swell that would take her through the narrow channel in the reef and out to sea. But off to the north something caught his eye. Rennison passed him the telescope. Tatsuo adjusted the eyepiece and focussed. Emerging from the headland outside the reef he made out three ... no, four large native war canoes. Thirty armed men apiece. With the stiff ocean breeze blowing in from the sea Tatsuo could just, barely, distinguish chanting and a rhythmic thrumming of war drums. And they were heading to cut off the *Beacon*.

'This is bad,' Selma said. 'I just know it.'

Approaching fast, the canoes split into two lines of attack.

'Quick, fetch guns! Rennison, you and me, into the tender.' Tatsuo stayed fixed to the telescope. He heard the pop, pop of distant gunfire, but the *Beacon*—although she had now cleared the reef— was pathetically outnumbered. With a fresh southerly in the tender's mainsail Tatsuo and Rennison skipped across the lagoon.

'Now what?' Rennison shouted through the wind, spray whipping his face.

'Make sure those rifles are loaded.' Tatsuo held the tiller steady. 'But hide them under the tarp.'

'And then what?'

'And then ... I'm not sure. I'll let you know when we get there.'

'Oh, Christ!'

Beyond the coral reef the war canoes, low in the water, were difficult to see. But Tatsuo knew their paddlers were strong and that the canoes moved fast. He held the tiller firm. With the escaping pearler well beyond the coral reef, Tatsuo could only make out the top of *Beacon*'s mast over the rise in the coral. She was now on open water. But the canoes were out of sight behind the reef.

Rennison was nervous. 'Where are the canoes?'

'Can't see them.'

Instantly several more distant gunshots were heard.

Minutes later the tender sailed level with the reef's channel to the open ocean. Suddenly the war canoes appeared. They paddled into the mouth of the channel. They had abandoned *Beacon* and were turning back.

'Oh! This doesn't look good.'

The canoes surfed over breakers rolling into the lagoon. One hundred and twenty armed warriors paddled towards them ... at a frightening pace.

The chanting and war drums grew louder. Closer.

'We ... we can't outrun them ...' Rennison's words broke through the terrible fear clogging his throat.

Tatsuo heard shouting from the shore. He turned. Another hundred or more savages gathered on the beach. They cheered and danced, building into an animated frenzy. The war canoes passed through the reef channel into the lagoon and approached at speed. Again they fanned out. They surrounded the tender.

'Jesus.' Rennison swallowed hard. He dropped to the bottom boards, picking up a rifle. He checked the bolt action.

'No!' Tatsuo yelled from the tiller. 'Put the gun down. With any luck they'll be friendly.'

The first canoe drew close. There was no option. Act submissive.

'Friendly?' Rennison said nervously. 'They don't look friendly.'

'Reef the sail.'

Rennison didn't argue. Tatsuo braced for conflict.

Immediately a familiar voice ...

'Cap'n! ... Hey, Cap'n!' the familiar voice shouted across the water.

'Will?'

Young William pumped the air with excitement. Tatsuo stood, scanning the approaching war party, finally catching William's scrawny white figure amongst the natives.

And look at you, lad!

William was balancing awkwardly, waving frantically, while Chief Sulufou sat on the stern seat, grinning with approval. William was naked to the waist, his face adorned with war paint and wearing brightly coloured plumes in his hair held by a headband. Tatsuo had never seen the lad so excited. The canoes surrounded them and a dozen hands secured the tender alongside.

'Samoa!' Rennison yelled out. 'Samoa! Sis, is that really you?'

Tatsuo scanned the other canoes and saw Samoa—dripping wet, but safe. She must have jumped overboard from *Beacon* and been rescued by the warriors.

'What the hell?'

Tatsuo hoisted William, who was closest, into the tender.

'And where did you come from?'

'From what I gather, Cap'n, word came to the village that you were in danger, that another whitefella boat was attacking you.'

'Really?'

'Aye, 'cos there was a sudden commotion and Sulufou was angry and then I was dragged along. I didn't have a clue at first, 'til I seen the *Beacon*. Bloody Bligh took shots at us. What's Bligh doing here, anyway?'

'Long story, Will,' Tatsuo said over his shoulder, preparing to help Samoa on board.

'Did yer find the gold, Skipper?' William asked.

'Like I said, it's a long story.'

Tatsuo helped Rennison lift Samoa into the clinker.

'You alright?' Tatsuo asked, barely concealing his concern.

'Oh, I'm just dandy,' Samoa gasped, the ordeal having fueled her adrenalin. 'Just terrific,' she said, her words spilling from her like bullets from a Gatling gun. 'Brilliant. Couldn't be better. Kidnapped, manhandled. Shot at. Nearly drowned.'

'Shot at?'

'What?'

'You said "shot at."'

'Well, it felt like it.'

Samoa looked back at her saviours, who made no bones about staring at her in her wet clothes, which clung to her body like a glove. Tatsuo noticed also. It left little to the imagination, black man or white man. Tatsuo wanted to hug her there and then but it was neither the time nor the place. They exchanged smiles.

'Sorry,' Samoa apologised, melting in Tatsuo's presence.

'For what?'

'For sounding ungrateful. It's just that … well, I thought …'

Tatsuo silenced Samoa by taking her hand. He squeezed hard.

'There's no need to apologise.'

Samoa smiled. She took in a deep breath. 'Let's get back to the *Mystery*.'

Tatsuo singled out the chieftain watching the unfolding events from the comfort of his stern seat on board the largest canoe. He placed a balled fist against his heart and nodded a serious smile. The old native returned the salute, barked orders at the warriors and they parted ways.

'I will forever be grateful to them,' Tatsuo said, watching the sleek vessels cut through the water like mystical sea creatures.

Rennison hugged his sister. 'What happened?'

'Well, I was below deck,' she said, 'when I heard the gunshots. Gunshots!' She reiterated. 'Those monsters were shooting at the natives.'

'Yes, we heard. Then what?'

'Well, with all the commotion I managed to get on deck unnoticed. Then I saw the canoes. And I thought, *God, we're all dead. These natives mean business.* But then I saw William.' Samoa looked at William. 'And weren't you a sight for sore eyes!'

'So how did you … what did you do next?'

'Well, I realised William was there, and I recognised the chief …'

'Sulufou.'

'Yes, Sulufou. I couldn't believe it.' Samoa was prattling again, excited.

Tatsuo could not have wished for a better outcome. The woman was fearless. She was a woman after his own heart. Many other women, or men for that matter, would have capitulated under the circumstances. Now here she was, bursting with enthusiasm, her long blond hair wet and matted from her swim. It took a near catastrophe to realise how fond he had grown of this … this Scandinavian, German, English woman, or whatever she was. Samoa broke away from her brother's embrace and took Tatsuo by his wrists.

'Brannon,' she managed to say between breaths, 'that disgusting man, and some of the others, fired shots at the canoes.'

'Yes. Were any natives killed?'

'No. They were trying to scare them off, I think. But as the canoes got closer they wounded one or two.' Samoa snatched a breath. 'I made a run for it, but Bligh caught me by the leg,' Samoa hadn't finished yet, her words rushing forth like a whitewater rapid. 'So I grabbed his bad arm, the arm injured from the cyclone at Turtle Neck Island, and I twisted it.' Samoa bunched her fists before her and wrung them like she was wringing laundry. 'You should have heard him scream.'

Rennison laughed. 'Good for you, Sis.'

'And he let go?' Tatsuo said, grinning with admiration.

'That's when I dived overboard and the first canoe picked me up.'

'That's when they gave up the chase?'

'Yes, well they saved my life.'

'Pity …'

'Pity?'

'Sorry, that sounded wrong.' Tatsuo shook his head. 'I meant it's a pity they hadn't captured the *Beacon* with all that gold on board.'

'The gold!' For a moment everyone had forgotten about the gold.

'So you did find the gold?' William asked, incredulous.

'Yes.'

'How much?'

'How much? Enough to buy Australia.'

'We're rich.'

'You mean … we *were* rich.'

'What do you mean *were*, Cap'n?'

'It's a long story, lad.'

'That bastard you call Bligh,'—Rennison's face reddened—'stole it from us,'

'What? How?' Will asked, incredulous.

'We were ambushed, held up, robbed at gunpoint.'

'How on earth did he know where to … I mean how?'

'It's a long story.' Rennison tugged at the ropes on the mainsail. 'We need to get back to the reef,' he said to Tatsuo. 'Right?'

'Aye.'

'And then what?' Samoa asked.

'We chase after them, that's what!' Tatsuo said, grinding his teeth, watching the *Beacon's* sail fade over the horizon.

Chapter Ten

The channel between Nagho ni ara and Nggela Island to the north

It was no picnic for a sailboat in the doldrums. The sea was a millpond, while the sails hung limp in anticipation, like an oversized suit of clothes draping a man who's lost half his body weight fasting. All on board the *Beacon* were desperate. In their haste to escape Half Moon Reef on the west coast of Malaita they hadn't refilled their water kegs.

Bligh rationed the water. After three days of calm, all the gold in the world couldn't buy the crew a drink.

So *Beacon* was easy pickings for a German admiral, Admiral Gustav von Stosch, steaming southeast across the Solomon Sea on board the SS *Prinzessin*. The German gunboat was returning to the Shoal of Ghosts with unfinished business with a German fugitive they had marooned on the shoal earlier. A fugitive they knew as Horst Schwarz, alias Rennison Plum. Yandina Island, only two days sail northwest and the supposed site of the Chinese treasure ship, according to the fugitive, had proven a wild goose chase, and Admiral Gustav von Stosch could not believe he had been so gullible.

Greed will do that ...

Now, here they were, half a day's sail from the Shoal where they had marooned *'that lying bastard—Horst, Rennison, whatever the bastard's real name was—*and here was the first lugger they had seen in a fortnight. A sailboat stuck in the middle of nowhere.

'Another gunrunner, more than likely.' The Admiral exchanged a villainous grin with the German ship's captain, Captain Herr von Schtumpf. The captain was of the same opinion. Luggers had been selling the natives guns for a few years now, and all those guns seemed to be trained against the Germans.

If Bligh looked worried, he had good reason. Half a ton of gold was not easy to hide, and as they had not expected to be boarded any time soon, they had hardly hidden the hoard.

The German steamer reversed engines, to drift alongside the *Beacon*. Bligh noticed with interest that the German gunboat's for'd gun was badly damaged, and if he didn't think it unlikely he would have guessed they had been in a scrap, maybe with the Royal Navy.

'Who ees da *kapitän*?' Schtumpf called through his speaking horn, in his faltering English.

'I am!' Bligh called back to the SS *Prinzessin's* bridge. 'Captain Bligh!'

'Bligh?' If the German captain thought the name was familiar, he couldn't quite put a finger on it.

'What can I do for you?' Bligh asked, fidgeting anxiously.

'Ve are coming on board.'

'On board. What for?'

'We have goot reason to thinking you have guns on board. Many guns to trade in thees islands.'

'Guns! No. There are no guns on board.'

'Ve are sending men onto your boat for inspection, *ja*.'

'You can't do that.'

'Oh, but I am thinking, *ja*, ve can. Ve are German Imperial Navy und thees ees international seas, *ja*.'

There was nothing Bligh could do besides signal to the men closest to hurry below and make certain the gold was covered. Immediately a dozen German marines dropped over the side of the German ship and onto the deck of the *Beacon*.

Less than five minutes had passed when the sergeant of the guard reappeared. 'Best you come on board, Kapitän. See for yourself.'

'Guns?'

'Better than guns, sir.'

It took ten minutes to help the old Admiral onto *Beacon* but he had been told it was a sight he should not miss. His imagination ran away with him, eager to see what all the fuss was about.

'*Mein gott!*' In the hold the old Admiral picked up an ingot, hefted the weight and grinned. He could not believe what he was experiencing. He inspected the markings. 'A Chine stamp,' he noted to the German captain. 'This is the gold we were looking for,' he said. 'See the Chinese markings?'

'Unbelievable. How?'

Back on deck Schtumpf confronted Bligh. 'Vere did you get thees?'

Bligh was assailed by a combination of anger and fear. He refused to answer.

'Get that gold on board the *Prinzessin,* now!' Admiral Stosch ordered his marines.

Although he could not understand German, Bligh understood the order. 'No!' he exploded. 'No! That is my ... our gold.'

'Vell it ees for da Vaterland now,' the captain laughed in English. '*Ja.*'

'Thief! You can't do this!' Bligh flew at the first marine appearing from below deck with an arm full of ingots, knocking him to the deck. Immediately he had a rifle muzzle hard against the back of his neck.

'Be calm, *Kapitän* Bligh, or I vill feed you to ze sharks.'

'But you can't ...' Bligh was near tears. 'It is ours. We earned it.'

'Stole eet, I am thinking. Now eet is for da Vaterland.'

Bligh started to plea further but he was silenced with a sharp rifle butt to the shoulder. The pain was unbearable, shooting down his wounded arm, and Bligh sat heavily before he fainted.

Once the gold was safely on board the SS *Prinzessin* the Admiral barked orders from the bridge.

'The admiral, he say all aboard your tender,' the English-speaking sergeant told Bligh.

'What?'

'Get into your tender, you can have sextant, nutheen else.'

'Why … what …'

'NOW! *Schnell* … English bastards.'

The last of the marines hurried from the hold. 'Done?' the sergeant asked.

'*Ja*, all done.'

'Goot.' He turned back to Bligh and his crew, all looking extremely nervous. 'Get into your fuckeen boat. Now. *Schnell*. Bastards.'

'You're not stranding us out here in the tender?' Bligh's words were futile.

'You have about ten seconds.'

'What?'

The sergeant and the last marines scrambled back onto their ship, where the captain on the bridge called back to Bligh and his crew with his speaking horn …

'*Funf … vier … drei … zwei …*

Suddenly a loud explosion blasted the bottom out of the *Beacon*. The lugger listed to starboard and while Bligh's crew endeavoured to catch their balance, the German ship steamed off to put some distance between itself and the sinking lugger.

Before Bligh realised how dire his situation was, two smaller explosions finished the job. By the time the men had fought each other for position in the *Beacon's* tender, the lugger's bow nosed skywards before sinking stern first and disappearing forever.

Bligh looked like he wanted to cry. To come so far …

German bastards!

Bligh's right-hand man, Brannon, wasted little time having the crew erect a spare oar as a mast. A small emergency sail kept in the tender's locker was soon set.

Bligh finally resigned himself to trying to survive. 'By my reckoning we are a hundred miles east of the island of Nagho ni ara,' he told Brannon.

Neither Bligh nor Brannon mentioned the darkening clouds to the native divers. The dark clouds gathering to the east, and blowing in their direction. Yes, the stillness was deserting them but what was replacing the calm looked worrying. Within the hour they enjoyed a stiffening breeze. But with eight men on board the tender was cramped and vulnerable.

'We have a fair wind behind us, men,' Bligh said. 'If we can keep up the pace we should reach land in three days.'

'German bastards,' Brannon growled, his fists balled and keen to punch something, anything.

'Did you see their for'd gun?' Bligh finally asked Brannon.

'Aye. They were attacked by the Royal Navy.'

'Attacked!'

'Aye. I overheard some men talking when they were stealing our gold.'

'Oh?'

'I heard "*Englische Marine*" and it means English Navy, so I got to ask one of the crew, who spoke English.'

'And?'

'He said they were ambushed at Wakanai Bay in Bougainville. He said the *Englische* shot at them like the cowardly bastards they are. Now he said he will be longer than he hoped getting back to the bars and whores in New Guinea.'

'Why?'

'There's damage near the ship's waterline as well. They'll need repairs, so they're headed to Buala on Santa Isabel Island where there is a German settlement.'

Bligh knew Buala well enough. The Germans had declared a protectorate over the island 12 years earlier in 1885.

'That's all very well, but of no use to us.'

With the gold on board the SS *Prinzessin* locked safely in the hold, Admiral Stosch and Captain Schtumpf were two contented sailors. The men enjoyed a late lunch, finishing with coffee and schnapps in the captain's stern cabin. They were alone.

'Half?' Schtumpf queried the Admiral's judgment. 'Do you think we can get away with half?'

'Of course.' Stosch skolled his schnapps and refilled his glass. He and Schtumpf were both over the moon. What had been the chances of apprehending the lugger with the gold?

The admiral ran a hungry eye over the remains of the meat platter on the table before them.

'We will have to pay off a few people to silence them, like the purser,' Stosch said, 'but we can easily skim half.'

Captain Schtumpf had to pinch himself. Was this really happening? 'How did they find the gold before anyone else?'

'Who cares, my friend? Who cares?' Stosch plucked up a cold sausage and bit into its spiced filling. 'Think about what you are going to do with your 20 per cent.'

'Twenty per cent?' the captain coughed. 'What do you mean 20 per cent …'

'Ha! I am just joking with you. Pulling your leg.' Stosch wiped his greasy lips on a serviette.

'Joking, huh? Of course.' The captain managed a strangled laugh. But inside his stomach knotted. 'I must return to the bridge, give the order to sail to Buala for repairs, before we sail to Herbertshohe,' he said, Herbertshohe being the settlement on the German-occupied section of New Guinea, also known as Wilhelm Land.

'Wait.' The Admiral gulped another schnapps and thumbed tobacco into his Meerschaum pipe. 'We have unfinished business on the Shoal of Ghosts.'

'Horst Schwarz!'

'Yes.'

'I'd forgotten about him.'

'We had better be certain the British fell for our plan.'

'And be certain he isn't starving there.'

'Exactly.' The Admiral set his pipe aside for a moment—there was meatloaf remaining. Folding two thin slices of *leberkäse* together with a pickled onion, he crammed it into his mouth. 'Also we must be certain he doesn't know too much, and, besides, he betrayed us both, sent us on a wild goose chase.'

'Let him die there. We have the gold.'

'It is tempting. But as you well know, my friend, we have other duties.'

'Then I will direct the ship to the shoal.'

Next morning. The Shoal of Ghosts

The SS *Prinzessin* sailed through the night—no problem for a steamship in the doldrums. Now, however, stillness had been replaced with a heavy swell, turning into rough seas, where changing seasons created conflicting wind directions. By sunup they were anchored 200 yards off the Shoal of Ghosts. There was no sign of the man they had marooned here.

'Can't see any sign of life,' the captain muttered, his bushy eyebrows fluttering above the binocular lenses.

'Give me those.' Admiral Stosch wrestled the glasses from the captain. He focussed on the rocky outcrop and shuddered. *What a god-awful place.* 'Where *is* the fool?'

'Maybe he was rescued.'

'Rescued!' Stosch harrumphed. 'Out here? It's unlikely.'

'May I suggest he's hiding in one of those small caves, sir?' an officer on the bridge suggested.

Stosch harrumphed once more. He had not as yet partaken of breakfast and was feeling cranky. 'Send a shore party over, and be quick about it.'

A sergeant of the marines returned half an hour later. Unable to land because of the rough seas, they had sailed the perimeter instead. There was nowhere to hide, except the shallow caves, and they appeared to be empty. 'Nothing, Captain, Admiral. No sign of him.'

'He's definitely not cowering in one of those caves?'

'No, sir, it's very doubtful. Besides, if you don't mind me saying, sir, wouldn't you come out with your hands in the air, grateful to be taken aboard ship, even as a prisoner? I mean, look at the place—it's terrifying.'

'Maybe he drowned.'

'Or committed suicide.'

'Or went for a swim.' This thought gave them all shivers.

The admiral weighed his options. He would just have to hope the man was dead. 'Then we shall steam directly to Buala for repairs, and then it's back to Herbertshohe in New Guinea.'

And then, the admiral wanted to shout out loud, *it's back to civilisation in Europe as a very, very wealthy man,* ja!

A day and a half later

Captain Bligh and his eight companions huddled in the *Beacon's* 15-foot boat. They had survived one pounding after another. The weather was unpredictable, and mostly angry. *Like a woman scorned.* Now, on day three, the seas were building and the men were terrified. To make matters worse, the clinker was showing signs of falling apart and they feared it would break up any moment.

Then, on the crest of one huge wave Bligh was certain he saw a ship, still some way off. With the black clouds overhead little light filtered through, but Bligh thought the ship was white-hulled. Could that be the German ship still prowling in the area? With mixed feelings he was deciding whether or not to tell the others when …

'Land!'

'Where?'

'Dead ahead.'

Men stood unsteadily, looking through the heavy rain that now hampered their vision.

'It's land alright.' The patches of white that Bligh had thought might be the hull of the German ship were bird shit, and a lot of it.

'Looks like a shoal—it's just a coral reef.'

'Well, it's better than drowning out here, lads!' Bligh yelled over the increasing storm and held the tiller straight.

Twenty minutes later the *Beacon's* tender entered the outer ledge of this coral outcrop. As uninviting as this shoal was, it was land, solid ground underfoot, for eight exhausted castaways. Bligh weighed his options. A huge surf was crashing over the jagged coral shore and the current was taking them in fast. There was no choice but to surf ashore and pray to God they would make it.

Either way, men, Bligh wanted to shout, *we're going for a swim!*

A returning wave, spent from pummelling the coral ledge, rolled back under the tender. The small boat dropped nose-first into the trough left behind. Bligh deserted the helm and prepared for the worst. The boat lifted on the next mountain of water. Ten feet, 20 feet in the air. Eight men gripped the gunwales and sucked in deep breaths. On the crest of the breaker—a mass of boiling whitewater—the boat turned broadside. They were at the mercy of Neptune himself. The boat capsized, flinging its passengers helplessly into the sea. scattering them like skittles.

The tender shattered onto the coral, shredding into tinder. Four men were dragged under the shoal ledge to drown immediately. Bligh and Brannon, and one other in the stern, were washed onto the shoal as the clinker broke up. Wounded, badly lacerated from the coral, they dragged themselves to the only high ground. A shout had Bligh turn back. One of the native divers, whose legs were clearly broken, screamed out for help. But as they watched, another wave washed over the man and dragged him back out to sea.

Crawling, exhausted, gasping, the survivors made it to high ground, a small steep-sided mound of coral. The only native diver to survive was bleeding profusely and there was little Bligh could do to help the man. Nearly drowned, wounded and miserable, the remaining gold thieves took in their godforsaken surroundings. On the one hand they *were* alive … yet on the other hand …

Bligh knew the Coral Sea. He recognised the shoal and his heart sank even further, for he knew now exactly where they were …

On the Shoal of Ghosts.

The *Beacon* proved easier to find than those aboard *Mystery* expected. After crafting a new rudder, they had sailed silently off into the night even though storm clouds gathered on the horizon ahead. While the mood on board the *Mystery* was at a low, William's tales of adventure with the savages put the occasional smile on their faces.

William told of how he'd befriended the younger natives, who took him to a secret place half a mile inland, well off the pathway, camouflaged behind a thicket of poison-leaf *nalato* bushes. Here he found a miniature communal hall built by the younger boys in the village. It was a faultless copy of the adult communal hall. Inside were the boys' own trophies, skulls of rats and iguana and lizards preserved over smoke.

In the short time he was there he learnt how to hunt with a bow and arrow and a few words of their language. But then urgent warnings came to the village about the unwelcome strangers boarding the *Mystery* and threatening the bones of the whitefellas' ancestors so revered, lying on the reef seabed.

The rest was history.

Mystery sailed through the bad weather and into the night after the storm blew east and the worst of a short squall passed overhead. Tatsuo and Horace knew these waters well and were confident, sharing the helm through the long hours of darkness. Tatsuo was keen to sail back to north Queensland as soon as time permitted. He hoped to track down *Beacon* by asking around the islands, if they were smart enough and fast enough.

Of one thing Tatsuo was certain; that amount of gold made men greedy and loose-lipped. They were likely to be exchanging ingots for cash and splashing money about on booze and whores.

'And,' Tatsuo reasoned with his passengers and crew, 'where better to start, than Bona Bona Island off the south coast of New Guinea?'

By first light the next morning the weather had settled and Tatsuo estimated they were 20 nautical miles east of Guadalcanal, when Horace noticed flotsam and jetsam floating on the surface.

'Looks like wreckage, Cap'n,' he told Tatsuo. The others gathered at the rail.

'That's wreckage, alright.' Rennison pointed out what appeared to be a section of a wheel housing. The debris trail became prolific, with many smaller items floating with the current. But no one expected to find a portion of the stern nameplate bobbing on the waves. Horace fetched a long-handled fishing gaff and hoisted the piece of timber on board. There was enough remaining of the nameplate to read …

'B—E—A—C ,' Samoa read aloud, astounded.

'*Beacon!*'

'No!' Tatsuo felt sudden defeat. 'Not the *Beacon*—Jesus, no.'

Rennison studied the floating debris field. 'There doesn't appear to be any sign of the tender here. Maybe they saved themselves.'

Tatsuo's first thought was, *Who cares if they got away or not.* 'The gold's gone down with the lugger.'

'Maybe, just maybe, they managed to save the gold,' Rennison suggested hopefully.

'Half a ton of gold in a 15-foot clinker? I don't think so.'

'But they may have salvaged some of it.'

'Possibly.'

'I mean, if that had been us we would have managed a few bars each, would we not?'

'Fine. Let's say you're right. But they could be anywhere.'

'Look, we're in the channel, aren't we?'

'Aye.'

'Well, there are many shoals here. I mean, I was marooned on one, for Christ's sake.'

'Shoal of Ghosts.' Tatsuo studied the current. He checked the sun, making a debut after days of bad weather. It was true there were many shoals in this area, and, as far as he could ascertain, the current and wind were in favour of the Shoal of Ghosts. 'What have we got to lose?'

'That's the spirit,' Rennison replied.

'Bligh's also a good sailor,' Tatsuo said. 'As much as I hate to admit it, he knows the sea; they could have made it to Guadalcanal.'

It was bittersweet for both parties. Bligh and one other survivor, his right-hand thug, Brannon, stood at the pinnacle of the shoal's highest point and waved their shirts in a frantic attempt to attract the attention of the vessel several miles out to sea. Morning had arrived, offering a pleasantly calm sea, the calm after the storm. Offshore, various dorsal fins patrolled the waters, reminding the castaways of their dire situation. Lying at their feet was the native diver who had bled to death not long after they'd crawled ashore the day before. Gathering about the base of the pinnacle were hundreds of the shoal's fist-sized orange crabs. They could smell blood.

Bligh lashed out with his boot, crushing the closest as a warning. All night they had been keeping the crabs at bay, but now an element of confidence returned. 'They've seen us! They've seen us!' Bligh yelled as the sail turned towards the shoal. But the moment the ship went about he realised it was the *Mystery*.

Bittersweet indeed.

'Is it them, Cap'n?' Horace asked anxiously.

Tatsuo pressed the spyglass hard to his eye. 'You know what,' he said out of the corner of his mouth, 'I bloody well think it is.'

'Really?' Selma grinned. She was spoiling for a fight.

'How on earth did they end up there?'

'Yep, that's Bligh, alright, and his mate Brannon.'

'Brannon!' Samoa felt her teeth grind.

'You done good, Cap'n.' Horace slapped a hand on the skipper's back.

'And,' Tatsuo added, his eye remaining glued to the glass, 'the bastard's stopped waving.' Tatsuo had a wry smile. 'He's recognised us. Oh sweet Jesus, isn't this justice, eh?'

Rennison took up the spyglass. 'Bligh, you thieving bastard.'

'Horace,'—Tatsuo grinned—'fetch a rifle.'

'A rifle, Cap'n?'

'You're not going to shoot him?' Samoa said. 'Surely?'

'Why not?' Selma said through gritted teeth.

'Now, that's an idea,' Tatsuo replied, grinning, 'but, no, I'm going to scare the bastards.'

Tatsuo trained the telescope across the shoreline and made out pieces of wreckage from the tender, scattered along the coral ledge. 'But if that's the *Beacon*'s tender splintered on the coral, which it must be, then we can say goodbye to any gold.'

With such a calm day dawning, it was another hour before the *Mystery* furled her sails and dropped anchor in deep water 20 yards off the shoal. Even the birds seemed to have settled.

'You dog, Bligh!' Tatsuo yelled, his words travelling clearly across the calm of a perfect day. 'Looks like you got your comeuppance!'

'Thieving bastard!' Selma screamed out.

Bligh stared back, a picture of desperation, with pleading eyes. He looked miserable and weak from exhaustion, and his shoulders sagged in submission.

'Where's our gold, Bligh?'

'Parley,' Bligh called back. His voice was broken and frail.

'What?'

'Parley ...' Bligh motioned with his hand for Tatsuo to come ashore.

'He said "parley,"' Samoa said. 'He wants to talk.'

'He wants us to save his arse, that's what,' Selma said. 'Let him rot there, I say.'

Pearl had her say also, front paws up on the guardrail, barking at the pathetic sight. Bligh was pleading, beckoning them ashore.

'Why should I give you the time of day, Bligh, you thieving bastard?'

'P-please.' Bligh's voice was weak. 'We need to talk.'

'What?'

'We need to talk.'

'Talk! Why? Clearly you've lost the *Beacon* and our gold, you thieving mongrel.'

'No. Not at all.' Bligh brightened somewhat. He had an ace up his sleeve. 'I know where the gold is.'

'It's all lies,' Samoa said to Tatsuo, too angry to speak to Bligh.

'What do you mean?' Tatsuo called back. 'You know where the gold is?'

Horace shook his head, exasperated. 'It's on da sea bed, Boss. Dat where da bloody gold is.'

'The *Beacon* was sunk, was it not?' Tatsuo asked.

'Aye. But we were …' Bligh paused a moment as if the memory was too raw for him to say the word 'robbed.' 'We were robbed.'

'Huh! You expect us to believe that?' Rennison shouted.

'Robbed by who?' Selma yelled out. 'Blackbeard the pirate?'

'Maybe they buried it somewhere,' William suggested. 'On an island.'

'They just want us to save their arses.' Rennison said, running the lens over the shallow caves beneath the castaways. 'Where's the rest of his crew, anyway?' he asked the others.

'It might be an ambush.'

'Where's your crew?' Tatsuo yelled.

'Gone … They're all dead. Drowned when we wrecked here.' Bligh remembered the body at their feet. '*He* died last night,' he said, kicking the cadaver.

'So who robbed you?'

'We need to talk … on board the *Mystery* … I'll tell you everything.'

'Tell me now.'

'No. Take us aboard first.'

'It could be a trap,' Rennison interjected.

'Give me that gun,' Selma said, reaching out for the loaded rifle in Horace's hands. 'I'll shoot the bastard myself.'

'No. Truly,' Bligh pleaded. 'You *must* believe me.'

'We *do* know where the gold is!' Brannon now managed to shout.

Before anyone aboard *Mystery* knew what was happening, Selma fired off a shot. The bullet slammed into coral at the castaways' feet and orange crab shell and guts sprayed about. Bligh and Brannon skipped on the spot.

'Don't shoot!' Bligh begged, his voice cracked and terrified.

'I trust you were aiming at the coral?' Tatsuo asked Selma over his shoulder.

'Aye.' Selma seemed momentarily satisfied. 'But I tell yer...'

'Don't shoot,' Bligh said anxiously. 'We meant you no harm back at the reef.'

'No?' Tatsuo pointed to his head. 'I've still got a lump on my head where you hit me, Brannon.'

'He meant to cause you no injury.' Bligh spoke for Brannon.

'No! But what part of *you stole our gold* don't you get?'

'We know where the gold is. We can help you retrieve it.'

'Where is it, then?'

'I'll tell you when you take us on board.'

'Selma,' Tatsuo shouted for Bligh to hear, 'shoot them!'

'Aye, Cap'n.' Selma shouldered the rifle.

'Just a scare, mind,' Tatsuo said quietly.

The Enfield kicked into the old ship cook's shoulder as another bullet thundered from the muzzle. Another crab exploded amongst shards of coral.

'Jesus!' Bligh cried out. 'Please, I beseech you! Don't shoot!'

'The gold?' Samoa called out.

'The gold is safe.' Bligh remained crafty.

'Fuck him, fuck you ... f-fuck! B-bullshit! Don't trust 'im Cap'n,' William spit out.

Bligh looked beyond exhaustion; he was weakening further, the ordeal having taken its toll. 'Please, Tatsuo, I beg you. Take us on board. I am telling you the truth.'

'Bah!' Selma raised the rifle. The two captives cowered. Tatsuo reached out and pushed the gun barrel down. He eyed the castaways carefully. The Shoal of Ghosts was a terrifying place to be stranded, but Tatsuo wasn't feeling benevolent. Neither was Rennison, and he knew the perils of the shoal intimately. But both men wanted that gold, and if there was a single word of truth in that dog Bligh, then they needed to know. The swell was picking up and the tide changing. The *Mystery* tugged at the anchor chain. 'Horace.'

'Cap'n.'

'You and Will get the tender in the water.'

'Cap'n? But …'

'Do as I say. I'll go and talk to the bastard. If there is any truth in what he says, I think we need to know.'

'I agree,' Samoa chimed in.

'I'm coming with you,' Rennison declared.

'Selma.'

'Aye, Cap'n.'

'Keep a bullet in the breach and a sharp eye.'

'Aye, Cap'n.' Selma loved the sense of adventure she had with her beloved Captain Tatsuo Gaston. She knew exactly what the boss had in mind. *Watch his back.*

Minutes later, while Horace and Will kept oars in the water at a safe distance off shore, Bligh limped to the coral ledge, as close as he could. Brannon seemed worse off.

'You're a thieving bastard, Bligh,' Tatsuo said. 'You've got one minute to convince me why I shouldn't leave you here to die.'

'Please … Tatsuo. I … I'm sorry.'

'Sorry doesn't cut it. The gold?'

'The gold is safe. We were robbed at sea, in the calm two days ago.'

'By whom?'

Bligh, cagey as ever, prevaricated. 'Ah … well …'

'By who, Bligh? Who robbed you?'

'Like I said, take us on board and I'll tell you everything.'

'The gold! Where is it?'

'I'll tell you when you take us on board.' It was Bligh's only trump card.

Tatsuo turned to Horace and Will. 'Take us back.'

'Aye, Cap'n.'

The oars dipped. 'No! Wait!' Bligh screamed.

Tatsuo, his back to the sea, held up his hand to his rowers. 'Well?'

'It was stolen from us at sea, like I said. I know where they're taking it. We can retrieve it. I'll help you.' Tatsuo turned to his rowers once more. 'It's the only security I have,' Bligh pleaded. 'If I tell you, you'll abandon us.'

'Try me.'

'Tatsuo. Please.'

'Take us back,' Tatsuo ordered the crew.

'It was the Germans!' Bligh screeched. Tatsuo looked back to Bligh, who sighed the sigh of defeat. 'It was the Germans,' he repeated in a lower voice.

'The sauerkrauts?'

'Aye.'

'The SS *Prinzessin*?'

'Aye.'

Tatsuo turned to Horace and Will. 'I heard the Germans were cruising the Solomons. It's possible.' Tatsuo faced Bligh. 'When?'

'I told you. Two days ago.'

'Where?'

'Here in the channel. They are headed for Herbertshohe in New Guinea, but they received damage at Wakanai Bay.'

'Damage?'

'They got in a fight with the Royal Navy, apparently.' Brannon limped to join Bligh, and now Tatsuo could see he was badly wounded, worse than his skipper. 'The navy crippled their for'd gun. You should have seen it. And we know for a fact they need urgent repairs and are on their way to Santa Isabel first.'

'The Royal Navy. Do you know the name of the ship?'

'No, but I have a suspicion it was HMS *Pride* from Thursday Island.'

'Your old friend Captain Reynolds,' Horace muttered.

'Aye. Sounds like it. Jesus.' Tatsuo looked at the sorry sight standing knee-deep in water. He certainly had no empathy for the two mongrels. Why, he'd drown them himself if need be. But he had made a deal, and, besides, if he found Bligh was lying he could still throw the bastard overboard.

'Get as close as you can,' he ordered his rowers.

The waves washing onto the shoal were in the castaways' favour. They waded in until they were up to their chests, where Tatsuo managed to throw them a rope and the two men were soon on board the tender.

'If I find you are lying to me,' Tatsuo said to Bligh, 'so help me, I'll maroon you on the first island we come to.'

At sea aboard HMS Pride

Captain Jonathon Bourke studied his Admiralty charts of the Solomons, although he prided himself on knowing the area reasonably well. For the Army captain's benefit, he flattened the maps onto the chart table, weighting two corners with his tobacco pouch and sextant.

'They will head for home ground—here, Herbertshohe in northern New Guinea,' Bourke said, stabbing his finger into New Guinea like it was Emperor Wilhelm's eye. 'Agreed?'

'Agreed.'

'But we also holed her just above the waterline.'

'Ah, yes,' Reynolds had been meaning to talk to the maverick sea captain about that second, most unnecessary shot. But the right moment had eluded him.

'So, my thought is she'll sail to Buala where the sauerkrauts have a German base. It's only small but they'll be able to do repairs there.'

'You think so?'

'I know so. I can read that sauerkraut captain's dirty little mind.' Bourke cracked his knuckles. 'So, if we sail north up the coast of Malaita and sail west across Indispensable Strait here,'—Bourke ran his long gnarly finger across the representation of water—'and keep to the east coast of Santa Isabel, we may just cut them off. They will be sailing slowly, remember, with that hole in her side.'

'Ah, yes, that second shot,' Reynolds started.

'What of it?'

'Do you think it was necessary?'

'Bloody oath, I do.' And Bourke shot Reynolds a dark look ...
Don't you dare question my actions.

Chapter Eleven

Buala—German Settlement—Santa Isabel Island.
Lutheran missionaries settled the coast of Santa Isabel under a German Protectorate, not unlike the Spanish had done centuries earlier. But while the Spaniards were looking for gold, found none and left empty-handed, the Germans envisioned a bigger picture. A small community grew and those savages of the island who insisted on practising their age-old traditions—like headhunting and cannibalism—occupied areas away from the white settlers.

Now, in 1897, the community of Buala housed a blacksmith as well as those plying other necessary trades, and it was the services of this blacksmith that the SS *Prinzessin* required.

Tatsuo anchored *Mystery* some miles south of the Buala Bay in a protected cove. They would have to be vigilant. Tatsuo still didn't have a plan, but if Bligh was telling the truth and the gold *was* indeed on board, then he would think of something.

Tatsuo studied his charts. 'My guess is we have a three-mile hike to Buala,' he told the others. 'The terrain doesn't look too difficult to traverse.'

Together they inspected the shoreline from *Mystery*'s deck. 'Looks like it'll be mostly beaches and headlands. Too easy.'

'What's the plan, Skipper?' Selma asked.

'Plan … you and Pearl guard the *Mystery*. And you,' Tatsuo said to Bligh, 'I want you and your mate ashore.'

'We can't possibly walk,' Brannon grumbled. 'Not with our injuries!'

'No. But you're going ashore and you will wait where William here will keep an eye on you.'

'Cap'n?' William asked.

'After you row us all ashore, Will, you and Horace can push back into deep water and watch these two from a distance. I'm not leaving them alone on the *Mystery*.'

'Aye.' Will looked pleased with himself.

'You best stay with Selma,' Tatsuo ordered Samoa … and waited one second for the reaction he knew was forthcoming.

'No way,' Samoa started. 'I'm coming with you.'

Tatsuo simply grinned. *That woman was certainly headstrong.* 'I thought you'd say that. But if you're joining Rennison and me, you'll do as I say.'

'Aye, Cap'n,' Samoa clicked her heels in jest, saluting.

Tatsuo shook his head and smiled. 'Alright, let's do this.'

An hour and a half later Tatsuo, Rennison and Samoa crouched behind a rocky outcrop off Buala Bay's southern headland.

'Eureka!' Tatsuo cheered. 'They're here.'

The German ship was anchored in the bay. Tatsuo focussed his spyglass, running a keen eye over the ship 300 yards distant. He then cast an eye over the surrounding waterway and shoreline.

'Well done, Captain Gaston,' Samoa quipped. 'You know these Germans.'

'Well, in the Pacific I do. She's quite the handsome ship, eh?'

'If you can call a ship handsome, then I guess she is.'

'SS *Prinzessin*,' Tatsuo read the stern nameplate aloud. 'It was built as a passenger ship ten years ago, before they fitted her with guns and put her into service here in the South Seas. See the damaged gun? Bligh was telling the truth for a change.'

'Yes.' The sight of the damaged 15-centimetre for'd gun turret put a smile on Samoa's face. 'That's totally out of service.'

As they looked on, they noted activity around the ship. A maintenance barge moored next to the *Prinzessin* supported the blacksmith and his offsiders and it appeared repairs were well and truly underway.

'She has a damaged hull as well.'

'It's just a quick patch job, by the looks of it,' Tatsuo said. 'She'll be up on the slips when they sail her to Herbertshohe.'

'Now what?' Rennison asked.

'We'll wait till nightfall then I'll swim out and board her.'

'Board her? How?'

'Up the anchor chain.'

'Are you serious?' Samoa asked. 'And then what do you hope to achieve.'

'Well, I'll confirm that the gold is on board, for starters.'

'And then?'

'I'll make off with as much gold as I can carry in a backpack.'

Now Samoa realised why he was carrying a large canvas sack.

'What if it's locked in a vault?'

'I know these ships like the back of my hand. It was built as a passenger ship. There is no vault. The gold will be stored in the stern, near the captain's cabin, most likely in the saloon store.'

'This is crazy,' Samoa said.

'I've been on board that ship, Sis,' Rennison said. 'Tatsuo's idea could just work. I was interrogated in the captain's cabin, and what he says is correct. We could bring the tender in close when the village is asleep. Look, the maintenance barge is on the side of the ship facing the sea.'

'Madness.' Samoa shook her head. 'How about a diplomatic, legal approach?'

'With the Germans? Right. Pigs might fly first.'

Samoa sighed in frustration. 'What about crew?'

'That's what makes my plan so simple. Everyone's on shore,' Tatsuo said. 'Here, have a gander.'

He passed Samoa the telescope. Samoa noted half a dozen crew on the main deck, and that was about it. She checked the shore. The village dwellings were quite sparse, with several bamboo and grass huts built on stilts well above the high tide line. The ubiquitous communal hall was central, and off to the north she could make out more of a European influence with clothes drying on lines, wooden water barrels and other necessities of modern civilisation. Further north, on the outskirts of the village, Tatsuo could just make out laughing and chatter amongst the trees, where most of the German sailors had set up camp ashore and many appeared to be preparing meals. Two pig carcasses rotated on spits and the schnapps was pouring freely. Suddenly, without warning ...

'Vell, vell!'

The German voice sent a shiver down Tatsuo's spine.

'Vot have ve here?' The German officer spoke good English with a heavy accent. Tatsuo, Samoa and Rennison, lying on their bellies on the sand, looked up into the menacing spectacle of half a dozen German marines, all pointing rifles at them. 'Up! Up! *Schnell*!'

Tatsuo stood biting his lip, angry with himself, angry that he had brought Samoa along. Offering Samoa his hand, he hoisted her to her feet while Rennison brushed himself down.

The officer reached out, taking the telescope from Tatsuo.

'I'll be having thees—*danke*.' He inspected the instrument with reverence. 'You may like to learn, eet ees thees what give you away, *ja*.'

Tatsuo realised the sun had been reflected in the lens. '*Und* eet ees made by *Smith Royal Exchange London*,' the German said of the eyepiece. '*Vunderbar*. Goot lens, thees.'

The German officer collapsed the spyglass, draping it around his neck with its leather strap. For once Tatsuo was speechless. After all, what was there to say? 'Alright, start ze valking. *Eins, zwei, drei*.'

Tatsuo's mind scrambled. He would have to play the diplomatic card. Say he was looking for a friend who had gone missing. *Yes, that's it, another lugger. Bligh maybe? No, not Bligh—these bastards sank Bligh's boat and left him for dead. Think man, think.*

They were marched into the village, while a young marine rushed ahead with a message for Admiral Stosch. The overweight, sweating admiral approached lazily from the village to meet them and then stood waiting, his face red-blotched from the tropical heat and overindulging in food and schnapps. A native boy stood at his side, holding a straw parasol over the admiral's head to keep the sun off his bald pate. The admiral stood barefoot in the sand, the better for his oncoming gout. The German ship captain wasn't far behind.

'What do we have here?' the Admiral asked the guard in his own tongue as he wiped his sweating neck with a handkerchief. 'Spies?'

The marine was explaining how he had caught them when …

'Horst!' Captain Schtumpf hurried forward, taken aback to see Rennison standing before him; and with another man, an Englishman by all appearances. *Und* a beautiful *fräulein*.

'Horst Schwarz?' he said in greeting.

Rennison's face blanched. 'Captain Schlewig-Holstein,' He replied.

'Horst Schwarz?' Tatsuo repeated.

'I thought you must have been washed off that godforsaken shoal,' the captain told Rennison, speaking German.

Tatsuo flinched. 'Did I hear correctly?' he asked Rennison. 'Did he just call you Horst Schwarz?'

'Yes.'

'And this is the man who marooned you on the shoal?'

'Yes.' Rennison took a step closer to the marines.

Tatsuo took note. *Is he drawing a line in the sand here?*

The captain took the opportunity to eye Samoa. 'Ees thees your sister of vot you spoke?' he asked in English.

'*Ja.*' Rennison answered. *Now* he had crossed the line. He didn't dare to look Samoa in the eye. The penny dropped.

'*Ja?*' Samoa shouted. '*Ja?*'

'Oh, haven't you told your sister yet?' the captain said in his native tongue. 'Tut-tut. You *are* a negligent brother. Yes, very negligent.'

The captain turned to Samoa. 'Samoa … isn't it?' he said in English. 'Horst … Rennison, whatever, he is one of us, *fräulein*.'

Samoa stepped in to attack her brother but was stopped by two marines.

'You are joking!' Samoa shouted at her brother. 'You are joking, are you not? Tell me this is all a mistake.'

Tatsuo fumed. 'He's not joking.'

'Rennison, tell me this isn't true.' No answer. 'RENNISON! Look at me!'

Rennison looked his sister in the eye. '*Ja, es ist wahr … Schwester.*'

'I'm not your sister!' Samoa screamed.

'Take those two to the lockup,' Admiral Stosch ordered.

'Wait!' Captain Schtumpf stepped between the prisoners and the marines, before having a quick word with the Admiral, who capitulated.

'How did you arrive at thees island?' the captain asked Tatsuo.

Tatsuo remained silent.

'He has a pearler, the cutter *Mystery*, anchored south of here,' Rennison answered for Tatsuo.

'You're a piece of work, you are,' Tatsuo said, stepping towards Rennison. But he was grabbed from behind and his arms were pinioned by a marine.

'*Und* vot are you doing here?'

'Fishing!' Tatsuo said the word clearly, underlined with contempt.

'Fishing, eh?' The captain looked to Rennison for answers.

'We stopped at the island for fresh water and were on our way to the village to see if we could trade for a couple of pigs and fruit.'

Tatsuo looked Rennison in the eye. *He hadn't mentioned the gold!*

Schtumpf pushed out his bottom lip in contemplation. What Rennison had told him made sense. He exchanged words with the admiral before addressing Tatsuo once more. As far as the Germans were concerned, they had already sunk one lugger and had an altercation with the Royal Navy, albeit in international waters, even though they—the Germans—had been provoked. But it was imperative they return to German New Guinea, as soon as it was possible to repair the for'd gun and the hull. Besides they had the gold.

'You'll return to your ship,' the captain ordered Tatsuo. '*Und* leave immediately. I do not vont to see you again, *ja*?'

Tatsuo wasn't waiting to be told a second time. He grabbed Samoa by the arm. 'Come.'

'*Nein, nein.* You leave *fräulein* Samoa.'

'I'm going with him,' Samoa made to hurry away, but a quick nod from the captain had her secured by a marine.

'Get your hands off me!' Samoa fired out like an alley cat. Tatsuo stepped in but was rebuffed with the muzzles of several rifles.

'Take her away.' The captain looked at Rennison. 'And you, my friend, follow me to my quarters. We must talk.'

'You've got that traitorous bastard,' Tatsuo shouted, 'Samoa's coming with me.'

'Do you vont your freedom or not?' The captain stopped momentarily, back arched, chin high, arms folded.

'You go,' Samoa called out to Tatsuo as she was taken away. 'Go!'

'She vill come to no harm, providing you leave thees island, now!'

Tatsuo shook himself free from the restraining arms and watched Samoa being dragged away, wrestling three marines. Samoa fought hard. As Tatsuo watched, steely-jawed and angry, Samoa looked over her shoulder one last time, managing to mouth three words. *I love you.*

'Leave!' Captain Schtumpf ordered Tatsuo. 'I von't tell you again.'

The officer of the guard stepped forward, clamping Tatsuo's arm and shoving him away. 'You heard ze *Kapitän*, go!'

Tatsuo's chest rose, his body rising two inches above the officer. He said nothing, but snatched his spyglass from around the man's neck. 'That's mine,' he said in a low deep growl, and disappeared back into the jungle.

Tatsuo ignored Bligh and Brannon who were waiting his return. He waved to Horace and William and the two rowed close to shore. Tatsuo waded out and climbed aboard. 'Back to the *Mystery*.'

'What about them?' William nodded to Bligh and Brannon.'

'Leave them.'

No one argued. William and Horace rowed towards the *Mystery*.

'Where's Samoa, Cap'n?' Horace asked. 'And Rennison?'

'Prisoners!'

'What?'

Tatsuo told them everything.

'Bastard. Now what?'

'I need time to think.'

Chapter Twelve

The timing could not have been worse. Nine hours after leaving Buala the SS *Prinzessin* was running at three-quarter steam off the northeast coast of Santa Isabel Island. Captain Schtumpf was pleased with the temporary repairs to the hull plate and was thinking that if all went well the weather would remain in their favour on the way to New Guinea and they would arrive there in less than a week.

Tatsuo anchored in a sheltered cove on the east side of an unnamed island at the very northern tip of Santa Isabel Island. Smoke rose from villages in the jungle but the natives were an unknown. However, short trips ashore for fresh water and coconuts went unmolested. Either the savages didn't know of their visitors' presence or they had decided to leave the whitefellas alone.

Tatsuo was morose. He was a bear with a sore head. Cursing the Germans and cursing Rennison, he defended Samoa.

'She's probably in cahoots with her brother,' Selma, who could never keep her opinions to herself, said. 'Ever thought of that?' She scowled and spat a glob of betel nut over the side.

'It doesn't look good, Skipper,' Horace agreed. 'Such a nice young lady, too.'

'I refuse to believe she is working with the Germans.'

'Fuck'em, fuck'em … Cap'n Tat-Tatsuo. Jesus … Cap'n!' William snatched a breath. 'Remember I seen her talkin' to that man on Thursdee Island? Talkin' German.'

For Tatsuo it just didn't add up. 'You weren't there,' he argued in Samoa's favour. 'You should have seen her face when she found out her brother was in bed with the Germans.'

'All the same,' Selma said, 'we've been anchored here five days, Cap'n. How much longer are we goin' to wait?'

'True, Boss,' Horace said, nodding solemnly. 'What *is* the plan, anyway?'

Truth was, Tatsuo didn't know himself. Blinded by love, he was hoping fortune and fate would intervene and deliver him the answer. 'I figure they have to pass by here, savvy?' he said.

'Aye. We all agree with that, Cap'n. But when?'

'It's only a matter of time.'

'Time!'

'Then we can follow ...'

'Follow a steam ship, with us under sail!' Selma shook her head.

Tatsuo had a wild plan to follow, or at least catch up with, the German ship in New Guinea, and rescue Samoa from there. *Love is blind,* Selma thought, still shaking her head. *Then, again, life's never dull with Tatsuo Gaston around.*

'And what about the gold?' Tatsuo reminded them. 'Those bastards still have our gold.' Tatsuo's face darkened even more. 'And make no mistake. It *is* our gold.'

Selma frowned. 'If Bligh was telling the truth.'

'Oh, I have no doubt about that. It all adds up.'

'If it's on board it would be well guarded.'

'Aye, it would. But they have to take it off at some time.'

'Then what?'

'I'll think of something. Even if we only get a few bars of gold each, I'll think of something.'

'I think yer dreamin', Skipper.' Selma was about to go below deck when ...

'C-captain! Look!' William jumped up on the locker hatch and was pointing out to sea.

Steaming hard through Manning Strait, between them and the next large island of the archipelago to the north, was a ship, several miles out.

'If I didn't know any better, I'd say she looks like the HMS *Pride*,' Tatsuo said.

'It *is* the *Pride*,' William said.

'So the Royal Navy are here. That bastard Bligh was telling the truth.'

'Aye.'

'She's sailin' east.'

Tatsuo picked up his spyglass and scrambled up the ratlines. 'That's her, alright. I wonder if she's looking for the *Prinzessin*?'

And that was when the timing couldn't have been worse.

No sooner had those words spilt from the skipper's lips, than in the distance another large ship could be seen, also well out to sea. It appeared from the south, hidden until now by the southern promontory sheltering their safe cove, and only visible to Tatsuo now because he was elevated up in the rigging. The second ship was travelling off the east coast, heading north, and it was white with two funnels.

'Another ship!'

'Where?'

'Heading north. It's the *Prinzessin*. I'd bet my life on it.'

'You serious?'

'Aye. Bloody hell, I'm serious!'

'Well if it never rains, it pours.'

Selma shielded her eyes from the sun as the German gunboat appeared from the cover of Santa Isabel. 'Do you think the Royal Navy's seen the Germans?'

'It's too much of a coincidence. I reckon they've been looking for them.'

'Aye, and they had an altercation recently,' Horace said. 'Maybe the Navy is going to have another go at her.'

Suddenly Tatsuo had a vision of Samoa on board a sinking ship. And then there was the gold. 'Weigh anchor!'

'Weigh anchor? But, Tatsuo,' Selma stammered, 'hve you forgotten that's the Royal Navy, and the last time we saw them on Thursdee Island they fired artillery at us from the fort?'

'Aye, and we had guns on board. We haven't any longer.'

'Yes … but …'

'Weigh anchor. That's an order.'

'Aye, Skipper!' Horace leapt into action. 'What's the plan, Boss?'

'We have little choice, my friend. We will expose ourselves to the Brits. We have nothing to hide, and together we arrest the *Prinzessin*.'

Selma looked confused. 'Arrest the German ship?'

'Look, we aid and abet our British *friends*, retake the gold with their help, and save Samoa. It's a win-win.'

'And give the gold to the Royal Navy?'

'Not all of it.' Tatsuo was raving. We found it; we can claim it back in a court of law. At least we know where it is that way. Sure, we won't win it all back, but most of it.'

Frantically he unfurled sails. The others were a little slow. 'Jesus! Does anyone have a better idea?' The crew looked at him with vague expressions. 'Or do you want to lose the gold to Germany?'

'Christ, no!' Now Selma leapt onto the ropes.

'Will.'

'Skipper?

'Get that bloody anchor up, fast.'

The Royal Navy's HMS *Pride* had firepower, but the SS *Prinzessin* was far larger, and faster. Only her patched hull slowed her. Captain Herr von Schtumpf ordered an officer to fetch the admiral. The captain was worried, and with good reason. Admiral Gustav von Stosch limped onto the bridge. His leg pained him and he suspected his gammy foot was a sign of oncoming gout. But this didn't hold back the old war veteran and glutton from his favourite pastime, eating and drinking. The admiral's steward rushed in behind him, tugging at a white serviette still tucked into his collar.

'What is it, *Kapitän*,' Stosch asked. 'What's so urgent?'

Schtumpf passed the admiral the binoculars. With half a bottle of schnapps under his belt the admiral took a moment to focus, and a second moment to register. 'Is that what I think it is?'

'Royal Navy? Yes.'

The admiral remained focussed on the British gunboat, still several miles west. 'And they're coming after us, aren't they?'

'Yes, Admiral, it looks that way.'

'How did the dogs find us?'

'Educated guess, I would say.'

The admiral thought of his altercation with the arrogant Royal Navy ship's captain, Captain Jonathon bloody Bourke—*Bastard!*— and ground his teeth.

On board HMS *Pride*, Captain Jonathon Bourke was a happy man. His hunch had paid off. The Germans had been making repairs at Buala and now here they were, heading north for New Guinea … running with their tails between their legs for the protectorate of Imperial bloody Germany.

Although HMS *Pride*'s own repairs to the valves in the main steam pipe had slowed her down a day or two, Captain Reynolds, too, was ecstatic that Bourke had anticipated the Germans' move. Reynolds stood on the *Pride*'s bridge, feet planted firmly apart, tongue resting on bottom lip, and eyes sharply focussed on the white two-funneled ship which he could see some miles off through the binoculars.

'That's her,' he said with measured satisfaction. 'That's definitely her.'

'Bloody oath, it is, Rafferty!' Captain Bourke's gravelly voice announced, 'Enemy in sight!'

Rafferty! Captain Bourke had made the habit of calling Captain Reynolds by his middle name, after he'd read it on official papers days ago. And Reynolds hated his middle name. He wasn't that keen on the name Gerald, either, but he'd been born with it.

'So what would you like me to do, Rafferty? Ram her?'

Of course Captain Bourke was thinking of the yet to be tried iron ram just below the waterline on the *Pride*'s bow, an innovation of the Royal Navy when the ship had been built back in '85.

'Ram her? Hardly. We will board her and take Rennison Plum into custody, as was the original plan.'

'Rennison Plum. I'd forgotten about him,' Bourke said. 'Are you certain he's on board?'

'Oh, he's on board, alright.'

'And what if they don't co-operate?' The sea captain cracked his knuckles in a sickening act of crepitus, the popping of joints. 'Which, Rafferty, I've got to tell you, I doubt they will,' he continued.

Reynolds pinched his lips in what could only have been called a grimace. The ship's captain, Bourke, was a menacing man, well over six feet, muscled and afraid of nothing. Yet Reynolds decided to speak his mind.

'I must ask you, old chap, to please refrain from calling me Rafferty. It is most unendearing.'

'Unendearing?' Bourke massaged a finger along the Sevastopol scar running down his cheek and eyed Reynolds a moment.

'Please,' Reynolds added.

'Hmm. Sure thing. What would you like me to call you, then? Gerald?'

'"Captain" will be fine.'

'"Captain"?' Bourke looked hard at the army captain a long moment. 'I don't think so. I'll call you Gerald. I'm captain.'

Nearly three hours later

As the SS *Prinzessin* headed north inky clouds gathered, spiked occasionally with needles of lightning, but Captain Herr von Schtumpf and Admiral Gustav von Stosch were nervous for another reason. Off to their port side and sailing parallel with the *Prinzessin* for half an hour now, was the Royal Navy's HMS *Pride*.

'What are they playing at?' Schtumpf said, ashen-faced.

First Lieutenant Anton Kruger was the first to notice. 'Look *Kapitän*, they are signaling.'

From the starboard bridge deck of HMS *Pride* the Royal Navy signaler relayed the British admiral's message: 'Slow ship to three knots. This is an order.'

'An order! Who do they think they are?'

'*Kapitän*?'

'Ignore them.'

'I beg your pardon, Admiral, but I think they mean business. Remember what happened at Wakanai Bay?'

The Royal Navy semaphore signaled again; the six-shuttered signalling lamp with its black-and-white-striped louvres flashing the message: 'Slow to three knots immediately. We are arresting Horst Schwarz who we know is on board the *Prinzessin*. Prepare to be boarded .'

'Pre … prepare to be boarded!' The German admiral was fuming.

'We have little choice, Admiral,' the captain argued. 'Our for'd gun is damaged, and they outgun us.'

'You keep this ship full steam ahead, *Kapitän*. Full steam ahead, you hear me?'

'As you wish, Admiral.'

'And 'head into that squall, man.'

In all the excitement the ship captain had hardly noticed a squall brewing further north.

'They're ignoring orders, Captain,' the Royal Navy signaler told the bridge.

The expression on Captain Jonathon Bourke's weathered face turned into a dark smile. He looked at his first officer. 'Fire a warning shot across her bow, if you please.'

On board *Mystery*, now sailing through a rising swell, Horace studied Tatsuo, who was at the helm, focusing on the converging ships.

'I don't like the look of the weather ahead, Cap'n. There's bad weather approaching from the north.'

'Nothing we haven't been through before!' Tatsuo yelled back over the wind and spray.

But that wasn't Horace's only concern. 'I'd jus' like to remind yer, Cap'n, that the last time we seen our friend Cap'n Reynolds there, he took potshots at us from the fort, remember?'

'Aye. Only too well.' Horace hooked an arm around the ratlines to steady the spyglass. As he focussed, he noticed a puff of smoke from the muzzle of HMS *Pride's* 12-pounder gun and imagined he heard a subtle boom. A plume of water immediately lifted 50 yards off the German ship's bow.

'They mean business, Cap'n!' Horace called out.

'Aye.' Tatsuo had heard the big gun also. 'We're in luck.'

'Luck? Is that what yer call it?'

'Aye. The Royal Navy's doing our dirty work for us. They're arresting her at sea.'

'Jesus, Boss, I hope yer know what yer doin'.'

'Have faith, my friend.'

On board HMS Pride.

'Full speed ahead,' Bourke ordered.

The order was relayed via the telegraph down to the engine room. Engineers shoveled coal furiously into the furnaces. The boilers glowed red. The pistons wheeled and pumped, and HMS *Pride* powered through the waves.

'As soon as we are up to speed,' Bourke barked at his helmsman, 'we'll cut across the bastard's bow and force her to slow. And then, Gerald, you may board her and take our fugitive.' Bourke narrowed his eyes, salivating with the thought.

Captain Reynolds was an army captain. Whilst he was accustomed to sea travel, the thought of cutting across another ship's bow while travelling at speed on the open sea … quite frankly, daunted him.

Such a manoeuvre was always fraught with unexpected possibilities. Captain Schtumpf pushed the SS *Prinzessin* full steam ahead. Now both ships were racing side by side. Captain Jonathon Bourke stood at the entrance to the *Pride's* starboard bridge, glaring through the spray-streaked window at the German bridge. Their admiral, a fat, arrogant sauerkraut known as Stosch, whom Bourke had already met, and hated, stared back. Bourke jammed a half-smoked cigar into his mouth, sparked it and rolled it to the corner of his mouth.

HMS *Pride* had an unexpected edge in speed over the larger German vessel. Slowly the Royal Navy gained a ship's length on the converted passenger ship. Perfect timing was of the essence. Captain Bourke drew in a lungful of smoke, enough to choke a lesser man. 'Helmsman.'

'Captain.'

'Prepare to slice across her bow.'

'Aye, aye, sir.'

This manoeuvre would be his coup de grâce. Time to cut across her bow. *Scare the shit out of the German bastards.* Force them to capitulate.

Bourke gave the order. 'Hard to starboard.'

'Aye, Captain. Hard to starboard.'

The Royal Navy gunboat steered hard right. With both steam engines at full throttle the ship closed the hundred-yard gap between the two ships. As HMS *Pride* turned, the SS *Prinzessin* approached at a similar speed. All on both bridges stood to attention. The *Pride* was well on target, a full ship's length in front of the German ship. It was perfect timing. They would cross in front with 50 yards to spare, when …

A loud explosion in the HMS *Pride's* engine room heralded the failure of one of the new valves in the main steam pipes. The engines slowed and the ship lost precious power.

Bourke reared up like a grizzly bear. 'What-the-hell?'

HMS *Pride* slowed steadily. The comforting throb of the engines vanished. Army Captain Reynolds' eyes widened.

'What's happening, Captain?'

This wasn't in the manual. Captain Bourke was immediately a deer in the crosshairs.

'Captain Bourke ... what is happening?'

Bourke ignored the army officer and yelled down the speaking horn into the engine room. 'What's happening?'

'Lost power, Cap'n!'

'I know that! Jesus Christ, man! Why?'

'The new cross heads, sar. They're failed.'

'Jesus-Christ-Lord help us!'

Through the bridge window the SS *Prinzessin* loomed like a giant whale. 'Keep hard a'starboard.'

'She's as hard as I can get her, Captain!'

It was all in slow motion. Dreamlike, really. Captain Bourke, Captain Reynolds, three officers and the helmsman could see clearly onto the bridge of the steaming German ship. And their German equivalents looked back with faces frozen in disbelief ... and terror.

The distance between the ships shortened.

Fast.

Slow motion evaporated. Life sped up. Someone shouted,'Oh, Mother Mary ... Jesus Christ!'

Captain Bourke watched over the *Pride*'s bow. A collision seemed imminent. It would be a port-side ram. The German amidships rushed by.

Bourke caught sight of the lifeboats swinging on davits. German sailors and marines along the port aft rails scattered, screaming and yelling.

The distance closed, 20 yards, ten yards. It was close. Very close. But there was the chance they would miss by a hair's breadth.

'B-Bourke!' Reynolds shouted.

'Brace for impact!' Bourke roared.

The Royal Navy gunboat rammed the side of the German ship some 20 feet from her stern flagstaff. The noise of the juddering shredding of metal panels was horrendous. The rudder and propellers were sliced off and cast into the depths, followed by ten metres of the after part of the ship. This exposed the sailors' after-mess. These men had had no idea, no warning. The iron ram of the conqueror-class gunboat shredded the rear of the SS *Prinzessin*. The British ship suffered minimal damage. Sure, some of her port-side superstructure was thrown into the sea, but she coasted clear of the collision site virtually unscathed.

The ram, it appeared, was a huge success.

Without engines, it took HMS *Pride* a mile to finally stop. Meanwhile, all the Royal Navy could do was crowd at the stern and stare at the unintentional carnage they had left in their wake. Captains Bourke and Reynolds stood at the guardrail; both men were wide-eyed, mouths open, and speechless. As they looked on, helpless, the SS *Prinzessin* initially took on water slowly. But as the stern filled she tilted faster and faster. The bow rose from the waves. And slowly she foundered, stern first.

All aboard the *Mystery* watched the unfolding drama. They were aghast. Why would the Royal Navy commit such aggression? As they raced to the scene, fast as the wind would take them, Tatsuo watched the German lifeboats launch awkwardly. They filled with survivors rapidly. If anything, it appeared the Germans had suffered loss of pride more than loss of life.

Although the squall mercifully passed, the seas remained rough. Tatsuo trained his glass onto the motionless HMS *Pride*. Confused as to why she should anchor a mile away from the German ship, he watched two cutters under sail launch from the Royal Navy gunboat, each with an armed crew.

'Samoa,' he prayed.

Selma stood amidships, dressed in oilskins, her long grey hair wet from sea spray.

'The gold,' she said with reverence.

Tatsuo placed a hand on her shoulder.

'All that gold, gone … for what?' Selma said. A large wave rolled under the keel and Selma lost balance, sitting heavily on the sail locker. 'I can't believe it. I honestly thought we had a chance to get some of it back.'

'Me too.' Tatsuo took a mental bearing, noting the nearest headland on the northern islands of Santa Isabel. 'That gold's in a thousand feet of water by now, Selma,' he said, trying to keep steady despite the rolling deck. 'Maybe it was meant to be.'

The Royal Navy cutters met the German lifeboats only moments after the SS *Prinzessin* disappeared beneath the waves. Tatsuo remained a mile distant, watching procedures through his spyglass. He could only imagine the exchange of dialogue, the altercation between the two groups after such a hostile act, although Horace was of the opinion it had been an accident. An attempt to threaten gone wrong.

'What *are* they doing?' Tatsuo muttered, the lens tight to one eye.

Horace stood firm at the helm. 'What's that, Boss?'

'It appears the British are taking prisoners. But it's too rough to tell.'

Moments later the Royal Navy cutters left the Germans to their fate and sailed back to HMS *Pride*.

'Now what?'

Tatsuo looked at his mate. 'Horace.'

'Aye, Cap'n.'

'Take us in close to the Germans.'

'The Germans, Cap'n?'

'Aye. The Germans.'

The crew of the *Mystery* sailed as close as they dared to the German survivors, 60 in all, in lifeboats. Although the seas were up, Tatsuo estimated the Germans only had a three- or four-mile sail to the nearest land, from which he knew they would make their way back to Buala to the south.

'*Sprich Englisch*?' Tatsuo yelled to the nearest lifeboat, warily keeping his distance.

'Eef you come looking for gold,' one man who recognised Tatsuo from Buala and guessed the gold to be his purpose called, 'it is on the seabed.'

'I seek an Englishwoman on your ship. Samoa Plum.'

'*Ja*. Woman ees always bad luck on ship, I'm thinking.'

'Where is she?'

'Your English friends take her.'

'What?'

'The English, they sink us, then they come and take English *fräulein* und her *bruder*.'

'"Bruder"? You mean "brother," yes?'

'*Ja*.'

Chapter Thirteen

Ten days later. Bona Bona Island off the south coast of New Guinea.

The smoky steam from the bêche-de-mer smokers permeated the bay of Bona Bona, where the air was still, like the calm before a storm. Tatsuo dropped anchor and inspected the sky. Indeed, bad weather was brewing and he was glad to have made landfall before it arrived.

On shore the cicadas were at fever pitch. Maybe they, too, knew a storm approached. Ah Sin met them on the beach looking resplendent as usual in his dark blue robe with a colourful pattern of red, gold and green,yellow silk trousers and his gorget made from hundreds of tiny shells.

Horace and William dragged the tender to the high-tide mark and buried the anchor in the sand.

'My fren, my fren,'—Ah Sin was genuinely pleased to see Tatsuo —'I did not expect to see you so soon.' He paused to acknowledge Horace, William and Selma.

'It is good to see you, too, Ah Sin.' Ah Sin's two beautiful bodyguards joined them on the sand, but remained in the background with their hands crossed before them. This did not go unnoticed by Tatsuo.

'If you're looking for my pistol, ladies, I lost it,' he told the two women. Ah Sin translated and they nodded to the affirmative. Neither smiled.

'Where is your beautiful fiancée?' the tall, dark and handsome Chinaman asked.

'It's a long story, my friend.'

'Well, we have plenty of time. Come.'

Distant thunder followed lightning flashes on the skyline and the spill of sunlight was lost behind a black horizon a moment later. Within minutes the rains started. Heavy rain, large fat droplets bringing with it a humidity only known in the tropics. They hurried into the *palace*—Ah Sin's bamboo, grass-roofed communal hall—where several women were preparing yet another feast, and the aromas seduced their appetites.

'It is fortunate you arrived when you did,' Ah Sin said. 'We can offer you shelter and a feast.'

'Aye. I thank you.'

'But I will be asking you a favour in return.'

'Oh?' Tatsuo said warily.

'But sit, let us eat and drink—I am famished. We can talk later.'

The favour turned out to be a delivery of three tons of smoked bêche-de-mer, to be taken to Cooktown and delivered to a Chinese merchant, Chung Zen. There was just a cargo tariff to be negotiated, but as Tatsuo's hold was near empty he was happy for any trade. He did, however, have three crates of bibles to dispose of, now that Samoa and Rennison were out of the picture.

'So tell me, your fiancée Samoa, what happened to her?'

Tatsuo didn't need to be reminded. Just her name caused him angst. *Yes indeed, what happened to her?*

Tatsuo went on to apologise for telling a mistruth, but explained that Samoa had been his passenger only. He explained that for diplomatic reasons they had decided to masquerade as an engaged couple. Ah Sin listened attentively while Tatsuo told the entire story, including his connection with HMS *Pride*.

'The *Pride* passed south of here heading west a week ago,' the Chinaman said. 'Heading home to Thursday Island, I should imagine.'

'Are you certain?' Tatsuo inquired. He was hoping to arrive at Thursday Island before the HMS *Pride*, especially Captain Reynolds.

'Yes, I am certain. Danish Tom was here five days past and said he passed her at sea.'

'Tom the Norwegian?'

'Yes.'

Tom was known to hail from Norway, but everyone knew him as Danish Tom. He owned a bêche-de-mer lugger named *Moira*. A small man, he was normally happy, but when drunk he was a murderous villain.

'He said he tried to avoid being seen by the gunboat's crew,' Ah Sin said. 'Luckily the Royal Navy paid him no heed.'

'The bibles I spoke of,' Tatsuo said, 'are you interested?'

'I am interested in all trade, my fren. Bibles I can sell to passing missionaries and God knows we have plenty around the Pacific these days.' Ah Sin had chuckled quietly at his own jest. 'God knows … missionaries … God knows.' He laughed again. But Tatsuo's mind was elsewhere. 'But, I am only interested if the price is low,' the guileful Chinaman added. 'Bibles aren't as popular as your English novels, *Moby Dick* or Charles Dickens, you must understand.'

With the storm's passing came a fine rain, a wet mist, the type of rain that soaked through, even oilskins, it seemed. With Selma and William retired in their bunks for the night, aboard the *Mystery*, Tatsuo and Horace inspected the bibles. They would take them ashore first thing in the morning and then depart for Cooktown and home.

Hooking a lantern overhead, Tatsuo looked on. Horace prised the lid from one of the crates. 'Dem look in good condition, Cap'n. Should bring pretty penny, I'm thinkin'.'

'Aye. You ever read the good book, Horace?'

'Nar, can't say I have, Boss. Can't read that good nohow.'

Tatsuo lifted a copy free from its tightly packed box and flicked through the pages. 'What the?'

'Jesus, Cap'n … is that … is that real?' Several five- and ten-pound notes sterling fluttered to the deck.

Tatsuo unhooked the lantern, the better to see what was before them. The bible had been hollowed out with a cavity to fit the banknotes exactly. It was packed.

Tatsuo looked at Horace; his jaw dropped. Horace scooped up a handful of notes of various denominations, but all were engraved with the seated image of Britannia in the top left corner. 'Dem look real, alright, Skipper.'

'Bloody oath, they're real.' Tatsuo snatched another bible—it was the same. Then another and another. Each bible was filled with several hundred pounds in sterling banknotes. They both let out a whoop, bringing Selma and William scrambling from their bunks. 'What is this?'

'There's thousands of pounds here.'

'Thousands and thousands!' Tatsuo upended the crate. Each bible was filled with money. He crowbarred the lid from the next crate. Same. And the third … same. Every bible was filled with banknotes. Tatsuo sat heavily on a keg. 'This is crazy.' Even Pearl was roused from her reverie, curious to discover why the humans were so animated, sniffing at hundreds of notes scattered on the deck.

'Samoa was taking this to the missionaries, wasn't she?' Selma said.

'Aye. But bibles only. I have a feeling she knew nothing about the money.'

'She said Rennison sent her a letter, ordering the bibles. She was to have them sent as cargo to Mist Island. It was only at the last minute she decided to come along … to look for her brother, like.'

'So Rennison knew about the money.'

'Had to.'

'Where did the bibles come from?'

'I seem to recall her saying she brought the bibles up from Sydney,' Tatsuo said. 'Four crates in all.'

'Four?' Selma mentally counted three.

'We left one behind on Mist Island, remember?'

'Yes. Those Lutheran missionaries must have gotten a nice surprise when they opened their crate.'

'Maybe, or maybe not. Maybe they were supposed to get them.'

'I don't know about that. Because Samoa was supposed to leave them four crates, but she changed her mind at the last minute. If they were expecting more they would have said so.'

'That's true.'

'What would missionaries want with all this money? And where did it come from in the first place?'

'Who … who cares, fuckem …' William fought his tic. 'B-but is it legal?'

Tatsuo placed a hand on William's shoulder. 'Don't know, Will,' he said in a quiet, calming voice. 'Legal? Who knows? But it's bigger than simple missionary work.'

Selma's eyes remained wide as she held several hundred pounds in a tight fist. 'What are you going to do with it, Cap'n?'

'I don't know. I honestly don't know. I'm thinking we go back to Thursday Island.'

'Thursday Island? But I thought we was goin' home, Boss.' Horace's brow wrinkled.

'That was the plan. But this changes everything. I suggest we hang about for a few days on Thursday, make our presence known to the authorities, and see if anyone comes forward asking about it.'

'And then tell them about it, do you mean?'

'No, Horace. If we did that, everyone would be making a claim. No. But if it does belong to anyone there, then they will be in touch, that's for certain.'

'What about Captain Reynolds of Green Hill Fort?' Selma asked.

'What of him?'

'Well, he will come for you, Cap'n. He weren't exactly happy when we left Thursdee Island in a hurry.'

Tatsuo smiled. 'No he wasn't, but he would know by now we witnessed the ramming of that German ship.'

'Aye, someone would 'ave recognised us. We was 'ardly discreet, eh?' Horace agreed.

'Th-that's a point,' William said.

'So, crew,' Tatsuo continued, 'we have that over him, do we not?'

'The ramming?'

'Aye.

'Possibly.'

'Besides, we've done nothing wrong.' Tatsuo winked at Selma. 'What has he got on us? Naught. The guns have gone. There's only this lot.' Tatsuo nodded to the cash. 'Oh!' Tatsuo suddenly realised. 'I see what you mean. Regardless whether he knows about this money or not, he is going to search the *Mystery* for contraband, like guns, isn't he?'

'Aye.'

'Then we'll do what the pirates used to do hundreds of years ago,' William managed an uninterrupted sentence before the excitement caused him to tic once more.

'What's that, Will?'

'Fuckem… fuckem, fuck … we'll fuckin', fuckin' bury it.'

'Good thinking, Will.' Tatsuo grinned at the thought. 'We'll bury it somewhere remote, then sail into Thursday. Then when we leave for Cooktown, we'll recover it and do the same down there.'

'What, wait and see if anyone comes forward asking about it?'

'Exactly. Then we'll wait a month or so and then split it four ways.'

'And if someone, like the authorities, comes forward to claim it, what then?'

'We'll tell them, "What money? Oh those bibles! We jettisoned them overboard during a storm."'

It took the best part of the morning to load and secure Ah Sin's produce in the hold of the *Mystery* before they slipped away on the outgoing tide. The entire village came down to the water's edge to wave farewell.

'Do you reckon Ah Sin will wonder what happened to the bibles?' Horace asked Tatsuo, standing proudly at the helm. There had been no more mention of them.

'I don't think he will be too bothered, Horace.' Tatsuo was deep in thought a moment. 'Can you imagine if we hadn't opened those boxes, if we had just sold them to Ah Sin for a pittance?'

'Doesn't bear thinkin' about, Boss.'

'Aye.'

'W-what will we do with the empty bibles, Captain?' William asked.

'The bibles, Will?' Tatsuo's long dark hair brushed across his face with the wind 'Toss 'em overboard, lad—feed 'em to the fish.'

Chapter Fourteen

Ten days later. Northeast Horn Island, Torres Strait Islands archipelago. Two days' sail east of Thursday Island.

Selma had reservations. Rambling Jack wasn't the most inspiring name for a man Tatsuo insisted was as trustworthy as one's own mother. But Tatsuo was adamant. Rambling Jack, a loner with scrupulous morals, who had lived alone on Horn Island for 40 years now, was the man to entrust with the banknotes—12,000 pounds' worth, in fact, after they finally counted them … a number of times.

Ten days earlier Selma had emptied out several large jars of preserved meat that she'd discovered in the galley store. If it wasn't half rotten, it was entirely rotten. The contents were heaved overboard—along with the hollowed-out bibles—and the jars were aired on deck for several days.

'Fuckit,' William said, triggered by his tic. 'S-Selma, they still stink real bad.' William laughed and succumbed a few more times to his tics before rolling the banknotes in tight rolls tied with bootlaces to fit into the airtight jars.

'All ready, Cap'n.'

Tatsuo looked at the stone jars lined up along the sail locker, 20 in all, each crammed with pound notes in various denominations. 'Christ, Selma, did you wash the jars first?'

'Of course I did, yer cheeky bugger.'

'Well, Jesus, they still stink. Alright, then, get their stoppers back in.' They were ready now for burial on Horn Island. But the mystery behind so much currency hidden inside bibles plagued the skipper.

If only we knew for certain, we could safely keep it. Did Samoa know about it? I think not. So Rennison knew, but what was he planning to do with it?

There were more questions than answers.

Horace snapped Tatsuo from his reverie. 'Will I take her straight in, Cap'n?' Horace at the wheel held *Mystery* on a direct course for Rambling Bay, the name Tatsuo had bestowed on Rambling Jack's promontory on the northeast of Horn Island.

'Aye.' Tatsuo took up his spyglass, and panning the shoreline he recognised the hermit Rambling Jack immediately. He was sitting on a log mending a fishnet. Old Max, a blue heeler, guarded the beach the best he could for his years, barking furiously at the new arrivals.

Rambling Jack had few visitors, just a handful of pearlers who worked around the nearby islands and reefs and brought him supplies at odd times. Supplies like vegetable seeds for his garden, sacks of flour and sugar, chickens to breed and cats to keep pests away. Old Max the blue heeler tolerated the cats, just. Jack also loved to receive newspapers and books, and as he kept a diary he would be given reams of paper, pen and ink.

'What would he want a diary for?' Selma wanted to know when she first heard about it. 'Every day would be the same, wouldn't it? Fish, cook, eat, sleep?'

'Rambling Jack is a smart man, Sel'. He has an interest in migratory birds, believe it or not,' Tatsuo said. 'Migratory birds, marine life and plants. He keeps records.'

'Well, well, look what the cat dragged in.' Rambling Jack stood barefoot in the shallows, steadying the tender as it came onto the narrow beach. 'Tatsuo Gaston, haven't seen you for a while ... *and* yer 'aven't changed, yer 'andsome bugger.'

'You neither, Jack, still the fighting fit old hermit of Horn Island.'

'Enough of the *old* bit lad, I'm only seventy-four.' Jack grinned, showing yellowed teeth with gaps and red gums. 'An' you, too, Reaper, skinny bastard, as ever.' Horace smiled at his sobriquet. 'An' Selma, aren't you a sight for sore eyes?' Jack looked at William. 'Is Selma still burning the arse outa them pots … William, Will, ain't it?' William nodded, smiling. 'Say, don't suppose yer brought me some books? I got nuthin' to read. Read 'em all, what the lads brought me, oh … ah … four months ago now. Read all the *Illustrated London News* copies, *The Strand Magazines*, the *Halfpenny Marvels*, then all the books Banksie left me nine months ago … ah … *David Copperfield*, *Vanity Fair*, *Great Expectations*, *Far From the Madding Crowd*, then there was, what's it called? … ah … *Wuthering Heights* … Jesus Christ, that was a buggered up relationship, then …'

Now I remember why he's called Rambling Jack, Selma thought, smiling to herself.

'Sorry, Jack, no books, I'm afraid.'

'Oh, more's the pity.'

'But I brought you some flour, a bag of coffee beans and whiskey.'

William fetched several canvas bags from the tender while Horace lifted three-legged Pearl onto the sand to have a sniff about with her old friend Max the blue heeler.

'Now yer talkin' my language.' Jack reached out and took the whiskey, uncorked the bottle and took a swig. 'Oh, sweet Jesus, that's good. I ain't had a drink o' the good stuff since Christmas.'

Rambling Jack's abode was a driftwood affair. A shanty in the true meaning of the word. He had a chicken coop, well fenced, as the odd crocodile was attracted to the clucking and scent of live fowls, and several cats roamed about killing vermin. There were pigs somewhere, too, because Tatsuo and his crew could hear the squeals and snorts in the undergrowth nearby. Jack ate well, his diet being mainly turtle meat, fish, eggs, vegetables from his own garden and mangos when he could find them.

William saw movement out of the corner of his eye in the mangroves, a hundred yards away—what he'd initially thought was a log, moved! Horace noticed also.

'I see old Bertie still 'angs about.' Jack had told Horace about the 15-foot saltwater crocodile named Bertie, after the Queen's dead husband, Prince Albert.

'Aye.'

'I reckon dat bastard's grown since I seen 'im last.'

'That'd be right. 'e's getting' a bit cantankerous of late,' Jack said. 'Snatched one o' me chickens last week. I don't know 'ow the bloody chicken got outa the coop, neither, but Bertie snaveled 'im in one gobful.'

'You still feed him, then?' Selma asked.

'Aye. Scraps when I got 'em. But it ain't much.' Rambling Jack heard bottles clunking in one of the bags William carried ashore and guessed it was more whiskey. 'Here, lad, let me carry that.' Jack peeked inside. 'Another five bottles o' whiskey!' He was chuffed.

'Aye. But don't drink them all at once,' Tatsuo said.

Jack took another swig at the open bottle before asking, 'Well, yer sure as hell didn't come ashore visitin', then. What was yer after?'

'We want to hide something here, Jack, bury it, behind your shack, maybe, and come back for it in a week or so.'

'Bury something? Like what? Not a body, I hope.'

'No.' Tatsuo laughed at the thought. He explained everything— Rennison, Samoa, the bibles, the cash and the reason why they needed to hide the money briefly before sailing on to Thursday Island. 'I know the money is in good hands with you, my friend.'

'Hmm, are you certain?' Jack bunched his lips in a smug face.

Tatsuo had known Rambling Jack for many years, and although he was known to enjoy a game of cards when the opportunity came his way, Tatsuo knew he could trust the old hermit with his life.

'Yes, I'm certain,' Tatsuo said. 'Besides there's 200 quid in it for you.'

Jack whistled. 'What am I goin' to do with 200 quid?'

'You'll think of something.'

Barking drew everyone's attention to Pearl, who had wandered close to Bertie the crocodile, who was minding his own business and basking in the sun. The three-legged dog took an instant dislike to the old salty and barked loud enough to send the great croc into the water. Pearl ran to the water's edge.

'Pearl!' Tatsuo shouted. 'Here, girl.' He put two fingers to his lips and let out a shrill whistle. Pearl looked about, barked at her master, turned back to bark once more at Bertie's wake, and hurried from the shoreline where she ran off into the scrub with Max.

'Don't know how you live with the bloody thing, Jack,' Tatsuo said.

'Oh, me and Bertie go back aways. We tolerate each other.'

With the 20 pottery jars of bank notes buried in a shallow ditch behind the shanty and carefully camouflaged with bark and bracken, the *Mystery* set sail for Thursday Island, two days away.

Thursday Island.

It was like Captain Gerald Rafferty Reynolds had a sixth sense. It was early morning when he swept the Green Hill Fort telescope across the harbour, focussing on movement in the bay.

'The *Mystery*,' he sighed contentedly out of the corner of his mouth, more to himself than anyone else. 'Tatsuo Gaston, you mongrel pirate bastard. You've got a cheek sailing back into *my* port.'

Down on the calm waters of Port Kennedy, *Mystery* dropped anchor and furled sails. They had moored amongst dozens of other pearlers and bêche-de-mer fishers, all waking to a new day. Many nationalities were represented, from Filipinos to Chinese, Malays to Indians.

'Will you look at that?' Tatsuo grinned at Horace as various bare backsides presented themselves to the new day, completing ablutions before breakfast 'I reckon every arse in Asia is represented there.'

Horace chuckled, and then grew serious. He wasn't convinced his boss was doing the right thing. He would have much preferred to sail directly to Cooktown. But he suspected, as did Selma, that a young blonde woman was also a part of Tatsuo's plan.

Samoa, Tatsuo thought. Not a day went by when he didn't think of her. There wasn't a moment when he didn't fear what had happened after the sinking of the SS *Prinzessin*.

Horace lifted his cap to scratch at his sweaty scalp. 'Now what, Cap'n?'

'We wait.'

Waiting was not Horace's forte. 'Wait?'

'Aye. Wait and see if anyone approaches us enquiring about four crates of bibles.'

Captain Reynolds turned to a knot of soldiers mingling lazily about the parapets of the fort. 'Guard!' he yelled. 'Sergeant Maples.'

'Captain.'

'I want a dozen men at the double down to the bay. Arrest Tatsuo Gaston on board the *Mystery*. Sergeant, you bring the prisoner directly to the fort for interrogation.'

'Interrogation?'

'Yes. Do you have a problem, Sergeant?'

'No, Captain.'

'Then make haste.'

'Yes, Captain. Ah, Captain ...'

'What?'

'What charge, sir?'

'Resisting arrest.'

'Resisting arrest, sir?'

'Yes. Last time he was in port he ignored my request to return.'

'Aye, sir.'

'At the double. Understand?'

'Yes, sir.'

'Corporal Browning,'

'Sir.'

'You are to join Sergeant Maples and remain on board the *Mystery* with five men. Search the vessel thoroughly. And I mean *thoroughly*.'

'Yes, sir. Am I looking for anything in particular?'

'Contraband, arms, anything you can find so I can throw the book at the bastard and lock him up.'

'Yes, sir.'

Selma finally appeared above the companionway, her hair done neatly in a chignon. *And was that a clean blouse she was wearing?*

'Are we goin' ashore?' Selma wanted to know, ''cos I need groceries.'

'Aye, Selma, we'll go ashore. We need to make ourselves available … for anyone to ask about the bibles, like … the better for people to approach us.'

'Like them soldiers?' Horace said, pointing out two navy wherries rowing towards the *Mystery*.

'Oh.' Tatsuo swallowed hard. It wasn't like he hadn't expected them, but seeing two boatloads of armed soldiers approaching was a little daunting. 'Looks like I'm going for a visit to the castle sooner than later.' Tatsuo looked up towards the hill fort, and attempted a smile.

'You've got a bloody nerve!' Captain Reynolds barked at Tatsuo the moment he appeared under guard in the Green Hill Fort guardhouse.

'Nerve?' Tatsuo feigned ignorance. 'What makes you think that, Captain?'

Reynolds stood and walked around a table to confront the … *the Japanese French fucking mongrel fucking pirate.*

'Sailing back into *my* port as if you own it.'

'Your port? I wasn't aware you owned it, Captain.'

Reynolds flinched, his fists balled. He badly wanted to punch Tatsuo—*here, right now.*

Corporal Browning interrupted the moment. 'Captain Reynolds, sir,

'Yes! What?'

The corporal silently shook his head.

'Wait here,' Reynolds spat at Tatsuo. 'Watch him,' he ordered the guard next to his prisoner.

In the corridor. 'Nothing sir,' Browning told his captain. 'The *Mystery* is clean as a whistle. There's nowt, no contraband, nothing at all, sir.'

'Did you search the hold properly?'

'Yes, sir. Nowt. Just a cartload of stinking smoked fish.'

'Did you look in the bags?'

'Certainly did, Captain. We opened several bags indiscriminately —just rotten fish.' For a man who enjoyed eating kippers, this was a strange description of the Oriental delicacy smoked bêche-de-mer.

'Shit!' Captain Reynolds stormed back into the guardroom, hooked his hands onto his hips and yelled at Tatsuo, 'Did you sell arms to the natives at Wakanai Bay on Bougainville Island?'

'What?'

'I said, did you—'

'Yes I heard what you said. What the bloody hell are you implying? You know it's illegal. I don't trade in arms.'

'Liar. I was there. We were attacked by a German landing party, but the savages had guns and—'

'Saved your arse.'

'I beg your pardon!'

'The word around the islands is that the … *savages*, as you call them, saved your arse when you were attacked. The word is the savages made the Germans run with their tails between their legs.'

Reynolds' face had gone from red to beetroot. He turned to the three guards and the corporal standing to attention in the room. 'Leave us.'

'Sir?'

'I said, leave us. Bugger off. NOW!'

The soldiers hurried from the guardhouse, their young faces holding back smirks and their tongues loose and ready to spill the beans around the town.

Reynolds slammed the door shut and turned on Tatsuo once more. 'Let's get something straight. I don't like you, savvy?'

'Oh, really.' Tatsuo acted disappointed. 'And I thought we were getting on so well.'

'I know you sold guns to that crazy Maori woman—man, thing, whatever the freak is. Hatsie Raven belongs in a circus.'

'I don't think her followers would agree with you there.'

'I don't give a damn what those savages think.' Reynolds paced the room. 'I know you sold her guns, and when I prove it you'll be charged and locked up here at the fort where I can keep an eye on you for the next ten years.'

'Can't help you with the gun-dealing accusation,' Tatsuo said calmly. 'I wasn't there when you had your arse saved by … *savages*. But I *was* witness to another event off the north coast of Santa Isabel Island.'

Captain Reynolds changed colour faster than a kaleidoscope viewer could be twisted. His voice lowered. 'What on earth are you talking about?'

'I was there when you rammed the German ship, the SS *Prinzessin*.'

Reynolds' mouth opened and shut like a freshly caught fish cast onto the deck.

'Wh … what … ? You're talking gibberish, man.'

'Oh, am I? I know what I saw. And I have three witnesses to back my claim. You were on the bridge, cocky as a rooster, when HMS *Pride* used her ram to sink that German ship. Now that, Rafferty, is an act of war. You've been a naughty boy.'

'By God, I should have you whipped. If you were in the army I would—'

'Gerald, darling, there you are.' Briana Pledge, Reynolds' fiancée, barged into the room without so much as knocking. 'I've been looking all over for you.' Briana let out a small gasp at the sight of Tatsuo. 'And Tatsuo! Fancy seeing you here.'

'Briana,' Captain Reynolds said, flustered, 'what are you doing here?'

'Oh, I just arrived on the steamer *Guardian*. Daddy's with me.'

'Dadd… General Pledge?'

General Pledge arrived on his daughter's heels. He pushed into the room with the air of a king. With swagger stick in hand he hooked his hands behind his back and thrust out his chest, chin high. 'Rafferty…' The general glanced at Tatsuo in his seafaring garb. 'Everything alright in here?'

'Y-yes, sir, G-General.'

'Tatsuo Gaston, General.' Tatsuo stepped forward and thrust his hand out to greet the general, who had little choice but to shake it.

'Tatsuo…' The general racked his brain. 'Now where have I heard that name before?' He looked at his daughter. 'Ah! So you're the Tatsuo my little princess speaks so highly of?'

Reynolds ground his teeth.

'I'm the only Tatsuo I know of, General, so I must be the same.'

'Of course this is he, Daddy.'

General Pledge was looking at Tatsuo's bare feet in an unsubtle way.

'Please excuse my dress General,' Tatsuo said. 'I've just returned from the Solomons.'

'Ah, Captain Reynolds here was also there recently.'

'Yes, sir.' Tatsuo looked to Reynolds, who was feeling extremely uneasy. 'Gerald and I were just comparing notes.'

'Oh?'

'Yes. Word is, the Germans have been trying to add all of Bougainville to their protectorate and that they have a gunboat in the area.'

'Yes … well … I don't know about that.'

Tatsuo studied the general a moment and deduced the old man knew more than he was letting on.

Briana slipped her arm through Tatsuo's. 'How long are you here for, darling?'

'I … ah …'

'He was just leaving,' Captain Reynolds said. 'Weren't you?'

'Oh, I was hoping we could catch up before you leave again,' Briana said. 'I don't suppose you can make it to Darwin for our wedding?'

'Briana, dearest,' Reynolds interrupted, 'you couldn't possibly expect guests to travel all that way—'

'On the contrary,' Tatsuo replied, grinning. 'When is the wedding?'

'Exactly one month from today,' Briana said.

'Then I shall do my utmost. Thank you.' Tatsuo paid his compliments to the general. As he was leaving he had a thought.

'One last thing, Rafferty,' Tatsuo said, turning to face the captain, who was in danger of shattering his teeth he was grinding them so hard. 'Rennison Plum?' Tatsuo noted a slight twitch in the captain's eye at the name.

'What of him?'

'You know him, then?' Reynolds shot a glance at the general. *Clearly, I've struck a nerve*, Tatsuo thought. 'Is that correct, Captain?'

'Ah, yes. I have made his acquaintance.'

'Do you by any chance know where I might find him?'

'No!'

'He found passage on the SS *Normannia*,' the general said.

'Oh! So you knew him, too, sir?'

'Yes,' General Pledge said. 'Why do you want to find him, Mr Gaston?'

'Well, I'm really trying to locate his sister, Samoa.'

'The pretty blonde lass?'

'Yes, yes. You've seen her?'

The general looked at his future son-in-law. 'Tell him, Rafferty.'

If anything, Captain Reynolds appeared to sulk. 'They accompanied me on my return from the Solomons,' he replied.

'They did?' Tatsuo smelt success. 'How? I mean, how did...? Where were they?'

'They were at a mission on Rennell Island and asked for passage to Thursday Island.' Tatsuo knew Reynolds was lying, but that didn't matter. Now Tatsuo had confirmation Reynolds must indeed have rescued them from the Germans. *And the stupid bastard didn't realise Rennison was a German spy.*

'They sailed on the *Normannia*?' Tatsuo asked. 'When?'

'Four days ago.'

'For England, right?'

'I should imagine so.'

Tatsuo bid Briana and her father farewell and retired, somewhat deflated, even tossing about thoughts of following Samoa to Europe. Captain Reynolds hurried after him, catching him at the fort gates.

'We're done,' Reynolds told his rival quietly, out of earshot from loose-lipped soldiers.

'Done?' Tatsuo bunched his lips. 'If you mean you'll back off from harassing me if I keep my mouth shut about the ramming business, then, yes—we're done.'

Reynolds gave a stern nod and turned on the heels of his boots. Tatsuo just couldn't help calling out, 'I'll see you in Darwin!'

Reynolds stopped dead in his tracks and turned hard to face his pirate nemesis. 'You turn up at my wedding, and I'll fucking shoot you myself.'

Tatsuo found Selma with the tender near the slip yard where she was sorting groceries to be taken out to *Mystery*.

'How did it go, Cap'n?' Selma asked. 'Alright, by the looks o' yer.'

Tatsuo returned a weak smile. 'It went as well as could be, Selma. Thanks for asking.'

'No mention of bibles crammed with money?'

'No, Selma. God knows what their purpose was.'

'So we get to keep the loot, then?'

'Hopefully. But we're not out of deep water yet.'

Tatsuo looked out to sea between Hammond Island to the north and Friday Island, south, towards the Torres Strait and Arafura Sea, and imagined the SS *Normannia* steaming away at 15 knots with Samoa on board. The thought of having missed her by only days tugged at his heart.

'Where are the boys?' Tatsuo asked of Horace and William.

'Gone to the chandlery. Said they'd be back by noon.'

'Good. I'm keen to leave Thursday behind us.'

Return to Horn Island.

Four and a half days after having left Rambling Jack, the *Mystery* returned, dropping anchor off Horn Island. Here in the bay the wind had died. It was hot.

'106 degrees,' Tatsuo read aloud the brass thermometer screwed to the bulkhead at the entrance to the companionway.

'106, eh?' Horace whistled. 'Bloody feels like it, Boss.'

Tatsuo scoured the shoreline for the hermit. 'No sign of our friend,' he told the others. There was no smoke from a cooking fire, which was unusual, and no sign of Max the blue heeler. 'Will, launch the tender.'

On shore, all was still. The air was stifling and it seemed even the birds were too hot and bothered to sing. Tatsuo looked toward the mangroves nearby. There was no sign of Bertie the croc, just his ominous tracks in the mud leading into the water. Behind the shanty a million cicadas made their incessant racket.

The shanty was empty, and so were the whiskey bottles—well, three of them, at least. They lay where they'd been discarded amongst other stone jars and empty glassware in a corner of the hut.

'Jack one thirsty bastard, Boss. 'e drunk three bottles o' whiskey already.'

Tatsuo shook his head. 'I trust he's had company! Three bottles?'

A meat-safe swinging from a rafter contained some roasted turtle meat. It had hung there long enough to attract flies, and a day-old damper sat on a chipped blue and white plate where it had been abandoned. An open pot of marmalade was crawling with wasps.

But there was no sign of Jack.

Horace and Will spread out, calling out the old man's name. Cats prowled about the scrub at the back while chickens scratched around the yard, where the coop had been left open.

'Jack!'

Silence.

'Where *is* the old bugger? Spread out,' Tatsuo ordered. Moments later Horace's broken voice called out from behind the shanty.

'Boss ... Cap'n.'

'What is it?'

'Better come see, Cap'n.'

Will appeared from the direction of the mangroves as Tatsuo joined Horace along a path behind the shanty leading to a lagoon a few hundred yards away.

'Oh, sweet Jesus!'

Jack lay where he had died, his right arm missing completely, along with his right foot. Clearly he had bled to death.

William's tics triggered. 'What—what the ... fuckit ... wh-what happened?'

'Croc?' Horace asked Tatsuo.

'A croc would have dragged him back into the water,' Tatsuo replied.

'Maybe he fought it off and managed to crawl this far.'

'Or,' Tatsuo looked back along the path towards the lagoon, 'maybe he was fishing in the lagoon and a shark attacked him ... Christ!' Tatsuo had a sudden thought.

'What?'

Tatsuo rushed to where they had buried the stone jars of bank notes. 'No!'

Horace and William stood next to the empty ditch.

'Who? How ...?'

And lying next to the ditch with his head split wide open was Max the blue heeler.

'It wasn't a croc or a shark.' Tatsuo picked up a machete lying nearby. 'Someone found out about our stash.'

Chapter Fifteen

Weeks later

Tatsuo had been morose for weeks. Ever since Dhai—whose life had been lost so needlessly to a misunderstanding and a native spear ten years earlier—no one had stolen Tatsuo's heart like Samoa. Samoa, the castaway baby, named after the island on which she'd been spared, 27 years before.

Rambling Jack often visited Tatsuo in his sleep, seemingly haunting him. The guilt he felt for endangering Jack's life rivaled the love he had lost in Samoa. The best Tatsuo could do was keep busy and prepare for another sail through the trade winds of the South Pacific, transporting more bêche-de-mer for Ah Sin, maybe. Or sailing further afield to Fiji, and then Tahiti—who knew?

The day they docked in Cooktown Tatsuo was keen to empty *Mystery*'s hull of Ah Sin's three tons of smoked bêche-de-mer.

Everyone worked together—Tatsuo, Horace, Selma and William. Tatsuo hired six native lackeys also, along with a bullock dray. The loading, hauling and unloading was hot, exhausting work, but at least Tatsuo could take his mind off Samoa.

Chinese importer-export firm Ewo Hong of Canton—owned by elderly merchant brothers Lee & Chan Hak-kan—took delivery at their warehouse situated at the top end of Cooktown's main thoroughfare, Charlotte Street. The sprawling timber structure tiered down the muddy embankment to where six Chinese junks and a dozen sampans listed precariously, loitering lazily in the mud, taking siesta in the low tide and the stinking heat of the new season.

Each sack of the three tons of smoked fish was inspected carefully. Lee and Chan seemed happy and all were in agreement that Ah Sin's product was always the best quality bêche-de-mer, the literal translation of which was 'spade of the sea,' also known as trepang, or sea cucumber.

Tatsuo dealt with Chan, as he spoke better English. 'Fwee tons at 90 pounds a ton,' Chan said, sitting at his desk, looking up at Tatsuo over the top of wire-rimmed spectacles. 'Is two hunert an' 70 pounds —you agree, my fren?'

'Aye, Chan.' Tatsuo used his neckerchief to wipe sweat from his brow.

He would keep ten per cent of the cash—less expenses for the lackeys and wagon—and purchase a cashier's cheque for Ah Sin at the Queensland National Bank, also in Charlotte Street. At Chan's instruction, brother Lee fetched a cash tin from a large iron safe in the office and started counting out the notes in various denominations. Immediately Tatsuo sensed something familiar in the transaction, a permeating stink he recognised but could not quite put a finger on … when it dawned on him.

'Where did this money come from?' he demanded unexpectedly. Lee and Chan were immediately evasive. Chinese businessmen took transactions seriously. *What was this, a threat?*

But Tatsuo had dealt with these brothers for years.

'Chan, this money,'—he held up a handful and sniffed it—'where did these banknotes come from?'

'Why? Why you ask?'

Tatsuo knew if Chan suspected the notes were stolen the accusation would silence both Chinamen.

'Why you ask?' Chan repeated. 'Money good.'

'Yes, I know money good. But I … excuse me one moment.' Tatsuo collected up the full amount, 270 pounds, and went searching for the others. He found Horace, Selma and William under the shade of coconut palms, looking hot and bothered.

Horace found enough energy to bounce to his feet. 'Ready to go the White Horse, Cap'n? Bloody hot sittin' 'ere.'

Tatsuo said nothing. He shook the notes under Selma's nose. 'Smell familiar.'

'Phew, not nice, Skipper. Where 'ave the Chinamen been keeping that, or shouldn't I ask?' She broke into a lazy cackle. Horace and William agreed.

'Ah, shit!' Horace turned up his nose. 'Dat smell like Selma's cooking.'

Selma punched Horace in the arm for his trouble.

'That's the money we put in them jars,' William said, his young nose more refined than those of the others.

'That's what I thought.' Tatsuo marched back to the Chinamen, who had hastily re-locked the safe.

'Chan, Lee,' Tatsuo asked as diplomatically as possible, 'I've got to know, please—where did these bank notes come from?'

Silence. Extracting an answer to such a question would be akin to extracting blood from a stone, and these two brothers were suspicious and superstitious.

Tatsuo decided to appeal to their conscience. He told them the story, including details on the murder of Rambling Jack, an old man murdered for money, and how old Max the blue heeler had been bludgeoned to death.

'Killing, even animals,' Chan said sadly, 'leads to misfortune.'

It worked. As it turned out, both Chinamen had known Jack; they had bought from him when he had brought pearl shell to sell.

'He good man, Jack.'

'Aye. So will you help me?'

Chan finally opened up. 'Chen. He buy *Ching Shih* from us. Two thousand pound he pay.'

'*Ching Shih*? A junk? A ship?'

'Yes. She good, fast ship, werry stwong, good price.' Chan looked at the payment in Tatsuo's hand. Suddenly it seemed like blood money. 'That money we take from Chen.'

'Benjamin Chen, yes?' Tatsuo asked.

'That what I say.'

Tatsuo knew Benjamin Chen well. He was from Taiwan, of mixed race like Tatsuo, half Chinese, half European. He was also known as Timberfist, on account of having only one hand, the other having been lost using explosives to catch fish. The stub on the shorter arm was rigged with a wooden block into which an iron hook was screwed. As useful as this was, it could prove a liability occasionally; like the time it became entangled in an anchor rope and pulled him overboard, dragging him 30 feet down to the seabed. On that occasion he'd twisted his body around several times to unscrew the hook and swum back to the surface. At least that was the story that Chen told.

Tatsuo knew Timberfist based himself in Dutch New Guinea, where he traded as a merchant carrying anything that made money, especially from the lucrative blackbirding trade. But the way Timberfist practiced it, it was more like slavery. Natives were promised good wages and living conditions. But they received neither.

It was rumoured Timberfist had once found a centuries-old merchant junk wrecked off the coast of Vietnam in which he found a quantity of valuable porcelain, which he sold to a dealer in Hong Kong. Owing money all around the islands, Timberfist denied this financial windfall, of course; he was always the secretive type.

But Tatsuo had moored next to his 30-foot junk, *Jasmijn*, named after his Dutch wife, at Thursday Island a year or so before, and recognised the coral-encrusted four-foot tall pottery urn tied to the main mast, used for water storage, as a Ming wine vessel, possibly late 17th century—the same period and origin as the valuable porcelain.

Now of course, Benjamin Chen was in the market for a new ship, his precious *Jasmijn* having been damaged on a reef off Lizard Island on the Barrier Reef, where she'd lost a cargo of cedar. But rather than repair her, he must have thought why not buy another with the cash from his ill-gotten gains at Rambling Jack's Bay?

Tatsuo knew heavy gambler Timberfist was dishonest, a liar, a cheat and a thief, but he was not known as a murderer. Although, it was rumoured, he had once thrown a pregnant native overboard because she was a burden.

Despite being a town with a large transient population, Cooktown was still a small place where gossip cloyed the settlement like the suffocating weather. Tatsuo's first move after depositing Ah Sin's money at the Queensland National Bank was to meet up with his crew at the White Horse Hotel, refresh himself with a well-earned beer and plan their next move.

Tatsuo had made enquiries. 'Benjamin Chen is going nowhere soon.' 'He may have purchased a bargain from the Hak-kan brothers, but the bamboo-fibre sails are rotting and he must replace them with canvas.' Tatsuo spoke of the junk's iconic red sails, dyed with bark tannin extracted from oak trees. 'This will delay any departure by at least one week, as the sails have to be made specially.'

'Who told you this—Yorkie?' Selma asked, referring to a local aborigine who traded in information for grog money.

'Aye, Yorkie.' Tatsuo noted Selma's head shake. Yorkie could be unreliable.

'What else did Yorkie tell yer?'

'He told me Chen's been on a bender at the Sovereign.' Tatsuo spoke of the Sovereign Hotel on the corner of Charlotte and Green Street. 'He's been cashed up lately, Yorkie said. He's been buying lots of temporary friends with rounds of drinks. And he's been losing at the tables, although Yorkie assured me Chen's luck changed for the better this afternoon, and he was going hard at the poker with a bunch of drovers up from Townsville.'

Selma finished the last of her quart of beer and her sigh of satisfaction was contagious. She looked into the depths of the empty tankard a moment, deep in thought.

'What's the plan, then, Skipper?' Selma swiped her arm across her mouth left to right, removing the deposited froth. Hotel owner Ma 'Breaker' Bentley kept a sharp eye out—she was like that—and three more brews were pumped from the wooden barrel under the bar. *The beer might be warm, but it was bloody wet.*

'The plan?' Tatsuo said. 'I'm going to search the ship, that's the plan.'

The others knew this was madness, but the money was theirs. There would be no assistance from the law; they would simply have to fight for it, if necessary.

'What makes yer think it's on board, Boss?' Horace said.

'He's living on board, so where else would it be?'

'What about his crew?' Selma asked.

'Yorkie said there's only the cook on board, an old Chinese bloke, deaf as a post. The crew are enjoying time out until the sails are fitted.'

'And his wife?' Selma wondered.

'Jasmijn? She has a cousin who lives five miles south of here and Yorkie said last he heard she had gone to stay with the cousin for a few days.'

'Hopefully she's still there?' Horace said.

'Aye.'

'Tell yer what, Cap'n,'—Horace swigged at his ginger beer—'I'll go pretend I'm drinkin' at the Sovereign and keep an eye on the bastard. I'm jus' 'nother blackfella to the half-caste mongrel. If'n 'e make a move I'll hassle him in the street, hold 'im up, like. Will, 'ere, can be waitin' across the street. When 'e sees me 'e can come warn yer.'

'That'll work.'

'What can I do?' Selma asked.

'Stay safe.'

'And miss out on the fun? No way—we owe this to Jack. I'm comin' to watch yer back.'

Two hours later it was dark, dark enough to make a move. Angered by the image of his old friend Rambling Jack hacked to death, Tatsuo 'borrowed' a small clinker that was tied up at a nearby jetty and rowed out to the junk *Ching Shih.* The large Oriental ship was now afloat on a high tide. It was after nine and the cooler night air kept the diehard drinkers and gamblers at the Sovereign's bar and card tables.

Tatsuo rowed around the junk. There were no lights, no lanterns, just darkness and quiet, a quietness interrupted by distant drunken laughter along the waterfront hotels, or, occasionally, by the splash of a powerful armoured tail as a crocodile caught a barramundi in its hungry jaws. Tatsuo secured the clinker and climbed the junk's anchor cable. Slipping over the bow rail he padded barefoot across the deck. He passed silently by the mizzenmast and the open galley. There was no sign of the old Chinese cook. Presumably he had gone ashore also. Tatsuo continued to the stern castle, where a low doorway led to the captain's cabin. Tatsuo wasted no time searching Benjamin Chen's private trunks. He fossicked through boxes and drawers, trunks and linen coffers.

Nothing.

Tatsuo had dropped silently to his knees, and was fishing for travelling chests under the main cabin bed when …

'What are you doing here?' Benjamin Chen's wife was barely visible, clothed in an Oriental black-silk pants suit. She stood firm, veiled in darkness. 'Well?' she insisted, her cold tone manifesting menace.

'I … ah …' Tatsuo made to stand.

'Slowly! Put your hands where I can see them.' Tatsuo noticed she held a small pistol, a derringer, and it was aimed directly at him. Immediately, as Tatsuo turned to face the woman, his profile was revealed by moonlight reflected in off the water.

'Why, it's Captain Gaston of the *Mystery*!'

'Jasmijn Chen.' Tatsuo turned slowly. The two knew of each other, but that was the sum total of their relationship. Tatsuo forced a pathetic smile, recognising the double-barreled Remington Model 95 with its nickel-plated finish and walnut grip as an inaccurate weapon, unless fired at short range. And Jasmijn was less than eight feet away.

'I … I was just … ah … looking for Benjamin, actually,' Tatsuo said lamely.

'What? Sneaking about my ship like a thief in the night?' Jasmijn's excellent English was delivered with a thick Dutch accent.

Yet Tatsuo detected a break in her voice, a lack of confidence.

'True, Jasmijn. I was looking for Benjamin.'

'You lie!' Jasmijn jerked the gun. 'Hands where I can see them.'

'Easy, Jasmijn. Be careful where you aim that thing.'

'Light that lamp so I can see you properly.' Jasmijn pointed to a spirit lamp on the cabin desk. 'You'll find matches in the top drawer, if you haven't already noticed,' she said with sarcasm.

Tatsuo lit the lamp and, lifting the glass chimney, he tweaked the burning wick, illuminating the cabin. He could now see the middle-aged woman clearly. She was tall, slim and quite stunning in her Oriental dress. But it was hardly nightwear. It was then that Tatsuo noticed the travelling trunk on the bed, filled with women's clothing and personal items. If Tatsuo didn't know any better he would suspect …

'Going somewhere?'

'None of your business. Now answer the question, what are you doing here?'

'Looking for Benjamin.'

'Don't lie!'

'Look, Jasmijn, put the gun down and we can talk.'

'Oh, do you think I'm stupid? Give me a good reason why I shouldn't shoot you here and now.'

As threatening as this comment appeared, Tatsuo took a gamble. 'Now, Jasmijn, you don't want to be arrested for killing me and being charged for murder along with your husband.'

Jasmijn couldn't comprehend this sudden change to confidence in this Japanese Frenchman's tone. 'What are you talking about?'

'Look, I don't know whether you were personally present or not, but I know for a fact that Benjamin killed Rambling Jack on Horn Island.' Jasmijn eyes gave her away. She knew something, alright. The woman looked long and hard at Tatsuo.

'Well?' Tatsuo asked.

'Well, what?'

'Were you on Horn Island recently?'

'What if I was?'

Tatsuo flinched. This was akin to a confession. 'Answer me this, then. How did you know Jack was hiding all that money?'

'What money?'

'The money buried behind Jack's hut.'

'Don't know what you're talking about.'

'Oh, don't lie to me, Jasmijn. That money belonged to me and my crew. Jack was safekeeping it for me and you and your husband killed Jack for it.'

Jasmijn looked pale. Her mind was awash with decisions. 'I had nothing to do with Jack's death,' she finally said.

'Oh?'

Silence.

'Speak to me, Jasmijn. What happened?'

'I was aboard the *Jasmijn*, our old boat.'

'Yes, I know the *Jasmijn*. And … ?'

'Look, the killing was an accident.' Jasmijn was weakening. Truth be known she had been tormented by guilt since the day of the killing.

'So you admit it, then?' Tatsuo stepped forward and the pistol reared up like a striking cobra.

'Back!'

'Easy. Easy does it. I just want the truth.'

'Then let's get something straight. I admit nothing. I was on board the boat when Benjamin went ashore.'

'What were you doing there?'

'We went to Horn Island as we were in the area and Jack owed Benjamin 180 pounds.'

'For what?'

'Gambling. Jack lost big time at poker. It had been seven months and every time we paid him a visit Jack never had the money. Then we stopped by the island as we often did, and this time Jack says, "I've got the money. Wait here while I go fetch it." But Benjamin followed him, thinking Jack was up to no good, and he catches him digging up a jar of banknotes. Well, Jack turned around and caught Benjamin and he went crazy, attacking Benjamin, who stabbed him with a machete. He didn't mean to kill him, it was self-defence.'

'Then why was Jack's body dismembered?'

'Benjamin tried to make it look like a crocodile attack.' That made sense. 'Then, when Benjamin checked, he found lots of jars buried, hidden in a shallow hole.'

'You've just admitted that you are an accessory to murder.'

'That's your word against mine.'

'I haven't got time for this,' Tatsuo said, growing impatient. 'Look, Jasmijn, that's my money. I buried it there for safekeeping—I want it back.' Tatsuo caught Jasmijn looking toward her luggage and had a sudden thought. 'You *are* leaving, aren't you?' Jasmijn was not a good liar. Her face reddened. 'Wh-what are you talking about?'

'You're leaving Benjamin, aren't you? While he's drunk in the hotel, you're shooting through.'

Tatsuo stepped over to the bed and tipped the trunk upside down, looking for the money.

'How dare you!' Jasmijn stepped back two paces, keeping her distance, with the pistol still aimed at Tatsuo's chest. But Tatsuo was calling her bluff, doubting the woman really wanted to do him harm.

'Where's the money?'

Jasmijn also grew impatient. 'If I tell you where it's hid I want half,' she said, knowing she didn't have time for this altercation.

'So it *is* on board?'

'Yes, and well hidden.'

'Then where is it?'

'I said I want half. I'll fetch the money, we go halves. I leave Cooktown immediately. No police. Agreed?'

'Half! Forget it! No.' Tatsuo was close to retrieving his money. But not close enough. 'Why should I let you have any of it?'

'I want to get away from this godforsaken country. I want to get away from Benjamin. I'm sick of his drinking, his womanising, his abuse. I'm a city woman. I want to return to Rotterdam.'

'You're an accessory to murder, Jasmijn.'

'Look. I'm serious. I'm not playing a game here. I want 25 per cent, at least.' Jasmijn was growing desperate.

This crazy sea captain was jeopardising everything and there was no time to waste. But she recognised determination in Tatsuo's eyes. He was going nowhere any time soon. Jasmijn dropped the pistol to her side and tears welled in her eyes.

'I just want to get away from here!' she cried out in frustration.

Tatsuo stepped forward carefully and took the pistol from her. 'You're not a killer,' he said softly. 'Now show me where the money's hidden.'

'What's in it for me?' she asked weakly.

Tatsuo wanted out also, and for both their sakes—Benjamin Chen could return any minute. 'I'll give you 1,000, Jasmijn, and that's more than you deserve. It is stolen blood money.'

Jasmijn capitulated. 'It's in here,' she said, leading Tatsuo to the storeroom off the stern cabin, where Tatsuo saw two hardhat diving helmets and suits hanging, drying.

'I didn't know Benjamin was into pearling,' he said.

'He's not.'

'Then why the suits?'

'Benjamin has hired two Filipino divers. The plan is we leave as soon as the sails are fitted for Santa Isabel Island.'

'Santa Isabel? Why?'

Jasmijn looked at Tatsuo long and hard. 'Look, Benjamin will return soon. We must act quickly. I will show you where the money is.'

But Tatsuo had a gut feeling more was afoot than he'd expected. 'Tell me first why Benjamin wants to sail to Santa Isabel.'

There was no reason now for Jasmijn to hold back. Her heavy bosom rose and fell with a deep sigh.

'Gold,' she said. That magic word resonated around the cabin.

'Gold?' Tatsuo repeated.

'Yes. Benjamin has heard on the grape vine that a German ship was sunk only recently off the north coast of Santa Isabel Island. There was supposedly gold on board. He has the location marked on a map and the services of a German officer who was on board.' Jasmijn shrugged her shoulders and huffed. 'So he says. There is even an "'X' marks the spot" on the map, according to the story.'

Tatsuo shook his head; *how readily rumours start*, he thought.

'Well, I have some bad news for you, Jasmijn. I was there, and I saw—'

'You were there? What do you mean?'

'I was there when that ship sank.'

'What? How?'

'Doesn't matter.'

'But—'

'It was the SS *Prinzessin*, right? A German gunboat sunk by the Royal Navy?'

'Yes! That's the name, the *Prinzessin.*'

'I saw the whole thing, and I can assure you that German ship sank within minutes in a thousand foot of water.'

'No. That's where you are wrong.'

'Pardon?'

'You are wrong. The survivor told Benjamin—'

'Who is this survivor?'

'He was one of the last to be picked up after the officers saved themselves and left the site. He said the ship is caught on a coral ledge in less than 80 feet of water. A hundred yards either side and the ship would have slipped, as you said, into a thousand feet of water.'

'You said there was a map. Have you seen it?'

'No.'

'Have you met this survivor?'

'No. But Benjamin told me the German has been back to the site since and he swears the top superstructure of the *Prinzessin* can be seen in 30 feet of water on a low tide.'

This was remotely possible.

'Then why would he tell Benjamin?' Tatsuo asked, referring to the German survivor. 'I mean—Benjamin? Really? Of all people…'

'The German needs divers. In exchange, he is offering the location. They are to share the spoils fifty-fifty.'

Tatsuo nodded toward the upended travelling chest. 'Then why are you running away? Why aren't you hanging around for this … gold?'

'Because I don't believe the gold is there, and I don't want to be arrested as an accessory to murder. It's only a matter of time.'

'Fair enough. So where's the money?'

Suddenly a deep voice resonated. 'Well, well, well!'

Tatsuo and Jasmijn twisted about to face Benjamin Chen, propped against the bulkhead to the main cabin. 'You bitch!'

'Chen? I didn't … I wasn't expecting you back so early.'

'You bitch! You lowlands dog!' Chen had heard everything. 'The cook said you had company.'

He was drunk and angry. Whilst he gripped the doorframe for support with one hand, he clutched a long-pointed sailor's knife in his other.

Tatsuo's discovery that the gold was still within reach was cruelly shattered by the realisation that his life was in danger once more, threatened by an unreasonable man who had nothing to lose, and plenty to gain if Tatsuo was dead.

Chen lunged.

Tatsuo leapt aside but in the confined space the dagger point lanced his upper right arm. Dodging right, then left, he caught Chen's dagger arm and, twisting it, he delivered a left hook to the man's jaw. The blow caused Chen to stagger backwards. He straightened and lashed out once more with the blade.

The point caught in Tatsuo's tunic. Tatsuo raised his right arm, brought it down hard. Chen dropped the dagger. Cursing, Chen thrust his body forward. Tatsuo caught him by both lapels, throwing him sideways against the writing desk. The lamp crushed under his weight. The glass smashed. Chen fell to the floor … and the damaged lamp spilt its fuel which poured off the desk, soaking Chen's clothing.

Flames chased the spillage. A tongue of purple, red and yellow lunged towards Chen and he exploded in flames.

Screaming, Chen rolled on the cabin floor. Tatsuo snatched bedding and tried to extinguish the flames, but the bedding caught fire. Chen's scorched skin instantly blistered. The pain was unbearable. Chen crawled screeching to the stern deck. He pulled himself erect at the guardrail, but a light breeze fed the flames. Chen's body became a torch. He screeched in agony, his flesh crackling and burning; the skin on his face bubbled, his hair blackened and fire seared his eyes.

Chen leapt overboard.

At the same moment the bamboo superstructure of the *Ching Shih* caught alight like paper.

'No!' Jasmijn screamed out, more in shock than pity. Tatsuo rushed to the port side facing the sea. Only white water revealed where Chen landed. Instantly, there was movement … Dark, ominous shapes snaked from the mudflats, slipping silently into the water.

The fire on board spread.

Flames licked, teased and danced their way up the masts, attacking the bamboo battens; tarred ropes burned like the wicks on firecrackers. In the cabin, more inflammable spirit dripped through the decking, down the companionway, seeking fuel … of which there was a great abundance.

A final garbled scream drew Tatsuo's attention back to the rail. The crunching of human bones was sickening, yet death came swiftly.

'Jasmijn!' Tatsuo shouted over the increasing inferno. 'Jasmijn!'

The woman had gone to fetch the money, the cursed banknotes that had caused nothing but doom and misery.

Tatsuo sprang to the cabin doorway. But inside was a furnace. The heat was intense. The cracking and snapping was deafening. Instantly a whoosh of combustibles exploded below the deck.

'Jasmijn!' Tatsuo cried out.

There came no reply.

Tatsuo had no choice but to save himself. Suddenly he was conscious of his own name being called.

'Tatsuo!'

Tatsuo's name was shouted over and over from the docks. The flames were fierce and the smoke thickening. Tatsuo was now aware the wharf had drawn a crowd, and waving frantically, screaming his name, were Selma, Horace and William …

Family.

Tatsuo took to the anchor rope as it caught fire. But the borrowed clinker broke free and also caught alight. Tatsuo was climbing down when the rope burnt through. He dropped gracelessly into the muddy water and promptly sank. He struck out for the surface. Surfacing, gasping for air, he looked about him. The clinker was ten feet distant and burning, while the water all about him bubbled red from flames and Chen's blood, and saltwater crocodiles fought over Chen's bloody carcass. In the blinding, muddy water something hard and fast grated by Tatsuo's leg. Tatsuo kicked out. The croc turned toward him in a mad frenzy of gorging. If anything, the clinker was now further away. Tatsuo had no choice. He struck out for the shore. Behind him dark, sleek, prehistoric shapes weaved after him.

Two crocs … three.

They followed with stealth and cunning, barely leaving a wake.

William and Horace launched a dinghy and pushed off from the shore. Tatsuo was a powerful swimmer but the bastard crocs were closing fast.

Twenty feet from shore, Horace screamed, 'Swim, Cap'n!'

William rowed like a champion. Tatsuo caught the dinghy's bow head on. He hooked his hands over the prow and Horace leapt forward,nearly joining the skipper in the water. William pounded an oar into the head of the first salty. Tatsuo hoisted himself upwards and somersaulted into the boat. Horace landed on top of him. Now with three at the tiny bow, the small craft nearly capsized. Another croc launched itself at the boat. Its giant head rearing up from the water … hissing … jaws gnashing.

Will struck out again … and again.

Now several crocs surrounded the tiny tender. The water was turbulent, like a whitewater rapid; the only difference—it was muddy, bloody and black as death. Instantly a shot rang out. A rearing croc rolled over, falling heavily back into the water, a bullet lodged in its throat. Another shot sizzled by Tatsuo, slamming into the eye of another croc. Marksmen on the wharf took up target practice. William sat heavily back on the bench and rowed hard for shore. At the water's edge Selma had no end of supporters. The dinghy was dragged away from the water's edge, while some of the more aggressive crocs dared crawl onto the embankment. Only the yells and shouting of drunken revelers sent them back into the water.

It had been close. Too damned close.

Tatsuo sucked in several deep breaths. He slowed his racing heart and finally took in his surroundings. Like it or not, he was the centre of attraction. But now the excitement was over and the crowd dispersed. Tatsuo looked over at Horace, equally enervated.

'Jesus Christ, Horace.' Tatsuo burst out laughing, an anxious, nervous laugh. 'Your face sure is white, for a blackfella.'

Behind them the *Ching Shih* was a bamboo bonfire. There had been no sign or sound from Jasmijn.

'The money, Boss?' Horace finally asked.

Tatsuo nodded to the burning junk.

'It was never meant to be, Horace,' Selma said, putting an arm around her old mate and sighing. 'Blood money, all of it.'

Chapter Sixteen

Next morning.

Tatsuo wanted to sail off towards the horizon, to nowhere in particular. Simply weigh anchor, set the sails and go wherever the wind took him. But the police had other ideas. Tatsuo spent three hours at the police station preparing a written statement, including information on the death of Rambling Jack, whose death Tatsuo did not wish to be accused of. The statement read like an adventure novel and the police struggled to believe the 'banknotes in the bibles' narrative, but as all evidence was now ash drifting out on the tide towards the Coral Sea, there was little anyone could prove or disprove.

Selma, Horace, William and Pearl met their captain outside the waterfront police station, where they had waited patiently.

'Another stinker,' Selma said, looking at the clear sky.

Tatsuo smiled warmly at his cook. She was a solid part of his life. She had fed him for years, and did a bloody good job of it, most of the time. Great with fresh fish. But she baked lousy cakes. Tatsuo looked up at the sky also. 'A stinker, huh? Yes, well, we're not here to talk about the weather.'

'It's not too early for a drink, then,' Selma said. She didn't give a stuff whether the others would join her or not. Despondent after the last few days' bedlam, Selma was about to head for the White Horse when abruptly Pearl sat up and barked. The old three-legged red setter suddenly took off down the docks towards the passenger steamer *Cassowary*, recently docked from Darwin.

'Fuck. Fuckin' dog.' William twitched as his Tourette's struck again. 'What's she up to …?' … twitch …

Mystery's crew was watching the dog limp, run crookedly and hobble towards the steamer, when it became apparent she was rushing to greet someone.

'Now what?' Tatsuo eyes narrowed, adjusting to the bright morning sun, still low in the sky. The *Cassowary* sat high in the water and the gangway swung at a steep angle. Then, amongst the hot and bothered passengers alighting, one figure stood out. 'Is that … Samoa?'It was apparent the person saw Tatsuo amongst the townsfolk arriving to greet the ship.

'Samoa!' he yelled out. Samoa waved back. At first she was hesitant, her greeting apprehensive, as if she were uncertain of whether she was in fact doing the right thing, following her heart.

'Samoa!' Tatsuo cried out unashamedly. He hurried to greet her. What had been intended as a warm hug became a passionate embrace. 'Samoa, you came back.' Tatsuo's arms tightened and Samoa showed no restraint. Tatsuo pushed back briefly. Face to face. 'Samoa. Is this really you?'

'Yes,' she whispered in a husky voice. They kissed, a long passionate kiss. A risqué, public kiss that would have been frowned upon in Sydney or Melbourne. But this was the wild frontier. Tatsuo finally came up for air. 'I never thought I'd see you again,' he said, his voice breaking. He wiped a tear from Samoa's eye. 'I thought I'd lost you,' Tatsuo said.

'And me, too.'

They stood face to face, at arm's length, holding both hands, studying each other for what seemed ages, until they became aware they were holding up passenger traffic. 'I thought you were on board the *Normannia*, on your way to London,' Tatsuo said, leading Samoa away as they walked hand in hand.

'I was.'

'What happened?'

'I jumped ship in Darwin.'

'How did you know I'd be here?'

'I didn't. It was just a wild guess.' Samoa pulled Tatsuo close once more. 'I would have kept looking until I found you, my darling … You crazy man.'

Tatsuo had no control over his emotions. 'I love you,' he said and, with the crew standing by, Samoa answered with a silencing finger to his lips.

Suddenly Selma spoke up. 'Christ, you two, are we goin' to celebrate at the White Horse or what?'

The White Horse Hotel. One hour later.

Samoa took Tatsuo aside. 'Alright,' she said, taking a deep breath in, 'I think it's only fair you know what's been going on, but I must insist it is our secret.'

'Oh?' It was time to be serious. Tatsuo was apprehensive. Some things, he thought, he would prefer swept under the carpet. 'Ah … what?'

'Come,' Samoa insisted. Excusing them both from the rest of the crew she led Tatsuo outside.

Cooktown was embracing a new day. The tropical township had been buzzing with commerce since the arrival of *the Cassowary*. But no one took notice of the handsome couple at the side of the hotel sitting on a stack of kitchen firewood, huddled in conference under the shade of the veranda. Samoa did not hesitate. 'Rennison …'

'Ah, Rennison. I was wondering when you'd mention him.'

'Yes, well, Rennison worked for Whitehall.'

'Whitehall? London?'

'Yes.'

'In politics?'

'Not exactly.' Samoa placed her hand on Tatsuo's arm. 'He … ah … Rennison was in espionage.'

'A spy!'

Samoa pulled a face. More a *keep the voice down* cringe, really. 'Yes, I suppose you could call him that.'

'Well, he either was or he wasn't.'

'Alright, then,' Samoa whispered, 'he was a spy,'

'Devil's blood! And I thought he was in bed with the sauerkrauts. I knew there was more to Captain Reynolds' story.'

'Captain Reynolds?'

'Yes.' Tatsuo recounted how the army captain had told him he'd found Rennison and Samoa at a mission on Rennell Island and how 'you pleaded for a passage back to Thursday Island.'

Samoa shook her head. 'Reynolds pretended to take us prisoner after the sinking of the *Prinzessin.*'

'I thought I had lost you that day,' Tatsuo said. He explained how he'd witnessed the whole altercation.

'You were there?' Samoa was incredulous. 'I recall talk on the bridge of the *Pride*, how a pearler was in the area and might have witnessed the event, but I never guessed it could be you, my love.'

'Aye. It was me.'

'Why were you there?'

'Looking for you.'

Samoa took Tatsuo's hand and squeezed hard. 'That was the most terrifying thing that has ever happened to me. I thought I was going to drown that day.'

'Yes, well. I thought I had lost you, too. But go on … Rennison? When I last saw you at Buala on Santa Isabel, Rennison was in cahoots with the Germans.'

'He was.'

'What?'

'This is where it gets confusing, especially for Rennison. He was a double agent.'

'Double agent? How's that work?'

'He worked for Whitehall, but infiltrated the Germans, and with his fluent German and knowledge of Germany he managed to convince them he wanted to work for them.'

'The Germans?'

'Yes. So then he would learn all he could and report back to Whitehall.'

'Jesus. Now that is gutsy.' Tatsuo whistled and Pearl hobbled around the corner on her three legs. He gave her a good head rub and the devoted hound curled at his feet. 'So who was the German bloke you met on Thursday Island the morning before we left?'

'He was a consulate official dealing with Rennison. He thought Rennison was on *his* side, but he was wrong.'

'So what were you doing meeting him?'

'I was trying to find out about the Lutheran Missionaries on Mist Island. I had telegrammed the German consulate in Sydney to try and find out about Rennison. Don't forget, I didn't know Rennison was a double agent at that stage. But as Rennison was working for the Germans, the consulate would tell me nothing. They denied any knowledge of a man called Rennison Plum.'

'You mean Horst Swartz?'

'Yes. So you knew his German name, then.'

'Aye.'

'That's when I discovered there was a German representative on Thursday Island, so I arranged to meet him.'

'They told you in Sydney?'

'Exactly.'

'So what exactly was he up to, this spy brother of yours?'

Samoa looked about surreptitiously once more. 'He was infiltrating German intelligence. Gathering information about Germans setting up naval bases in New Guinea and the like.'

'But why did the Germans maroon Rennison on the Shoal of Ghosts?'

'Well, that was supposed to have been a clever ruse. He was left on the reef and the information was leaked to the Royal Navy. The Germans knew the Royal Navy were in the area, and that they would have no choice but to rescue him.'

'The Royal Navy?'

'Yes. Making Rennison a believable contact embedded with the British. That's in the Germans' eyes. But all the while he was working for Queen and country anyway, and all the while he had vital information regarding German bases in the Coral Sea. This also explained where he had been the past five years, since I last saw him.'

'Confusing.'

'Very. What made things awkward for Rennison was when his beloved sister, yours truly, turned up in the Pacific. Then he had another worry.'

'The Germans didn't know about the gold, either,' Tatsuo told Samoa. 'It was only when the German captain, who I think has turned out to be a renegade, searched Bligh's boat, the *Beacon*, caught in the doldrums at sea. He was looking for guns, but found the gold, our gold, which Bligh had stolen from us. They took it and then scuttled the *Beacon*. I don't think the German captain was going to declare that gold to his sovereign. Well, not all of it, anyway.'

'Gold and greed go hand in hand.'

'What about the bibles?' Tatsuo asked as a throwaway question.

'Oh, golly,' Samoa exclaimed, looking surprised. 'I'd forgotten about them. Where are they?'

'I left them on Bona Bona,' Tatsuo lied. 'To be handed out to missionaries.'

'Well, that'll be interesting.'

Tatsuo studied Samoa's reaction. 'Why?'

'Oh … Lutheran bibles handed out to Catholic missionaries, or whoever.'

Tatsuo looked Samoa in the eye and had no doubt then and there that she knew nothing about the pounds sterling concealed in the bibles. Tatsuo described the discovery.

Samoa was dumbfounded when she heard about the hidden banknotes. 'That would have been intended for Rennison to purchase favours and land from the natives on Bougainville, to disrupt the German occupation.'

'That makes sense The money was all in pounds sterling and mixed denominations.'

'How do you mean?'

'Well, it wasn't in Deutschmarks.'

'Oh. He never mentioned the money to me.'

'Forever the secret agent, huh? Where is he now, anyway?'

'On his way to London.'

Tatsuo leant forward and stole another kiss, a passionate kiss that sent prickles down Samoa's spine. Tatsuo stood abruptly and offered his hand. 'Come.' He dragged her to her feet.

'Where?'

'I have unfinished business with the crew … and with you.'

'Oh!'

On board the *Mystery*, Pearl took it upon herself to undertake guard duty in the shade of the sail locker, while her master and Samoa slipped below decks.

'What are you up to, Captain Gaston?' Samoa giggled.

Tatsuo said nothing. He dragged a heavy carpetbag out from under his bunk. Samoa looked puzzled. 'What's that?'

'Surprise.'

'Oh? For me?'

'For all of us.' Tatsuo hefted the bag with one arm onto the bunk, flexing muscle. He pulled back the flap, inviting Samoa to see inside for herself.

Samoa's jaw dropped. 'G … Gold!' The four lettered word demanded reverence. Samoa stood frozen, staring at ingots of solid gold. 'How? I mean … I thought the gold was lost with the *Prinzessin*.'

'It was. Well, most of it.' Tatsuo had kept the gold a secret until now and the response from Samoa was reward enough.

Samoa instinctively reached in to touch the shining bars, taking two hands to prise one free, mentally weighing it. 'H-how?' she stammered.

'Do you remember when Horace was hoisting me from the wreck site and the diving platform got stuck?'

'Yes.'

'And Bligh was aboard the *Mystery*?'

'Yes.'

'Well I suspected something was afoot and stashed these bars in a contraband locker I built into the keel of the boat some time ago.'
'For smuggling?' Samoa raised an eyebrow feigning disapproval.
'Well,' Tatsuo grinned. 'I suppose you could say that.'
'How many are there?'
'Six.'
'And the others don't know about it?'
'Not yet.'
'Tatsuo Gaston, you never cease to amaze me.' Samoa dropped the bar back into the bag with a satisfying clunk only gold on gold could resonate. Tatsuo resealed the carpet bag, shoving the gold back under the bunk. 'Let's go break the news,' Tatsuo said. 'I can't wait to see their faces when I tell them.'
Samoa didn't move. 'What's the hurry?' Samoa's skirt fell to the deck and she stood before him naked but for her Parisian undergarments. Tatsuo stood fast.

'Wh-what's the h-hurry?' Tatsuo sounded rather taken aback. He cleared his throat. 'Hurry? Why … ah … There's no hurry.'

The invitation made Tatsuo light-headed. He had not been with a woman for quite some time, and especially not with a woman he knew deep in his heart that he truly loved. Not since Dhai had been lost to him ten years earlier had he felt such passion. Samoa stepped from her attire. Her nakedness took Tatsuo's breath away. Her chalk-white breasts and womanhood—itself a neat tuft of blonde—were accentuated by the suntan she'd acquired during the past months in the tropics. Samoa took Tatsuo in her arms. They kissed once more, a wet, intense kiss of submission, an embrace of totally intoxicated passion. Samoa felt Tatsuo's arousal. Not since that moment in the cave all those weeks before had she felt such desire. Samoa unbuttoned Tatsuo's britches while Tatsuo ripped his shirt free, exposing his chiseled body. He hoisted Samoa into his arms. She wrapped her legs about him and, overbalanced, they crashed against the wall in unbridled passion before falling heavily onto Tatsuo's bunk.

Selma was no fool. She read the signs.

The time elapsed was a give-away, for starters. But then there was the teased hair, the touching, the shared impish grins of two people in love. It was infectious. Selma read the two contented faces like she could read a recipe for blancmange.

'You took your time … Captain.' Clearly Selma had relaxed tenfold over several whiskies. Now the bar was filling steadily. Tatsuo said nothing at first. 'Will,' he finally said.

'Cap'n.'

'Get more whiskey, lad.'

Minutes past. William returned with a bottle while Tatsuo's damned smile was starting to aggravate Selma. 'Do you want to tell them?' Tatsuo asked Samoa. 'Or shall I?'

'You tell them,' Samoa grinned back.

'Tell us what, god dammit?' Selma grumbled.

'What would you say if I told you you're each a gold bar richer?'

'What the hell yer talkin' about?' Selma banged her empty glass on the table.

Tatsu went on to explain, while they all looked on, disbelieving. 'Samoa,' Tatsuo demanded confirmation. 'Tell 'em what you saw.'

Samoa nodded acknowledgment.

'The contraband locker?' Selma conceded.

'Aye.' Tatsuo glanced to nearby tables. 'But let's keep our voices down, huh?'

'They've been there the whole time, eh?' Horace asked. Tatsuo nodded.

'You're a bloody genius!' Selma poured herself a stiff whiskey.

'Why didn't yer tell us before, Cap'n?' William asked.

'I thought it best I keep it to myself until now, in case we encountered another mongrel like Bligh.'

Tatsuo, with Samoa's blessing, went on to explain Samoa's brother Rennison's involvement in all the shenanagans.

'There's one more thing,' Tatsuo told the gathering casually.

'What's that, Boss?'

'What would you say if I said there's half a ton of this …' Tatsuo looked about surreptitiously. The bar had now filled, but there was not one of the gathered imbibers who had a clue. 'Of this *gold.*' Tatsuo's last word was spoken in a whisper, spiced with a rakish grin and the gemstone sparkle of his blue eyes.

'What? How?'

'I have it on good authority that the German gunboat, the ship that had our stolen gold on board, the very same ship we witnessed being rammed by the Royal Navy, sank in shallow water.'

'What? But we saw—'

'I know what we saw. But it's in 80 foot of water, not 1,000, caught on a reef where a precipice drops away sharply on either side.'

Four pairs of eyes looked back at the skipper. Tatsuo explained Benjamin Chen's plan to salvage the treasure. He told them about Jasmijn and her story. 'And, unfortunately for them, they have all passed on.'

'So no one knows about this?'

'I'm afraid we have one rival.'

'Who?'

'A German survivor. He was the one who approached Chen to dive on the wreck.'

Samoa asked, 'And he is … where?'

'That's the bad news. I don't know who he is or where. But the good news is he is now without a partner, since Benjamin Chen is dead and his ship the *Ching Shih* is no more. For the moment, time is our friend. So, are we all keen to sail?'

'Aye, Cap'n! Bloody oath, we are!'

'But, all the same, the clock's ticking, as they say.' Tatsuo shot four fingers of whiskey and hoisted his quart chaser of ale high. 'So, like Robert Louis Stevenson wrote in his book *Treasure Island*, "Drink up, me hearties," we've work to do!'

THE END

South Seas Pearling

The early luggers were versatile pearl shell gatherers, when much of the shell could be gathered from reefs in less than four feet of water at low tide. These luggers were 27 feet long, eight feet in the beam, with a cabin aft with lockers and bunks for the crew. With masts, sails, oars, anchors and chain they cost 65 pounds each in the early days, the 1860s. Each boat was capable of collecting 2500 pairs of shell before returning to shore, usually in six days of gathering. The shells were opened as soon as they were taken ashore, and the oysters were allowed to rot in the sun for 24 hours before cleaning. An average pair of shells weighed in at four pounds (1.8 kilos), and on average it took 900 pairs to make up one ton in weight. Once delivered to Sydney the shell would sell for 150-180 pounds sterling per ton.

In the Torres Straits 1897 was a record year for the pearling industry, with 260 boats bringing in 1,257 tons of shell gathered, at a value of 126,024 pounds sterling. These pearl luggers, ranging in size from ten to 30 tons, were crewed by 1,600 men. At the time, Japanese and kanaka divers were earning up to 120 pounds a month, a lot of money in those days.

Cyclones during the wet (monsoon) season were always a concern. But many pearlers sailed with the attitude that if they stayed well north of Cooktown they would be comparatively safe, as most cyclones seemed to occur further south. Unfortunately, this rule of thumb was shattered in 1899 when the Bathurst Bay cyclone devastated the pearling fleet. On the Saturday night of March 4th about 60 luggers were destroyed, damaged or lost, with the loss of 300 crew members, while 100 aboriginals living in the area were drowned—washed out to sea—trying to save the pearlers.

Craig Godfrey loves nothing more than to weave adventure, mystery and mayhem together, incorporating colourful characters from all walks of life. Born in Hobart in 1952, Craig has traveled extensively, which has given him many of the experiences and escapades he so enjoys putting into print. These include working in the early 70s as a chef for a restaurant owned by figures from Sydney's criminal underbelly, and cooking in Darwin when cyclone Tracy destroyed the city.

After decades in the hospitality industry—and nearly 40 years after opening The Drunken Admiral Seafood Restaurant

—Craig decided to hang up his apron and leave family at the helm in order to indulge in his other passion, writing fiction.

Craig has published 18 previous titles, and is currently writing the seventh book in a series called *Shadow Hunter*, in which Caspian Hunter travels to Van Diemen's Land from Birmingham in 1855 to take a position as second in charge of Hobart Town's fledgling police department. His adventures around the waterfront inns are boundless.

The chef of a Hobart waterfront restaurant called the Hook, Line and Sinker is the protagonist of a series set in modern times. He and his partner, the assistant curator of the Tasmanian Museum, continuously find themselves in trouble, whether it be solving the disappearance of rare art works on Tasmania's west coast, caught in hang-glider dog fights over the Caribbean Sea, finding their way out of the myriad of tunnels under the battlefields of Flanders, or being imprisoned by antiquity thieves in Venice. Number five in the series has recently been completed. Other action-adventure novels are set in 1830s Van Diemen's Land, the Tasmanian wilderness of the 1940s, and during a murder investigation in Sydney and Darwin in 1974.

In the 1990s Craig independently shot two feature films: *To the Point of Death,* a murder mystery set in Southern Tasmania, which aired on television; and *Back from the Dead,* a splatter comedy still available online. He wrote, produced and directed both.

Craig's life has been busy and interesting, to say the least.

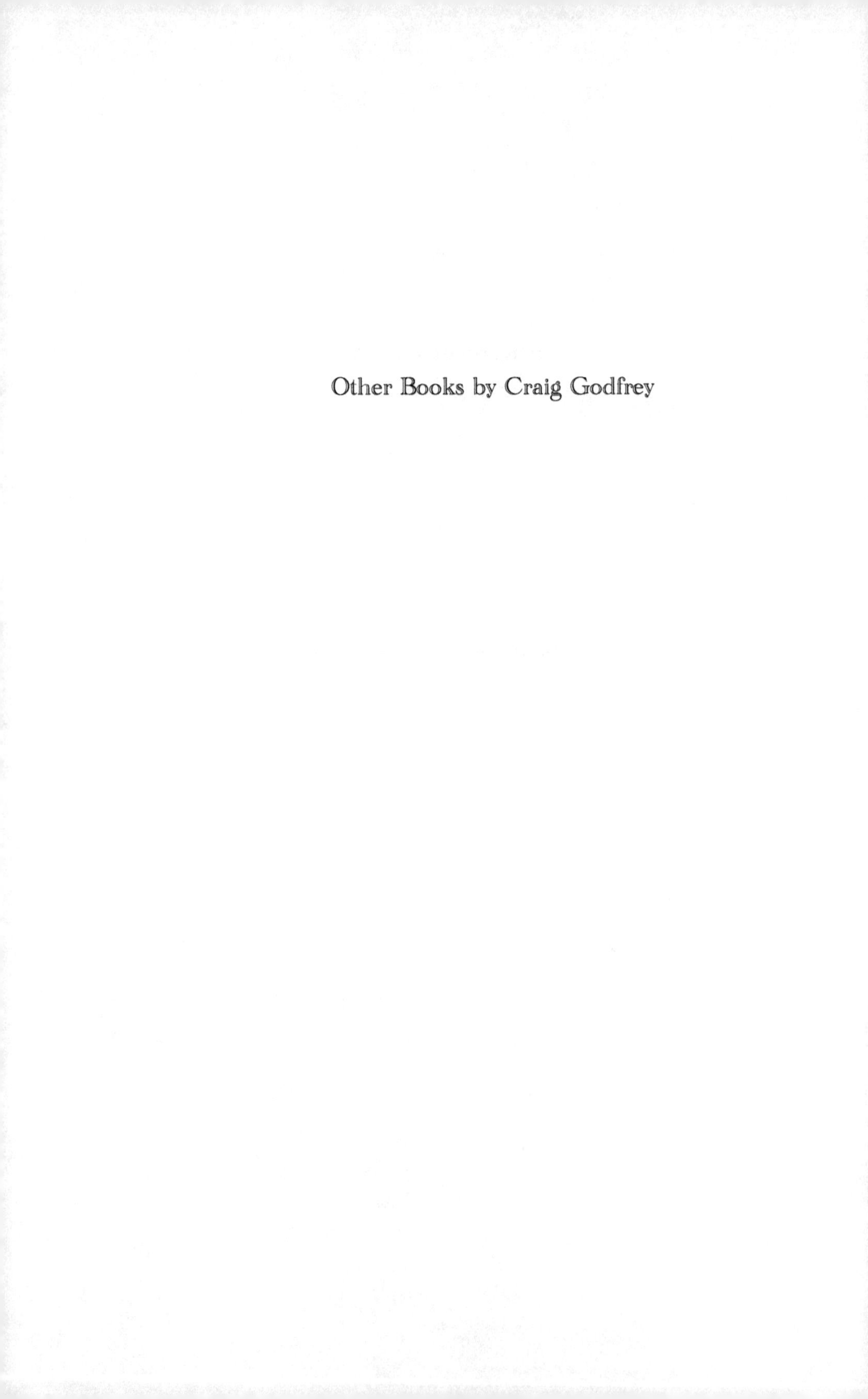

Other Books by Craig Godfrey

Taken to The Grave
BY
Craig Godfrey

This adventure continues....

Nineteenth Century Van Demonian sleuth, Caspian Hunter, is a colonial lawman deeply immersed in the life and crimes of Hobart Town, where convicts transported from Mother England form a majority of the population. Caspian and his decidedly unconventional associates are sworn to uphold the law where lawlessness is almost a way of life.

The fledgling colony includes newly pardoned convicts – 'ticket of leave men' – on a sort of parole. Misfits and unsavoury characters come this remote outpost of the British Empire to get as far away as possible from whatever lives they seek to leave behind.

But by the middle of the century, free settlers are arriving in ever greater numbers from Britain. Hobart Town is blessed with one of the world's most beautiful deep-water harbours, so it also attracts sailors and whalers. And it is rapidly becoming prosperous. There are inns aplenty, and a growing number of enterprising ladies are skilled in the arts of making sailors, whalers, gentlemen and even lawmen briefly happier and certainly poorer. This is Caspian's town.

A murder most foul committed with the most blunt of instruments, a hot flat iron, leads Caspian to the prison hell of Port Arthur, traveling on a railway man-powered by convict slaves, and an illicit liaison with a British Army officer's wife. The motive for murder: a diamond worth a king's ransom, hidden in a most incongruous place.

PENMORE PRESS
www.penmorepress.com

1814

BY

CRAIG GODFREY

1814 is a tale of two hemispheres and a man and a woman who initially shared little but the English language. Of a man of peace – a doctor – ensnared in the violence of the American revolution, forced to flee the former American colonies of King George III. Of a very young woman fighting for survival amid the injustice, poverty and corruption of early nineteenth Century Britain. A woman who is unjustly sentenced to transportation to Van Diemen's Land. British 'justice' was harsh beyond belief at this time and at its worst in its treatment of female convicts.

At this point in history Britain and particularly the Royal Navy were all powerful and the American doctor sought anonymity under a new identity. He 'signed on' with a group of sealers who had their own notorious empire in the remote islands of Bass Strait. These sealers, to this day, are recognized as the most evil of men.

It is in this lawless world that two good people meet. This is a world the writer/ historian and master story teller Craig Godfrey understands very well. Though fictional his characters fiercely illuminate the times, the remoteness and the people that populate these colonies.

PENMORE PRESS
www.penmorepress.com

The California Run

by

Mark A. Rimmer

New York, 1850. Two clipper ships depart on a race around Cape Horn to the boomtown of San Francisco, where the first to arrive will gain the largest profits and also win a $50,000 wager for her owner.

Sapphire is a veteran ship with an experienced crew. Achilles is a new-build with a crimped, mostly unwilling crew. Inside Achilles' forecastle space reside an unruly gang of British sailors whose only goal is to reach the gold fields, a group of contrarily reluctant Swedish immigrants whose only desire is to return to New York and the luckless Englishman, Harry Jenkins, who has somehow managed to get himself crimped by the equally as deceitful Sarah Doyle, and must now spend the entire voyage working as a common sailor down in Achilles' forecastle while Sarah enjoys all the rich comforts of the aft passenger saloon.

Despite having such a clear advantage, Sapphire's owner has also placed a saboteur, Gideon, aboard Achilles with instructions to impede her in any way possible. Gideon sets to with enthusiasm and before she even reaches Cape Horn Achilles' chief mate and captain have both been murdered. Her inexperienced 2nd Mate, Nate Cooper, suddenly finds himself in command of Achilles and, with the help of the late captain's niece, Emma, who herself is the only experienced navigator remaining on board, they must somehow regain control over this diverse crew of misfits and encourage them onwards and around the Horn.

PENMORE PRESS
www.penmorepress.com

SILENT from The Shadows
By

Craig Godfrey

Nineteenth Century Van Diemen sleuth, Caspian Hunter, is a colonial lawman deeply immersed in the life and crimes of Hobart Town, where convicts transported from Mother England form a majority of the population. Caspian and his decidedly unconventional associates are sworn to uphold the law where lawlessness is almost a way of life.

But maintaining law and order is not a simple task, as Caspian records in his own words in this, his ongoing saga.

Tasmania's history will never be the same.

Vampires! The ignorant rant, as mysterious murder victims appear around Hobart Town's environs with inexplicable puncture marks to their throats. Anarchy threatens the island.

The Measure of Ella
by
Toni Bird Jones

The islands frightened her with their uncivilized rawness. They looked like a place where anything could happen, a godforsaken outcrop at the end of the world.

Sea-faring chef Ella Morgan is an honest woman — until her life falls apart. When her dream of owning a restaurant is shattered by the death of her father and loss of her inheritance, she is suddenly alone in the world. Desperate for money, she signs on as crew for a Caribbean drug run, only to find herself fighting for her life in an underworld ruled by violent men.

Set in the Caribbean, The Measure of Ella is a dramatic story of love, murder, high-seas action, and the consequences of pursuing a dream at all costs. Like Patrick O'Brien's novels, including Master and Commander, The Measure of Ella captures the breathtaking and perilous world of blue-water sailing. Like Girl on the Train, it unwinds with gripping suspense from a woman's point of view. With its brave, strong, complex female protagonist at the helm of a high seas adventure, the novel is entirely unique.

PENMORE PRESS
www.penmorepress.com